*The Fire Above,
the Mountain Below*

THE GERMAN LIST

The Fire Above, the Mountain Below

REINHARD JIRGL

Translated by Wieland Hoban

LONDON NEW YORK CALCUTTA

This publication has been supported by a grant from
the Goethe-Institut India

Seagull Books, 2021

Originally published as *Oben das Feuer, untern der Berg*
© Carl Hanser Verlag, Munich, 2016

First published in English translation by Seagull Books, 2021
English translation © Wieland Hoban, 2021

ISBN 978 0 8574 2 779 3

British Library Cataloguing-in-Publication Data
A catalogue record for this book is available from the British Library

Typeset by Seagull Books, Calcutta, India
Printed and bound by Versa Press, East Peoria, Illinois, USA

CONTENTS

They guard the ashes
and they stamp out the embers.
— Proverb

CHAPTER 1

— *Ba-boom* — *Ba-boom* — The-beating of my heart — *Ba-boom* — *Ba-boom* — incessant beating. Frightful heart. How it !resists, shaking the chest cavity with its hammer blows against the-end. Constantly twitching, stamping heart. !As thecold from night hours penetrates the=flesh. Grabs it — *Ba-boom* — the flesh is still resisting. When will it stop resisting. Surrender. Flesh in this place where all fleshlythings must perish — *Ba-boom* — — *Ba-boom* — the-beating-heart is The Problem. Before you die, kill your heart. Better if humans had been born without hearts. Even better if no one had been born at all. *I shouldn't have.*

But you brought me into-the-world in 1956 in the unassuming street village of Kaltenfeld, 10 kilometres south of here, and had to leave me 3 years later. Mother. Father. :SOMEONE took me, your 3yearold girl, away from you. They said you were !spies. *The spies Irma and Alois Berger were found guilty of espionage and sentenced to 15 years in prison.* (Manyyears=later I read those lines about the court's verdict printed on an old thin-yellowed piece of newspaper with the pungent smell of the past. . . . .) It took me a long time to make the-connection between !these=lines and you=MotherFather. :Spies were caught spying & punished : the spider weaves its spider's web, the snake squirts its snake poison — the tautology turns you into a process of nature. And next to the announcement an over-contrasted black-and-white photo of you, so that you Both looked as if you were infected with the dark plague-spots of deviousness. But I didn't set eyes on these two photographs, the only 1s I ever saw of you, the ever-strangers, until muchlater, when it was too late for you; and: itwas a !greatrelief for me. Because now you couldn't take me away any more. — That was why, at=thishour on a winter's day in late October 2012 which had begun prematurely with frost&snowstorms, I was able to sneak to the cemetery here in Birkheim and to your grave, to visit in death you who had been strangers in life. Your grave vanished long ago, even without the snow — flattened — & yearsago the-cemetery-administration expanded the cemetery's rubbish heap, enclosed by wrought-iron railings, over that patch of soil. The dead under all the rubbish. (?Are your bones still lying down=there, 2½ metres under-theearth = as per regulation.) ?What might you look like, Mother Father, now in your forgotten death, freed of all the passions of the-flesh —: I should check. But the rubbish heap has grown too high under the snow, theground no doubt frozen too hard to dig with my hands, and: I didn't bring any other tools. Except my voice. So I'll bring you back with my voice. I needn't be scared of waking you. The-dead are always=awake. They want to pay their=debt from their=lives for theworld-of-the-otherdead. *You owe theworld 1 dead.* ?Do you remember. No. !What did I ?do. I brought my=dead back up.

This was the=place for your grave, just as I was shown for the 1st time manyyears-ago by the people I had always taken for my=parents. *Listen to the snow. The whispering of the snow.* Say the-dead. *Snow that falls too early in the year, !those are our voices. You must try hard if you want to hear us amid the rustling of the crystals, the frozen stars that fall to earth. We are here. You will now learn Everything. Now you are old=enough.* I hear the man I always thought to be My=Father say to me. He was standing

4

at the grave next to the holly tree, so that his voice seemed to be coming out of the bush. It has grown tall over=theyears, as I now see, probably approaching 10 metres; its slim, hard evergreen leaves, slightly curved, are like little boats carrying their heaped cargo of delicate, light October snow. The stone bench, now crumbling at the edges, lichen-scarred, but still standing=here and over-time embedded at=thefoot of the holly-stele as if in an alcove, with enough space for a man, and now a frosty cold creeps into=me as I sit. ?Howlong will It. . . . . take. But the heart. My heart. Keeps beating. Warm. Blood-warm beating. On and on. My heart. Now I, who was not meant to be, only have you. So I will stay here, will compete with frost&snow, and see if It stops my heart before the end of everything I have to say to you, Mother Father, from my life, lost bit-by-bit. Then, !finally, we will be able to stop, to forget ourselves and Everything. Finally !forget Mother Father. You both died in 1979 *under-suspicious-circumstances* (the-people dully murmured, they didn't dare do more than murmur) : your=deaths were the last I heard of you. But !What you had been through, !What had happened to you and !Why — I only learnt of allthat muchlater. First it was only !thisshock: those I believed to be my=parents (that is, I never thought about it; what child ?!doubts the authenticity of its parents) & whom I grew up with, Martha & Paul, and whose surname I shared; suddenly I was meant to believe they were !not my ?parents. They had adopted me when I was 3 years old, I was suddenly told; but I hadn't known Anything about That in=the-years=of my-childhood until the=day they told me That.

At-the-time an amnesty on the XXXth anniversary of the GeeDeeR in October 1979 : various prisoners were released from the-captivity of a prison into the-captivity of a country. (?Why had they even been arrested, ?what had they ?spied on : ?who

were my=real-parents. . . . . and ?What were they really.) : My
parents are !strangers : *Now the=real-parents will come & take
you home with=them.* I=was=sure of that once I had found That
out. For 9 years !thisfear. . . . . I ran trembling to the bathroom
to vomit. With burnt breath, a feeling set in that I hadn't known
before: fear of falling through the familiar, solid ground, which
suddenly seemed full of holes, unsafe, brittle, mocking & full of
betrayal : when I looked up from the toilet bowl, my face wet —
the towel on the hook, ?wasn't it blowing in a draught of inde-
terminable origin — in the corner the bathroom's only floorboards, ?weren't they bent, yielding, to ?break at the slightest
touch — the wallpaper was peeling off the acute-angled bathroom wall in long garlands, as if from rotten fruit — the brown-
glazed boiler teetered, threatening to fall on me with its full force
of hot water — and between the cracks in the floorboards a
many-voiced whining reached me from Some=Below, not melan-
choly or afflicted with pain but almost lurking and poisonous or:
completely soundless, a growing wailing from the mouths of
lunatics who were being kept=Down=there —!now: enormous
black hands spread their fingers across the steamy window from-
Outside, they would push it in, a moment later slithering dark
arms would reach in=here from-Outside — find me — grasp,
grab me, drag me Outside — : — They, my=true-parents, that
sent thesearms=thesehands, now they would come & take me home
with=them; apparently they had theright. From Outside, already
close to the window, laughter from a man's throat, mocking, dark
& full of anger. — 9 years later both your=deaths. When I learnt
of it: !joy. (:Joy, bright, but only secret joy to be hidden from
Everyone; I had long since learnt to havetopretend). For now you
could no longer take me with=you from My=world. . . . . Since
then you can only come after me in my dreams. . . . . I wish I'd

never learnt anything about you, then you would have stayed what you always were for=me: nothing. ?Why, Mother Father, did you ?do something that they could accuse you of !espionage for. ?Why can't people ?keep=quiet, born as lowly-people & shoe-horned into the-lowly-life of themasses, grey in=thegrey of their little existence.

Your dying, Mother Father, began 1 early winter's morning in Kaltenfeld. That's like a shard in my=memory, left over from a picture that was definitely complete once, — but the=moment it happened this picture already shattered into sharp-edged fragments that cut into my=memory, unintentionally, and: I couldn't have said afterwards !what these particles were supposed to mean. Only this=1 shard was left : from-outside someone was banging on the front door & gruff raw men's voices called out names & the-command to open the door !immediately. I only remembered that again on-the-way=here, hours ago, when I looked out of the train window at the flat landscape moving slowly past, a landscape of abandoned life with its old black-brown spruce trees, between and behind them the sounds of depleted woodlands. *They stand self=confidently, self=belonging in Their=space. These spruces. The restricted area once began not far from here & 5 kilometres later the-border. . . . . That scar that was torn open again by your espionage, because you, Mother Father, thought you knew that This Wound was an incurable wound as long as various people, on This side too, had painted their brown-shirts red, those tough thick coats of red oil paint, when the-time came to change paint pots & the-slogans to keep up business as usual: as knew-people at their oldposts.* . . . . Then the front door was opened by an undefined figure (Father, you), hesitantly & questioningly, barely a crack, then immediately slammed back in response with an icy draught from

outside, thespilling of official force into the hall, strange fright-
ening angular dark-green uniforms. Figures seemed bigger wider
than the narrow corridor, so that They threatened to push in the
walls doors in the flat with their brawny steaming bodily masses.
But no: there was also 1 slight man with flickering glances behind
strong spectacle lenses. His hair was thinning, his complexion
chalky, his skin full of pimples and warts. This slight wiry man
bent thebodilymasses of the policemen aside, stepped through a
fleshly Scylla & Charybdis towards you, Father (whose appearance I still can't remember, even now just a silhouette, the something of an anonymous body —), planted himself in front of you
— you must have been taller than him, because I remember that
the stranger, with his pimply face & burning red eyes had to look
up at you menacingly, then over at you, Mother, who were holding
me=pressedagainstyou, as if you wanted to make me disappear
into your clothes (yes: into this warm sleep-smell of your dressing
gown, that was where you were trying to push me, to hold me in
this fruitful stable-warmth of a mother animal) : the little thin
man in a coat that was muchtoobig was now holding a note (the
paper pale as his face) close to his spectacleyes & a crusty voice
read Something out — (:later I found out that it was the-arrest-
warrant for you Mother Father. . . . .) — Then two thick strong
hands grabbed me, tore me away from you Mother, shoved me
out of the room, the hall, out of the flat, pushing more energetically than a 3yearold can walk, so men's arms lifted me off the
ground (my left ankle struck the edge of a step with glaring pain,
theshock at theroughness choked the tears), and Out onto the
street — immediately I was grabbed by a frosty wind, its hard
ice-hands slung needle-sharp hailstones in my face. I looked for
help, for other hands that might want to hold me, saw the grey-
plastered cracked wall of the house, a white curtain was twitching

in the window of the neighbouring flat, — I was pushed hastily in front of a car shed, two doors held wide open, the hollow maw of the opening loomed large as it came towards me, I was pushed inside into musty sweat-air, it swallowed me, barely any breath. Black. — I didn't know It back then: for=me this was the beginning of a life that (as I now know) would become the life of a beetle. *1 of those summer&autumn insects that is supposed to expire with its season; only sometimes 1 of these creatures outlasts its=time and: finds itself, confused unsure uneasy, in a later time of year & still alive. Now snow covers this beetle-world, where even the most ordinary activities from earliertimes seem useless. Everything strangely removed from the world. The small legs, numb from the unfamiliar frost, sticking out of a snow (:!what a peculiar material: loose as summer sand, but smooth with no foothold, sparkling gleaming like cold fire in the stagnant icy taste of water) that, moulded into a crater, covers the walls that the little legs are struggling to crawl up, and: after a short time the plump insect inevitably slips back down the ice-slicked snow cliff into the (for a beetle) yawning depths of the crater. It seems, always deeper than the last time. Thus ends a beetle-life that outlasts itself for unknown reasons.* — For what I had Then, when I (the 3yearold child) was brought to my adoptive parents and lived with=them, that was All that would belong to=me, & that had been ordered that frosty morning 53 years ago. At the same time it was the 1st day of All=my lifelong forgetting.

First making fine dust like pale billows of smoke — drifting unclearly in the grey of the late October day —. When I slipped on my brown woollen coat before, on the long-distance train that went to Amsterdam, just before getting off in Stendal, the cloth wrapped itself around my body, and suddenly the feeling: *your last warming piece of home closes around=you with this rapid swing of a coat* (I hadn't noticed my shivering before). Suddenly, enclosed in its warmth, something I had long missed poured into=me: confidence — *you're doing Everything right. Good that you're On-the-way.* Just a bit of warmth, no more than that. From-now=on Something-Else. . . . . will begin.

Then, when I stepped onto the narrow, crooked worn-out platform for the regional trains & had to wait because the train to Birkheim wasn't ready, the 1st tiny dunes, fine as dust, gathered around my shoes: !snow —, mist rising from the ground made the grainy snowflakes drifting through the air invisible, the thin draughts of air tasted blandly cool and white. (*My shoes are much too thin; I'll end=up* —) *j j jjjjjjjjjjjjj* All the station noises already sounded muted, as if wrapped in cotton wool; the forenoon hour in this premature start of winter drew in its shoulders like the fore-dusk, like a child born old and: unwilling to grow any more. With small steps, slowly secretly, as if I was afraid of falling or giving someone a fright in the grey air, I walked up-&-down the narrow snow-covered platform, so far the only 1 waiting for the train. — The snow grew stronger — the flakes spun to form spiral veils in the grey air, ghost swarms of migrant birds sent out their shrill calls, — air swirls moulded the snowflakes into long thin tubes — pale-soft arms that wanted to grab me — ?free me from the-fists that still held me in their grip since Then, since 1 early morning hour — — :!Abang. A!heavybang. Stormthunder. It crashed down like a ball of steel with an angry din. Winter-storm. Thestorm sticking out of the whirling snow. A blinding beam of light hissed across the windscreen of the dark limousine — bright yellow firebolt — Asmash crashbang as giant claws ripped the car body —: a flash of lightning had struck the vehicle and hit the windscreen: — and dispersed as fire-rain, inside=the car the faces snow-pale. As if thelightningbolt had made all the blood in those bulky bodies evaporate. *?Did the-officers catch sight of The Boss of the Other=Higher-Agency, their terror before this paragon of rage towards them, who always felt they were in the=protective-bunker=of-theirpowers : unassailable, justified by the law-of-the-strongerstate.* — But the car with its passengers was not split apart by the lightning, it didn't even smash the windscreen, no one was burnt; it's not as easy as that. But thelightning did shatter something=in=me that I couldn't put in words back then (all I remember is the thin taste of blood in my mouth), later on I found out what thelightning had broken apart: primal trust. The primal trust of the 3yearold child, and I felt thiswound. . . . . only muchlater. *Because childhood is over when you !know that you must die. I shouldn't have.* — The car wouldn't start. As if the car with the three men who forcedme|betweenthem had sped into a block of steel. For a longtime bright flurries of sparks danced before their flashed eyes — while the car had long set off again, with me and: my guards who had COLLECTED me. — ?What else happened. Forgetting. That's my=steel-block, the-forgetting that happened immediately in the subsequent=years. My memory always drove into this steel block at=thatpoint. ?What's behind thissteelblock. . . . . except the broad expanses of ?my=fear. . . . . Suddenly it was there: the figure of a man. At the front of the platform, almost at the end, with his loose coat the colour of coal dust flapping around his slim body. He stood still. The face of the stranger, turned away from me, seemed to be looking at the ground; freezing, he buried his hands in his coat pockets. No baggage in sight that belonged to him. And even when the train approached and stopped for boarding, the stranger didn't move.

The carriage was well-heated, — slowly thecold let go of me, I was sitting in a window seat as the only passenger on the

train. The suburban train left the station with a quiet hissing &
murmuring of the motor —. As I drove past the stranger, who
had stayed on the platform, he raised his face for a moment: an
extremely pale, narrow face whose age I couldn't guess, the
mouth scar-thin; he looked directly=at-me. Was it a ?smile that
reached for=me from the corners of his mouth —. — The short
train swam soporifically along its route, stopping at deserted stations; faded crumblyold brick, old doors now covered up with
boards or metal sheets, broken windowpanes. These buildings
like shipwrecks, swept to the shores ofmist, coasts on the rigid
cold sea of endless everthusness between the-villages. No one
who visited them any more. Pelted with snow they crouched low,
played dead. On the station signs, once newly installed, now
splattered with snow-white, one could only make out ice-olated
letters; on the brick fronts of the old station buildings I read the
black letters in old German type against a once-brightly-painted
background, each name with a full stop at the end. **Messdorf.** I
remember, and **Hohenwulsch.** Then the-ride continued — like
endless dreary monologues about alwaysthesame things. I rarely
saw anyone board the train. But the closer we got to the final
stop, Birkheim, the more: men women, wan village figures, heads
covered faces frost-red and full of calm, with no anger no reason
to be amazed. They brought in the smell of snow, stale-cold gusts
of air that blew around their close life everyday habits — the
same air that probably hung over the countryside Outside.
Autumn-empty ploughed earth, the furrows filled with snow and
smoothed, cornstalks protruded, the black of the forests gradually filled with grey —. In here was an accumulation of warm but
cloudy air, which immediately changed the incoming smell of
cold&snow into the ever-same ancient stagnant travel air of all
trains, this indifferent, sullen sluggishness and aversion=to-

Everything in the air molecules. The people who got on uttered a greeting into the carriage, a short sound. Then schoolchildren tumbled in, noisy giggling babbling, feet scraped, trampling snow off their shoes. Frosty fingers hastily scraped across little rectangular pieces of plastic from which thin cables extended into their ears; satchels swung crookedly on their backs. — Then, during the-ride, stripes of drifting snow rose to the train windows as thin white lines of force fields from strange magnetic distances turned whirled from invisible grey heights. Birkheim, the magnetic pole of my journey into misfortune. No doubt the thread-thin snow field lines extended from There — from A=particular= place. They grew denser, tighter. (Wouldn't surprise me if there were crackling clattering in=them like ice-cold electricity. The-voices of all the travellers that ever took this-route=here, they were trapped inside them. Now I hear them, these-voices, asking quietly hesitantly like children when they lose their way.) — We drove deeper and deeper into the premature winter — a journey intofatigue — a block of greyair (the voices of the-absent locked inside it) turned to lead by all things peaceless, preventing sleep with fever-points of pinpricking attentiveness to the smallest jolts of the rails (the-voices : ?must I hear them ?already), — invisible activity, — the-lurking —. Bentgloomily and waiting at some of the stops-on-the-route, flat dull hours without time. — — !*That's the fifth one.* I remember speaking those=exact words aloud while pushing the cigarette smoke out between my lips with a hiss, as if I had to breathe against strong gusts of wind, & pressed the stub into the ashtray. That was the-perpetrator in my fingers, the perpetrator I could now squash in the ashtray. *So that's the fifth one.* When I got up behind the desk, my gaze fell on the pinboard opposite: 4 large colour photographs, different sizes, of women — the youngest 20 years, the oldest 43 — all blondes.

Their looks were also conspicuously similar in other ways, as if they came from the same family. — And all=of-them were from moderately well-off backgrounds with siblings. My subordinate, Inspector Möller, had noticed this; his comment on it was like a casual hand gesture. I nodded equally casually, as if I had long been aware of the fact. Frozen smiles on the photos, carefree & as if the red lips with the glinting white incisors in their slightly-open mouths were the bait cast into the-currents of the-human-flood, fishing for attention & appreciation, which women of all=ages are capable of. : These are photos of the dead. Women caught in=the-net of a cruel fisherman. And these photographs= there-on-the-wall with their temptingly smiling faces seemed obscene compared to those otherphotographs of the same women; the photos from the crime scene: bodies & clothes torn up, the blood-smeared leavings of a serial-killer, — in the swollen, violated & shattered faces on !these photographs, fear and hor-ror were frozen=into-eternity; their features had slipped away too quickly even for the-chisel of suffering, death was faster. In the faces around the mouths on the body in the genitals — that was where the perpetrator had raged. We=at-the-station assumed that the-perpetrator had to be a man (though we hadn't found any traces of his manliness on any of the dead women). The per-petrator had not only spared the other parts of the women's bodies, he had actually protected them from his=rage & the scalpel — had even wiped the blood&dirt from the mutilated mouths & genitals carefully off the neck, breasts, thighs, combed the blonde hair; his=frenzy was directed at the orifices. And when the firestorm of his rage had gone out, he scrupulously sewed up the orifices of the murdered women, even the eyes, ears and nostrils, with a thick black thread. Always the same yarn, always the same stitches. The perpetrator wanted to command the women to absolute silence. Then he laid the bodies on moss in little wooded areas or inside flower borders in parks — *laid in state* was the phrase that came to mind when I saw them. (The fact that I was still capable of !these feelings after thirty-years=in-the-homicide-squad didn't bode well for the rest-of-my=time=as-a-policeman. I had hoped to get hardened over-the-years, more self=assuredly impervious to the horrors of reality. . . . . But the opposite happened: thefears grew, came over me more quickly. The skin gets thinner. . . . . over The Void.) All the dead women dispatched in the same way = the same perpetrator each time. That was our assumption. Soon 1 more photograph would be smiling at me from that wall=there & the other=from-the-crime-scene would preserve the bloody madness as a computer file. — Then (I still remember it as=clearly as if I'd stepped outside myself & a camera was pointing her cold eye at=me, and I could follow all my own movements with it, which seemed to belong to anyone except me) I saw myself slowly rising from my chair, buttoning up my jacket, & this man (who was supposed to be me) left his room, guarded by the old stagnant cigarette smoke hanging in the air, followed his colleague Möller, who had come to my room in the 1st floor especially from 'reception' (as we called the complaints office), where he was on duty for-the-day, knocked strangely quietly at the door, & then, very carefully, as if he feared an outburst of anger or despair from me, placed his words. — Boss. Chief Inspector. Downstairs there's a man, the father of a 55yearold woman. She lives with him and he says she hasn't come home in half a week. Hasn't been in contact either. I think you should have a —

Möller was almost 20 years younger than me, his=rank was below mine, he was meant to be my successor. Still, in-allthe-seyears, he had never addressed me as *Chief Inspector*. He had been sent to this station at Alexanderplatz a few years after me, he was still in training then. He came from some backwater in Brandenburg; I was from Hanover. The deal was originally that I'd only come here for 1 year, *!re=organize the-place*, as my-superiors had put it —; — but then I stayed.

Inspector Möller-from-Brandenburg tended towards a= certain chattiness: he had evidently preserved the last of his youthful precociousness in a taste for expressions; turns of phrase that he used to conclude almost every explanation, statement or remark, which gave a man in his late30s a hint of premature mouldiness, as if he were still wearing his father's old trousers. —: A manner that could drive me up the wall. He also often confused the-sayings & phrases, disfiguring them into involuntarily comical sentences that were so stupid they could almost have been profound. The last time we found a woman's body, when it was clear to all of us that it had to be a serial offender, he added in passing: *So now we know !which side the wind's blowing on.* — And the longer The Cases with this serial offender occupied us day-in=night-out, the more similar I found his blathering to the photographs-from-the-crime-scene. So I was grateful to him for refraining from his clever-dickery for once on the way=down to 'reception'. As quiet as he rarely was & almost carefully, walking in front of me & making sure I was following him (as if I didn't know my way around our spacious headquarters and might get lost in the labyrinth of floors hallways stairways or: as if was afraid I'd pull out & leave him=alone with allthework) he went down the steps to the ground floor. *The-fifth-one.* These 3 syllables, they dug deeper=intome with every step I took. And I also realized: *The intervals are getting shorter. The fifth one. Noteven 1 month since the last.* Then we arrived at the office=on-the-ground-floor.

16

In the area in front of the wide counter with a total of 4 desks not separated from one another, it was rather like a refugee camp in medical emergencies at this hour of the morning: excitement tumult bickering of lamenting women's voices, shrill as the Balkan&Orient, feet scraping, fists banging on wooden tables, sour black body fumes — coming going, uniformed officers intervened — and on the sidelines of thisactivity, sitting on 1 of the old chairs, was the man Inspector Möller silently gestured at, the father of the missing woman. I introduced myself, the old man looked up. His face bore that expression found in people who think they've already said Everything about themselves and others; he seemed talked-out, was beyond anger and resentment about his-fate, not even surprise could sneak into this calm face, which showed that he, this old man, even lived beyond bitterness. Maybe his features had once burned-with=passion, — but they had long since cooled off like an old piece of iron. But where the-flame had disappeared, that was where burns were still left as signs of a long forgetting —. I took him out of this reservoir of noiserage&fumes and led him to my smoky office (Möller followed, bravely keeping quiet). There the old man sat with the same posture, with the same averted, cooled-off face that he had downstairs at 'reception', as if he hadn't even noticed the change of location. I gave him time. He would start talking. — Hissing of the hydraulic brakes — then the train stopped. Arrival in Birkheim. My steps went down to a platform in ankle-deep snow. The three platforms, unusually long, stood out like extended snow-covered sand banks from the waters of a river hidden by ice. Maybe the people who built these long platforms had made them suitable for ICE trains to stop here, as originally intended. The ICE trains never came; their line went elsewhere. — After emerging from the underpass I stepped out into the station square, looked around: bus stops, bicycle stands, — everything Here rejected me, my search for memories could not penetrate this solidwall of new buildings from the lastfewyears. ?No recognition. !But yes: the tall chestnut tree at the end of the median strip in the station square, it still spread its leafless branches& twigs, now highlighted by thick snow, over the square placatingly —. It was the-good-acquaintance who is=there every time and spoke to=me now too. A man, wrapped in a military jacket, set his hastyshort steps against thedriftingsnow, plodding along under the white-bearing chestnut tree to a different station building: a new 3-floor clinker-brick construction, box-shaped, the front made of industrially produced bricks interspersed with oblong rows of windows. This building had replaced the old barracks-like works canteen & the station building for the secondary line which once had the handless clock on the gable, gaping through the years like the blinded eye of Polyphemus.

Isolated bell strokes from the nearby town through the grey snow-whirled air — made me think of church steeples, two or three in the centre —: towards the bells, that was where I had to go now. I remembered that much. —

The houses didn't speak to me with so much as a syllable, old, newly built, renovated houses; foreign was this town with its narrow alleys, now blocked by snow, whose various windings all led towards the main road, banal was the road bridge across the black-flowing River Jeetze, arrogant — still — was the high pointed brick facade of a secondary school, hostile was the Lüchow Gate, only reluctantly allowing me to pass through; 2 square columns of grey weather-beaten stone, like old decrepit guardsmen with no mission, sullen & long since abandoned in doing their duty, each squeezed under the snow caps on two giant trees: chestnut on the right, acacia on the left. —:*Baobab*

trees :two frozen baobab trees suffocated by snow arms —
(:?*where did that idea come from*) — the bell in the nearby tower
of St Mary's Church with several snow-muted damply shaky
strokes, jingles on the winter fool's cap. 2 + 4: the arithmetic of
the Lüchow Gate = ?What's the ?result. The milky grey of the
snow and the slightly darker grey of the sky, full of haze and
dense flake-whirls, added a hint of crumbling lenience even to all
the things that were waiting morosely in oblivion, just as there
seemed to be a lasting exhalation of surly forgiveness attached
to the whole town —. (?*Why are you pausing for so long in front
of these remains of a gate* —! *Fool: keep going, no one's going to
ask you for the result of the calculation here.*) Right after that,
as if on an island enclosed by winter-marked trees, St Catherine's
Church stood firmly there with its stout, tapering tower (it was
from here that the noontime bells rang out through the snow-
silenced air before; now it's quiet and thick). Small shops with
their window displays like colourful patches sewn onto the
white snow fur; heavy & broad-shouldered, a transport truck
pushed its way through a street — (I look up at the little street
sign on the house wall, read:) Mittelstrasse —:*suggestive, isn't
it.* Mittelstrasse, which ends, in the gaping, hollow-mouthed
opening to the brick building of a gate. *Gate devours street, gate
devours city.* Tenaciously slow and hiding undersnow, probably
fearful of voracious gates, a whole small town with its low timber
houses & the sparse traffic ploughing through the white-covered
roads. Silently the place sent me on my way — it still had enough
power to reprimand me : !Nothing to see here. I wanted to be
polite, did it the favour of seeing & hearing Nothing. The white-
covered line of buildings along the road, the houses, the small
shops, seemed like an encounter with someone I'd heard a lot
about a longtime-ago. Accordingly I'd painted a=certain picture

of this person for myself, and: now, as this stranger=himself came towards me, holding his straight road-arm, marked only by a few tyre-tracks-in-the-snow, out to me —; I didn't recognize him. The whole town sank slowly into-the=snow and the grey-dimming day as into a valley of lost courage —. — But I, I still felt It, it was even stronger=now than in-the-train : thepull coming from a=particular place, aimed at !me — it was there, into-the=centre of this pull, that I had to go. I felt It, but I didn't know the-way=there, only remembered that It was located at the town's exit, but in ?which direction. When a taxi appeared in front of me from thedriftingsnow, I flagged it down. Told the driver my=destination. He, looking at my small travel bag, ventured a bland joke and asked if I wanted to ?move in there. (*If you only !knew.*) But I didn't answer, then the driver was quiet too. The taxi to the cemetery. Took me to a small gate (hardly bigger than the entrance to an allotment) of spear-shaped iron stakes. On a stone column the little marble plaque:

Parish of St Catherine's Church

Neustadt.

On the right behind the gate was the little chapel. Yes: !that was The Place. This is where It comes from.

And the snow-whirls thickened spiralled into-the-air swept across the untrodden white ground like bright tiny birds — wind shaped their flight into swarms, their spinning formed tubes in the air, gusts forced them between frost-clad long grass into back roads & along the main avenue — they flew whirled and dispersed —. And avenues and paths the trees shrubs fences and the graves — buried by the snow like people buried by their lifetime. *I shouldn't have.* Now I heard thevoice very clearly. It came closer. It was luring me, I wanted to go to=it — right into the middle of The Force Field. This !weather. So much !snow. Dense as thewall in front of a bigroom. I have to get closer to thiswall. Want to get deeper into thesnow. Into this bigroom. Thevoice will be there. Must get to=It. Must hear. Want to hear thevoice again of that man whom I took for My Father as a child. : — *Born on 15 October 1956. When we took you with=us Back-Then= 3-years-later from that-orphanage, that was in October too. Martha & I had !finally been granted permission by the-authorities to adopt you. !What !greathappiness. For old=communists like us the month of October is just a lucky month. So for=us=at-home you were called: October. That's you, Theresa. You already learnt as a child what many people only experience with age: most relatives are the-dead.* Yes, it's !his voice. The voice of the man I had not only called *My=Father* in-theyears-of-my-childhood, but who also felt like *My=Father*. But the waves of feeling too had to break on the hardrock of-the-facts. (I also remember how, at least in-my-early-years, the silhouettes of a man a woman appeared in=me, and kept appearing, because the-neighbours, whenever they found me playing alone in the street, told me other things about My=Father and My=Mother. They were shrewish, coarsely hissing voices that sent their=words hailing rapidly down on me like knives. *I shouldn't have.* Then I would cry and run away every time — deep into the streets & alleyways of thetown. And then when I got lost, when I asked the scarred, taciturn houses of the-strangers. . . . . ?if they hadn't seen Myfather & Mymother, those dirty sooty houses didn't answer, and: I was left lonely as a stone in the middle of the pavement, then slunk on slowly and covered my face, contorted by crying, with my hands —. It was often evening by the time somestrangers or maybe a policeman took me by the hand & brought me back to where My=Mother and My=Father lived. That was what They=

always said to=me.) In the early years of my=childhood I didn't want to hear !whatever Anyone said to me. It was never defiance or stubbornness; I just didn't hear Anything that I didn't know already. It seemed thosevoices=of-the-adults=above-me were speaking in words of snow. And those words already melted on their lips and fell down before me as bright raindrops; then dried up in-the=dust. Thisdust changed into sludge from somanywords, solong & insistently did the-adults keep going on=at-me. But I always jumped through the puddles in the little light-coloured dresses, tiny shoes and white knee socks of my=childhood, the shoes squelched in the mud, I laughed aloud about it and: heard Nothing. That was me. But that was also !agreatdeal that I didn't hear. Later, as some1 else, some1 older, I made an effort, wanted to catch up on Everything I'd missed when I=was-a-child. I always wanted to be=Thebest. In life at university in my job. But even back then, there was already Somuch=in-me from years when I had to replace All-that I didn't know with All-that I thought up instead. Now That collided with Everythingelse, and: I, who had heard Nothing before, know heard Everything, but understood Nothing. And so, once again, I remained a stranger before thevoices=of-the-strangers. That's me. And sometimes a smile turns towards me from the-lips=of-the-strangers. Smiles from men's lips. What do they ?mean by That. But It is reaching= for=me. The last time was on the platform in Stendal, when I saw the stranger from the train as it was already leaving, he was standing on the platform in his coat of coal dust and smiled at me. Back then, that other man who I did not know was *My=real-father* also smiled at me. I can remember that much about him. But I can only recall his friendly mouth; his face his form and that of the woman, whose warm smell of sleep from her dressing gown I still sense sometimes, like a deep memory seemingly from a time before me, and who I would later realize was *My=real-mother*, disappeared beyond my reach.

And yesterday, even before deciding to leave, I met that other man whom I had seen as *My=Father* in-theyears-of-my=childhood on my doorstep. He was wearing a thin coat the colour of old cement, his arms were hanging down on either side of his body, and his hands were holding several large bouquets; they seemed heavy, as it was clearly an effort for the man to hold them. His appearance had changed in other ways too, sunken cheeks, his eyes, deep in their sockets, gazed absently, his shoulders sagged and his legs and feet were heavy, like someone who had suddenly plunged into old age. Before I could say anything in response to the flowers he raised his voice, which rasped with feeble tinniness. He complained that no one ever put flowers on his grave — so he had to do it himself. — *I'll drive out to the cemetery & put flowers on my=own grave.* This notion seemed to amuse him, shrill bleating laughter from his mouth. I had !never seen Father like this before; theshock at his appearance & especially at this macabre joke of bringing flowers for his own= grave sent Fearful Words into my throat: — *But !Father, you're !not dead. !Stop making jokes like that, you're scaring me. !Father* —. — But I think I only managed to say the last word out loud. The man I shouldn't really have called Father any more turned resolutely to leave, as if my words hadn't reached him atall or: as if he didn't want to hear Anything from me. Hesitantly, doddering and obviously disoriented, he went along the busy avenue — his steps were wobbly and unsure — he wanted to reach the tram stop on the median strip. But if he was heading for the cemetery, as he had said, he was going in the wrong direction, the opposite one, which went not to the cemetery but to the city centre. I called out into the raging traffic at the top of my voice —, in vain, the old man was standing at the wrong stop, the heavy bouquets lowered to the ground like extinguished torches, and presumably couldn't see or hear me any more. When I was about to rush across to=him, the front door opened behind my back & my mother (my adoptive mother) came out. I didn't have any time to be astonished, as the woman had been dead for several years. She wanted to go on her=way in a fashionable autumn suit, but I held her by the sleeve of her jacket (the material felt cold, as if it had been taken out of the fridge) & asked her loudly & desperately to look after her old=helpless husband & help him with the flowers. The woman stopped for a moment, then said in an unwilling defensive voice: — *That's how he wanted it. So let him finish-it himself.* Her breath hit me, it was as cold as the material of her suit. Then the woman walked energetically along the pavement, further=along on her=way, without us. I was left alone in front of the house in which I'd spent the best years of my childhood and youth with my adoptive parents, who were Mother and Father to me and whom I loved before I found out about my true parents. Now I don't have anyone, I'm alone, just like those first hours as a 3yearold child when I was dragged from the house of my true parents.

The voice of that man, my adoptive father, will always stay with me. And it spoke now too, just like Backthen=Yearsago when he came here to this cemetery with me. Solemnly, with serious faces (I still remembered) he & I took the train for the long journey from Berlin to Birkheim; the man's voice told me he had found out Something manyyears ago, & that he had to tell me !this, now that I was an adult. And he revealed something that he called My=true-story = in !this-very-place in front of this grave next to a holly tree. Now I heard his words loud and clear one more time in the snow-sated grey air of this premature October winter hour. And just like before, I felt as if I was looking at a completely unfamiliar life that opened up before me, suddenly & unexpectedly, like an unknown house. — *Martha, my wife, became pregnant at last. After more than three years of marriage. We had wanted a child somuch, Martha even more than me. We had already accepted that It wasn't meant to be. In a sense that was even true, but not in the way we expected. Martha had problems from-the-start-of-her=pregnancy. The-doctors said she wouldn't be able to keep the child, her tissue was sick. . . . . (That was all they said. Probably not allowed to say more because Martha came from near Aue, & that was where Wismut was. . . . .) Uranium mining had hollowed out the area, and in places like the small town where Martha grew up, there were always gases pouring out of the cracked ground. . . . . The-authorities had set up big sprinkler systems above these places, and the constantly-trickling rain was meant to wash the toxic gases back into the earth —. Martha's childhood was in rain&mud. . . . . The lasting memento of her-childhood — her contaminated tissue. The-doctors advised her urgently to abort, there was still time for that. . . . . Martha refused, she wanted to keep=our=child. After the last consultation with the-doctors once she had made this=decision, Martha's condition improved. All her ailments disappeared almost overnight. The following weeks and months of her pregnancy passed withoutincident, the-doctors were amazed, spoke of a miracle; Martha gave birth to a daughter. We called her Rosa. The medical examination of the newborn revealed that her blood was sick. Verysick. . . . . said the-doctors & also that the child would stay alive for a few weeks at most. They would do what They could, in a children's hospital. The newborn would have to be moved there for that. A cure was possible, but They couldn't guarantee Anything. We had to agree, because we had nochoice. They took the child away. Without speaking about it, Martha and I secretly prepared, each on=our=own, for the death of our child. We lived still evenings, walked about quietly and with slow steps, the lamp in the living room seemed as if it was shining more dimly, we touched each=other gently and more often than before. Thus each gave the other what they could not have managed alone: thecourage to bid our child farewell. But the news from the children's hospital sounded better day-by-day, the child was recovering !astonishingly and !rapidly. Once again the-doctors spoke of a miracle; soon They would be able to give the child back to=us. That happened. All the dark shadows of fatal predictions & farewell disappeared like dust when Rosa — our child —!finally came home=to=us. Martha had also recovered in the meantime. Now, we knew, Now Everything would be fine. And were happy with Our=life. The child was a quiet creature, she rarely cried, slept alot. (As if she didn't want to stick out in thisworld or settle in for a lifetime Here.) One evening the child suddenly had a highfever. The tiny face in her little bed glowed on the big white pillow like a red autumn leaf in the early snow. We didn't have a telephone, I ran to a neighbour to call the-emergency-doctor. It was already late, the neighbour was sleeping, I had to wait a long time for him to open the door. By the time the-doctor arrived, little Rosa had died. After 2 miracles, the path of 1 life had quickly led to death. She was not meant to live any longer, noteven 1 year, our Rosa. So, unlike all the other people, she never had to experience the returning anniversary of her death.*

The maple leaves still glowingred through the ice-coloured crystal layers of young fresh snow, frozen furnaces in tall autumnal trees. And the invisible smoke trails of these frost-trapped flames are the paralysed shadows, cut out of the autumn sun by the same treetops just a few days ago. Some of their murky secrets have now been wrested from them, but not all by any means; & the all-covering, softly wrapping hands of the sudden frost now leave these once secret=filled expressions metallic light flat and narrow, like the androgynous faces of city women —.

— Now we grieved a second time. Everything before that, when we had already tried once to come to terms with the death of our=child, it now seemed like a drill for This Case. . . . . And Everything-bad always happens after all, even if It wears the mask of happiness at first. The-doctors, who had seemingly been wrong somanytimes with their predictions, in the end they weren't wrong, & they weren't wrong with their diagnosis that Martha wouldn't survive another pregnancy: we'd lose the-unborn and we'd lose each=other. That was what the-doctors professied. — Then we heard about children who'd been chosen for-adoption. First Thewar — then the-Post-War — unrest in the socialist=camp : 1953 in the GeeDeeR, in Berlin & the rest of the country — then Hungary — the-hunt for fascists in hiding, as they put It — a !conspicuous number of children who were. . . . . given up for-adoption. We heard what everyone heard about It. It was like flashes of lightning, evidence of a storm — far away; not here=among=us. Martha and I, we came from a work-ing-class background; we had no reason to distrust our=state, the-workers'&farmers'-state. —. — Our parents — Martha's parents Gustav and Hilde in Aue, my parents Franziska and Max in Berlin — were factory workers. They=all belonged to the illegal Communist-Party during the-Nazi-period. Puttingup posters= against : Hitler, handing out the-party's-texts, keeping forged passports for comrades who had to flee. —! those were actions that both our parents, each in their respective location, were involved. A number of summons to the security-police (neighbours. . . . . had denounced them); but nothing was proved. So they remained free. But: after that they were under-observation. . . . . With the advancing front-from-the-east Hilde & Gustav fled with their 12yearold daughter Martha on 1 of the last trains to Berlin. After-Thewar Hilde & Gustav joined the-SED; they were among the 1st members of the new party. They were workers among workers, they felt at home here. Their daughter Martha also became a member of the youth federation of the Communist Party, she was considered a party candidate. — The 1st party assignment took Hilde back to the small town near Aue: to her home town, to the- uranium-mines. . . . . Here they were to coordinate the-shifts & convince the-workers to do the necessary overtime & special hours. The-party-assignment separated the couple, because Gustav had his=work in Berlin. Martha used to work on the assembly line, a worker-among-workers, she could talk like the-men. She took her daughter with her, wanted to teach the adolescent how to talk to the-workers. So Hilde & her daughter Martha stayed with the-workers for manyshifts, they helped them where they could, spoke to the-dispirited & the-cowards. ?Was it thezeal of the two women, mother & daughter, ?or: the mere presence of two women in this men's world that impressed the-workers more. Either weigh, their visits had the desired effect on the-men. Unnoticed & secretly, but stronger-&-everstronger, thesickness was already grasping at=Martha during this time. . . . .

— Hilde's husband Gustav stayed where he had lived since the war ended: in Berlin, & worked as a precision mechanic at the reopened Borsig works in Wedding. After greatefforts he managed to convince his wife to return to Berlin. For the-functionaries at-the-headquarters in Berlin had heard of Hilde's successes — in the-work of agitation & perswaysion, as they called it. They had also got=wind of thezeal of her daughter Martha. (But the two women, Hilde & Martha, had just said what they thought in words that men could understand.) There were now bigger plans for them & so the-authorities agreed to their request for transfer to=Berlin, under 1 condition: henceforth Gustav would no longer work at=the-Borsig-factory in Wedding, but at the Elektrokohle works in Lichtenberg. (?Why. Gustav asked himself. Whether it was Wedding or Lictenberg: work is work. But kept quiet and agreed to the-condition.) Now at least he and his wife weren't only to=gether at the weekends.

— Already in Aue, at Wismut, the daughter Martha trained as a toolmaker. She completed her-training as a skilled worker; she returned to Berlin with her mother. Here the young-worker was employed at the Elektrokohle works in Lichtenberg, where her father also had to work on=party-orders. And here Martha met me, a precision mechanic 1 year older & a fellow comrade. We married soon afterwards. —

— After Rosa's death we heard for the 1st time about children who were given:up for-adoption, as one put It. Unexpected happiness often shines brighter than thesun. We-didn't-know-Then what we. . . . . had to know later. — Dry cracking sounds from the tall straight holly tree, like knuckles — the voice there=in-the-tree didn't speak, it had to swallow the-frost and snow, fallen down from theheights of a cosmos silenced in= the-ice. — Here=In-Thisplace, when I lost you for=ever as *My= Father*, that=1=cruel-moment many years ago, while you told me about my=true-parents at this grave=here —, I heard These Words for the 1st time. And I wish, as in the years-of-my=child-hood, I hadn't listened to Thewords=of-the-adults, which thawed from their lips like snow & then fell as rain into thedust at my feet. But now they no longer dried up into mud in which I could jump around with joyful leaps, laughing; now Thesewords grew into flames that reached for=me, blazing up, and took control of me for=alltime. . . . . & made me do what I did. — Yes, I heard them, Thesewords, every single 1 from you, who were no longer my father, only heard a voice from the holly tree next to a grave, the voice of someone now a stranger; youth is over as soon the words of others are the knives that lay bare the-bitterness in the soul's flesh. It is not yet one's own=bitterness; it's the bitterness of the-old who were there before you, & passed it on to=you like a cursed inheritance, the ulcer that grew in=you. Their words have the colour of-life: rusty pissy yellow. Now say what you want to say, Oldman, with the-words-of=the-old, which now and for=ever become !your=words in !your=voice.

— They were born, worked and they died. If life were as=short as=simple as this sentence, life would certainly be happier. But life lasts longer than a sentence. Irma & Alois, those were the names of Theresa's true parents. They were both born in the same village Kaltenfeld, 10 kilometres south of the district capital, Birkheim — Alois in 1930, Irma 6 years later — as farmers' children who had owned a few hectares of fields-&-woods since-time=immemorial. After Thewar, both Alois's and Irma's parents, who were now considered major farmers, were expropriated, they lost their houses farms & land. They were forcibly transferred & changed from farmers to workers at the chemical plant (it produced synthetic fertilizer) on the outskirts of Birkheim. Accommodation in old apartments damaged by-the-war, near the works, 1 room for two families, 1 kitchen, toilet in the backyard. They were treated like unwelcome=refugees. The two families divided up their=home by putting up old Wehrmacht tarpaulins they had pulled out of thedirt in the only room. They hadn't fled to=the-western-zones like many other dispossessed farmers;

they'd stayed on their=properties, either out of farmer's=stubbornness or because they missed the-moment to flee. But I think it would have been thestubbornness-of-thefarmer, who, like the captain of a sinking ship, would rather drown than abandon it, for-honour's-sake or: out-of-stubbornness. (But it used to be like That with-farmers & with-captains; Today the-people don't understand that any more.) Anyway, they had stayed until they were chased off their land. The chemical plant on the outskirts of Birkheim: In=Thewar over 1000 camp inmates were forced to-work=until-they-died there; it wasn't bombed by the-Allies. Work=there would only have been interrupted for a few days after=Thewar. Then the northwest wind was once more drawing plumes of smoke from the tall slim chimneys of the chemical plant — which was known in Birkheim simply as The-Alcid — the constant sulphur-yellow outline around a flat land covered in war-fallow fields —. The-rulers of the 1,000-year Reich had disappeared after 12 years. . . . . ; the-instrument of forced labour now law in the-hands of their successors, a Different Power, a Workers'&peasants'power that also knew how to punish with work. . . . .

The longer I listened to the old man & his steady, almost monotonous voice, which sought to avoid all heights of emphasis as well as depths of gloom and despair, looking at his face, I noticed that these features, which previously seemed like those of a person who has told all his stories, who has to make a great effort with every word, already spoken umpteen times, just to talk about it 1 more time, might be expressing something Entirely different. It seemed to me that, with his words, this old man was looking for Something that was not attainable Here&now. Because this 1 word=for-It is much too small to get What this old man may have longed for: forgiveness. Forgiveness for nothing less than almost hiswhole life. It was his=own search, here at the at the police station; because he could never believe in Anygod, and: not in Communism either any more, not in-years, he wanted Absolution for Hislife & that of his dead wife — but Absolution from ?whom. And this word forgiveness is always=toosmall, just like the other word: wrongdoing. For ?who can ?forgive another person and ?who can ?call-into-question another person? : only and only ever !That-person=themselves. — As if the-words had agreed to recite in only a few letters & short syllables what Most=People consider the-main-thing=in-life, and: what they can nonetheless never attain. And they die over that. This old man didn't want that. But he too could never find this=forgiveness, first of all because he was not talking to me, the unknown police-officer, but to a dead person. Actually two dead people, both lying buried & under a rubbish heap for cemetery waste (or: not even that, because their=remains had surely long been dug up & thus chased away a further time, this time not off but rather out of their land) on the graveyard of a backwater in the Altmark, the true parents of this woman whom that old man, her adoptive father, now wanted to report to me as missing. It's always the unattainable things that people say the most about. That's why their=stories will never end. Not until the verylastperson has disappeared off the face of the earth. Then there'll be silence. Human silence and human forgiveness. — Towards the end of the long straight road and now the main avenue of the cemetery, covered by a soft layer of snow, where the dull white of the flurries almost blurred one's vision, clearly undisturbed by the blowing snow as if moving behindglass in an otherworld, a man in a dark coat crossed the path with quick steps — maybe he was even ?whistling, or was it coming from the sharp lips of the wind — and disappeared into the more distant regions of the-cemetery.

— Flakes settled on the eyelashes like gnats made of snow, stayed for 1 2 blinks of an eye, — then thawed, new ones fell in their place. From the ice-cold stone of the bench under the snow-laden holly, frost crept first of all into the thighs, — it took blood, sent ice even into the finest veins, thecold seized the flesh in a firm=grasp, a clawed clutch, burning with frost. . . . . In=the-body wakefulness slowly burns up into ash-grey languor. (*Want to lie down. Stretch out —. !Ah my eyes are closing. Seenomore. Sleep. The heavy longing in my whole body, heavy as a millstone. A tired animal. Can't go on. Don't want to. Justsleep. — But the stone bench has no backrest, it's too short and to narrow to liedown. So stay sitting, upright, !won't freeze quite as much. . . . . Won't be. . . . . !socold —*) The silhouette of a figure in front of the teeming curtain of the-snow, it remained for a moment, like an echo, like a smile in a slowly-freezing face.

Milan's smile. !O that First Moment of an encounter. I crept from the basements of my humiliation at the Historical Institute to the washroom on the 1st floor. Downstairs, where I had been banished to=the-archive since the Great-Bureaucratic-Reshuffle (GeeBeeR) implemented the labels for *belonging / excluded* & I lost my position as a PhD historian — in=the-cellar, in the archive doing the job of an unskilled worker, Down=here the toilets were even out of order. Climbing the stairs into the atmosfear of rejection & thinly veiled malice among all the former colleagues who had been classified as *belonging* towards someone nolonger-belonging, someone demoted, her research area whyped out. (:?!Who on earth was still interested in *The Role of the Working Class & the Communist Party in Historical Class Struggles in the 2nd Half of the 20th Century* ?Today.) But precisely=!That was once my=research-project, & I'd been working-on=This keenly for-years, was on the point of making a completely unexpected discovery. My work and I, we=belonged=together. Jumped over all obstacles — a course like my previous=life: swift as an arrow & thesun of favour & my=successes was at the height of noon. *Your little girl is darting about in her white knee socks, flawless. Father.* That was The Beginning, smiling in triumph. The End was different, it led deeper down than weeping, and: I had neither of the two under control, triumph or weeping. *I shouldn't have.* But an end like that is never the definitive end. It goes on-andon. . . . .

The discovery to which My Work led me was emerging as someone so incredible so immeasurably baffling and utterly outlandish that It would hardly have been accepted by the-authorities — possibly THEY were about to declare me insane, certainly to take the-project out of my hands !immediately. . . . . THEY practically slapped me in the face with their scientific hands, as it were, referred even to the-little I had mentioned of This Discovery in my regular progress reports as *ludicrous, leading directly into the realm of idiocy, !completely !laughable, utterly !unworthy of a socialist scientist or a Normal-Person=of-Today, !against the !funda-mental insights of the Marxist understanding of his-tory* —: and Those were the most harmless accusations. Admittedly, my results within this research project were so !outlandish that I myself didn't dare to articulate Them in their full scope — and !not even Today —. I would only have had to gather a few pieces of material to prove the accuracy of all=my claims, yes: I !could have !proved them=All. — / In the spring of 1990 it was !over forgood. The New Directors of the institute didn't want Anything to do with my theories either, they reacted just=like my earlier bosses. : Had I managed to present my results before, under=the-old-conditions, I would have lost my position too. I'd have lost either way. — But what mattered today was:

my former function=at-the-institute was now considered an offence. I was the director of research for=years for !this=project. . . . ., which had previously received generous support from the-state. !I was responsible for the-distribution=of-funds — My=project had privileged status — & free choice of staff. Anyone I left was almost considered *unreliable* in=party-terms. . . . . Because THEY couldn't accuse me of offences in=democratic-terms after the GeeBeeR, THEY banished me (the-madwoman) to the basement without further ado. ?And the- colleagues: who had once scrambled to work=with-me on my=topic, for them, it seemed, the mere mention of that topic provoked nausea, like someone making them put old patina-green spoons in their mouths. But for days, since the toilet in the basement had been out of order, I'd been forced againandagain to ascend from the depths of the archive to the levels of those who belonged, had to feel the atmosfear of rejection coldness & malice that settled in the hallways as a=solid block of air along with the new plastic smell after the-re-novation of the institute. This breath came out at me from every room, and: colleagues-from-Before didn't know me any more. But the little closet of the ladies' toilet Up=here was always clean & even open to an undesirable coming from her basement exile. (For now: soon a sign on the door would deny me this room once=and-for=all: **Admittance for 1st floor staff members only!**). The plastic door handle placed itself in my hand with helpful willingness. The tiled walls twinkled in the white light. I entered, and gazed at my face in the mirror above the sink : *?What do you see.* I'd hardly shown my face to the glass before it mocked me with its question. And today, once again, it gave me the answer immediately: *Not a woman in her early 30s. You see an old whore.* I lowered my face sadly over my hollow hands, full of clear water. The cold freshness of the water burned on my face. My eyes-closed — —. *I shouldn't have.* But no one can drown themselves in their own hands. — Then I raised my water-soaked face to the mirror again —! :An unknown face, next to mine, leapt out at me: the face of a man. But this face didn't allow for any shock; the glass was so full of this man's smile that even the silver seemed to be pulsating, like the water of a sunlit lake with a mild breath of wind passing over it —. This smile filled the cool white room with the humming bee-fur warmth — flattering eye-hands reached for=me. So I didn't hear what the man was saying (no doubt little ironic jests about how he=a-man ended up in the ladies' toilets —); — I only heard the enchanting humming of his voice — saw That Smile and his eyes like darkly shining notes that coloured His Voice with the pitches of the summer day. Eyes face and mouth approached with the rapidity of a flood, — they shook the air in the little closet.

What I knew about him: years-ago this man had come from a Prague institute to this one in Berlin. He had done a PhD on the subject of the-relations between the Czech and German populations since the-Middle-Ages; a study that quickly led him into-politically=sensitive areas, as it also concerned the period from the late 19th to mid-20th centuries: changing occupying powers — dispossessions flight expulsions, sometimes of the One population and sometimes the Other, & amid that the pre-carious=role-of-the-Soviets. . . . . After completing his PhD in 1985 he was meant to continue his studies on This Subject, to deepen them, *uncover new sources*, as they put it. That was why he was sent to this Berlin institute. With the subject-of-expulsions of Germans from the Sudetenland, the man called Milan had expelled himself: from the calm & honour of the academy, from Prague to East Berlin, from the sonorous past into the New Concrete. Red Milan — left here=at-the-institute in the Great-

Bureaucratic-Reshuffle, not condemned to descent=into-the-base-ment, to the archive where the Worst Cases, like me, are left to rot; he, a Czech, wasn't thrown out, we don't have anything against foreigners : march of the-staff to kowtow, to swear fealty to the Renewed Administration — *Each an egg will quickly lay / Then success will come that day* & !Up to the 2nd floor, to the academic sanctuary of the luck-sure-y class. (— *But even there the loo falls apart sometimes, & you have to go down here where I came up to, and: on top of that, you have to go to the wrong department, the ladies' toilets : otherwise ?whoknows, we might never have met=eachother*). In this setting, dulled by talk wanly overthought & remodelled into clever Getonwithit-groups by the-epics of pragmatism, invisible to those who cannot *see*. I saw him, often and often, in the corridors, in front of the lift, in the canteen, — he was cloaked in invisible clouds, I couldn't get through to him. He probably never knowticed me. So I thought. And now heard from his mouth, suddenly so close, that he'd been looking for !me all=the-time. The basement exile of dim lights and dim-witted dull work (what a !joke to call that work), the parched need that had ruled me until just now, had lost its power in one moment of smiling. Milan. We arranged to meet in the evening.

!How the hours flowed into one another from evening-to-evening and night-for-night, leaping over the daily sorrow like splashes of sea foam. *And I couldn't take my eyes off him. Couldn't deny him a single hair of mine not a fingertip's skin. My One=and=Only. Your basement-dwelling child, Father, !what leaps.* —

— Let's go on holiday. Together. End of August. — — Where to, Milan. — — That's a !surprise. — *Foaming and wine and the skies coloured violet* — —

NEW YORK. Rain when we arrived, coming down pitilessly with no hope of ending. The greyfloods changed into light fluxes, scattered in puddles they flowed away like shrill rivers of colours. The car roofs glistening with moisture like diamond eyes, thehonking boxed its way warmly through thevening, colourful steam clouds floated around us — we were no longer on the earth, we'd stumbled into anenormouscave. Long pointed apartment towers that leapt out of an invisible sky and only kept still for a moment, taking a run-up to their ClouldEarthJump, protruded into Manhattan, vertical dreams, all times & styles that ever came over from Europe trapped=inside, set up as statues of marching capricious angels of glass stone concrete, in love with their own reflections, and thelights congealed into gossamer oily waves, therain flowing down their graceful flanks —. The yellow taxi took us further to the asphalt-hot wind shifts in scarlet & gold flames slicing with long blades ghost lights shooting glass-dazzling spray streams in fine veils bleating with its horn & clanging burnt into the rain-heavy night sky vault over thecity & pressed into the whirling exhaust clouds of the multi-yellow-coloured metal stream car-to-car, then finally hurled down the lines of avenues glowing in the night fever & starting a!new in the heat-soaked steam-hot air block after each ending over&over=again — —

Anything live shrieks red. The scarscrapers wreathed in purple, a king's robe wrapped around all the carcasses. On the landing stages of South Manhattan. The docks. The heavy smells of all seas all people. Fishflood oilflood mudflood meatflood human flood. . . . . Dead fish on the pier, screeching clouds of seagulls cormorants swirling around prey. Cadaver food for cadavers. In the iron-blue light the broken bodies. The great cave-vault of New York. The skies so distant, steaming from cracks in the stone

in the asphalt. Skyscrapers, the lighthouses for all sailors of rage
& seething pleasures. The sky and the earth exchanged their
places, familiar since-time=immemorial, turned over: the Empire
State needle-thin, honed from the sky as a fang, we took the ele-
vator and went down to all the clouds. 96th floor, gazes : all the
high higher highest buildings bared their teeth. Beaten into the
body of acity. Awholecity as prey. — ?Will you marry me. —
Asked Milan and looked at me. I took my face out of the clouds
and threw myself into=his. Silent on the platform, thick storm-
arms roaring around us. The swishing carried my Yes to his ears.

BROOKLYN BRIDGE. Iron & wood, smoke-black sand-
stone, the path from one nocturnal shore to the other riveted on
with dazzling big-eyed chains of lights. — It must have happened
there, by that dark mighty pillar: a strange accident years-ago.
— Milan began. — A woman died in it, along with a creature
that was said to be like a dog and a human. Nobody knew what
it was. The woman was driving in her car from Park Row
towards that approach=there to Brooklyn Bridge. She wanted to
dodge what she thought was a stray dog running across the road
— lost control of the car and crashed into that bridge pillar. It
was said that the dog — an unusually large animal of almost
human form, !very strange — had been tied to the pillar for many
days. Now, in !the-very-moment the woman was driving towards
the bridge, the animal, almost starved to death and mad with
fear, finally tore its leash and rushed right into the road, ran
into=the-car the woman was sitting in — to its freedom, which
only lasted seconds. And ?do you know what's funny about the
story: the husband of this woman had hired a hitman, he wanted
to get rid of her, who knows why people want to get rid of other
people. Anyway, he felt remorse & did away with the killer. His
wife stayed a-live. Until she encountered this manimal on

Brooklyn Bridge. She had escaped the killer and died in the accident. ?Isn't that tragic.

— ?How do you know All=that.

— A writer talks about it in a book, some German. I don't know his name, haven't read the book either. And the writer has been dead for-years, I think. Come on, let's go back. — His hand closed around my hand.

Dull hazy morning hour — the field of stelae formed by theapartmentblocks, woven into the fine cocoon of an already-approaching autumn. Strange the silence down=in-the-street-canyons — as well as noise honking stamping rumbling the shrill cries all silenced by a large white mist-world. —. My face dipped into wet air at the open window on the top floor of thehouse, — and: a strange sound, the only one I could make out clearly from the Great Fog-Silence: a wavering, whirring twittering very close to me, bright & moving away at an incredible speed before disappearing in the canyons between the high-rise buildings. *!No bird can fly that fast. ?What is that.* And a few moments later it came back — whistling twittering wavering frantically speeding upwards through the air. Then, on the roof of the building next door, which was slightly lower, I saw a man: he raised his right arm, swung it far back — and threw: — boomerang. — Said Milan's voice next to me. !Look how it flies away, like some unknown whirling bird between the skyscrapers far above the streets of Manhattan. The people=down-below can't see it, don't even know that it's=there. You can only see and hear it Up=Here; when it flies off — and when it comes back. Again=and=again. — Those were the first hours without rain and it was our last morning in New York. *I shouldn't have.* Back in Germany: living in a small toxic-tasting coin again. I'd barely got back from New York before I got a phone call summoning me to the personnel manager at the institute. I could guess !what He wanted from me, I'd been expecting it for-a-longtime.

The personnel manager, several years younger than me, imported from Württemberg in 1990, was called Schmitz; but at-the-institute he was known only as *Mr Whistly*. That was due to his appearance, especially his manner: everything about this thin, lanky man seemed pursed into a pair of lips that were about to start whistling. He had a swaying gait with large steps and wide, flapping arm movements, as if he didn't know what to do with his long thin limbs. With his head (the hairline already receding) always cocked slightly to one side, he turned his slim face towards people, peered with beady little eyes, and his taut lips always seemed on the point of smirking; one almost expected him to begin every sentence with 'Well-lookat-!that'. But this man was anything but cheerful; his outward appearance belied his ruthless nature, and the clever glances he used like a-needle to skewer the others could have been the glances of an exterminator, as if he had to inspect any area he entered for pests & as if no matter where he looked, all he expected to find was vermin. As soon as he laid eyes on 1=of-those-woodlice gnats bedbugs again, his eyes said: *Well-lookat-!that: another one. I !thought as much.* Then he immediately employed his=methods. After 1990, in — the =course of the Great-Bureaucratic-Reshuffle, he showed that same exterminator-style in finding a number of former secret service members informants big & little snitches &, faithful to his duty, kicking them to-the-curb (though sometimes the curb was located a few floors higher; the gravity of-careers has its own=rules).

Mr Whistly told me to come to his=office before even starting work. I had barely entered the room (he didn't offer me a seat) before he revealed the reason for this appointment.

He spoke of *restructuring=the-institute*, of *downsizing-&-reju-venating-the-body-of-personnel* & of *lowering-institute=costs* — in short: the man was telling me to hand in my-resignation. (This would save the-institute A Lot of money). Un-for — — tunately (the broadness of his clever dicktion stretched the word out like a saggy hammock) there would !not be any possibility of com-pensation or similar firenancial arrangements, *Mr Whistly* emphasized. With that, he considered the matter settled. But he did add that in the case of a-resignation=on-my-part he would certainly be willing to put in a word for me elsewhere in order to find a position for me. Otherwise. But he didn't finish the sen-tence; looked at me with his pursed face, thin lips & cocky eyes. This figure seemed to exude a sharp-edged smell wherever it appeared, as if knives were being sharpened. / I felt nausea rising, turned around & left the office wordlessly. Later I handed in my-resignation.

In the following weeks, when I went to interviews with other personnel managers in the hope of a job, they always demanded a reference from my previous employer. That meant I had to phone *Whistly* every time, tell him what I wanted & ask him to send the assessment to the respective address. Every time *Mr Whistly* expressed great pleasure at the New Chance I had found, and provided his support. Gave me addresses to contact, saying that !he had sent me. It was just a tad strange that this never led to any employment —. — By chance I discovered that as soon as I had accepted his offer & put the receiver down, *Mr Whistly* called the other personnel manager & urgently !warned him not to employ me at !any cost. As for my=documents, he could leave them where they were for awhile. *Mr Whistly* was a man who !enjoyed doing his job in the-New=Way & showed it; his cunning smile was in-reality the grin of the victor who had Full

Authorization for his actions. Arseholes can be leisurely about their=jobs too. And so I asked myself, considering the many thousands who died daily: ?Why can't !he=of-all-people be ?one of them —

When I collected my things from my workplace in the basement that morning, after my appointment with *Whistly*, I took all the materials for my earlier research project with=me: all documents, all electronically-stored data. No one had shown any interest in them since my demotion, no one would miss those-things. I thought. And ascended for the last time from the-basement=of-my-banishment. *Not so far from all things, Father, that building bridges-of-repair across the abyss-of-ending is impossible. Gold became silver, silver became flesh. Then the millstone. And at=the-end The Prize of Love from the One Person who once sent you out. That's the certainty in=fairy-tales. ?But what's certain in this-reality. You girl, Father, has become cautious and steps from 1 rotted, cracking board to the next, the wobbly planks tied with coarse ropes from this Other Reality. Father, I know you won't be able to help me any more now; and you don't know how to help yourself either. Lownlier than ever — and times of victory, vanished for now.*

Once again the storm raised its fists and drove snow-whirls over the area, pressed into a densewhitewall. Then, as if a giant-mouth were exhaling icy masses of air, ahowl shot through the sky, — and the snow-whirls and storm suddenly collapsed into themselves. The sky now calm in grey. Only iceolated little flakes rushing about, like schoolchildren late on their way home. A smile on frostbitten lips, lips like glass, and this smile settled in (*feel the tearing in the corners of my mouth, can't stop it*), now it didn't want to leave the mouth, the freezing face —. — — The two children, Irma & Alois, grew up with their parents after they

43

had been forcibly:transferred to Birkheim. The-state-border=
with-the-west also grew, spread out, became harder, more impenetrable. — As if the words spoken to me by the old-man=there
at the table had been a password, one of those ancient initials
full of depictions of death and lost life, one-of=those oldstories
returned, compulsively, immutably, — and I no longer had to listen to the narrator, because I had already heard Everything that
These-Oldstories could tell a dozentimes, so often that I've come
to think These-Stories were spawned by my=experiences, and so
now too, I heard myself inside=me continuing with my voice &
my own words: *Now & again one hears shots at people — fugitives — who want to get across-the-border, through black &
silently-waiting woods; the-shots often hit them. . . . . Then the
people fall in the sand, where not one blade of grass grows
because plant toxins ensure a Clear Line of Fire, sometimes they
aren't dead : they scream theirpain into thenight. Then packs of
dogs come running, shortly afterwards the soldiers. Drag the
bullet-shredded, bleeding flesh out of the dirt, throw It on a
truck, drive away with it —. — But more often, after warning
shots have burned glowing trails into The Darkness, the-border-
soldiers catch the fugitives in front of One of the fences, in front
of barriers, barbed wire. In the shrill glare of the searchlights the
chalk-white faces like bloodless masks in thenight, animal fear
in huge eyes that stare at the soldiers running towards them; —
then dogs barking, boots trampling, torch beams flailing across
the pale faces like slaps; yelling, throwing to the ground, the dog
bites going up&down the bodies, handcuffs, taken away. The rear
lights of the patrol cars die away in smoky shreds of the night —
—, and silence returns to this district of easily acquired death.*
I've heard that sooften in-the-years since my arrival=here that
now feel as if I'd seen It myself, & again-&-yet-again. *And in*

these daydream visions I'm the-fugitive and: I'm the sentry who confronts me, the would-be escapee, with my submachine gun at the ready & the bloodthirsty dogs tugging on a taut leash. With each return of this vision the taste of heavy bitter earth trampled grass and blood, a view into the barrel of the submachine gun, the weapon's round opening, little black maw of death; and: the eyes bitten to pieces by the glaring light with which They drag me out of the sheltering darkness & throw me to the ground in front of the flashing dog teeth by-the-fence. . . . . , which I can never overcome. Later THEY didn't want to shoot the-fugitives any more, THEY needed the flesh of the-fugitives alive, preferably unscathed; to sell-out first the prisoners, then Anyone Else who might bring in some MONEY=HARD-CURRENCY.

But those, as I say, were just the words of my own Inner-Voice. For this man sitting opposite me certainly wouldn't have been able to utter anything of that kind, even Today, after the former present had been fading for somanyyears; he believed he was still connected soclosely to those times, now only ashes, that he probably wouldn't have admitted the difference between imagination (his=ideal) and: reality (that is, what ideals always become as soon as people turn them into deeds), even Now. Because yes: what remains of those-times are a few buckets of ash, greasy insubstantial dust on allthe dust heaps from the-times=before; — but anyone who pokes around in it will soon find remnants of embers, glowing spots of flame-coloured shimmering that can't light any more fires, they're too faint for that, and if one exposed them to theair, they'd quickly go out, yet these ember lumps are strong enough to burn one's fingers —. — That's what I suspected; there'd be no point asking him, the old man, about it. (People always defend their=deadlove more passionately than the-dead whom their=love left by-the-wayside.) So now I

heard the old man's voice speaking alone again, heard him continue his=own Oldstory.

— Irma & Alois didn't want to stay in Birkheim after their
parents died. They moved back to Kaltenfeld: the house of Alois's
parents stood derelict. (Irma found her parent's house inhabited
by strangers termed=*repatriates*.) 1 half of Alois's house also
belonged to strangers now; just decrepit leftovers for the former
owners. Better leftovers than Nothing : Irma moved in with Alois,
and they were married there in 1955. Together=they made a
greateffort to renovate their run-down half of the house. For the
farm & land no longer belonged to them; after the land reform
& after the-expropriation=of-the-majorfarmers they had to live
in their former house as tenants & virtually to work on the property, which was now an eLPeeGee, as farm hands on the soil of
their ancestors. Henceforth life could only seem like an exile=in-
a-foreign-land to them; the confrontation with their neglected
house, which no longer belonged to them, was like the disturbing,
unsettling sight of a closer relative who one hears has been
released from An Institution. They stood before it in the bright
daylight as strangers. Without anything to hold on to, they fell
apart=inwardly. But they had to do !Something. They siphoned
off various building material from the eLPeeGee's supply to
renovate their=part-of-the-house; they reported sick all=the-time.
?Why work for strangers on their own farm. . . . . Now the money
would come by-itself. They became a nuisance for the-authorities,
who couldn't convict them of theft & simulating-illness, they were
considered unruly, irredeemable; They wanted to get to=them. —
1 year after they married, Irma gave birth to their 1st child: on
15 October 1956 in the village of Kaltenfeld a girl. Theresa. —

The old man spoke these words as if he had to give a-report
of some wrongdoing. His right hand reached into the inside

pocket of his jacket with a calmly resolute gesture; as if I had asked him for it, he pushed a photograph across the table towards me. The controlled nature of this arm movement was matched by the austerity of his accompanying voice: — You'll need a photo of her for the-investigation. — As if wanting to prove the old man's coolness wrong, his other hand, empty, opened in my direction with an imploring gesture.

No one in=the-room said a word. (Möller cleared his throat awkwardly.) The paper made a scraping sound on the bare wood of the table.

Meanwhile the old man continued in a calm, but veryquiet voice: — Alois & Irma both died in=the-same-year, 1979, *death under-mysterious-circumstances*. That was what people whispered. People never manage more than a whisper, otherwise they'd choke on The Truth.

I didn't touch the photo=before-me on the table, shied away from it. ?Maybe I really thought that the=moment I picked it up, this woman would really become *a case*, the fifth victim=of-a-serial-offender we had so far failed to catch. So I left the photo in front of me for a moment, stared at it. Not a portrait photo of this woman, probably a photograph from a late summer outing to the town's environs: a small meadow on the edge of a forest or park, the trees in the background lowering their ample leaves close to the soil like greenish-black clouds; in front of that 2 parked cars (VW & Renault in blue & grey), and in between long thin grass standing high and looking fluffy, like yellowish fur, closely surrounding the woman's legs, covered by long white linen trousers. The grass almost reaches the woman's knees, her height maybe 5 foot 7, slim figure, but with nice womanly curves. (The trail slightly curving through the soft, dense grass field shows her path to that point; she must have taken it shortly before the photo was made, as the trampled grass hasn't recovered yet.) Her stance is relaxed, arms hanging down on both sides of her body around a blouse with a brownish-yellow pattern and a belt of the same colour, like a caftan (a watch on her left wrist), and she's smiling at the-observer. The blouse is cut low, down to where the breasts begin, with shadows there on the bare skin and on the left side of her face, while the whole right side of her body is illuminated by the copper-tinged light of an afternoon sun. The woman's shiny blonde hair, styled into wavy locks, ends just above her shoulders. The features of her slim face, half in the shade and half in the light, are smoothed over by a static smile. The thintaut lips, painted veryred, show her white-shimmering upper row of teeth, the corners of her mouth inscribe a few vertical, half-round folds into her cheeks that underline the cheerfully=relaxed nature of her expression. Her eyes are in the shade, narrow, screwed up as if dazzled by sunlight (which is impossible, the-light is coming from the side); it seems as if her face can't show that smile very often; this woman seems a little unpractised in cheerfully=relaxed gazes.

— She studied history. And philosophy. At the Humboldt University in Berlin. Did some specialized work there recently. — The old man added this like an explanation, as if to justify the severity and: lack of cheer, which he too had noticed & viewed as a fault, he showed while gazing at this portrait.

— ?How old is the photo. — I asked the man. — — Not old. — He replied immediately.

— Perhaps 2 years. I was the one who took the photo. On an outing to —, I don't remember where that was.

But she looked younger on the photo than a-woman=in-her-mid-50s. We had to enlarge her face for the mug shot. Shortly afterwards I had the following detail in front of me: narrow

woman's face, surrounded by wavy blonde hair, a mouth unac-
customed to smiling, veryred & slightly too severe, but a dimple
was visible on her chin.

— Death under-mysterious-circumstances. — I repeated the
old man's earlier words to tear myself away from this photograph
and my dark suspicions. . . . . — — ?!What : ?What ?do you
mean. — The old man's eyes may also have been=fixed on the
photograph of his adoptive daughter; my remark had torn away
his glances, with which he clung tightly to the picture, as if I had
struck him. He stared into my face in shock.

— You were speaking about the death of her parents, Alois
& Irma, in 1979, and you said: death — — Under-mysterious-
circumstances. Yes. I said that. — Now there was almost relief in
his voice, as if the-cup-of-bad-news from my hand had passed
him by for now. (After all, one expects Bad-News from a detective superintendent as soon as he starts a conversation, which
can become an interrogation at any moment. For=me it was
always-the-same moment that kept returning : the face of my
later second wife, Regina, in the hours of our first encounter: the
sunshine of joyfulness and carefree laughter shimmered in her
face; but when I told her I was a policeman, a cop=at-the-DCI
— then something like frost shot into her eyes, the laughter
stayed in them but it seemed to harden like plaster. And I saw
joyfulness and cheerfulness from the other side, as it were. It
stayed like that, I never saw that once=first fresh honey-sheen of
laughter in her face again. Now we've been married for almost
twentyears, we're at home with=each-other, live in our thoughts
& words, know each other with our hands feet elbows knees and
shoulder, the chewing sounds at mealtimes & our sleeping faces,
but only rarely do our hours of intimacy now have the same scent
of freshly-cut flowers as they once did.)

CHAPTER 2

The wanderer comes to an inn.
He has his property with him.
He wins the steadfastness of a young servant.

But I was wrong about that. The relief in the old man's voice was only feigned, it even seemed mocking, sarcastic. And suddenly The Voice of this almost ghostlike man, his hair turned grey by time & disillusionments that had recently brought him disappointments, by losses & grief, surged up, — an unexpected power of rage went shot through his body like electricity in a thunderstorm, straightening his limbs, his chin jutted out and his eyes smouldered; he'd have liked nothing better than to bang his fist on the table: —!They didn't have to come back from their graves as if they'd been buried prematurely. — Therage slurred his words, they raced along, but his face was not turned towards me; his fierce words struck the corner of the ceiling: — The-undead cling to the last rough breath-rope — they could stay lying there all those=years until they rotted and beyond, Twoandahalf metres=Undertheearth: !they didn't matter any more. They got what they needed: their=stone with their=names on it: Alois and Irma Berger. Each at the head of the grave. What put them=there came Back=Up again without any ghosts & resurrection. It climbed through flattened earth by=itself — went through the cracks in the layers of dirt & time. — Then the old man took his hand and wiped the anger from his face.

— And now Everything took its-course : It found ears, nestled firmly=in-the-brains, & finally perched on people's-tongues
: Certain-Things were given voices again. There they were again:
these-Oldstories. . . . . — He had to catch his breath. But he
hadn't finished his narrative rampage yet. — And ?do you know
the ?best bit: !coincidence. All !coincidence. None of it was a
result of exposed espionage (as the prosecutor claimed in=court),
that nonsense about col-laboration-with-the-class=enemy, malicious treason & allthat pompous rubbish THEY always have
at=the-ready whenever some state needs enemies. !Noway: those
two were much — much too simple for !that kind of thing and
much too far away from Anything one could call. . . . . politics.
Anyone who was a vaguely good judge of character would've
noticed That right away : but nobody was !supposed to notice
it. !That was the-point. And the 1st one to be executed by judges
like that is always Common Sense. — He gave a short, dry cough.
— They were just troublemakers, and THEY had to turn them
into that first by taking away their=family-home & their=measly-
farm, and: for SOME PEOPLE. . . . . they were in:theway. That
was all. This whole damnbusiness just fell on their heads :
Newton's apple & political gravity, if you will. But whether it's
a crab apple or a road apple: either one of them can fall on somebody's head, assuming one gets tooclose to it: to the arse-of-
politics. — And then he had himself=under=control again.

I hadn't interrupted him during his=run, even though I hadn't
understood a word of what he was getting at. But now the old
man could carry on, he found his slightly monotonous voice
again & took up his account with his head slightly lowered, the
way an old packhorse takes up its rope & theburden. Theburden
of his story about the *mysterious-death* of two people, Theresa's
true parents.

— But she'd be the 1st without any siblings. — Möller's voice, bright & loud, butted in tactlessly, with the cockiness he had whenever something occurred to him. We, the old man and I, started up as if awaking from a spell. But it was true, Möller was right; I looked up, so did the man opposite me, we looked at each:other. His gaze seemed disturbed, almost fearful or: trembling briefly, as if before another fit of rage.

Attentively. Waiting patiently. None of the intrepid eagerness of an investigator in the eyes of this inspector, oho: this !chief inspector, this man already getting-on-in-years. Attentively, yes, patiently, but with a calm, unswerving constancy he casts his=glances at me. As if they were solid walls, & only between them, on a narrow eye-path, the passage for my words. Must be- !careful, mustn't scrape against thewalls. !No more evasions now, no escape from Everything I have to say. He's giving me time. Isn't pushing me. Out of politeness or with the concentrated matter- of-factness of a doctor inspecting an X-ray. This removes him from a personal judgement on the-patient, which, assuming the- doctor would even make a judgement outside of his=field, would be completely irrelevant for the illness. These grey-green eyes gazing calmly, steadily at=me. Not implacable, but demanding. They wouldn't let go now. Even seems to be coming closer, this attentive grey-green of two eyes, — closer and closer — and now they start turning slowly, this well-defined twofold round eye — as if looking into the funnels of two maelstroms, the two pupils the dark centre, the eye-in-the-eye —; as if two currents were sud- denly forming from a calm, wave-smoothed sea beyond all tides & all lashing breakers in this massively=still mass of water with two thirds of awhole planet's weight — currents that slowly but surely touched thewaters=allaround more&more and set them in-motion — making them spin faster and faster — subterranean

*deep bubbling roaring raging rises as if from behemoth lungs —
already thecurrents are pulling Everything near&far towards=
them grabbing=it sweeping it along with=them & dragging it
away into these ever faster-circling whirling depths of two bright
centres growing clearer with every word —.* NOT YET DON'T
LET ME DIE NOW THAT THE WHOLEBUSINESS IS JUST
ABOUT TO —

*Yes, Nothing that could offer any support or shelter now —
yes: ?why shouldn't it be like=that : all that has been, whether
Great or small, revolves precisely=around-These=two-centres,
these two eyes of two maelstroms, two people long dead &
buried —; that It was !them & It is !them, seemingly so insignifi-
cant so contemptible / ephemeral, even more fleeting than a
cough from the throat of-leviathan, that hardly anyone knew
their=names and: even fewer wanted to keep them in=mind
for longer than a breath : And yet :* AND YET IT WAS BECAUSE
OF !THEM ONLY=!THEM AND STILL IS NOW&HERE
THAT ALL THESE=OLDSTORIES. . . . . TOOK PLACE.
IT WAS FOR THEM THAT ALL THE TEARS FLOWED,
THE-HEAVENS CRACKED & OPENED UP, & DISMAY
HATE CONTEMPT MALICIOUSNESSES & ALLHORRORS
POURED DOWN WITH HAILSHOWERS OF BOMBS
GRENADES TORE CITIES & PEOPLE APART WITH
KATYUSHAS MENCHILDRENWOMEN CRUSHED UNDER
TANK TREADS, FRIGHT & OUTRAGE SHOT UP FROM
THE DIRT&BLOOD OF A-WHOLE WORLD AS A NEW
SEED BUT THE ROT OF THE OLD WAS ALREADY OR STILL
AT ITS=CORE — *then I began with the twisted* WE *in my mind,
& these typical=human feelings & forces were also defeated once
again & again with hail or fire or storm tides or other despair,
and finally everything fermented into the meaningless dirt of*

53

oblivion. !That's It, Inspector : !Chief Inspector, and !that's why I won't escape from you, and don't want to escape, but want to say Everything that's been inside=me for=so-long out loud & not spare anyone. !Least of all myself. And all the explanations, proofs, conclusions and truths whose accuracy I too was con-vinced of = so infused with that I didn't see the thin rusty chains-of-thought which could actually !never have given these IRREFUTABLE FACTS *a foothold on the sludgy bottom-of-the=matter, didn't see them my whole=life : I believed !somuch. . . . . in the-con-crete,* ROCK=SOLID=TRUTH *of these loose flighty idea-things that poison living experiences with their ascending miasmas —:* AND NOW I SEE THEM=ALL DRAWN DRIVEN TORN EQUALLY INTO THEGREATCURRENT AND THE MOST BRILLIANT PROOFS=FROM-BACK-THEN NOW FLOATING BELLY UP LIKE SHOALS OF DEAD FISH *— but now: now I'm !free : !free=through=speaking.*

— Willfried. His name is Willfried. With 2 Ls. It always gets misspelt. And Nothing makes him angrier than !that.

— ?Who is this Wilfried.

— You see: you also pronounced it with only 1 L.

— But no one can hear it that precisely.

— Because it's always=misspelt & therefore mispronounced, I can hear it. Chief Inspector.

— But just now you — (clears throat) — — so ?who is this: Willfried-with-2-Ls. And ?how do you know this=whole story. ?Who ?told it to you.

— Theresa's brother is called Willfried. —:Möller, whom I took to be dozing out of boredom and disappointment over what the old man had said so far, shot up from his chair at the word *brother*; we gave each other a quick look : (So she !does: !she has siblings too.)

No doubt the old man hadn't even noticed our reactions; he was already immersed in his=accounts again. — Several years ago, we — my wife Martha was still alive — received an anonymous letter. It was a real tale, actually: the story of our adoptive daughter Theresa. To thisday I'm not sure who wrote it. But probably the author of that letter died long ago too. The whole letter was written in an even, unexcited hand, I thought it must have been written by a woman, I could almost hear the stranger's voice while=reading: carried by a deep, tearless sorrow — that was how she spoke the lines with unexcited but steady implacability, with words that sounded like some old murder ballad from long ago. The lines — I kept thisletter, picked it up once again before coming to the station to see you — the lines of this writing are still unfaded, even after somanyyears, peaceless, as if they'd been written in a special ink, & all the violent acts of those times have not only left the blue, regular fabric of this writing, but instead have imprinted themselves on all times after that, as if the ink strokes were still=damp & copied themselves firmly & clearly onto the empty pages of all future things that would come into=contact with Them. If this story is true, and I've never doubted that it is, then for=us, for my wife Martha and myself, it was The Turning Point in our life. I can say that with !no reservations. And we also knew that we could only tell Theresa Allthat once she was old enough for=thisstory. But to=this=day I still don't know when that=certain age=of-old=enough starts. Perhaps I told Theresa about It tooearly; perhaps It would always have been !tooearly for=her. She had a very sensitive, dreamy nature that can feel the tension in any events.

— *Had* a sensitive nature. ?Why do you say: *had*. — The words almost slipped out by-themselves. But the old man didn't let it interrupt his=story. He wiped his eyes. — I thought the long-time after her youth ceremony would finally have been the-right=

time. So we went to Birkheim, my wife I and Theresa, to the town's largest cemetery, where — according to the anonymous letter — Theresa's true parents lay buried. We found the grave exactly in the place described, next to a tall holly tree, & there we told Theresa thestory as it had been told to us & also what I'd found out about it myself. Because back then I started researching, as far as possible, about Theresa's parents. Much to the annoyance of certain=authorities. . . . .

— When Irma Berger was finally arrested with her husband — after several open or covert acts of spying intimidation sum-mons-to-the-authorities — in February 1959, it was at the start of her 2nd month of pregnancy. But even she didn't really know !that at the time. Because they say that with-women the-period gets interrupted in situations that are so dangerous to=their=own-lives that the possibility of New-Life is lost. She probably only became aware of her=condition in custody. Daily-prison-life in the GeeDeeR in the late 50s: ?shall I ?tell you something about it, Chief-Inspector-from-Hanover, that might ?interest you. Every-time, after all, has its=own-reason just as every-church has its=saints. And from reason, everytime also develops its=own punishments & the-treatment of offenders. This produces differ-ent form of meaning that are necessarily impossible to understand in othertimes. Especially when it comes to !what's considered worthy of punishment and !how people could then endure !Those Hardships & !Those Ordeals at all. Because outside their=time, the-reasonable & the-saints are stupid & ridiculous, and all tribulation just seems bizarre; decorations for the-games=of-horror in history. Later on, people drive busloads of history-tourists to such places, & they, gobbling icecream chocolate & popcorn and pointing their digital cameras at every rusty nail, let the chatty museum guides explain Everything to them that can't be explained. — (He cleared his throat.)

— Today I could say plenty about That, as far as the-cruelties of those 50s in this-country are concerned; back then I never wondered ?what happened to the-enemies=of-the-GeeDeeR in the human cages behind thewalls & steel doors. And I neverreally thought about the-women who gave birth while-in-custody. ?What happened to ?these=children. ?Who brings the up & ?where. I didn't ask myself any=of-that back then. But I was sure the right-thing was being done, just as I was sure that our=state leadership always sought what was best for=us=the-people. And what was best=for-us would be best=for-the-wholeworld too. : But some-times when I was at the train station & saw the paddywagon, Green-Minna they called it, & saw the figures that were herded out & ordered to line-up-in-rows, some of them already wearing the black garb with broad yellow stripes down it, the-prison-uni-form; how they were rushed across the station courtyard into the-prison-train, the Grotewohl-Ex-Press, by armed police with their menacing dog squads —: then I got a feeling inside=me like hoarfrost, freezing me from-the-inside. . . . . And later on I tried every time to remember the faces of those prisoners; but all I managed were silhouettes, just the stereotypes : grey masks of men&women-in-prison-uniforms, and one time a large brown case in the hands of 1=of-these-men. ?Why did I always have to think of !that case —. Everytime they disappeared in the dirt-green tin wagons with the narrow, barred windows; the hoarfrost inside=me kept on freezing me for a while —. And those were the=moments in which I consciously sucked the breath into=me, I practically listened to the inflow of theair with the atoms of all those who had to *disappear*. . . . . , who weren't people but *Our=Enemies*, which concentrated in the wind & airstreams to form air walls that I had to breathe against every time I filled my lungs and: which still crept into=me & made me freeze in the hoarfrost —. But I wanted to !fight Against-It, not let myself be poisoned, & so I always remembered Our=State's Men, and the hoarfrost=in-me thawed, thefrost of doubt melted: for ?why should These=Men, who had once fought with-the-resistance= against:the-Nazis (as They said), Now that they=were-in-power, ?not want what was best for the-people; ?why should they think & act ?differently from me & many like me. —

With a jolt, the old man sat up straight in his chair, at first I thought he wanted to jump up & rush to an imaginary black-board to demonstrate the course of his life to me & Möller in chalk.

— ?!Why should I have had doubts about the WE & the US. The-state came to me & Martha with the guarding arms of friendship, THEY brought us gifts with full kind hands; we were among the first eSEeDee members, and were then, even though we were still young in-years, already considered *Old Comrades*. The-state paid for our qualification; from a simple mechanic to a dispatcher-for-transportation — we, Martha and I, travelled all over the country through this profession. We saw Alot, including things it would've been better not to see, for reality is acid for the flesh of ideals & dreams. But even now, we had our=firm= viewpoint and didn't doubt the goodwill of this state we viewed as our=one: THEY only wanted the best for us — so THEY took it from us. But the 2nd part of that, we didn't know it back then, Martha and I. And when we finally had Theresa with=us, whom we=secretly, just=between-us, called *October*, our=happiness began and: our=misfortune too. But we didn't know about the misfortune yet; we !finally had a daughter, even if it wasn't our biological child, and we were happy. !Yes, I remember that feeling, because that happiness was something we had created=ourselves. We didn't yet know that happiness always has to be invented, otherwise there is no happiness, least of all happiness-for-humans. But with this happiness, misfortune came towards us — not slowly but suddenly — in the form of a letter, it stepped into our home like the ghost of the unredeemed past that remains Ever=Present : the story of what happened to Theresa's parents. It was as if death had struck again. But this time it didn't take away the child, this time death — gradually, day-by-day & as long as it stayed in our=home — It took away : our *faith*. It took what we thought was the best thing we had: the love for our state, our trust that THEY wanted thebest for=everyone. — (Now the old man wiped his face once more, his hand leaving red marks on his forehead as if he'd tried to plough through his brain —) — But !that was exactly why THEY had arrested Theresa's parents, these descendants of major farmers who had now been dispossessed by that same state: for them too, THEY only wanted what was best, except that for us, this=best-thing was the other side of the best; I never knew before then that even the best things can have at least 2 sides. —

(He coughed croakingly into the palm of his hand, nervous. Thought for a moment. Collected himself.)

—!That was exactly where their=story and the story of our misfortune began. First it was just the-story, 1-of-many of people resisting the-measures of the state that had followed the land reform. The village of Kaltenfeld was not far from the-border with Lower Saxony. Many of the dispossessed farmers & various former Nazi-Party-members had fled there. If one believed the-papers & the-news=in-this-country, !all the surviving Nazis had gone !there, to-the-west, our=GeeDeeR was considered *Nazi-free* (:and no one, it seemed, noticed. . . . . Anything about this word; no one seemed inclined to remember Anything=Particular in relation to it, for whenever such remembrance is painful, one avoids the pain and the remembrance, & then the Old can be sold as New. And sometimes the knowledge lies *in* the words and *in* a slip of the tongue.) But !that was exactly It — (the old man writhed) —!That was It, & those who had fled-to-the-west had also taken the news over=there about rural-conditions=here & what had happened to the-dispossessed who hadn't run off but stayed.

— They were still young people, Irma 23 and Alois almost 30. And had grown up as farmers' children. The early years of every-person's life make them merge with the place and the region where they were born. Thatsjusthowitis. After returning from Birkheim to the village of Kaltenfeld, to the region of their=childhood, they were met with the contemptible sight of a Strange Land: the expropriated land. And there was a man who worked for the-authorities in the administration, a small wiry person with a balding head & an oversized mouth full of bad teeth with wide gaps between them, making it seem as if the mouth took up his entire face. I got to know this person. When he spoke, it seemed as if he first formed his wide mouth into the necessary shape and only then placed the appropriate words in it, which meant that only oversized words — phrases — could come out of that oversized mouth. People (in secret & in whispers) called him 'Pigtooth'. No one dared speak badly of him out loud, because he was The Party Secretary of that administrative district (&, according to rumour) a !particularly vicious-bastard= in-the-firm. . . . . If you follow — (:I nodded) — — Nobody could say where the man came from; he was one of those swamp plants that sprout up after every change of faith. Wherever That-Man turned up, conversations stopped and all joy disappeared; people adopted a servile manner, but anyone could see how much they=all !hated That-Man. And that=very-man had the two of them, Irma and Alois, in: his-sights : they were like 2 thorns in his side, he wanted to see !his=workspace 'cleansed of enemies'. And if, instead of just suspicions & the-disgrace=of-their-birth, he had had anything concrete to use against them, He would've seen to their arrest within the hour. . . . . One can always find reasons to send other people to-their=doom in a world where Everyone is sniffing around for reasons & proof. But that would turn out !differently too. ?Do you think I could have a glass of water. It's very stuffy in —

Möller was already in motion (with strange eagerness) to get him what he wanted. While he was out of the room, the old man continued. — It was coincidence, as I already said, that 1day led a man to the ½ a house of those two, Irma & Alois, in their rural hardship: an acquaintance of their late parents, a shady character who travelled back&forth across the-border for certain-transactions — in a word, smuggling. And he was the one who —: then Möller re-entered the office holding a large glass of water and placed it wordlessly in front of the old man, who reached for it eagerly, — he emptied the glass in heavy gulps. Then wiped his mouth with the back of his hand and continued his story where he had left off: — He was the one who brought them !The News, not just some hearsay but official documents —!proof — which showed that their greatest adversary, this eSEeDee functionary with the oversized mouth, he'd been their greatest adversary once before: used to be a functionary in the party with the other name: eNeSDeeAPee. : His=party-membership-book lay there with his own signature, as well as the membership form, likewise signed by him. There: in front of them both, on the worn-out crumbling oilcloth spread over the only table in the little kitchen area. The stranger drank the liquor he had brought with him, & his little eyes, which seemed to be swimming in spirits, repeated to them

what his lips had already stated: — With !thesepapers, the
Pigtooth is !donefor. If you make the wholething known. And
because stories without people aren't stories, you=both have to
get !loud about your=story. Have to sound the !alarm. Really
kick up a fuss. You have to !stand up to shut that Pigtooth's
mouth & cast down the one who wanted to cast you down. Now
it's !your=turn. I'll help you, — said the lips & the squinting liquor
eyes, — if you tell me abit about !What's going-on=here so that
I can turn it into a !reallybigstory for BILD. — The weak glow
of the kitchen lamp mingled with his boozebreath — that's how
I imagine the scene that evening. And the two of them, who suddenly had a backbone again, who stood upright, must have felt
as if they were suddenly holding The Weapon in=their-hands with
Which they could shoot-down everyone who wanted to bully &
finish them: they caught a whiff of life's happiness & of justice
— o yes, certainly — & so they agreed to-Everything the liquor-
eyes had offered them.

The old man asked for a little water again. I motioned to
Möller to bring a jug & 3 glasses. This time I didn't let the old
man continue, but told him to wait until Möller came back.
Peculiar silence in a room burnt-through from the Dark Centre
by the invisible field lines of fate; — quietly deadquietly I could
hear them crackling. —

Then Möller came back, carefully placed everything he had
brought on the table, decorated it as if we'd gathered for a cosy
get-together at a garden party. — I suspect that things=took-their-
course from there. — Möller, visibly at pains to move the old
man along in his story, burst in oafishly with this stupid=hack-
neyed phrase while arranging the glasses and the glass carafe,
dewed by the cold water, on the table (all that was missing was
for this Brandenburg allotment-garden-thinker to add a plate of

biscuits). But my conversational part:ner, the old recounting man, almost seemed to welcome the crude interjection, because it absolved him from the details that, despite the many hundreds of similar cases & repetitions of such similarity in the sequence arrest — interrogations — imprisonment — abuse — more inter-rogations — & then the show trial & The Verdict: the prison sentences that were handed out in those days, unimaginably long for a human life, as if we were living in Biblical Times when the main actors took hundreds-of-years to grow old —: that he would nonetheless have had to mention in each individual case, the special kind of horror inflicted on each individual person; but the-platitudes postponed this necessity of narration to the Day-of-Judgement (I saw the old man drinking with relish).

But before the final judgement there are still the errthly ones. — Wellnow, — the old man remarked in a broad voice, still sated from the water. — Anyway, Thebigstory was printed by BILD ?or DER SPIEGEL = the BILD for better-off people or: those who think they are. Samething. And Thebigstory was, as is almost-always the case with suchthings, less interesting to the-people than to the-police, namely, the-GeeDeeR=police. And ?how did the-wholething come ?out: !now the Pigtooth !finally had his weapon to use against Irma & Alois Berger; !now thebigwords filled thebigmouth all the more — he didn't see it only as attack on him=self, in=hisperson He saw the-party & thus The-State denounced dragged-through-the-dirt. . . . . In the paper that had touted thisbigthing, the writer claimed that in 1956, a whopping !42 per cent of members in the GeeDeeR People's Parliament were former eNeSDeeAPee memers; the article contained columns with the respective names. !That was thereal=blow: acase of !espi-onage. And because the vehicle=forthiswholestory, so to speak, was that little clown of a party functionary in the administrative district of Kaltenfeld, anyone could count on 2 fingers !who was behind this in-sighting article=in-the-western-press. The boomerang flew —, & came back & struck the heads of those who had thrown it: Irma & Alois Berger. No more happiness, no Golden Bridges to the Golden West, no extenuating circumstances : the boomerang they had thrown, it threw them down with the full-force of judiciary's power. . . . . — I looked the old man in=the-face, watched his expression as he got to !this point in his account (I had detected something unpleasantly malicious, a snottiness in his tone coming from the old sordid, cynical brazenness of the-loser=at-the-end from whom the-pleasure=of-victory had ultimately been swiped away in the decisive endgame, decades after this case) : as if I were standing on the edge of a sea cliff and looking down into An Abyss full of an unholy dark foaming of grey waves that always collapsed at the zenith of their power, died off, and only the impetuous knife-bright squalls from those raging waves remain awake & hissroar against the moreandmore crumbling steepness of this once seemingly firm&secure shores. That was what I saw in=the-face of the old man. Yes, the old man had spoken before of the turning-point-in-their-lives, his and his wife's, and I didn't doubt that he had told me The Truth. If anything, it was probably an understatement. For I could imagine that, with each new find from the life&death of Theresa's parents, he had also been taken away step-by-step from hisworld of convictions & faith in the-absolute=rightness of His=World & His=Truth — but not to the firm ground of a New World where The Truth would be at=home, together with happiness & life, but rather to an uninhabited porous unsafe terrain full of uncertain, malice, deceptive mirages that were supposed to represent truth, in a word: into the world of those who must always & at-alltimes be viewed by authority as the-disciplined. To see !their world & even to know that they !existed — this man had been spared that until now. From that point on, he wanted to look more precisely at His=World and all the people in it who had always been His=Surroundings, that is: from the side. That was probably how he discovered — this is what I assume, at least — what anyone in his situation can discover in such activities as soon as the warm enshrouding dust cocoon of belonging is blown apart : a society of careerists, fellow=travellers, hypocrites & slyly-calculating yes-men (whose No can simply be an even more wicked Yes), and: all=this is all the stronger, clearer & more enduring the more deeply a society viewed like that is kept= under=control by some miss=belief: whether in a sacrosanct or a secular belief. . . . . And what was especially repulsive & danger-ous are those short stages in which the believer hominids change their=gods, with no difficulty, just like an old shirt. *But !why their=gods : their=alibis, whose protection allowed these hominids to act like pigs for a while in their existence & Afterwards they didn't even want salvation, because they had the=prospect of something !muchbetter than salvation: instead of the old self=certainties (the cathedrals of slogan baroque built by prole-taryan internazionalism by the sickness-of-communism :the everyday tongue exposes the infamy of the slogans as soon as it utters them — certainties & slogans perish & what had forced the heart of the time into a concrete stranglehold as firm as a stonewall — crumbles into dust, a Nothing of dust trembling away out of ancient, now-powerless hands. . . . .), now the knew self=certainties: during the One Night of completion in the Great-Bureaucratic-Reshuffle they stood ready, radiant & beaming like over-decorated Christmas trees in front of the-people=in-their-night: daemocracy & freedom. — What made such god-switching so easy was not the-slogans, not the-ideas that seemed connected*

to it, not even the-politics, just the homogeneity-of-the-subjuga-
tions. . . . . And this homogeneity can be recognized always&
everywhere by the-hominids as a familiar farmyard smell during
their idol=hopping. Caliban recognizes his=familiar visage in
every mirror under any-circumstances. Because a world war
broke out in this part of the earth over 70 years ago& 12 years
later a people were annihilated in their own fire, in the blood of
millions of people, and the-hominids=in-this-country lost the war,
which wasn't even !their war, all the more mercilessly, whereupon
anentire=nazion was branded collectively= guilty, with the strange
result that suddenly there were no more losers anywhere. So then,
on the one side of the-winners, the-cleverest of the-burnt broke
up everything nazional into small handy shards with shops that
were solvent again, cleaned up and straightened around the bro-
ken edges. While on the other side of the-winners in awar that
was full to the brim with blood & crimes like an immeasurable
bomb crater, the other part of a loser=people that could pretend
they had won thewar too, and could thus feel doubly like victors,
had risen from thedirt. Many little candles of penance & triumph
burned with their sharp flames on the scaffolds altars animal
fences & melted down to the faith-tallow of the knew-humans.
— But whatever the-outfit's called, the inner=order is always=the-
same. And because these zeitgeist-hominids seem to be steeped
in that, such god-switches always take place very smoothly. And
the last of these switches in this=country was over 20 years ago
: the Great-Bureaucratic-Reshuffle, the GeeBeeR, in the course
of which I was transferred in 1991 from Hanover to this place,
the police headquarters in Berlin, my lost marriage with Lena
behind me and another woman ahead. Regina. In-our-early-
days I went home to Hanover at the weekends. There I was soon
met with Lena's suppressed tears. She could hardly speak to me

without choking. I tried to console her, said things like Tempo-
rary & We'll-soon-be-together=again. Every meeting was burdened by sorrow, dull and grey like resentment. The few words
we still spoke to each:other were witless & gloomy. Then we
stopped. ?What had really ?happened: Lena couldn't take our
constant separations any more, and she=herself couldn't endure
this inability; she couldn't forgive me for forcing her into This-
State. Too long a farewell makes things rotten. Of all the things
I !can't do, the most prominent is my inability to console, either
myself or others. ?Which of us would be the 1st to not take That
any more. Then, 1 day, I returned from Berlin unexpectedly :
another man at her flat, a !black man. The woman had literally
taken him in off the street. — *The man & two others were standing
in front of the house one evening*, she told me (while the black
man rolled his eyes and stared at me, no doubt expecting me to
grab him beat him & throw him out). — *The three blacks-on-
the-street were arguing when they came. One stabbed his friend
& ran away. Paramedics police. But this man=here, after they let
him go at the police station, as he'd done Nothing, he returned
here at night to the place where his friend was stabbed to death.
He screamed lamented loudly in his language, wailed, the street
echoed with it — screams like a storm*, Lena said, — *then like
the gurgling of streaming water, it wouldn't stop, neighbours
were shouting abuse at him, yelling for !quiet; soon they'd call
the-police. Then I took him from the street. His sorrow was like
mine. Since then he's lived here.* Lena stood in the room with her
arms hanging down. The black man was squatting in the sofa
corner, still staring at me, ready to jump, expecting blows.
Coldrage shot through me. But I kept my self=control, I didn't
strike him or Lena. The two seemed like uninvolved strangers,
?why would I ?hit them. I pulled a few things out of the cupboards.

Before I left I said into the coal-black face with the uncompre-
hendingly rolling eyes that the-police here in Hanover were very
good, they'd quickly find his friend's murderer. Then I went to
the door. Again Lena's tears, but I was already out of reach of
them. I shut the weeping of Lena, my former wife, in the flat. At
the time I had photographs of Lena with=me in a paper bag
whenever I travelled. The paper had meanwhile been torn in
many places & I kept it together with sticky tape; a patchy bag,
like the forgiveness that we had to keep repeating just to carry
on. But forgiveness: ?for what. And at some point this forgiveness
was like a paper bag patched together with sticky tapes, so there
was Nothing left that could let us forgive. — Then Berlin: I'd
dragged the-unrest over here with me, my despair over a lost
marriage. I lay sleepless for manyweeks beneath the sky of this
city torn by noise&light, floodlights from the building sites, in
dust shouting machines roaring, a constant yelling in my head.
Even after the-divorce from Lena, long after I'd taken all
my=things from the old flat & brought them to Berlin, I came
back a few times, the way I used to. Stood in front of the house
a long time, in front of the door, her name on the little plate next
to the doorbell; it was still my name, she didn't want her maiden
name back. I looked up the house wall at the 5th floor. Crept
around the building for hours. When it grew dark, there was
nolight in her windows; black rectangles, the life in them gone.
Each time I left without going to see her. That's thetruth. It
seemed better that way. And sittingthere alone in my police quarters until late at night: *Again I didn't die, I who once lived.* And
switched off the TV. The room and I plunged into the stagnant-
cold night. . . . . — Then I slowly found my feet on firm ground,
together with this other woman whom I met in a bar where I had
been going for-awhile to find distraction on some evenings.

Regina. I was not only the oldest by far among the guests scrab-
bling about in that little basement room in noiselight&smoke; I
also clearly didn't look as if I belonged there. Neither did she.
Perhaps that was why I caught this woman's attention. We got
into=conversation pretty quickly. She was from Potsdam, born
there in 1960 (:calculate: today=1991 = so 31); but stayed
here=in-Berlin after studying medicine, works at a medical centre
as a paediatrician; the-children in her daily work are children=
enough for her, she didn't want any of her own. She emphasized
that right at the start. First she lived in the Mitte district with her
husband; then the-divorce just under a year ago. On the outside:
a determined woman, play-full with a refreshingly open laugh;
kitsch-resistant; filled with a primal feminine courage she had
evidently managed to preserve throughout her life. On the inside
(but I only discovered That muchlater) her strong form is sometimes abruptly interrupted by almost childlike sensibilities, she
gets upset, cries; recovers quickly, but the inner out-burst stays
in her constitution and her perceptions like a scar. So her Inner
Face was probably marked by countless deeper grooves & folds;
whereas her outer face, with its dark complexion, had remained
astonishingly smooth for her age, without ever relying much on
cosmetics (— *I just have good-genes*). She may have been looking
for youngmen here=in-this-club; but she had to realize that a-
woman Overthirty is already beyond a=certain equator of youth.
She had been looking for theyoungones and: had found her own
kind; we already left together that First Evening, barely knew
more than each other's names. But I already sensed then that all
firmground is just on-credit; that for every person who receives
that ground, many others have to get stuck in the quicksand
of thistime, because the-balance of all fortune & mis-fortune is
ultimately even. — So for-hours this old man has been sitting in

front of me in my office, having originally wanted to report his adoptive daughter as missing; but after being unexpectedly cast like flotsam into the rapids in the river of someone else's life, I=myself am in this-current, which flows everfaster like time as soon as a great, yet unknown event lies ahead — at first one can only suspect It from the flow of the water —. *He, this old man, had to circle in this current like the whirlpool at the bottom of a waterfall, following the same course for ever&ever. And always passed the same places on the shore whose support he had long stopped reaching for: the 'Old Comrades', the-party-toadies-from=Backthen, who met up in their pub backrooms & faded dull clubrooms when 1=of-their-champions wrote a little book from which they trumpeted the-litany-of-justification to their like-minded=cronies. The way they clung out-of=defiance to their old outfits, the flat caps on their thinning cemetery-blonde hair, the little wrist-bags dangling from their forearms, like on old gay men, their paunches bulging out from light-grey anoraks or shit-brown faux leather jackets, creeping through the streets in brogues as the eyes-&-ears-of-the-party, like in the Old Days, & pumped full of beer on their one-hour run, their triangular mouths full=throatedly blasting out their trashy slogans time-after-time as a chummy group, all=ways munching on their rancid old soul-lard sandwiches with political crackling, once rendered from the rinds of their swinish ideas; ensembles of unconditional opinio=nation & murderous staidness, dismissed & tossed on the pensioners' scrap heap at closing time for lemurs. Many had effortlessly withdrawn from the eternal whirling of their=for-mer=scheming long ago, had joyously reached for the roots of their reshuffled bureaucracy, which —!that was what they knew & !that was what they expected — gave them security=again. Subalterns are !always=needed. And so, if they're still alive,*

they're on firmground again, with their old shirts jackets caps &
old brains. For One Thing is genuinely !different compared to all
the changes in previous=times : less blood flowed, there were
fewer and fewer dead bodies. As if blood & corpses weren't com-
modities on the markets here anymore. — But he, this old man,
stayed in the whirling current, didn't even try to stretch out his
arms for 1 of those tough roots that presented themselves to him
too from the firmshore of the keep-going-as-always & stretched
especially towards him, this once privileged man Now&today,
from-allsides : !No. He !didn't grab them. I could see that,
because this old man wouldn't have been sitting here=with-me
otherwise. He had !refused the-offers of=rescue. *His refusal cer-*
tainly wasn't out of heroism, neither out of shame or remorse
about his=time-as-a-functionary nor out of pride or loyalty. He
would have had other=reasons for it. For with the Knew
Daemocrats, the profiteers of the GeeBeeR with knew-self=cer-
tainties-&-slogans : change-the-world again, now with digital-
networks, eco-logism & private-happiness — *from which these*
middle-class creatours come along high&broad with their dreary
little tragedies about careers kids & consumerism, grounded with
greed & obsessive-perfectionism — *a sour Biedermeier : the old*
man can't & doesn't want to have anything to do with them;
such slogans & manners are too smooth for him, too meagre, all
dreary ghosts of dreary ideas; they no longer reach him. And that
must be what repels him, this old man, precisely=these self=cer-
tainties which these knew world-savers trust in like their brand-
name clothes, which make them feel cosy & safe. But that's
exactly how old people behave, old & fixed in their=familiar old
& fixed views, however knewly-polished they may be. And he
knows he's old him=self. Any old person who seeks the company
of old people might as well be six-feet-under. He also seems to

sense, and this apprehensive conviction is something he shares with me, in a certain way, that even these Knew Self=Certainties were based on fraud & illusions — their unspectacular wretched demise will soon take place under higher & higher ash-mountains of burnt money & collapsed number-columns (It already stinks of sickly sweet fumes from the mouths of the Knew Idols, at-their-feet the burnt-out celebratory fires of the soulful) — ?howmany doomsdays can 1 person take. — In the old man's face, hewn by the chisel of the years, I see the-aversion towards everything that used to surround him, and: before rejoining those! Old turned coats he'd sooner choose the nothingness of his solitude and the poison dust from all his lost faith. —

But it seemed to me that the old man was waiting for me to say something, to question him again about that 2nd child, the boy called Willfried with the strange second L in his name.

And because I said nothing, he started speaking again. No, he didn't speak; in a renewed outburst he screamed: — It's because of !Him that Everything happened the way It did. !Much more than that: because of !him, whom Irma Berger gave birth to in=detention, only=because of !him. He's the Big Evil Centre, the Black Hole in Heaven=Onearth, believe it or: not. Everything revolves around !Him=alone. To this day and beyond. And ?why not. ?Who says that war&battles murder&fires and All Horrors with hecatombsuponhecatombs of dead and mutilated can only be caused by Caesars & leaders or some crummy oaf-ficials, former teat-chers, lore-yers whomanaged to become presi-dents or chance-llors & by luck are allowed to finger The-Red-Telephone when the-whirldbank calls & tells them !What's-to-be-done. ?WHY ONLY-THEM AND: NOT SOME TOILET CLEANER A WAITER OR INDEED A WILLFRIED-WITH-2-Ls = A PRISON-BASTARD BORN IN BAUTZEN TWO, THE SECOND

HELL BEFORE THE FIRST —: ?!WHY NOT !HIM, THE ONE EVERYTHING REVOLVES AROUND. — Thus screamed the old man, loudly and even more loudly, his voice becoming shrill — and screamed more things that I understood even less than the previous ones —. — Then nothing but screams of deepest dismay that struck the walls of my little office as if they wanted to smash through them. — Once again the old man sought to compose himself, wanted to speak clearly: — If someone gets hounded by the-mob he has to — has to at least have some1 who can — I should know. After all, I was the one — the one who — — But his breath failed him. — There are times —, his rapidly-breaking voice tried to pick itself up again, and repeated: — There are always times —, then he collapsed in his chair —, and would have fallen to the floor if Möller hadn't caught him & carefully laid him down while I called an emergency doctor. — —

There we stood, Möller and I, around this motionless old man on the floor. Stretched out, his body seemed much larger than suspected, and didn't move. In my office, & it felt louder than all the work noises from our surroundings in the massive, bulky heft of this high&broad-walled giant memorial to ancient petrified police=power, thesilence crackled darkly.

After the doctor had declared the old, motionless man dead & the body had subsequently been removed from my office, Möller and I remained in a state of indecision in that room, which suddenly felt frosty. I looked over repeatedly at the photograph of the blonde woman called Theresa. The photo was still on my table, I hadn't brought myself to attach it to the pin board with the rest of the deadwomen. — ?Did you understand any of what that man was ?going on about. — I bluntly asked my younger colleague. He didn't look up, maybe he'd expected a question like that; he kept his eyes lowered to the place where the dead man had lain. — The missing woman has a brother. That means she does fit the pattern of our-killer. — He finally murmured in the same tone of voice as the old man. — The man used to be one of the privileged, it seems he didn't get his act together 20 years ago. And in-the-time=before-that he made good use of his=privileges, for him & for his adoptive daughter. That much is clear. Got her Everything that was possible in that country, & even abit more than was possible. You have to under-stand, Boss, only the-select-few got a place to study philosophy Backthen. He removed all obstacles in her path, smoothed the-way for her wherever he could. She was bred into a pedigree mare from the best Red Stable. I know purebred girls like that. Had a thing for 1 myself once. — — And: ?what came of it. — I asked deviously without looking up. — — Nothing. — Möller pretended he was looking for something in his jacket pocket. — It was hopeless anyway. She was the purebred horse on a classless track. — (He laughed sourly.) — And I was the crummy cop, and just a trainee cop at the time. Ohwell: if you're born a tadpole you shouldn't try to be a salmon. — (?Maybe !this story was the cause of Möller's later odd sayings —.)

But Möller continued, now he came back to Theresa: — And then: the crash, the end, Backthen after thatnight when the-new ones came. That hit them both hard, her & her adoptive father. Presumably they were tooclosely entangled with the Old Conditions to make the-transition now, like many-of-their-equals. Oh well, some people give up the ghost when they're standing in front of a ghost train.

I had feared some comment of that kind, and glanced over at him.

— The brother's name is supposedly Willfried with 2 Ls. — Möller quickly added when he saw myglance. — That was all we could get out of him, wasn't it. — And pointed at the place on the floor where the old man had lain. — — And now we have to find this brother too. — — Yes. That's right. If there's anything in the files or the computer about this Willfried — presumably his name's Willfried Berger — then — — Yes. I'll havealookrightnow. — Möller responded helpfully. There was something else that seemed to be preoccupying him. — ?What did he mean by the Evil Centre that everything revolves around —:?Do you think he is; he was — was —. — Möller searched in vain for the right word.

— Maybe someone who's lost his=faith has also lost faith in reasons. Faith in the fact that Everything has to be a consequence of something-earlier because the-world supposedly consists of causes & effects. Perhaps That's what he meant. — And looked into Möller's wide, amazed eyes. — You're asking me if he was ?crazy. Maybe. A person goes crazy if they can't believe in this ironclad law of causalities any more. — — B-But — (it occurred stutteringly to Möller) — we don't have anything else. In our profession. — — Explanations are overrated. — I replied gruffly, tired of the subject, then turned to my desk and left Möller standing there.

So I knew, now that the old man was gone and couldn't tell us any more, that I would have to put together the remaining pieces of the story, & these remainders are always the !largest part of the whole, by myself. More than that: I had to check everything I had learnt — laboriously reluctantly & certainly inaccurately, because — ?what had the old man said about the-people before: they'd choke on The Truth otherwise; — to check all these fragments, organize them, because I had a vague feeling that !they would also be The Key to the other 4 murders. For that I'd have to retrace the old man's path backwards through time, step-by-step. Yes, I'd gather them=all together & see if they produced anything. That's my job.

But one thing is certain: she, Theresa, whom the old man had given us=policemen the task of searching for; to find her, dead-or-alive, she, if she was still alive, now she'd be all alone again, without her last protector who was her father and not her father, though probably a better father than her biological one had ever been. And she'd have no idea about her new loneliness. . . . .

But now I knew !where I could find her. Called my-colleagues in Birkheim, told them what was going on. At first they didn't believe me. I insisted, & before I hung up, added in a command-ing tone: — And let me know !today if you find the woman. If the whole thing is a mistake I'll take !full-responsibility. — Conversation over. 5 cases solved through 1. But The Case would begin after that. I had to start right-at-the-beginning.

First a call to Möller-in-the-house. — You & I, we're going to Birkheim & Kaltenfeld. Tomorrowmorning. — I was just about to hang up when I remembered: — And somethingelse: bring the printout of the computer file & Everything you can find about Willfried Berger. See you tomorrow. —

At night the old man who'd died in my office yesterday, car-diac arrest (the-medics had remarked), came to my bedroom in the pale shimmer of morning. When I noticed him in the doorway I leapt high out of bed, stood naked in front of the man, who looked mutely at me with his angry grey face. His mouth his lips=shut=tight, he finally stretched out his right arm towards me —, the wizened fingers, spread out and bent into a claw, stabbed against the skin of my chest — + slowly his hand entered my flesh like pale soft dough. Baffled, I stared at this motion, amazed by the painlessness, no blood, I felt nothing except a slight pressure inside my chest; the old man plunged almost his entire forearm in my body. — Now it's !your turn. — Said the old man's grim voice. He pulled his arm out of the deep wound with a jolt, + in his outstretched hand lay a bloody, twitching Something. But not my heart; it was the skinless body, in tiny miniature form, of my 1st wife. Lena. A few more twitches, like a chick that had fallen out of its nest, then the little body lay still + dead. — My heart : but my heart is my dead wife. — Spoke my stumbling voice. The old man remained motionless, insistently held out the hand with the tiny dead body + the severe, stone cold eyes gazed at me demandingly, they seemed to ask: ?What else. — He was right. ?!How was I supposed to live ?withoutaheart —. — At that, I recoiled with outrage, yelling: — I didn't !know that. — And exited sleep to enter the sparse wakefulness of morning. ?Had I really ?screamed. I looked across at Regina; she lay quietly under the feather bed, buried in sleep. *That's a different woman* —:Thus the last dream-arm reached for me. Sheet and bedspread clammy, sweat ran down my skin, thin rivulets of terror. Then more restless, evil leftovers of sleep. Dreams twitching like spots on the fur of a leopard-on-the-hunt. Timeandagain the predator's paws grabbed me, timeandagain they let me go — for the next shards of dream. This was the only one of them that stayed with me after waking up. A little more, then the alarm rang. Another day struck my burning brain — —

The weather had changed; warming breezes drew thaw into the premature winter, which could not stay. Thesky was dullgrey & damp, snowfalls now weighed heavy on the morning as dirtwhite glassy-wet masses stuck together. On the roads the car tyres hissed & sent doughy snow leftovers flying at the sides. The drive along the motorways & A-roads from Berlin to Birkheim took longer than such a distance normally would, traffic jams, a few accidents — the vehicles slowly threaded their way through road constrictions with yellow & blue warning lights flashing around them. — I only had a few free glances, and looked through Willfried Berger's file during the journey. My comments after skimming the documents: — After Irma Berger had given birth to the boy in-detention, he too, like his sister Theresa, was put in a home. But wasn't lucky enough to be adopted by good-natured people the way she was. It seemed he was already rebellious, dishonest, thieving and aggressive as an infant. He was pushed from home-to-home — — The-criminal-child. — Remarked Möller behind the steering wheel, didn't see me looking at him in amazement, just looked straight ahead. Further: — So he moved from home-to-home —, — and leafing through the few remaining pages — : — burglaries, theft, brawls & againandagain arrests, youth detention centre, out & back to business-as-usual — ?is that all. — — It's all we've got. Maybe there's more about him at the Stasi archives — for !sure, in fact — but we need special authorization for that. While I cursed, I looked at the only photograph of this man, a low-quality black-and-white picture that was over-contrasted, making the face look bloodless & flat as if cut out of a tin can : big dark eyes were concealed under heavyshadows which, in that face, looked like two boggy pools; the nose was strong & the chin small, but defiant. Yet the face as a whole had something withdrawn, an air of hidden furnaces, distilleries for anger & retribution. The light, short-cropped hair, the severe thin lips and the chin came closest to the photo of his sister. His left cheek was slightly sunken (evidently someone had hit him in the face & broken his cheekbone shortly before taking the-photo; those-dearcolleagues must have felt untouchable then if they weren't worried about capturing that kind of treat-meant on camera like a prize trophy.) —!Peculiar tattoos; so unusual that they were photographed separately at the-time. Not the usual stuff on the arms back chest & the rest of the basement-wall-white convict skin, looking like scribbles on toilet doors —:but the tattoos on his upper arms, neck, chest & back (though none in the face) made it seem like he'd been assembled from pieces of other people's flesh, sewn together with crude but regular stitches, calling to mind Frankenstein's monster : a patchwork human filled with stolen life. That way he can escape=inside=himself from one identity to another; & can't get hold of himself. —!But: the !seams —: the orifices of the murdered women had been sewn up in !thesame manner. — I cast a quick glance at Möller, who was sitting at the wheel and looking straight ahead at the road, but he still saw !what I'd seen and gave a little nod. He agreed with me. I closed the file.

Already late morning by the time the contours of Birkheim rose sluggishly from a trough, wreathed in grey fog, 2 church steeples a water tower chimneys roofs of houses etched themselves softly into the stagnant haze hanging over the town —. — In the narrow streets the snowpats were propelled across the pavements by hasty car tyres, smacking against the walls of old half-timbered buildings. The day flapped open like damp bedclothes, sweat & dreams in the morning, memory — memory of Lena, a dead woman in my heart (startled, I peered at the-driving-Möller to see if he'd noticed ?anything about me; but his face just looked at the road ahead) — and a bad mood caused by fatigue & unease came clouding up.

!What a bollocking I gave those !arseholes, those !morons with cowshit on their shoes & fluff in their heads — ?!is !that really their idea of ?administrative ass-istance. !!What are you talking about: ?no imminent-danger. I was wrong: you=village-idiots don't just have cowshit on your shoes, you've got cowshit in your heads too, you !incompetent cretins. We almost came to blows, there at the police station in Birkheim; would've loved to smash those well-behaved sandwich-eating faces in. Möller intervened, calmed things down. Luckily=for-me. I'd have made those clowns pay for Everything & even more than they owed. — But it was what it was: those clowns in Birkheim, those chicken-cops, had totally !ignored my call=yesterday and instead just done what they always=do: go-home-on-time. They didn't go out to the cemetery !immediately to find the woman, only !thismorning after work started, which in their case means: just now, the-minute you came in here, Chief Inspector, we were just about to —:?!Were they ?shitting me. They'd left the woman there in the cold&snow for !awholenight=longer. . . . . The chief dickhead stammered that it wasn't at all clear if the woman was really there=at-the-cemetery — and anyway — & there was still the otherguy who was being searched for nationwide — and the few people I've got here — always much too !fewpeople anyway — & that's why — & therefore — & so on. I almost exploded again. — All right: !get !going. — I said to the superintendent. — Take your fewpeople & come on: !!moveit. — I ordered (completely unnecessarily, as the colleagues-from-here had already gone out to the patrol cars); they'd called for an ambulance just in case, those super=brains. Just heard 1 of them murmuring to Möller on the way out, asking if the Chief Inspector (i.e. me) was ?always=like-that & ?if he maybe had a ?screw loose —. — I missed Möller's reply (it must've been short); we leapt into the cars, sped through the narrow streets full of wet snow with our blue lights on to Birkheim Cemetery on Lüneburger Strasse. —

She's !alive.

As we plodded through the cold-wet snow to the place in question at the cemetery, we saw the woman : small, as if she'd shrunk into a doll — that was how we found her, sitting on a snow-covered stone bench, motionless but seeming about to leave, as if she'd actually wanted to escape quickly from A Danger lurking in the tall evergreen vegetation behind her back; Something probably held her up before she could begin her= flight. She sat there, her bare hands clenching her tightly-closed thighs, her head slightly tilted and lowered as if listening to a veryquiet voice. While we approached she lifted her head slowly, as if rising from the depths of sleep, and gazed at us with con- fused eyes that seemed to come from otherworlds. A smile on frost-pale lips, and this smile had etched itself into her face of snow; and if she hadn't raised her head at once, we might have thought that smile was the serene smile of one frozen to death —. — Carefully the doctor and his helpers joined us, medically touched & auscultated the woman as she sat there rigidly (her glass lips moved as if whispering quietly) — but I was standing too far away from her to hear. In the meantime us=policemen had a look at the area=around the former grave. In the snow next to the woman on the stone bench was the imprint of a person who must have sat there. Although the thawing snow had widened & deepened the imprint, I could see that it didn't belong to the woman; it was clearly the bottom-print of a man. His foot- prints in the snow had likewise been melted wide open by the thaw, as if a golem had plodded through the snow here & up to the woman on the stone bench to sit next to her. ?What had he wanted from her. The doctor found no injuries to the woman. The tracks — they led over here from the end of the main avenue, and must have arrived only shortly before the snow flurries stopped in the night (the earlier prints had sunken into the heavy all-erasing white) — had already become unrecognizable, thawed away. And it seemed that the stranger had then gone back along his own tracks, like a wolf on the hunt.

— Second-degree frostbite, third-degree in some areas. — Remarked the doctor who had examined the woman. — Luckily for her thefrost wasn't as severe last night as it was the previous nights, and the thaw had started. Otherwise. — He didn't finish the sentence, turned around & got in the ambulance. I looked at the superintendent with ragefilled eyes: —!You'll hear from me. If you & your people had come out here last night after my call, we'd not only have saved the woman from seriousinjury; we also could've caught the guy who's being hunted all over the country. !You —. — And I wanted to fly Into=a-Rage again. Amazingly, the simple objection by the superintendent, spoken in an almost childlike voice like a schoolboy caught committing some serious, but unintended offence, calmed me. — ?How do you know that the-tracks=here belong to !thatguy. — — Because it's !My=Case. — I retorted arrogantly & with a resoluteness that tolerated no contradiction (because !that was all I needed: a debate with this yokel). The superintendent grew pale, but luckily refrained from any response and just gave a little shrug. — They drove off with the woman, to the intensive care unit at the local hospital. I was spared an encounter with death that day. —

But whoever looks for death will find it. A few weeks later I received the news of Lena's death. I remembered the dream, that dream where Lena was torn out of my body as if that were my heart. Violent death, evidently strangled. Said the message. (The black man she'd put up in her flat had disappeared. He was obviously the 1st option as the perpetrator.) The ex-wife of a detective inspector is murdered —:every profession has its=humour & its=tragedy. The oldburden of her=nameless-reproaches:to=me, from-now-on and for=my-entire-life it would weigh on me, would push me down(Always the unnameable anguish that pushes down the-hardest and: keeps us going day-by-day, even if only to escape thegrief over everything unnameable for a few hours, before returning later with even heavier weights for the leftovers of one's life time —) —

There was nothing left for us to do here at the cemetery in Birkheim. We'd go back to the woman when she was in a state to talk to us. (Then she'd have to be given the news of her adoptive father's death. . . . .) As we got ready to leave, the people from forensics also ended their race against the thawing snow.

Möller & I left for Kaltenfeld. As we reached the outskirts of Birkheim, going south along the B71 — the broad smooth route laid itself out before us into the foggy day through watery leftover snow — the heavy concentrated cloud-grey above the gently-curved line of the horizon suddenly lightened — and rays of cold silver coated the widely spread, waiting distance of a large, flat land —.

Kaltenfeld. One of many villages in the region that extend along the backbone of a trunk road & cling to the spine of an A-road with a few side roads branching off like fishbones. Always the same sight on those side roads: low houses, the odd farm on the village outskirts & a few workshops for agricultural machinery, & all roads disappear into field-lonely expanses —. There were 2 hotels w/restaurants here, Wiesengrund & Kaltenfelder Hof —:we parked the car there in the courtyard. Then we took a walk through the village, to the village centre, the fieldstone church typical of the region, whose steeple was reminiscent of a castle keep or a medieval prison tower. Surrounded by a small cemetery, out back in front of the fieldstone wall between bare black trees & shrubbery, was the vicarage. At the junction with the next side road, directly next to the massively built ochre-coloured headquarters of the 𝕶𝖆𝖑𝖙𝖊𝖓𝖋𝖊𝖑𝖉 𝖁𝖔𝖑𝖚𝖓𝖙𝖊𝖊𝖗 𝕱𝖎𝖗𝖊 𝕭𝖗𝖎𝖌𝖆𝖉𝖊, the-warmemorial for 14/18 with an engraved plaque on

a back background: 'Their all, their life, their blood they gave /
Their gift was sacred, their gift was brave / they gave it for us!'
:Only the 1st line was unquestionably true. Next to the house-
of-God the memorial to-the-gored. . . . . But further. Snack bar
(closed today) — Block's Bakery (lunch break until 3.30) — &
also on the other side of the village the fishbone-shaped side
roads flanked by low detached houses — and at the ends of the
roads a few farmhouses made of old bricks (:one of them must
have belonged to the Bergers, theplace where it all. . . . . started.)
The residential houses, the agricultural buildings, the bakery —
they'd almost all been renovated, no signs of decay. Yet these
houses didn't look glad in their new colours; they stood there
somewhat sullen & displeased, as if they had resisted those
paintjobs to the end. Now they looked ill at ease, like farmers in
Sunday best. They seemed extinguished, immobilized, the-life
seemed to have departed from them. Nonetheless, an uneasy
feeling that all the curtain-covered window-eyes were secretly=
staring at us, the-strangers, following our-every-step. At the shelter
for the country bus, between dirty snow that had been pushed
together into piles, 2 teenage girls were sitting and waiting, waving
at the passing cars with excited giggles. When they noticed me,
they too fell silent. What I registered as an annoying disturbance
from the 1st-minute-here was !thattraffic : cars lorries delivery
vans rushing constantly along the B71 — none of them stopped
— all the tyres hissing through the leftover snow&water on the
asphalt, like fits of senseless unstoppable outcries from an idiot
who keeps repeating the same thing again&again in a moist
squelchy voice — this dump, this road, this day —:*I've always
been afraid of the-country, of its inhabitants with their strange
mixture of stubbornness, insistence, deviousness, stupidity &
suddenly baffling friendliness. Allthat's out in the open with them,*

but the basic human traits are weighted !differently compared to city-dwellers; they're easy to see through, but their behaviour is difficult to predict for=outsiders. Yes, I've been afraid of the-country since-childhood. . . . . with its gloomy oldstories. — We had an appointment with the village administrator of Kaltenfeld. We waited at the hotel-reception for the man I had called & who, at our=request, had invited us quite straightforwardly to=speak at his home. He said that although he'd been here in=this-place for almost 15 years, in a village that meant as little as if he'd arrived yesterday. On the phone the man's voice had sounded young. He couldn't help us based on his own=experience, he said, but added that he knew a man in this village who'd watched the-arrest of the Bergers Backthen in 1959, & also knew about a few other connections. — Though always sceptical about this=kind of witness, I agreed; after all, I had to start somewhere.

!What a surprise when this village administrator we'd arranged to meet entered the hotel lobby: a small, slightly stout man (roughly Möller's age, so late 30s) with a gingerbread-coloured face looking out of his thick anorak, his cocoa-brown eyes and cheerful mouth beaming and smiling at us as if with greatjoy: an !Indian. He hurried towards us with his right arm extended, said his name (neither his first name nor his surname sounded foreign) & said in a clear, youthful voice that he was the village administrator of Kaltenfeld & was glad to welcome us to his village & his house. (The little round cocoa-eyes smiled cheerily at us.) Möller also seemed to have been caught off-guard by the-surprise; we followed the man down one of the small streets that led away from the main road and soon entered 1 of the low, likewise freshly-renovated detached houses w/ a tiny front garden. There was a bleak twilight in the narrow hallway; the man apologized for the absence of his partner (as he termed her), who had gone shopping=in-town. He had us sit down in the seating area of his open-plan kitchen. On the grease-yellowed wall above the stove, various steel frying-pans were hanging by their handles from individual hooks. Like black eyes, they gaped wide with amazement and displeasure while our host prepared coffee. Here=in-the-kitchen of the village administrator we awaited the man we were meant to speak to, a supposed witness to those oldstories that I feared. *Persistence is favourable.* (The black pan-eyes gawked stubbornly.)

Meanwhile I turned towards Möller, for something had occurred to me. — Did the woman-at-the-cemetery ?say anything when they picked her up and carried her from the stone bench to the ambulance. — — Yes. She did. I was close to her, but the words took such effort to come out as if she were trying to thread a thin yarn through a needle with frozen fingers. — — And ?what did she say. — — Just a minute, I wrote it down —: *I already know. Nobody has to tell me.* :?What can she have meant. ?Can you make any ?sense of it. — Möller closed his notebook & looked at me; I just shook my head.

The traffic noise came in from-outside, muted as if far away, that incessant fitful roaring, while a premature winter rushed back, restoring the lights to the season of colourful leaves. They'd had to hide under the frosty silence of the snow for a few hours. Now the maple leaves glowed red once more like flaming embers, their colours hardened by cold&frost. There they were again & burned, like all the other damned oldstories. —

—!That should !never have happened. No That was !not right. — The tall gaunt man had sat down at the kitchen table right after entering the room. He seemed very familiar with the village administrator & his=home. Spider-grey wisps of hair protruded from his worn-out black beret, which he still kept on here in the warm kitchen. From a long horse-face — the chin seemed so heavy that it dragged the upper features downwards into deep folds — gazed bright eyes, large and strangely withdrawn, as if he had to listen inside=himself to what an inner voice had to say about the matter. Sometimes he accompanied his words sparingly with his sinewy hands, cleft into countless little wrinkles, the rest of the time these old hands lay on the tablecloth like 2 small sleeping dogs. The man must be in his early 70s if he saw everything he claimed to have seen when he was barely 20 years old; but he seemed considerably older.

— It was just before 6 in the morning. On some weekday, I don't remember which one, I don't want to say anything that's not true. But it was February, February 19-59, when three big black limousines pulled up outside their house in the early morning, that is, outside the part of their previous house where they'd been allowed to settle just about liveably in 1 half. The name Berger still meant something here=for-us, at least, whether it was the old folks or their children. But they'd gone !totally !over-the-top. Wouldn't listen to us. The children as pig-headed as their parents — like banging your head against a brick wall. And the old Bergers had already come a cropper with a=certain wall. Anyway, when we saw this stranger turn up here, this shady former salesman & current newspaper=hack the two had got involved with, we sensed It wouldn't turn out well for them. Especially as everyone knew the-partynik'd had them on His=List for ages & was only waiting for a chance to grab them. We tried thebestwecould to !warn them to !drop their idiotic plan. But we were just the neighbours, and: ?who's going to listen to ?them. When this pen-pusher told them that the-partyman = their arch-enemy was

supposedly an old Nazi & the first thing they could think of
doing was to blare !That out inthevillage because they thought,
!Now they had thebastard who'd ruthlessly hounded them by
the balls & would be rid of him for=ever, & they wouldn't stop
making a racket & trumpeting propaganda —: that was when
they became a !danger to our=village. We had to do Something,
before the folks=in-Berlin gobbled us up once&forall — well
keep in mind that our=village was almost in the restricted area
— They would've !evacuated us right away in the first commando-
operation that came along, just ask someone from Jahrsau !What
THEY did to them, if any-of-them are still alive today. — It was
one of those winter mornings when pale cold light hangs over
theland like a frozen smell. I can still remember it like Today,
because I had to get up=veryearly & take the bus to the voca-
tional school in Birkheim. I was training as an electrical mechanic
at the pump factory in Birkheim, was in my last year at the
time. The twigs and branches on the trees and bushes stared at
the milky first light, white-furred from the hoarfrost, snow
grains drifted through the air, maybe it'd snow properly soon.
The winter cold had set in suddenly over-night, puddles and little
streams already blind from ice. The house the road the whole
area along with the people lay in cold silence, occasionally interspersed with traces of sharp bitter smoke from the chimneys of
the houses. I had just left the house when THE STRANGERS
came: THEY shattered the silence like thin glass. It wasn't even
6 in the morning when the three black limousines with Berlin
number plates, we all knew !Whom they belonged to: the donkey
caravan (as we secretly called it), invaded the village. THEY made
no secret of THEIR appearance, no effort to stay undercover,
everyone was supposed to !see&hear that THEY were=there &
!What was about to happen. THEY felt so !secure in THEIR

saddles, so !invincible. . . . . & !free from any accountability. The brakes harsh & abrupt, car doors flew open, firm energetic men's steps up to the door : THEY broke into the morning as one breaks into a house, the Bergers' house. I even heard the doorbell & thebanging on the wood — thenoise penetrated the still cold Februarymorningair as deeply as a drill. !No That shouldn't have happened. It was All just One Big Deal. . . . . But hardly-anyone knew that at the time; I & everyone-else here in the village certainly !didn't. We thought It was about something else, people said It was about Nothing=Less than World=Peace. . . . . That was what THEY had told us since-childhood & so we'd believed It. The-partyman (whom we secretly called The Pigtooth) knew that the stakes were high for=him; he set about this business properly & convened a public tribunal at the village hall. The male lead as a positive hero: he=himself; and: the negative heroes: the two Bergers & the rest-of-the-westernworld. The Bergers, standing in for the-westernworld, were made a proper example of. And at=the end, after his 3hour-mono=logue, the-partyman demanded that all of us present (& not 1 of us would've dared not to be present that evening) give our Full Support for all his measures against these-enemies-of-socialism :!that meant the Bergers, they were being sent-to-their=doom = *to re-education.* . . . . (we all knew !what That. . . . . meant.) But there was only 1 result of the vote: 100 per cent=unanimous in favour of the party-man's measures. So all arms stretched upwards in agreement in the hall's stuffy air, like bars of flesh to form a cage. And if we'd had 3 arms, the result would've been 33 per cent. ?!What ?else could we have done Backthen. . . . . except say yes. — But (as we only found out later) it was soon the end-of-the-road for Pigtooth as well. Because obviously the accusations against him were based on truth; the-partybosses=in-Berlin knew best-of-all

!howmany oldnazis had crawled under their=roof & were on-the-right-side again with their new party badges. There was no more denying it & thedirt had piled up so !high by now that it couldn't be swept under the cupboard without bringing the wholecupboard crashing down. If you follow. But the powers=that=be-in-Berlin weren't going to risk their=wholeoperation for some provincial nobody, some Pigtooth, who'd got the whole-thing started. Because, you understand, their self=image as an anti-fascist=state was the only thing THEY could use to justify all=THEIR brute methods. If anything broke up that foundation —!42 per cent oldnazis=in=THEIR=ranks — then !?what would become of THEM & THEIR=beautifulstate. So convening the-tribunal=in-the-village with allthe gimmickry & putting on hisshow had done the Pigtooth precisely sod-all good, even a 300 per cent vote in favour wouldn't have saved his skin; he was already done for the=!moment thebosses=in-Berlin heard about his past & were forced to listen to the kackophonous trumpeting of the-western-press. . . . . In short: the-partyman & Nazi was — removed. Notlong after THEY got rid of the troublemakers Irma & Alois Berger. We never found out what became of the Pigtooth. Maybe he and: the two Bergers encountered each other later: at the same prison=in-Bautzen. To be honest, I didn't think about him a great deal and the others=here probably didn't either. A Pigtooth comes, a Pigtooth goes. That's how it's always=been. —

— If you think about it: allthedeadandmaimed at The Border, allthosebrokenfamilies, like the Bergers, & they weren't even victims=in-the-name-of-freedom or some other noble ideal, nor weights on the scales-of-justice who, how shall I put it, gained their=value because they, and every single dead maimed ruined person, put !their=weight on those scales and pushed the rulers deep into the abyss ofguilt. But !no: that's !not how it was. Not

!atall. How It really was, that's something I and everyone-else
found out thatnight when the murderous arrangement was con-
cluded, so to speak, & The Deal was put into action openly: in
thenight of the Great-Bureaucratic-Reshuffle, when the kilometres of border-strip — very close-to-here as well — that normally
lay & lurked in the blackest of alldarknesses, suddenly flared up
with dazzling floods of white light like burning fuses; when the
bulldozers drove up to those murderous facilities from-1-moment=
to-the-next, illuminated by the glaring lights —: & commandos
speaking in a foreign language tore through thedarkness &
thedeathlysilence as only barking dogs submachine-gun salvos
or the-spring-guns used to — but those weren't military squads,
they were !work crews — : — ?!what was going on here. — It
didn't take long for us to see & to grasp it: these weren't soldiers
advancing, they were labour battalions, & they were taking
down all the border installations: the-guard-towers, boundary-
posts, the-barbed-wire, the-barriers & spring-guns, like some
abandoned factory — they even carted away tonneaftertonne of
poisoned soil from the death strip, — yes: to put thewholelot on
convoys of heavy transport vehicles & get it out of here : the-
rulers of this country that !flogged off their=own=border; they'd
!sold off the rest of their family-jewels to Americans Israelis &
Japanese now that the natives, i.e. prisoners, weren't fetching
enough western money any more. Still doing=business on one's
deathbed, now !that's loyalty to the citizens. And those border
installation were set up again in other corners-of-the-world, in
Texas & Israel: the-guard-towers, boundary-posts, the-barbed-
wire, the-barriers, the-highconcretewall & the-spring-guns —
:everything standing again & the same dirty-deals con-tinued,
just with different cusstumours and different slogans. And so
even Backthen, in the late 50s, the Bergers and their=children

91

were just tinylittle items on a bigbalancesheet; adeal that let everyone=involved, those who belonged to the bank, as it were, make a-killing. I and everyone-else here took awhile to grasp. . . . . the full scope of thematter. Because, how shall I put it, in a sense we=all had to look at our whole lives before that moment completely !differently. It was as if we'd suddenly grown new sensors thatnight-of-the-bigsellout, and: everything we'd registered in-the-years=before: allatonce it was invalid, false, completely !off. Only !now could we all see The Truth clearly in the sharp floodlights. But, as the saying goes, one always sees The Truth toolate; otherwise The Truth wouldn't have time to build itself up into The Truth. It's only through our blindness & our senses, which are too easily deceived, that something which should !never have become truth can become truth. — The old man's skinny hands stroked the table, as if to wipe the chalk writing from a blackboard before drawing new letters.

— 1st of all THEY dragged the 3yearold child, little Theresa, from the house & bundled her into the first black limousine. Right after that Irma and her husband Alois, each into one of the other cars. The car doors were slammed shut, the engines roared, and THEY would've have driven off the same way they came, as spook-y intruders into thesilence of our village —:if it hadn't been for the storm. Well, it wasn't really a storm, just 1 single stroke of lightning and a rumble of thunder —, then it was over. But !that-1-stroke, It hit the first black car : crashed against the windscreen like a burning tree trunk, sparks flying. I already assumed thatlightning must've wrecked the car along with its occupants & there'd be flames coming out of the cooler —; but nothing. There was just a dazzling flurry of sparks, as if a firework rocket had hit the car, raining down on the frost-hard road on either side of the vehicle — for a while the three limousines stood still,

Nothing moved, no one got out, they waited like mighty black bulls that needed a moment to recover from An unexpected blow. Then the engines got going again, they seemed to thread their way hesitantly, shaken up —; — in the triumphant knowledge that they'd been able to carry out their mission !unharmed, even by such natural=forcefulness, I positively saw the three cars stretching themselves under their shiny black paint&metal, as if they were preparing their muscles&tendons for a Powerful Leap, and they finally sped out of the village, — I watched their outlines blur in clouds of blue exhaust fumes. But I won't forget that morning 53 years ago. —

That old man certainly had a sense-of-drama; like a gambler, he'd saved his=trump-card till last. — As I said — (he continued) — I got my professional training as an electrical mechanic at the pump factory in Birkheim. The factory closed agesago; Backthen it was one of the main employers-in-the-region along with the chemical works & the furniture factory. In my early days as a mechanic I was often named as best-worker. After a few years I applied for a technician's job on the B. A. L. = the Baikal-Amur Line, the construction site of a railway line through Eastern Siberia that was over 3000kilometres long. They were looking everywhere for workers. For many=here !that was A Chance to get !out : to catch a glimpse outside their native=cesspits. Me too. And they actually took me (even though I wasn't in the-party and hadn't applied for membership); the manager appointed me. So I went there. —

The man fell silent, as if he still marvelled at this Today. Then he continued, & now his sleeping hound-hands awoke again, the bright eyes lost their glaze, now sparkled: — That was what I imagined the-foreign-legion to be like back then: some of the guys I met there were types I didn't even know !existed in this country. But not just best workers: I also met others who hadn't really been assigned there voluntarily. I made friends with 1= ofthose, we slept next to each other in the same dorm. !Funny type, already in his late 30s, which was much older than most of them, skinny but tough and with stamina, he was stronger than he looked. He'd been there a while, everyone called him 'The Ear' (because he supposedly had Perfect Pitch; he only told me his real name later). Because he'd been a sound engineer at the GeeDeeR ministry of foreign trade, did ?something he shouldn't have, but because he came from a family of High Functionaries, They couldn't just get rid of him the-usual-way; he just had to disappear for a while until Things-died-down. That's what he told me. I never found out !what kind of trouble it was; no one there talked about where they'd come from & stuff like that; for some of them, the B. A. L. was the ideal exile. There was just one thing 'The Ear' had revealed to me, because he knew he'd need me for That. During his service-at-the-foreign-trade-ministry it was part of his job to make tape recordings of all conferences, which naturally included conferences that hadn't officially taken place. Then he had to give the tapes to a courier-from-The-Firm (you know what I mean). But what nobody knew and nobody was allowed to know: he'd made duplicates of all=those tapes. *When you get back home*, he said to me on one of my last evenings there=at-the-B. A. L., *go to my flat & take the black briefcase home with=you that's hidden under the bottom board of the bedroom cupboard. Don't ask, just !do it. In the case there's a letter with an address, contact it. They'll send someone to pick up The Material. It's several tapes with !extremelysensitive material on them. Please do me that-favour when it's=necessary, you're the only one I trust. Here's the key to my flat in Berlin. You've got the address.* He pressed the little key into my hand & closed my fingers into a fist around it. — Well, I did him the favour. ?Maybe THEY hadn't searched his flat as thoroughly as they usually did because he was the son of a high functionary. Or: even THOSE=at-the-firm wouldn't have thought the man capable of !suchadaringact as these secret tape recordings, so THEY didn't really know what THEY should be looking for when snooping around in his flat. Anyway, I found the briefcase where he'd told me and took it home with=me. After my=time at the B. A. L. I came back here to the village, because my parents lived here. I don't know what happened to 'The Ear'; I never heard anything from or about him again. So I had to keep the briefcase at=my=place. I didn't so much as touch any of the tapes, let alone play them back. I don't know what It was about and I don't want to know. But maybe That Matter's ?important for you, Chief Inspector. Here's the case: take it, I hope the tapes are still usable after suchalongtime. —

We said goodbye to the village administrator in Kaltenfeld, drove back to Berlin. Möller was driving again, I was looking out of the window — : — *Under puke-grey snowpats beneath a heavysky full of rain the dead fields, and as soon as thesun burns down on them they give off such a sharp stench of liquid manure that it feels like a sticky wet coat of shit wrapping itself around one's body —:constant need for a shower. — And then under thisshit all the other filth: those ancient stories that are=always= there, merged with earth & slurry, never finished & done with but returning in the figures & voices of the-descendents, clinging doggedly to people like acurse. And !I, !I=of-all-people had to stumble into something like !That. Knocked from gang-to-gang like a billiard ball, have to listen to unsavoury=old-men with their*

drearystories, — have to look at dead, mutilated women; and
now on top of that I have to take this briefcase into my care,
touch the dull-black leather, flaked apart into countless islands
like a scab, as if I were touching the face of an old hag, quarrel-
some to-the-death, the likeness of an Erinys — now All=That.
.... is sticking to-metoo & I can't break away fromit : !Oh what
a !god=!damn..... — —

Later on during the drive I opened the case. I was immediately hit by compacked=technical fumes, a mixture of rotten
leather & sharp nitro, like a robot with bad breath. Möller also
grimaced but said nothing, coughed a short dry cascade & stared
ahead through the windscreen with the driver's obligation. — I
rummaged on bravely between the individual cassette boxes, a
good dozen 540m magnetic tapes, and written on the labels in
bold white letters: OR

WO

Then Möller glanced over after all: — Ohdear, those are
!muchtooold: from the 70s. You'll barely hear anything on those.
— He commented knowledgeably. — Had that problem with
my old tapes=athome too. The best thing would be to give
the=wholelot straight to the technicians for regeneration. — I
rummaged through the pockets inside the back & found an
envelope. Unglued (or: the glue had come off); I took out a typewritten piece of paper. Read.

The words essentially repeated what the man had told me; a
comment referring to the tapes promised internal state information that, because it offered completely new insights into the-
politics between East and: West, could or had already become
dangerous for the writer of this letter, and therefore — (I had to
unfold a 2nd sheet to read on. In the typewritten text, the 'n' constantly leapt above the other letters.) And was taken aback by

the address on the envelope, written in a jagged hand with scrawny bristly strokes desperately trying to be readable, in ink faded by theyears, to which allthis material was to be sent *In an emergency*. And then I didn't know if I should burst out laughing or get angry or feel ashamed for this unknown stranger : the-addressee was no less than the UN Human Rights Commission in New York City, New York, USA —:

—!Of course: ?who else. — I exclaimed. Möller looked at me in wide-eyed surprise and the car swerved immediately. I explained to him briefly !What was going on with this=bag & its contents. He muttered incredulously & raised his hand to his cheek. I knew !that was his reflex again. He had the unmistakable ability to contort his face briefly, as if he had strong toothache, whenever someone lied to him: it happened automatically, the way the-needle on a metre moves as soon as electricity goes through it. !That ability was the reason I liked to have him with me for-interrogations.

But I couldn't calm down: — All=that still seems so laughable & so touchingly misguided today, like when kids write letters to Santa Claus in the firm=belief that their=letters will !really reach The Greatman. And then a messenger-from-Santa or some other Duplo diplomat would come to them & grant alltheirwishes, because messengers-from-Santa could always pass through the-checkpoints between East and: West justlikethat with=their-bags. ?!What could have ?led this guy, 'The Ear', to believe he could use his=survival-insurance-policy consisting of illegal tape recordings at the UN Human Rights Commission=in-New-York of all places — which must have been something like A Magical Formula to this man that would suddenly make everything that seemed impossible work. And ?did he ?seriously imagine that just because it was addressed to The-UN, Everything would —

—!Good thing the man in Kaltenfeld never tried to hand in this case. — Möller interjected, skilfully avoiding a pothole. — ?Good thing : well, some put in this way, some put it that way. — The words slipped out. Then Möller had an idea: — Or: the other version: the man in Kaltenfeld didn't tell us the wholetruth. !Like Backthen he still would've kept his passport from his-B. A. L.-days for the Soviet Union !after he came back from-There. He'd also still have known enough people-from-There who could've invited him to their=places & that way he could've applied to the-GeeDeeR and: the-Soviet-authorities for the-visa & could've got it. So it would at least have been possible, at a High Risk, to smuggle !this briefcase to Moscow & from there to the US Embassy. But whichever version was true: this man, 'The Ear', like many=Backthen in this country, was: on the one hand heroic & clever ; on the other hand, daft as a brush and childish. — — Certainly not just in this country. — I responded. — In everytime heroism & stupidity are as similar as twins, they just look different at different times & in different places; but they have throngs of relatives. And with the Old Heroes it's always the-horses that survive, with the New Heroes the-brief-cases.

— But, — said Möller, quite astonished by my agitation: — That's. . . . . justwhat humans are like.

CHAPTER 3

— THEY aim for the liver & spleen. Rarely the face or other visible body parts. Blows to the liver only hurt later. Then thatpain is especially strong, you feel like you can't bear it, double over, whimper, roll on the floor, then you puke up blood — it takes a verylongtime for thatpain to go away. If the liver's already damaged, thepain keeps=comingback, even without new blows. Sometimes THEY break your ribs or fingers. No one sees !those injuries at-1st-glance either. !That's what counts. That's the difference between a-professional-thug and a-part-time abuser flying into a rage. THEY always=cover-up what THEY do to others : the-wardens, the-officials; most-of-all: the-other-prisoners.

— No punishment without reason, THEY rarely beat people for fun. THEY beat them when The-Hierarchy & The-Unwritten-Law=of-the-Prison !demand it. THEY can always find reasons for punishments — especially for newcomers=toprison : the !worst is if you get beaten and complain to the-staff about the-culprits. Then no one will protect you. Then !you're !in-for-it.

— No nightmares, !reality. !Your reality in blood & pain. You can't get rid of the treacly stale sticky taste of your own blood. And if you have to puke, and you do moreandmore, then you feel thepain again.

— Your=body throws back thepain inflicted on it: at !you. Because your=body has no one but you for its=pain. ?Whom else

99

should the body ?pass it on to. And it !has to pass on thatpain from beatings & rape, can't keep them to=itself. You want to ?die; the body doesn't want to die. From=now-on your body is your enemy too.

— Now you've got Nothing left. Nothingatall. Nobody. You're less than alone. . . . .

— Because what used to be your=body Now belongs to= Them. It doesn't protect you any more, your body, which used to be your=body. It causes you pain, longer than alltheblows last. But That: That's just the beginning, your debut as a political among the others. THEY deliberately lock you=a-political up with thieves conmen thugs rapists robbery-murderers.

— If you sing to the-officials & blow the whistle on the-enforcers, it'll be the last song you ever sing. No more blowing for you. At-night or at-work (in the tool shed or the storeroom) or in-the-shower The-Angel-of-Retribution will appear to you. . . . . Even the socialist-penal=cystem was not without higher-beings. Someone'll find you the next day between the dustbins in front of the kitchen or in the containers for dirty laundry. As rat food. That's what happens to all traitors, all spineless, double-crossing snitches. By the way, the-tipoff that it was !you who snitched on one-of-us to the wardens always comes from the wardens. . . . . : the-other-prisoners are your opponents; opponents can be negotiated with. The-wardens are your enemies; one doesn't talk to enemies; enemies must be !destroyed.

— There's only one person who's worse off than you: the-child-abuser. Even you can have your turn with him if you feel like It.

— Your beginning: the long polished hallways in shadowless light, the boot floor, germ-free self-free. You walk in the middle, holding the laundry packet & the dishes, escorted by two wardens, two officials (as they call them now). On either side the line of men in front of walls painted greyish-yellow. They eye you silently, your body, the way you walk; short comprehensive glances, demanding & cold. The way competing women usually size each other up with critical gazes. Theair=Inhere drained of freshness, neither cold nor warm, unaired air, so to speak, pervaded by the smell of disinfectant. Thelight=withoutshadows is just bright, not dazzling, not emphasizing anything, more like a coat of paint on the stagnant air. And the vague, gaunt faces, likewise unaired, against the greyish-yellow walls look just as whitewashed, scars & cracks as pale plastered wounds, once inflicted by storms that only This=Insidehere knows about.

— In all the eyes scrutinizing you rigidly & attentively, elusive waves of buried personalities flare up, gather themselves, as concentrated as The Eye of the Maelstrom on the-1-point: on !you=the-newcomer, the-political, the fresh meat. And in the middle of the hefty disinfectant smell, stale ammonia wafts towards you from somewhere like a knife cut into the block-hard vapour. And now you start to smell yourself: the odour of wretched fear-filled meat.

— You keep walking along the-corridor as THEY=silently order, the pristinely-scrubbed concrete lane that leads you deeper into theblock as if into a dead grey canal. !Hold your packet tightly=in-your-hands. Don't tremble. Don't wobble. : THEY see. . . . . Everything about you.

— If you get closer to one of the lurking men, you'll smell his broad sweat too. That means a threat & an offer.

— When you enter the cell where THEY order you to go, and there are other prisoners there, don't speak. Don't try to be chummy. Don't ask anything. Settle in silently & pointedly slowly.

The 'furniture' in the cells as a mockery of homeliness, oozed from the gangrenous brain-stumps of a puppeteer with a childish desire to torment his menagerie, out of the same joy with which snottylittlemisses-of-all-ages skewer flies alive on needles & let them twitch to-death : wobbly gangly rattly double bedsteads (always 2 beds on top of each other; for a wank you can turn discreetly to the wall; — but ?where's the wall to put the bed-steads in the middle); a joke of a table, stools that nastily pinch your thighs, a coldsorescabby enamel sink (yellowing out of the cell wall like a toothless bottom jaw); in the corner, with no enclosure, the openly fume-emitting toilet.

—!Avoid physical contact with the others (which is difficult in a cell). Knocking or pushing is considered an !attack, not an accident.

Thick jelly-coloured light skweezes through the bars and glass of the windows. Theair in the tightlittle cells has been breathed to death, worn out, exhausted like stagnant water in brackish underground pools reached neither by sun nor rain. Deadstale smell sticks tothecells. The smell of mechanically reg-ulated sequences: eat, shit, wank, work, go outside, shit, wank, sleep, wake up. The sticky air molecules like ghosts from this locked-away, obscenely intimate conglomeration of male rage, jammed into each other, forced into a rationed block of breath for shelved lurking flesh. . . . .

— THEY see you. Always. Everywhere. Everything you do & how you do it is language, communication, disclosure, information=for=THEM. Because THEY have to know !who you are : ?fearful. ?Violent. ?Needing protection. ?Mummy's boy. ?Faggot. ?Arrogant. ?Loner. ?Sheep. ?Snitch. ?Business type. ?Servant. ?Slave. ?Lord before lords. ?What are your strengths. ?What are your weaknesses. ?Are you someone who just wants

some=peace? ?Where can they get you. ?Which grouping=
Inprison will you belong to. You tell THEM with your gestures,
far better than with your words. Because most people have learnt
to lie with their=words, but no one with their=gestures-in=the-
long-run. THEY will find you. THEY will get you. One way or
another.

— You can get anything you want in=Here : from A for alcohol or A for an arse-to-fuck, via C for cigarettes (the main cur-
rency=here), D for drugs, F for better food to W for weapons.
You either have to pay with money or with other goods. The
prices are decided by The Boss of the respective grouping (!never
call it a gang). How to get hold of goods-for-trading is something
you'll find out when you've been in=here for a while : there are
certain=middlemen. . . . .

— Unlike life Outside, Everything in=Here is regulated
down-to-the-last-detail. There's justice=for-everyone. !What
justice means is decided by theprison. . . . . Someone who breaks
the rules once gets punished. Someone who breaks the rules twice
gets punished severely. Someone who breaks the rules three time
gets eliminated. Without-distinction-of-person.

*(The sharp-green plant smell of young cornstalks, cut out of
the heat-shimmering air on a hot summer's-sunny-day —:that
was what I wanted to smell now, to suck into=me. Like years-
ago Backhome. In some legends, demons live in=cornfields. In
the twilight they come for a child from-time-to-time. And that
person is never seen again —)*

— But what's stronger than thewalls-of-stone are thewalls
of hostility. !That's so concentrated & omnipresent that there's
no choice but to make friends with others. A perforated, shaky
friendship, but the-onlything there is Inhere. So !beware of inti-
macies; find someone you can trust.

103

The wings of the building stand pushed together, broad-shouldered, massive, brutish; something grimly assertive with no words, with its regular rectangular windows (mostly walled up with glass tiles) — arranged in rows & columns like the chart in a scrupulous, mercilessly listed balance sheet, burnt into broad-browed flesh-coloured clinker bricks — still baring its teeth today & for=ever. (Near the ground, between rougher cracks in the wall where the cement burst off between the bricks, one sometimes finds a pale green weed sprouting. But it doesn't finish growing, doesn't even go upwards properly; it remains the greenish juiceless scribble in which natures tries to assert itself Here.) Neither churches nor temples, castles or town houses or the villas of the richest, neither cult buildings nor pleasure domes, determine the level of a culture, but rather the structures built for punishment: madhouses, orphanages, prisons, work-houses. : !Those are the Inner Face of every culture.

—!You have the choice. Be who you are, otherwise you're !done-for. . . . . And anyone who doesn't know !who he is will learn it in=Here=Inprison. Dead=certain. If you want to be a trader, you have to start by joining the-other-traders. It takes a long time before you're=a=trader-yourself. !Never get in-the-way of Those-Others.

— If you want to belong to the body-guard of one of the bosses, you have to go-through-the-initiation: usually the punishment of someone who broke The Rules. First ask yourself if you're capable of paying !thisprice; if you're not and: still try to suck up to him, you're !in-for-it. THEY treat cowards the same as traitors. If you've got a big mouth, act the smart arse & get unruly, you'll be 'broken in' (there's noprotection from that, unless you've got a saw-toothed arsehole). If you're fearful, don't want any violence (like almost all politicals), you need protection. You have to pay your=protectors for that: in money or goods.

— But if you're someone who just wants to keep out of Everything, just have=some=peace & do his=time & not worry about anything else : !goodluck with that —

The man who had related this to me — as extensively & emphatically as if he wanted to prepare me for a-stint-Inprison — used to be an actor at a theatre here. He'd only joined this=profession late, he was already in his late 20s, and without graduating from drama school; a director had discovered him at an amateur performance during a workers' festival in a brown coal opencast mining area in Lusatia. The young man felt drawn to this amateur theatre group; a harbouring island inthestorm of contempt-towards-gays. . . . . Now he was to act at a Real Theatre in the role of 1 of the musical labourers in Shakespeare's *A Midsummer Night's Dream*. Since then this man had belonged to the fixed ensemble at this theatre (he referred to himself as only moderately talented, and wasn't cast very often). In the years=before, after repeatedly abandoning various professional training, the man had muddled through with menial jobs. One time he was a shunter-for-the-railway, then a storeman at the east station, a cemetery gardener & coffin-bearer, then a waiter & a storeman again — those were some of his jobs. Occasionally he also dealt illegally in consumer goods that were sought-after in=the-east: cassette decks, video recorders, oil-filled radiators, portable colour TVs, spare parts for cars & motorbikes. That slightly improved his=finances (with foreign currency too), as well as getting him acquainted with other young men. But he had to be on-his-guard in case he was pursued for an antisocial lifestyle: the shadow of prison followed him together with the rumours about his homosexuality. His *discovery=as-an-actor* by that theatre director happened one night in a well-known gay bar which the young man often frequented. At his jobs, none of

which he held down for verylong, he was generally welcome &
even popular; he always had a kindword for=everyone & never
considered himself above any work or overtime. His appearance
— with the never-fading vanity of actors, he showed me 1 of his
photos-from-betterdays: an oval & regularly-shaped face with a
friendly, soft gaze and a certain youthful cunning, though around
the eyes I saw the metallic shimmer of greed — had collapsed
over-the-years he had to spend Inprison; now his face looked
strangely pale, bloodless, too white, as if it'd been photographed
with a flash. — It was in 1967, a few cars pulled up outside the
gay bar late one night, men-in-plain-clothes got out, simply
pushed the doorman aside and & stomped into the bar. There
they grabbed a-few-guests at random & dragged them outside
into the cars; 1 of those guests was this young man. There was
no-doubt !who these men-in-plain-clothes were; they told the
man in-no-uncertain-terms what they wanted: —!*Nowlisten you
dirty little fudge packer, you've got 2 options: we'll beat your
pretty face to a pulp right here&now, we'll break your nose &
jaw, you can start by saying goodbye to a few of your front teeth.
Then you'll slurp porridge like your grandma, the only part you'll
ever act will be Quasimodo, and: none of your bum chums'll
show an arse hair's worth of interest in you any more, you stupid
shitty theatre=queen.* — (This was followed by a few blows to
the stomach for emphasis.) — *Or: you'll work for=!Us from=
now-on. We'll use you when & were !We need you. If you say:
yes, you'll go home tonight with your face intact. So: it's !your
choice.* . . . . — — !?What would you have chosen. One-of-them
smashed hisfist into my eye, to seal the deal as it were, then
THEY said: —!*You'll hear from us* — and threw me out of the
car Intothenight, blowing kisses; I fell on the asphalt like a bag
of rubbish. The next day at the theatre canteen — everyone saw

my black eye, but they assumed it was the result of an erotic conflict — I put my-colleagues=at-the-table in the picture (and knew word would get around in no time): I warned them not to badmouth the stateparty&authorities in=my-presence, because I !had to report Everything to THEM. . . . . But with !that declaration I'd gambled away my=future at the same time: because someone who was watching *me* had reported my spoken warning to *The-Firm*, & so THEY decided as quickly as possible to put me where THEY needed me : Inprison. . . . . They found more than enough reasons to chare and sentence me, my *Unsocialist Lifestyle* alone would have been enough. So I went in for the 1st time, On-a-secret-mission, as it were. And !Nobody, neither the-other-jailbirds nor the-wardens, could know about !It. I was to be a-prisoner-among-prisoners. And I !was a prisoner among prisoners. . . . . And I'd never get off thattrack again, not in my lifetime. Today I'm doubly useless as a person: an old convict, an old queer; I'm doubly meant Not to be.

— Inprison I always met a lot of precarious types. !You know that only too well. Chief Inspector. After all, you & your=ilk provide plenty of material for these institutions. At=alltimes. But I still remember this 1 you're asking me about, maybe because he was my-1st-political that I came across. Well, *came across* isn't quiteright, THEY promised that I'd be released from prison if I carried out my-mission !well, & they'd make sure I was assigned a-decent-job (!I, some1 untrained — that should've made me think), with my own flat in a place where Nobody would. . . . . know me & my=history, THEY also promised me a telephone & car. So: THEY set=me=on : Alois Berger.

— ?Why did THEY set me on a !political. ?Did THEY take him for a ?queer, and plan for him to ?fall in love with=me Inthe cell so that I'd get him to talk and & !betray him all the better in=thecocoon of infatuation. At any rate, THEY inserted me into his cell (a 2-man cell in which he'd already spent quitealongtime alone; his need for conversation was outsized by now). THEY had sentenced him to 12years because of espionage incitementagainsthestate & disparagementofleadingpersonalities. He told me that right-at-the-start, and when he recited the charges-from-backthen, it seemed that even after thislongtime (he'd already done 8years) his voice was made hesitant by disconcertment and amazement, as if he still had trouble relating these martial phrases to !himself. I noticed as soon as I went Intothecell: he's not gay. So the-plan-with-the-infatuation would take a while. Because Inprison they say: ?What's the difference between a hetero and a homo: 2 months. — But THEY needed !fast results, I'd found out later why. No, not gay. Just a sissy and a crybaby and above all a blabbermouth, that's what he was. ?But maybe in THEIR meatheaded stubborn psychology there's an equation: male crybaby + sissy + blabbermouth = queer. And as for political orientation, there didn't seem to be much there either. The justification for his=12year=sentence. . . . . was the granite slab that a lightweight like him could be squashed under in a flash. And !that's !exactly what THEY wanted: squashing, grinding up any&all, whether Big or small. Without exception. And if there was no one left to squash, THEY'd jump into the grinder consisting of their own knives. In a sense, THEY did act=ually do that decades-later —. — I met a few more of-these-politicals Inprison & it was almost always the same story : they had political dreams & some blabbed too loud while dreaming : disturbance-of-the-deathly-peace. That was All. ?Why did THEY always have to come down on those dreaming ½children like firing at sparrows with !cannons. But I suppose THEY !had to do that to display THEIR biting=qualities effect=ively-to-everyone.

— Well anyway, the guy I was supposed to pump for information: Alois Berger, he was whining the whole-bloodytime because of his wife, who was arrested, sentenced & taken away with him. She was at the women's prison, and she was pregnant when they arrested her & had to give=birth to their child Inprison. He started bawling everytime at this point in his=litany. !As if it matters a damn what side of the bars someone gets. . . . . shat into-thisworld, bars stay bars, on !allsides. But I didn't tell him that, I didn't want to spoil my chances with him. I tried to comfort him instead, & learnt a-fewthings in the process. When he wasn't bawling&whining he talked & talked, evidently it never occurred to him that Everything he said to=me was also going into otherpeople's ears. But !Bloodyhell !what !trivial stuff that was, essentially completely meaningless stuff he confided in me. !Espionage — hff, him a !spy my arse : he just lamented dayin=nightout about his=wife & his=child born Inprison in September 59, which THEY had taken from its mother right after its-birth, which had to grow up Withoutitsparents in-homes reformatories, and would've been !seven years old — and: he'd !never been allowed to see his=child or his=wife for justaslong. : ?!What was to become of this child and ?!what was to ?!become of him and his=wife — (&moretears & !boo-hoo-hoo=sobbing&slobbering). Honestly: I was !disgusted by the bastard prettysoon. And then thebawling carried on: about his other child, the daughter (I think her name was Theresa) —, who'd been taken away by THEM on-the=morning-of-their=arrest & later given up for-adoption; so she was lost for=ever too —:At that bit he always bawled so loudly that I had to hold his mouth shut long enough for him to calm down, otherwise the wardens would've come in & comforted him quicksmart with their rubber truncheons (his cold snot dripped through my fingers —).

Snivelling like an oldwoman, he always ended with a-sigh: couldn't everything be=like it used to. —: And I was supposed to report to THEM about familyslush like !that, muck like !that from the ?snot&waterworks. THEY expected to hear about spicy stuff, the wickedest !any=mosities, devious !conspiracies, !subversive= activities, !incitement (if only he'd called for a !revolt=Inprison — now !that would've been something to report), & THEY wanted to hear names names, of agents, co=conspirators, the 5th column & whoknowswhatelse —: I !had to offer THEM something weighty about him because THEY expected something weighty from him & from me. I saw it Backthen: THEY believed THEIR=own lies, THEY were the first to be taken in by THEIR=own-bogeymen.

— Then he calmed down for a bit & more or less stopped his bawling. But not for long, because there was news=for-him, but it wasn't good. THEY told him that his boy, this Willfried, who had once been taken in by his brother-in-law & sister, had now been 'given back', as it were, to=the-home; they couldn't keep him with=them any longer, because the child was *inherently evil*. . . . . That was all the information. But it was !enough. First Alois Berger flew into a rage, ran and rampaged about in the cell, pushed his bed over, yelled: his wife was a !Good Woman, so their=child couldn't be evil; this brother-in-law = this !swine, who-knows !what deal THEY=struck=with=him to put them, Alois & Irma Berger, Underpressure. ?And now the child was being held=captive at the-correctional-home —:then he had the next sobbing fit. Anger and: wailing, raging and: collapsing — I thought, !now THEY've donehimin for=!good. !?How was I supposed to ?get anything=useful out of such a wretched bastard crying his bloodyeyesout. !That was My Job, after all.

— So I had to embellish most of what he confided in me from
his mattress during allthose sweaty sob-soaked hours in the cell
pretty !heavily, add a lot from my own fantasees & fill it out with
scenes from plays I'd previously acted in : Shakespeare's a veri-
table treasure trove for That too: change the props, the names &
the titles of his plays and you've got Today=to-a-T. . . . . !That
way I could invent something usable & pin the-best stuff on him.
That bawling nitwit had no idea of the !great texts I was attribut-
ing to him — if I'd recited them to him he might not even have
understood them. I longed for a little style in his yammeriads, I
owed that to my=self. In every respect : THEY had repeatedly
mentioned certain parts of my face to threaten me, & !that
sounded like surgery. . . . . Most importantly, THEY determined
the-length of !my stay=Inprison by my successes. (Maybe I was
!toogood at-snitching; after that-case was over, THEY kept me
firmly=Inprison. I'd reached the point where I even believed the
fake charges they'd used to sneak me in Here. . . . .)

— Then I put the-bee in Alois Berger's bonnet about ransoming — especially of !Political Prisoners (PeePee) — by The-
West. THEY had given me The Tip & !That became a Real Hit.
At first he didn't understand !What I was getting at (he probably
didn't see himself as *political*, so this-ransoming=business would-
n't have been an option for him). While I was whispering details
to him, he gawked at me with wide, empty stares, as if he was
trying to measure the depths of a water butt. Then, !finally (the
material of my was getting pretty thin —), he !understood &
started up like an old diesel. He hugged me as if he was already
free and in-Theothercountry —; — which he was that night, at
least in=a-certain-emergency-sense. —

— But now he decided of-his-own=accord to !upgrade his
'titel' as a Political Prisoner for=The-West the way one gets=

dressed-up for an importantvisit. The sissy turned into a prickly character, with little iron spines; disobediences, impertinences to the-wardens, acts of defiance — & he talked big and bold — :!that was !exactly how THEY wanted him, finally he was playing his=role !correctly. His market value increased the wider he opened his gob & mouthed off — or should that be ?muth — & THEY had to impose Harsh=Punishments on=him —. — Anyway, I did my bit to egg him on, — but the-machine was already rolling very=nicely without my contribution. I was already counting (secretly) the days I'd stillhavetoremain=Inprison and: he was counting those to-his-ransom, which he thought was right around the corner. — On the side he became !amazingly good in-matters-of resist-stance : didn't justtalk big about de-mock-razy, free-dumb, Free Elections, you-man rights, but also pro-duced an illegal prison-paper, busily wrote articles on the socialist penal system & again about=Allthestuff he'd already fired like ping-pong balls into the heavystuffy prison air with his=speeches. Naturally I & my=handler also wrote diligently for the paper (but he didn't notice !that in his=conspirituality). Now he inter-fered in=Everything : while reading&writing these texts the memory of cosy evenings in backyard flats, bread and dripping crept into my mouth & the furry taste of bad red wine spread over my tongue. And I smelled the sulphurous coal smoke from old leaky ceramic stoves, winding its way in garlands into the agitated babble, looked into the excited, almost fever-hot faces of men&women (which I usually went to denounce that same-night) when they kindled their bitterly=maudlin manitou-festos & sly editawdrials in aggressively-tearful voices (and always with the feeling of shooting Maggie's Drawers every-single-time). And because the owners of the flats were usually painters or poets, they received visits in the afternoons & evenings, when the likes-of-us were !not allowed because there were Important-guests=Fromthewest, from: the-gallerist from Charlottenburg, the-publisher from Frankfurt or Hamburg. Now the raw-yalty were ashamed of their grimy backyard-household. The class society of the grubby urchins which these posh western gents were entering in search of the-reallyhotstuff=from-the-east : then the-dreamers suddenly had greed in their aye-aye-eyes, currency in their Wall-ets. Then posts & sinecures were handed out, & nobody, not even the-importantguestsfromthewest, got anything if WE didn't !want That. !Oh, I felt as merry as a bottle of red & highly conspiratorial, and: if I hadn't known that he was just cracking numb nuts in his writing, I'd have been the first to join in with his=song about a better so-shall-ism with a you-man fayce. . . . . — Now&again he'd get drubbed-by-the-staff, but to him !that was more like getting-dubbed=for-ransom, puffed-up words to go with his puffed-up lip. By now he was completely deluded, sure that he was right at the !top of the ransom waiting list. — But It !didn't turn out like that. It all turned out !differently. Honecker soit qui mal y pense.

And then the regenerated tape recordings from that ominous man they'd called 'The Ear' arrived at my office as well. Möller & I spent manyhours listening to these sonic documents, whose overarching narrative had large gaps, as if the covert copyist had been unwilling to preserve all those secret conversations in the ministry of foreign trade. Those voices resounded from the speakers on my desk as if coming from graves, word salad, dives in the cold phrase-sea, shark-toothed haggling in the realm of the dead. — For a long time we were both unable to grasp what we were hearing, even Möller with his=eastern-experience couldn't work out the terms that kept cropping up. There was particular talk of *products*, of *production figures, depletion, excess goods, product range* & more=of-the-same. ?Were the meetings supposed to be conferences on economic agreements from-GeeDeeR-days. That would make sense for a ministry of foreign trade. So the increasing rottenness that spread through GeeDeeR-society in all directions, its decline & finally its economic collapse were being presented to us —. But that was all old news; none of it could have got us=murder-investigators anywhere.

It was soonclear to us, Möller & me, that 2 negotiating sides — 1 East, 1 West German — conducted the official meetings on these tapes, while most of the recordings just documented secret=agreements between the GeeDeeR negotiators with=reference to imminent conferences. Presumably those negotiations between East and: West were to preserve the-status-quo on the one hand & on the other hand the-West-side wanted to 'soften up' the-GeeDeeR economically before going in=for-the-kill. — But if those kind of mashy=nations were made=public, was !?that supposed to ?shakeup anything Nowadays. Hardly. Because who cared about former conditions, except maybe priests & historians. So ?what good was allthatstuff to us=investigators. Evidently we'd been taken in by that self-important codger from Kaltenfeld. But we slogged on bravely, Möller & I, listening faithfully to the whole testimony of those voices from the dust of their graves.

Some confusion also remained about the sequence of the recordings. After listening many times, we decided on the order of the individual recordings. We kept to this sequence in our reports to the-superior-authorities. Because !that was odd : when word got out about the tape find in=the-department, the-home-office suddenly called. THEY commanded us to keep=quiet & demanded to have our report !immediately, as well as all the tapes.

— He definitely never noticed that I was thoroughly sounding him out & reported Everything=about-him. I'm sure of that. And in a way, he didn't want to know That. It probably never crossed his !mind that I=his-cell-confidant could be a snitch too, after Everything I'd done !for=him & !against=The-Prison. (The-Prison: over-time it takes on personified traits for the-prisoners, it seems to them like One Great Violent Person. . . . . : that one had to defend-oneself-against.) He seemed glad that someone was willing to listen patiently to his yammeriads & even give him tips=for-survival=Inprison. After all, I was his only real human= contact, outside of the-interrogations that THEY picked him up for at the most outrageous times. From-there he always snuck back into the cell, collapsed, cried, called himself a fail-you're, a worth=less pieceofcrap — & soforth. I sensed that THEY'd soon break him. . . . . I wasn't happy with that !atall, seeing as he was my-cash-cow that was supposed to help me get out. I had to do !Something. Had to 'sweeten' him again. And so I managed to arrange a meeting between him and his wife, whom THEY had locked up in the women's wing at the same prison. 1 meeting for 15 minutes — after almost 10years apart. . . . . —

— A corridor — long high-ceilinged narrow — connected the-men's-wing with the-women's, sealed off by several security gates. 1 guard at each gate. Normally it was !strictly prohibited for the-prisoners even to approach this corridor, and !impossible to cross over from either wing to the other. Also, the the-occupa- tion of the corridors & hallways was organized in such a way that no 2 prisoners could ever appear there at-thesametime. A complicated rotation system with a red light & sound signal, similar to the shunting plan at train stations, began as soon as one prisoner was picked up from his cell for-interrogation and another was to be brought from-there back to his cell; encounters, even just eye-contact from prisoner-to-prisoner, had to be !prevented. Everyone=here was Ontheirown, alone, & had to !know that at all times. — The meeting between the two took place at a late-hour, already after bedtime Inprison. It had to happen !quietly, almost like a spy swap. But the bootsteps of the-guards on the concrete sounded too loud, moving down the longcorridor with stone-like heft, the big bunches of keys in the hands of the-guards jangling brightly like thin glass tubes in the wind —. (THEY had switched off the loud honking signal that sounded as soon as one of the gates was opened, just !this once.) The corridor, dimlit only by the emergency lights, lay in murk like a coal mine. When THEY entered, the ceiling lights were switched on with a loud-bang: — lifeless brightness shot down the longhallway, pale as a corpse's skin (:the prison colour) — | — 2 guards led him to the last security gate, behind that the-women's-wing. The rattling of keys came closer from-there, — then two female wardens came around the last corner, and between them: the woman. THEY stopped. The two were still separated by the security barrier. The two forgot where they were, eyes torn open wide-amazed, arms hands legs were shaking, — then the little door in the gate was unlocked, the *clacka-chick-click* of the big key-in-the-lock gave The Sign : the man and woman leapt and flew towards each other, their bodies met and pushed together as if they wanted to burrow into each other, with arms hard as pliers they held each=other=tight. The man, taller than the woman, bent over her; the woman climbed up the man's form, wrapped her arms= around-his-nach=the-shoulders, pushed her thighs against his-body. She gasped — dug her head with the prison-short hair, discoloured to cellar-grey over-theyears, her chalk-white face by his neck — she breathed heavily as if the air & happiness were too much for her deprived lungs and her shrivelled soul —

sobbing waterfalls of sighs, her eyes blazed darkly, rolled upwards in their sockets so that a white semicircle appeared, like one of those dolls with the movable eyeballs, and her body did actually bounce back and forth once, twitched against the man's body as if being subjected to a painfully:sweet torture. And then, when his-hands=clasped=her-hips, the woman threw her wholebody against his neck his chest against the coarse material of the prison clothes (she almost knocked him down) — she seemed to be sucking on=him, him, slurping up this musty man in his cloth shell, soaked with fear&sweat&time, as if the prison smell that clung doggedly to everyone&everything were an exquisite, never-before-experienced fragrance. Her mouth wide open, the woman's body trembled against the man's, as if she were gasping for air and would have to perish like a fish catapulting itself out of the water with a silvery twist and flying towards the shore —. The=two stood like that, holding each=other=tight in their embrace, this most human of all human gestures, as if now they could not only take back the separation into woman and: man from-ages-ago, but also undo the other separation from almost tenyears ago in !thismoment=for=ever.

— Nothing happened.

— Themanthewoman, they just stood in the middle of the deathly pale prison corridor and held each=othertight. Not a word, just now&again a cloth-&flesh-muted sob from the woman, it was unclear whether out of emotion or horniness. Between them the quiet rattling of the key bunches in the hands of the wardens, standing there dull and wooden (their fingers were fiddling brainlessly with their keys), the over-sharp clinking like nails falling on the long hard corridor —.

— The guards from both wings, stiffstraight louts & musty pallid womanflesh overloaded with undisguised contempt, the purr-verted moral=enforcers who watched out not for indecent acts, but for conspiratorial words that THEY seemed to expect from the couple, stood around these bodies closed to form a sculpture of lost and once-more-found love, lurking in a semi-circle, eavesdropping on their every utterance. (They, the male & female guards, kept any sign of being moved by thisscene away from their faces; kept their bodies taut and straight as if wrapped in clingfilm. Maybe THEY feared being-reported for displaying-sympathy-with-the-class-enemy otherwise. . . . . The greater the-stifling of emotions among the male&female wardens on=duty, the greater Their-Inner-Rage=at-themselves, & the more relent-lessly they killed-off the feelings in themselves. The cruelties are not directed at the others first; they are applied to themselves to burn out those stirrings.) These guards stood like crudely-hewn stone pillars from a long-perished culture of Neolithic man=eaters. But these=two, they said Nothing, notaword from their=mouths that could have been examined by the-listening-guards and led to an !immediate termination of this encounter —; they stood, locked=in=embrace, and their=language, the sob-bing sighing cooing, was the primal language of all creatures beyond the batterings of brutish=humans. . . . .

— The sergeant of the guard who was in charge of this encounter cast an icy glance at his watch —: the agreed 15 min-utes were over —: a brief commanding gesture !immediately set the-guards on both sides of the gate in motion (with relief, it seemed to me). THEY grabbed the woman's arms and put their own around the man's shoulders. — that was how THEY undid the embrace and separated the two of them. For a moment the woman's arms remained in their clutching position, and the man stayed stooped as if his wife were still leaning against=him —, — then their flesh reverted to the-convicts'-bodies. THEY had feared screaming, protests & tears; — no more than a briefquiet sigh escaped their mouths, a little squeaky sound like boots squashing a mouse. Then THEY pushed each of the two away & back to their wing of the bigprison. . . . . The corridor with its gates lay cold and empty in the deadgloomy light with no shadows. —

— ?Do you know !what I (secret observer of this wholescene which I had enabled), ?what I asked myself at !thatmoment: ?Why don't they just let It be, because they !won't succeed anyway, they'll !never bring It off. All they'll do is have another-go and=another at bringing It off. Get stuck in the run-up, treadingwater-continuously. ?Why — don't they just —!let it — ?be —. !The question automatically burned itself into my mind, like it was etched with the tungsten filament of an electric heater, Backthen, when I saw those two lost souls, which they had long been without realizing It, in their=embrace. And now you can ask me !what I mean by It, by having-a-go and bringing It off. But no, you're !not asking, & that's the-wisest-thing one can do: !noteven ask about It in the firstplace. —

— And from !thatday=on Alois Berger confided in me even more unquestioningly, even more unreservedly and uninhibitedly than ever before (presumably not wondering for a moment !how a prisoner-among-prisoners could succeed in arranging !Such an encounter. : It's not love but gratitude that makes people blind, and the greater the misery they feel grateful for escaping, the blinder they are, even if it's gratitude for just 15 minutes of salvation).

— From-thatnight=on his=hope of being ransomed by the-west. Because now that they'd allowed him to come together with=her, even Inprison, the 1st instalment towards freedom sotospeak, then The-Outside couldn't be far away. He could already see himself and his wife striding through the-prison-gate hand-in-hand, the morning sun would be shining, & The Triumph over Their=Freedom as a new spine, heads raised to the daylight. (But imagining life=Inthewest, he couldn't quite manage !that.)

— Everything turned out differently. After longlongyears. . . . . On 7 October 1979, the XXXth birth-day=of-the-GeeDeeR, THEY, the state leadership, issued another AMNESTY. And those two, this time the amnesty applied to them.

— ?What's the 1st thing you'll do, now that you'll soon be back outside. — I asked him after the officer on duty who'd brought him the-message that he should !immediately pack his=things & prepare for-release had left the cell. !This message: !thebomb. He seemed dazed & numb from the force of an explosion, couldn't believe it at first, thought That was just another trick and he'd be humiliated all the more brutally afterwards. But I advised him to !hurryup with-his-packing, I knew This-Situation. In the midst of his=innerstorm I asked him again about his plans. Faster than a blink he answered with a flame-red face: — Look for my two children, Theresa and Willfried, and bring them home=to=us. Then Irma=I=the-children will be a real-family again. —

— He was as trusting as a child towards me. He should have known that by expressing !these intentions he was jeopardizing his newly=granted freedom. . . . . . So THEY took him away from me for=ever. — —

— And Today ?me : I'm old now. Not even grown old, I was already bornold so I had to age in my own way, a different way from other people: aging Inprison. I only count In=there. An old queer convict. I don't want to live Out Here any more. I'm already too old and everything connected to me is too old, it's decayed, battered. I don't belong Here, don't belong in This=Time any more. Can't join this race, the Hurry-of-Life, therush, thebigrush for Nothing. If I were religious I'd pray. For one of the incurable diseases: cancer, aitch-eye-vee (but Nobody wants anything to do with an old queer, so I'll have to stay-healthy). And I'm not religious, so there's nopoint to praying. But I hope. To die soon. Of all-the-people I've hated in my life, there was no one I hated more than my=self. Maybe Somebody has Something against old-queers=in-This-beautiful=healthyworld or: some1 I spied on & sent to=his-doom will find me & smash my head in. I hope he's a !good smasher & It goes quickly. That's compassion. It's all I want now. But maybe even that's too much.

— When the little gate next to the prison entrance was opened at the crack of dawn on 8 October 1979, 3 figures came out: my brother-in-law Alois Berger, & close:on:each-side one=of-these plain-clothes-men whose faces disappeared from every memory & never stuck. Figures from the vast mass of Teflon creatures. !Teflon — haha.

The man fiddled out a handkerchief, blew his nose, then adjusted his position on the chair in front of my desk; it looked like another day of long talks.

— I can still see the whole-scene before me now, as clear as it was — (he counted) — 33 years ago : with glazed eyes and sharp movements, these two men drove Alois along until they reached the station. They made sure not to stop once or allow any exchange of words or other contact with anyone. I suppose Alois had hoped that his wife, Irma, would be released at=the-sametime, because he cast a few searching glances back towards the gate. But she didn't come; either she was already gone or she'd only follow hours=later. He didn't know that all amnestied prisoners were released individually & separately from one another, because THEY wanted to prevent any-contact between them Outside too. So !every !single one who was released got their !own=privatescort like a celeb, isnthat ?funny.

— But I was there. At thatmoment. But kept hidden, didn't want to lose sight of the trio — so I followed them through the hazy morning light. Feel it again, the gossamer rain on my face. I zigzagged behind house corners so that the-guards, but especially Alois, wouldn't see me following them. He would've snitched on me to his minders without batting an eye, that's how !pissedoff he still was at me & Hedwig, who's my wife, because of Willfried & how we didn't keep him at home back then. That was why he and his wife had refused any visits from me & Hedwig to=them=Inprison, never answered any of our letters, and all parcels were sent back. They gave me & Hedwig the-blame for What-happened with their=Willfried. . . . . !Never forgave us over=alltheseyears. Not even in the hour-of-their-death. But I ask you, Inspector, ?how should we, me & Hedwig, have kept !Such-a-child. . . . . in our home. That Willfried, he wasn't a child, he was —. But I can tell you all about it, if you don't know thatwholestory yet.

Again he blew his nose into his handkerchief. The man looked at me and Möller with bloodshot eyes that revealed a life-long, now-faded discontent like leaves of dead water plants, he seemed to be waiting for something, — then he continued in his charred, self-important voice. — And so that morning, for the whole way from-the-prison-to-the-station, I squeezed into house entrances, driveways, against old shaky walls and fences in this decrepit backwater, which was held down sostrongly by the massive prison=complex that even this early morning calm still hanging over the streets & alleys — how shall I put it — seemed marked by something that'd been commanded, pushed down, made by force to keep=quiet, while inside, in-the-houses, something like life was incubating. Sullenness, grumpiness and resignation peered from every crumbling house wall, every blind-covered window & the locked front doors along the whole way. Yes, it's fair to say that. I still remember it exactly. Anyway. — He clicked his tongue against his lower lip. — The two retainers, who were holding my brother-in-law between-them & looking like caricatures of secret agents in their scruffy trenchcoats, stretched over their brawny bodies like old over-tight dressing gowns, evidently weren't interested in me (because obviously they'd noticed me following them long ago, hopping from corner to corner). Presumably they had orders to prevent any contact by released prisoner Number Such-and-Such on the way from-the-prison-to-the-station & then put him on the train to Magdeburg according to the rules, everything=else didn't interest them. (He must have had orders to go from Magdeburg !immediately to Birkheim, the district capital, to report to the authorities responsible for=him. Because Kaltenfeld was listed as his place of residence in the register.) THEY only released him & all the others who got out because of that-amnesty 1 day !after 7 October, because THEY feared pro-vocations on THEIR holiday or Whoknows !what THEY imagined might have. . . . . happened. Of course nothing would've happened, as=always. That's my opinion. But the ones who=most expected the-people to revolt were never the-masses=themselves but always the-secret-service-people. Well, & on 1=particular=day, or rather 1=particular=November-night, THEY set off the-revolt themselves, maybe to help THEIR fantasies&dreams-of-popular-revolt that'd been brewing for-decades finally become=reality, if the-people=by-themselves couldn't get it done & if nowadays a-revolt could only happen as a Bureaucratic-Reshuffle. The rulers just defected to=thepeople, probably because THEY thought, if it's going to be failure, let it be !their failure and: not OURS. That's why you won't find any of them today. But this Alois Berger they were pushing through the streets that rainy morning of 8 October 1979, he !had to feel with-every-step=outside that prison !never lets you go : the two guards-in-plainclothes deciding his path were like an arm stretching out further & further from theprison, a kind of tentacle-of-captivity if I might call it that, Inspector, a tentacle that extended and expanded into the streets of this place this area this country & this time, took=possession of Everything & transformed Everything into a construct=of-its-self. . . . . Now&again during the rush-to-the-station I caught a glimpse of his face (though he couldn't see me) : although it looked pale, unhealthy and even sickly, Something seemed to be going on inside — how shall I put it — there was a little inner flame glow-ing through that ashen skin, something that had been kept down for-alongtime & almost choked; but now it suddenly began to glimmer in the morning wind that was blowing in his face. And these-guards, even if THEY had know=ticed it, couldn't prevent that. I'd never seen my brother-in-law like !that, it was like seeing him for the First Time. At the time I'd hoped I could speak to him again, sort Everything out again, but I was fooling myself; me & Hedwig couldn't get through to him, and he refused all contact with us later too. Because !that was the-trouble in this country: people who wanted alone weren't allowed to, they were forced Intothecollective. But when someone needed Someone, then there was Nobody one could trust, then one was on-1's-own. . . . . And —

— And — And — And —: I let the man prattle on; after umpteen-years=in-the-homicide-squad I'd known my fair=share of windbags like him. Especially when these-types blathered about their=previous-life as if they'd done whoknowswhat for or against it; when actually they did what people usually do: wait, sit around, gape & toe=the-line. Afterwards it sounds like heroism (& maybe it actually is, especially Nowadays; better to do nothing than join in. . . . . And wait, because the-world keeps turning and an-Other-Life will come around : dead=sure). But having to ?!listen to !that stuff over&over again : bloody !time-wasters. I gave Möller a sign to take over (he knew what it meant, but still looked at me askance briefly) and let him carry on; left the office, closed the door behind-me; the-babble stayed trapped=inthere. (*Caught myself several times covering my ears during statements-from-witnesses —!don't want to hear any more, !don't want to hear anything; blissful=deafness to theflood of heaving, wrecking human=chatter — : — preferred response: favour unreason, unsense in=all-things — it menaces in light shades, burnt karst edges of expiring dis-quiet, —!there: a memory, !finally, some recovered sleep in the wickedly=sore wakework of the-job. . . . .*) Outside in the quiet hallway (it was probably gettinglate) I leaned the back of my head against the cooling wall. — *Gettinglate : time for=you to stop. !Hightime. It would be one of life's wonderful little joys if I could now ride my bike to my home town along the edge of a dirt path, following the bright trampled-down dust, which leads me along bends and U-turns past gardens and tall bushes full of lush green, at the end of a long day bright with the harvest sun, now going down beneath the rain-bearing evening clouds in the blue-grey air, damp with vapour. From the gardens, from the flowerbeds & enclosures, shimmering blossombrightly, many shiny little mouths with fragrant summer-flower breath —, and this little cycling tour would have no purpose, wouldn't take me anywhere, except to ride my bike to the end of a summer's day —. — That joy was over, the ability to feel it was lost, & the opportunity to repeat it had passed. But I know they still exist Today, these places that have fallen out of time, that escaped the paws of the active=life-sexploitation — you saw them yourself back then, out on the flat-lands of your home town: the unassuming country lane (which you knew from your childhood, and it still lay narrow in the overgrown meadowland, as it had before —); the scuffed kerb-stone at the corner of the old, long-deserted brick house; the crooked paving slab, it already stood out from the pavement decades-ago, crooked & worn-down; — & were still !there= today, even though you'd think something like !that — the nar-row useless path, the unnecessary scratched-up kerbstone, the wobbly, unsafe paving slab — would be the 1st thing to be removed by the hand=of-active-time. But !no : because only the things that were once of-use, that possessed=value & were employed, disappear over=time; while everything-useless is more likely to escape being used-up-by=time. !That's-you : the appear-ance of a useful shell on the-outside; burnt-up on the-inside. A little speck of ash in the-night. — And now life is too long & too hard for you, as for=all aging people : !toolong, !toohard. If only everyday had just 12 hours, 8 for sleep and the rest for work, or what people take for work. That'd be completely sufficient to wreak plenty=of havoc. But one would reach the end sooner.*

A sense=of-timing, that was something my years=on-the-job had instilled in me, & so I returned to the office just at=theright-moment, while this man, Alois Berger's brother-in-law, was still sitting in front of poor Möller talking. Now I !had to listen again, because now he was talking about Willfried, the son of Irma &

Alois Berger, who was born Inprison on 13 September 1959. And now I would learn that this Willfried-with-2-Ls was neither a ghost nor the invention of some hare-brained storyteller. This man, who'd probably murdered 4 women & probably many other people too, was farmore than Allofthat=together : in a sense he was the-embodiment of the goddamn=past that doesn't pass, never and nowhere. . . . .

— *For all our concerns, comrades, we shouldn't forget one thing: the profit target for the current year, in the amount of —* *Comrade Schneider?*

— *Seven hundred thousand in foreign currency.*

— *Comrades! This is an ambitious plan that places the highest demands on our current product range. Perhaps we can optimize a number of things. And bear in mind, comrades: time is of the essence! Make some suggestions!*

— *Well, the obvious course would be to expand the list of tariffs upwards by increasingly using products of Tariff Class 1, but —*

— *That would considerably weaken our economy!*

— *That's precisely what I was about to explain. And we wouldn't have good chances with the boss with this plan at the moment, after he expressly ordered restraint for this tariff class at the recent delegates' conference. For now, at least. No, comrades, our only choice is to increase the production rate for the middle and lower range of products in the hope —*

— *In the hope that the west doesn't notice? That they'll buy these products in greater numbers? And if not, what then?*

— *Well, we could upgrade precisely the lower product scale by giving them features that they didn't originally have.*

— *What do you have in mind, Comrade Abend?*

— *Well, it's very simple: we'll shift the comparative scale, the one our transactions with the west have been based on from the start, slightly towards increased negative actions — negative as we intend it, of course. And essentially harmless activities —*

— *There are no harmless activities in this context, Comrade Abend!*

— *Sorry. But I think you all understand what I'm talking about. You call that revamping a product. You know: taking up the good things from the west — if you'll allow the joke —*

— *And you really think, comrade, that the west will fall for that?*

— *Well, that's ultimately down to us. We have to present the products in such a way that the western media pounce on our offers and, just like BILD & DER SPIEGEL always do it, keep on spouting until every last man can recite the product names and assumes that the west discovered them and wrested them from us.*

— *I think that could actually work here too. For the western media, these kinds of presented products from our manufacture are the same thing a nice big shitheap is for bluebottles: if they see one, like it or not, they have to get on it!*

— *That's right. Never forget: the western media have always been our useful idiots.*

— *Alright then, comrades, agreed. Comrade Zeiger, your department at the HVA with the people from COSUBO will see to the suitable measures regarding the products in question. The report meeting — I know it's very soon — is in one week. Then we already need to have first successes to show before we enter the next sales negotiations with the west. As you know, comrades, one does not let one's opponent dictate the battlefield. The same applies to the sales field.*

    — Time, comrades, time dictates the battlefield. What can we do against time?

    — Well, we'll play for it.

    — Let's not get literary, comrades. We have our playwrights for that, they always do such a nice job. But time is of the essence for us, because we don't have any, comrades!

— Yes, me & Hedwig, we wanted to take=in this Willfried. Noteven adopt him, we hadn't planned that far ahead. First just take him in, to get the kid out of the-homes & the-prison-environment. That was what we wanted & that was our right, or rather mine as Irma's brother. So we wanted to help & keep their=child with=us until they, Irma and her husband Alois, had done their=time & were released from-prison. Then we wanted to give them back their=child so that they could be a real family. That's how we imagined it. — But for The-Authorities it !wasn't thatsimple. THEY started vetting us, you could say, me & Hedwig : the brother & the sister-in-law of a dangerous criminal sentenced for !espionage & !slander. . . . . : ?Are they=all=in-cahoots. Do they have ?connections to the class enemy. . . . . — Anyway, the-authorities did what they always=do: cause problems. Had concerns. Reservations. On the-back-burner — —. — — Muchtime passed —!years. The child was already almost 5, just 1 year & he'd start going to-school. The boy had already been through a few institutions & his=reputation was already in-place after those early years: brutal ruffian, thief, liar. With that label, because me & Hedwig still didn't give up & despite the-warnings from the-governors of those co-wrecktional homes, he finally did end up with=us, at=home with me & Hedwig. —

The man fished an envelope out of his inside jacket pocket, took out 2 photographs & placed them on the table in front of me. They were black&white-photographs from that time. — Here : this=one shows him when he first came to=us. —

I saw a boy who was quite tall for his age. He was wearing a knitted sweater vest with presumably coloured stripes across his chest, a pale-chequered shirt, dark shorts & light knee-length socks. He had thick shoes on his feet, like lead weights to stop him running away. The slight figure seemed held by the large hands of a man standing close behind him, Bernhard Mandt, which rested on his shoulders; the man wore an elegant frock-coat along with a light grey hat, and was smiling like a tenor. Next to the man, smiling in sunny agreement, his wife, Hedwig, in a grey Sunday dress : the ensemble for the Happy Family-photo=w/-child. (There was something chalky covering this picture, like many others from the early 60s; a cool returned= confidence after overcoming fear & poverty from a lost war.) — The boy's face was very well-formed, his hair, blonde, was cut in short back and sides with a crisp side parting. His nose, on the other hand, seemed strangely flat, as if it had been bashed in and the bone broken several times. That lent a coarse touch to his otherwise smooth, fine features; anything childlike seemed to have been beaten out of that face already. But then the eyes, set slightly too deep in their sockets, casting a frightful, suspicious, questioning look at the-observer; and this gaze was marked by an ageless sorrow that no longer knew anything of childhood. The lips thin, a straight, razor-sharp line that summed up the unchildly quality in this face.

And the other photo, taken some years later, showed an almost 20-year-old man in a challenging pose: standing with his legs apart, arms tensed on either side of his brawny body as if poised to attack, his hands clenched into-fists just waiting to strike. The features in the ascetic, haggard face, still smooth with no trace of a beard, were hardened, as if the taut pale skin had been galvanized. His jaw jutted out brutally, the lips were bitter & dangerously angry. They looked as if coarse swearwords, dirty jokes & degrading insults habitually spilled forth from them, thisfilth later being washed down again with hard liquor. Such lips, such a mouth wasted Nothing, never offered anything voluntarily; such a mouth knew no kisses, but knew bites all the better. The physiognomy of a criminal. Maybe the clenched fists were supposed to convey that he had !smashed the sorrow that had once held his being !once-and- for=all within=himself. His eyes, on the other hand, now showed a different gaze: a baffling gentleness, a knowing mildness that, the longer one looked at it, revealed itself as a verysmall, sharp burning core in the corners of his eyes. The eyes of a fanatic. This detail had almost remained invisible, as the picture had been taken by an official photographer who'd used dazzlingly bright lights : — The photo was for his application to join the COSUBO organization. . . . . — Explained Bernhard Mandt when he saw me looking=intently at this picture.

— That happened during the time in the late 70s when all living conditions in this country got worse again, the-party's-tone got harsher; the-need for employees at the COSUBO consortium grew considerably during-that-time. By then the boy had left us long-ago. After we, Hedwig & I, had to put him in=a-home again, yes: !hadto —: if I tell you !Everything that had happened with&around this boy over-the-years while he was with=us, then maybe you'll understand that we, Hedwig & I, had no choice but to turn him over to the-state & its-care again after 3 years — Today it's !easy to condemn us for that. — The man wiped his face with his handkerchief once again. Said nothing for a few moments, then returned to his=story.

When the boy was born on the prison's maternity ward on 13 September 1959, the prison doctor & his helpers thought the child was mute. When they lifted him out of his, he didn't cry. Not even when they struck him. A still, blind piece of meat. As expected: a weak child, almost a stillbirth. A moist, slimy film covered the little body and the shrivelled face, making it look sodden, and the furry first hair stuck to his head like damp felt — the skull and face and body almost seemed glassy, one could see fine little veins pulsing under the skin, like the-innards of those transparent fish, cataracts and blood fighting against the-shadows & havingtodie. The still-blind eyes wideopen, 2 diffuse holes in the skull, the eyeballs lead-white and the lids like parchment, along with the skin on the apelike littleclawyfingers. They took the newborn away from the mother immediately. They put him in=the-incubator & nursed the infant back to health with intravenous nourishment.

But they would soon find out that the child wasn't mute: he let out ear-piercing screams & cried in torrents all=days&nights — and Nobody or Nothing could calm him down. They almost put the child in solitary. Then, suddenly, he stopped screaming & crying. He had no tears left. Then they thought he was blind because he bumped into every object that was in-his-way, both when he slid about on the floor & later when he made his 1st clumsy attempts to walk; the child picked up more than a few cuts and bruises that way. But even then he didn't scream, swallowed thepain silently & bravely, and defiantly and stubborn as a machine, kept going the same way he'd crawled until he didn't bump into anything any more. (That seemed to confirm the suspicion of blindness, especially after one of the nursery school teachers carried out an infallible experiment, as she called it: she took a burning log from one of the coal ovens, held it in front of the child's face & jerked it towards his eyes —: the child didn't move a muscle, didn't flinch, didn't show any reaction, just stared quietly&stubbornly at the glowing wood. *He won't last !long.* That was what everyone thought; every day they expected his=end, they'd already reserved a box for the little body & the-papers for his death, all that was missing was the date of his descent to hell.) — But you know, Inspector, the boy was neither mute nor blind; I think he just didn't want to say anything; didn't want to tolerate the existence of things in his=way, that's why he kept running into:them until, as he imagined it, they had to yield to !him & !hiswill. (He certainly led the rest of his life following this infantile sense of defiance.) — So the boy showed no physical damage and grew, although he only spoke his first full sentences & learnt to walk reasonably confidently very late, at the age of 4. Afterwards the-authorities gave Bernhard & Hedwig Mandt permission to pick this boy up from the institution & take him home=with-them. That happened in 1964, at noon on a late September day. The child, Willfried, was now already 5 years old.

Hedwig stayed at=home, prepared The Food; she was expecting her=husband & the boy around evening. For that purpose she was already setting — refearently & solemnly — an !extra place at the living-room table. Meanwhile her husband Bernhard took the-train to the East German district capital to pick up the boy & had to fill out some more forms there. — Then, in=the-office of the-governor, led by a teacher, the boy finally appeared. Bernhard stood in the middle of the room waiting for him : the boy stopped in the doorway : no one spoke or moved. The boy with suspicious but vigilant eyes on the stranger : the man with joyful glances at the child : the governor hid his gaze behind thick spectacles & folds of fat around his eyes. The teacher stood there in her uniform like a dressed-up wooden figure. The air in the room was heavy and smelled of office.

Even when Bernhard, smiling cheerfully, squatted down & held out his arms to the boy, he didn't move. Only when the teacher gave him a shove in the back with the words —!*Go: !Getmoving. !Forwards.* — did the boy take a few cautious steps towards the strangeman who was squatting there in the middle of that blockheaded director, grinning inanely, & finally let the strangeman put-his-arms-around=him. The boy seemed to find that unpleasant; he wriggled beneath-his=touches —. Carrying the children's suitcase, they left thehome & quickly departed to-thestation & travelled *to your new town*, as the strangeman said to the boy to the boy. While they walked, the boy had to place his little hand in The Hand of the adult, and that was how they entered a flat that was now *your=new-home*, as the strangeman emphasized. Inside there was also the strangewoman, who started jumping about him as soon as he entered, wringing her hands, her eyes moist. The agitated voices of the two adults washed as waves over the boy's head, humming clanging laughing, they squeaked excitedly that he should say Something; he was silent. Then the woman ran her slightly podgy fingers through his thin brittlehair (:he shrunk back from this touch, hand shy like a beaten dog). Then he had to sit down at Their table, laid in white. Then the woman put a cushion on the boy's chair because he was too small, barely reached the table. The

woman used the opportunity for something one calls a pedagog-
ical remark: — *If you eat up like a good=boy, you'll soon be as
big as your father.* And looked at her=husband while she spoke.
The boy didn't react. A plate before-him, and the woman kept
piling more and more food onto it. — I remember it like it was
yesterday: we had beef olives with dumplings & red cabbage. —
The man swallowed the saliva of his appetite like Pavlov's dog.
And also enthused: — My wife could cook that In-her-!sleep. the
meat so tender, filled with gherkin onion bacon & mince, the
dumplings lay on the plate, bright, big and round like sumptuous
clouds, and the scent of the red cabbage was tangy and bayleafy.
The sauce smelt pleasantly spicy and warm too; allthat was new
for an-institutionalized-child, — it flattered the boy's nose. He
moved his mouth towards the edge of the plate, wanted to slurp
up the sauce, but the-adults told him with a laugh to stop. A hand
with a fork & a chunk of meat impaled on its prongs, accompanied by kind babblingwords, approached his mouth, — which
snapped shut. Devoured the chunk. And already opened again
in-expectation of the next mouthful. Andsoforth. The boy picked
up the last saucegreasy bits of food himself with his children's
fork & hastily wolfed them down. While the woman, her eyes
moist-red and her chin resting on her folded hands, watched the
gobbling boy with a benevolent smile.

During the day, because both adults worked & the boy had
refused, screaming and crying, to go to kindergarten — time-
after-time he ran off & roamed thestreets, they were afraid he'd
get run-over — he finally stayed home alone. He didn't have any
playmates; when he met with other children he soon started beating them up, so everyone steered clear of him.

When the woman came home from-work one evening, she
smelt fire from the flat. Smoke was coming out of the door to the

staircase in broad, thin wisps. And when she pulled the door open in horror, she stumbled into agreyblock of thick biting smoke. The boy had torn newspapers into shreds, made a trail of them going through the flat, grabbed the matchbox from the table & lit the paper trail at 1 end. He watched joyfully as the flame ate its way rapidly along the paper; but when it reached the carpet & thickacrid smoke & brightred and blue tongues of fire shot up from the synthetic fibres, the boy took fright and ran to the bathroom. He hid there, waiting, and the woman found him. She hastily put out the flames. To do that, she had to rush back&forth several times between the bathroom and living room with the water bucket, the boy watched silently with interest. When the man came home later on that evening, he already detected the sharp smell downstairs at the front door. After the woman, who was beside herself, had recounted the events in a halting voice, the child was fetched from the bedroom & confronted in the living room, in front of the wide, stinking scorched patch on the carpet. The boy kept stubbornly silent; they didn't hit him. — *?Why did you start the !fire.* They kept asking him. The boy had nothing to say, so he kept quiet. He was sent to-bed without any supper. — From-now=on there were often fires in that flat. One time the boy had folded some paper into houses above the kitchen stove & switched on the gas (they had kept all the matches locked=up since the 1st incident, but no one thought of the spark igniter for the gas) — singed scraps of paper swirled through the kitchen like glimmering swarms of moths, there was a sharp stench of burning. Such events & similar ones became more frequent; concerned neighbours asked the couple ?what was the matter, ?why there was smoke & a burning smell coming out of their flat so often, and ?why this-child was always at home alone —. — The two made excuses, citing the poor condition of the building & the stoves; they kept calling the-howsing-admin-istraytion about repairs, but so far no handymen had turned up — you know how it is with handymen — (they didn't say why the child was at home alone); the neighbours went away with a sigh. But the sighing of the couple wasn't down to any absent handymen. —

The woman gave up her job and stayed at home to keep=an-eye on the child herself. She followed his movements silently but constantly, didn't dare leave the flat any more. Acquaintances & neighbours who had often met the woman on the staircase, in the street or at the supermarket in the past asked ?what was the matter — ?whether the woman was perhaps ?ill —. And indeed, when the woman suddenly appeared in the street 1day after manyweeks, she seemed unsure of herself, barely spoke a word, the feverbulging eyes stood out from her very pale face with a disturbed, furtive gaze. — You need more !freshair & so does your boy. ?Where is he anyway. One hardly sees him atallany-more. — And so the neighbourly voices buzzed around her like wasps. — We have enough=air. — The woman whispered back & went on her=way, disappearing hastily through the front door. The neighbours gave one another meaningful looks.

Despite being watched by the woman, the boy didn't stop playing-with-fire; he cheekily set things alight directly under:her-nose. ?Had she given up keeping ?tabs on him. There was some-thing mechanical about it all: the boy set a fire, the woman came running & put it out. That was usually enough for one day. By now there was hardly a spot in the flat that remained untouched by these fires, a constant bitter stench of burning that stood in the old building's rooms like an invisible block. Once, when the-extinguishing was proving more of an effort for the woman, the boy went up to the crackling flames & pissed in the fire. From then-on he put out his fires himself. — After sometime, even without any fires beforehand, there were small a larger puddles all over the flat — behind the ovens, next to cupboards, wardrobes. The boy claimed there had been fires & he had put them out with water from a vase. By now thesefires seemed to have taken on a life of their own, as if it wasn't him, the child, who had started them, and thesefires had all been caused by a higherpower. — —

Because his date of birth, 13 September, was past the cut-off date for starting school, he didn't go there until he was 7. — I still remember 1 brief moment that day. The boy, his pointy school cone looked out of place on him, childish; he held the colourful cardboard cone away from himself like it was filled with disgusting rubbish. And looked up briefly, with a strange grin in his eyes that I'd never seen before in a child: a devious, deeply evil streak, a malice wrapped in silly smiles like the sickly-sweet goodies in his school cone. The boy kept his lips shut will grinning, like he wanted to cover up his teeth. —

Because he started school late, he was almost three quarters of a year older than most of the children in his class. He was unusually tall & brawny (a development no one would have expected when he was a baby, after almost dying). Just as he had beaten up his-playmates before, he now beat up his-schoolmates. No reason was needed; he hit them just for being in=his-presence. But now he not only beat up the other children, he also stole from them. After beating them until they lay at-his=feet, still and bloody, and didn't dare move, the boy helped himself. He robbed them with a determined, steady hand & took allthetime he needed — he knew neither haste nor fear of punishment for his deeds — he robbed the child=on-the-ground as if he were gutting a fallen animal. In that way he collected toys & smallchange. When he was *finished* with them, the beaten, robbed children ran to=their-parents with cries & complaints. Then the indignant parents appeared on Bernhard & Hedwig Mandt's doorstep; time-and-again they had to bow-their-heads, give back the-spoils & be thankful that the parents didn't press-charges-with-the-police. What they lost was their reputation & the goodwill of the-neighbours. The punishments which the boy Willfried subsequently received from his foster parents were endured silently withoutcomplaint, but also withoutremorse & without promising improvement. Now too, the boy said nothing in response to the horrified, angry & insistent questions of his newparents. He patiently waited for the-lectures to finish. Secretly he only seemed to be looking out for the next opportunity to beat & steal.

Because of his uncontrollable, unfettered aggression & recalcitrance, the boy was moved to a school for difficult & special-needs children already in his 2nd year. He felt out of place amid these-hordes of holing ruffians & dimwits; his academic performance at the polytechnic school had generally been far above average, & here all the more. Whatever learning material they gave him he could deal with off-the-cuff; but he didn't know how to sit down & cram. Though it didn't matter here. Because the stricter disciplinary methods at the school had no effect on the boy either, he was soon sent back to the polytechnic school where he had started off. There the-situation was the same as before: but now he did less beating, instead pressuring children to give him money & especially western-items they received now&again from relatives in *Gift Parcels — No Commercial Goods*: chewing gum, Matchbox cars, comic books, penknives, cap guns —. In exchange he offered these children His=Protection from other aggressive children, including ones from higher school years. Word got around that anyone who paid Willfried could absolutely=depend on Him. At the-parent-meetings, his foster parents had to endure one humiliation after another in front of all the other parents & the-teachers through the shameful reports about their foster son Willfried. But ?what could they do — they hadn't got through to the boy for a longtime; actually they'd never really got through to him.

Almost every day, the boy had to stay behind after school as=a-punishment for his undisciplined behaviour during lessons. He always complied without any visible emotion. He stayed for the required time in an empty classroom, just 1 teacher with him for super=vision purposes. Once the super=vising teacher asked him severely: — *?Are you !sorry.* — The boy started up from his lethargy. — *?What.* — — *The !things you did again today: ?are you ?sorry.* — she repeated, fixing him with a steely gaze. The boy shrugged. — — But you know, Inspector, I'm sure he didn't mean to be cheeky, he simply didn't know !What it meant to be sorry. Sure he knew the word, but he had no connection to it. And that was why he said to the teacher: — *?Why should I be sorry for something I did. If I was going to be sorry, I wouldn't have done inthefirstplace.* — Each time the-detention was over & the teacher sent him home, he left the row of benches slowly and deliberately and mumbled — *?Was that it.* — And it sounded as contemptuous as if he'd said: *?Is that all you've got you lit-tleshitheads.* — Later on he always said to the teacher on his way out: — *Seeya tomorrow then.* — & tapped his temple with the fingers of his left hand, the way plebs do at-work when they say goodbye to their colleagues before going home. — At some point they stopped making him stay behind.

At thattime Bernhard Mandt had begun an affair with a col-league; he only came home rarely. His wife Hedwig sat alone with the boy in the quiet flat. She suspected !what her husband was up to, but there was nothing she could do about it. Meanwhile she had stopped leaving the flat at all, not even to go-shopping. She was !verysick, she told the concerned & curious neighbours through the door crack when they came to ask after her. The-doctor had given her !strict=instructions to stay in bed. (A dull smell of bedroom & unwashedness wafted out of the flat.) So now&again the neighbours went to get the bare necessities for her. At the door she always got rid of the-helpers quickly, gave them themoney she owed them for the-shopping through the door crack with a pale shaky hand, thanked them in a wan voice & shut the door immediately. If it wasn't fumes of uncleanness & mould that emanated from the flat, it was veryoften that biting smell of fire, as the boy, almost 8yearsold now, hadn't stopped setting things alight; he kept finding new possibilities for it in the flat. (And the-people whispered & gossiped, put theirheads together, peered through the door crack inside=the-flat, saw the-rubbish all over the floor, the dirty scrunched-up bits of laundry; they hissed with outrage, spoke of vermin. . . . . & that Something hadtohappensoon because it !couldntcarryonlikethat : the-police had to come or the-health-department or the-welfare-office; but no one wanted to be the-first to do something. And Hedwig's husband came home lessandlessoften.)

In one of the next fires set by the boy, the woman didn't put out theflames the way she normally did. She stood rigidly before thefire, didn't move, stared like mad at the slowly-spreading flames. But the boy who had started it, the woman held him tightly=by-the-arm. He wriggled, twitched about, started to scream; he couldn't escape, the woman held=him there with unsuspected strength like a vice. Blankly, with wide empty eyes she watched as thefire ate its way into-the-flat —. Meanwhile the-flames in the living room had taken hold of the carpet the table-cloth the curtains, They leapt up thunderously with a bright red mass of fire, let the outlines of the objects, table sofa cupboard dresser, appear one last time in the wide swirling embers before They pounced on them & devoured everything with dazzling fire-colours. !Enormousheat, the glass in the picture frames burst, the wallpaper dissolved into charred strips and thefires were already racing into the adjoining bedroom of the couple, lunged crackling hissing at the disarranged bedclothes, a swishing whirling hot-throaty snarl shot out of theflames, as it they were screaming from within-them=selves with bright red voices of inexplicable power&rage, extearminating the silence & the need in these nar-row rooms with scorching breath — adream of !Fire !!Fire !!!Fire — the screams were coming from the house now, the flat=aflame, Nothing left to put out — —

When the-fire-brigade appeared in front of the house, the woman and the boy (her firmhand was still=holding him tightly by the arm) were standing in the frame of a window with heat-burst panes against a flame-surging background like a bright red painting — now the woman was !screaming too —!screamed & !screamed her mouth tornopen as if her=insides were driving the rushing heat out through the lips in her horrorstretched face, her hair already singed and her eyebrows, and the woman kept screaming, even screamed louder shriller than the lowangry hum-ming&roaring of theragingflames. . . . . — Only moments later, after a fireman-on-the-ladder had grabbed the woman&boy and dragged them out through the window & down several rungs — an arm of flame shot out of the window — tried to reach for the 3 people on the ladder — a scorching burstofheat swept over the rescued like a roar from the maw of a volcano.

When the man wanted to come back&home (from his mis-tress) very late that evening, he found his flat burnt out. Cold-smoky charred stench emanated from the soot-veiled empty window holes, greyish fire water left broad trails as it trickled down the house wall. In the street, paledirty glimmers lay in puddles, firefighters were clearing up their=equipment; a policeman approached the man, spoke to him. The man, chilled to the bones with horror, heard that his wife and: the boy were in hospital, he should accompany them to-The-Station as they needed his statement for a report. —!?*What kind of statement am I supposed to ?make. I want to see my wife and.* — The man's voice gave out. — *?Now — at ?thishour.* — The policeman looked at him askance. — *Visiting time at the hospital is over. So don't make anytrouble & !come with us.* — Disturbed, struck to the core by the firedamps of terror, the man followed, did Everything that was demanded of him. —

The fire & the water used by the firefighters had made several flats in the house uninhabitable; the tenants received — temporarily, it was said — other accommodation in a workers' hostel a few streets away. —

— At least there was one good thing about thefire: it saved us from having to clear up the total mess in the flat. From-the-authorities the 3-of-us got: a little room (roughly 15 m^2), a kitchenette with a 2-flame gas stove; toilet & washroom in the hallway shared by 4 people. At the weekends, when the-assembly-workers went home, we had the toilet & washroom all=to-!ourselves. My wife & I — the man remarked even now with a bitter voice — were forced to live in-those-conditions until late 1990. Everyone knows: housing in the GeeDeeR had been in a terrible=state for-years. It was only after the GeeBeeR was complete that we moved to a modest flat in a prefab housing block, the-rents had gone down because Everyone who could afford it had moved Out-of-the-Block. They used to be apartments=for=bigwigs & their=helpers, now the-former-bigwigs were moving away to the town's Better=Neighbourhoods.

— After we gave the boy back to-the-state in 67, we couldn't make special demands in terms of housing needs any more; we, my wife & I, were just bog-standard people to=The-Authorities now; no relationships, no Special-Status; Nothing that would've entitled us to privileges like a new place to live. People in the filth of General-Normality: that's what we were & what we were supposed to stay. But let's leave that for Today. — The man admonished himself & returned to The-Night-of-Thefire.

— That night, when the-police finally let me go, I ran at-once to the hospital where my wife and the boy were. — He over-whelmed the porter, who at first didn't want to let him in at-thishour & reminded him of the-visiting-hours; — the man raged, begged, sobbed & gave the porter money —; the porter let the man in so that there'd !finally be peace&quiet, but informed the-nurse who had the night shift on the ward. And so the man went to the room that the woman had to share with 2 other women. At first he didn't recognize his wife. In the blue emergency light she lay there verywan and mute in the palewhite pillows, her singed scalp concealed by a bonnet. She lay awake, her eyes stared at the man as if seeing him for the 1st time. The couple hadn't looked each=other in the eyes for alongtime. — *I won't go away any more.* — Whispered the man. — *Now I'll stay with you and the boy.* — — *I can cope on my own.* — A fragile voice fell from the pillow. — *We've !seen how you cope, haven't we.* — The man barked at her. The night nurse, who was mean-while standing there as a kind of warden, demanded quiet. — *You can be grateful THEY don't put you in-the-loonybin.* — His angry whisper was rough and scrapy. Then: —*!No: !enough. When the two-of-you, you and: the boy are out of hospital, Times Will Change.* — *You'll see,* he added in a quiet, gentler voice, — *Now Everything=will-be-alright.* — The woman's hand felt

144

rough, brittle, hot, it was trembling hard —. When it felt the man's hand it twitched, wanted to move away — but stayed there. — Morning light was already flowing through the streets when the man left the hospital bleary-eyed and shivering. It was one of those autumnal summer mornings when one doesn't know which season the coming day will choose.

Still living in their permanent=makeshift-accommodation, the husband-&-wife tried to change the boy seriously. Because he never had playmates and: no one in-school wanted anything to do with him, the couple gave him an animal for his 8th birth-day: a guinea pig. Without thanks, he took the terrarium to his corner of the room & placed it next to his toys. He sat in front of the glass container, looked inside & watched the animal darting around clumsily, and didn't budge from his corner. — But after only a few days the guinea pig lay dead in its cage. The short little legs stretched out from the bloated body, motionless and stiff, a little dead furball. Probably the man at the pet shop had ripped us off & sold us an old animal. When the boy found his guinea pig dead he !screamed wildly. Rampaged about, kept yelling at us —!*Murderers you !murderers* — because he thought we'd killed his=animal to punish him for some kind of disobedience. All=our denials were useless; for=him it was clear that we, Hedwig & I, were the murderers of his guinea pig. The boy shot like a cannon ball through the flat, which now had some make=shift furnishings, stomped knocked over threw against the walls whatever he got his-hands=on and could be moved. Bursting splintering crashing along with his inhuman stormlike yelling, hollow & hissingwithrage — from the mouth of a !child. We already thought the-police would come in any moment. I tried to catch the boy but he got away again-and-again. In a short time the room and kitchenette looked as if A Tornado had chewed them up. The hose came off the gas cooker, gas came hissing out sharply — I saw the matchbox on the table, he saw it too; we lunged at=it simultaneously, he grabbed the boy, I tried to wrench it off him — the toxically hissing stream of gas filled the little windowless room, already clouding the-senses —:!Not !That again. . . . . — I thought fullofhorror —!Anything but another Disaster — & reached for the boy, grabbed him & for the firsttime beat the-livingdaylights out of him; blood ran from his nose and mouth. Everything was quiet in=an-instant : as if hisrage had been choked by an avalanche, the boy lay on the floor after the blows, still, didn't move. Blood was still flowing from his mouth and nose. And even now: !no tears, not 1. Neither for the death of his guinea pig (maybe the 1st creature that had meant Something to him) nor for the beating. Sharp breath across his bleeding lips; the escaping gas hissing. I staggered over, attached the gas hose to the nozzle again. Meanwhile the boy got up from the floor, stood in front of me & in a defiantly emotionless voice gave me his usual — *Was that it.* — Then he took his little hand and smeared the blood from his nose and mouth extra slowly across his face — a wide, dark red trail —. Looked as if he'd crossed out his face with his blood.

— During the fit of rage, Hedwig, horrified by thepower unleashed by the young boy's frenzy, had fled to a corner of the room for=cover; now, as the-tantrum died down, she emerged & quickly took the terrarium with the dead guinea pig outside; the boy should not see That any more.

— The living-conditions=in-this-permanently=provisional accommodation — the makeshift solution had lasted for almost a year now — were, as I say, very cramped. 1 corner of the room belonged to the boy: he slept on a bed that folded into the wall, and at-night a curtain was drawn across it, it looked like he was

sleeping in a tent. We didn't want him to see as far as our marriage bed, you understand. One night my wife, who was always
a light sleeper, noticed the shadow of a figure standing at the end
of our bed. When the light flashed on it showed the boy standing
straight, holding a razor in his right hand. But he was holding it
by the blade, which cut verydeep into the boy's palm (:later his
1st scar, it must still be visible now), blood flowed down his arm
like rain from a roof gutter. The boy kept a completely straight
face, didn't make a sound; he stood in front of our bed, holding
the razor up threateningly, his blood streaming heavily.

— After that incident we realized: the boy was !insane. We
couldn't keep him with=us any longer. Someday he would've held
the razor the right=way round. . . . . — An 8yearold who wants
to !kill his family — ?where have you ever heard of anything like
!That, Inspector. — — Inwar. — Slipped out of my mouth. The
man, who hadn't expected an answer, gave a start: — ?What.
?What's that you say. — — Inwar = I mean there's stuff like that
every day. — I said more loudly.

The man gave me a strange look, — shook his head. — No.
We couldn't keep the boy with=us !anylonger. We !had to give
him back to where he'd come from. And if I'd just had 1 chance
to tell my brother-in-law !Everything I've told you, Inspector, I'm
sure Afewthings would've turned out !differently. Forsure. But
like that —. — Now the man was silent, as if thinking about
what he'd told me, in the hope of someday grasping that
All=That had in=deed happened to !him.

— After the boy left us, since then we never saw or heard from
him again, no call, no letter, Nothing. And the-authorities stubbornly refused to give us any information; pointed out with
crude=sneers that we were the ones who had given back *The Child*
(:suddenly he was *The Child*) because we'd proved incapable of

dealing-with-him; because we'd !failed as foster parents. . . . . And Those=Officials, they were right. So we stopped asking about the boy, because ?!who wants to have their nose rubbed in their-own-failure time&timeagain. We ho — we feared that the boy, that with !such a disposition. . . . . — well: that he might be dead —.
— Until 1day !this photo arrived. Notaword with it, just an enve-lope & this photo inside. That was typical of him. We, Hedwig & I, wondered ?what he was trying to tell us with this photo : a ?threat; ?was it a ?de-monst-ration — but ?whatfor. Because we couldn't know then that he wanted to join COSUBO = this state=murder-firm & did in fact work for-Them later; we & most-people=Inthiscountry didn't even know about the existence of such a company. . . . . Both This-Firm and its employees were part of one of the Biggest State Secrets. So ?what was Willfried trying to ?tell us with this photo. To this day, I haven't found an explanation for it. But it still gives me the !chills when I see !this-photo. Then Everything=from-Backthen comes back to me. — (The man didn't know anything about the others, the photos in this man's file with his twisted=tattoos. . . . .)

Back then the-police were looking for a young offender. But all investigations, all enquiries relating to his person, were soon terminated at-thetime, the-files destroyed, & any overzealous detectives who still wouldn't abandon their=investigations & keptgoing on=their-own=account, so to speak, were removed from office without-further-ado; they disappeared. . . . . That hap-pened during the time when COSUBO Ltd — the 'Commercial Subversion of the Opposition' — began its=secret=activities in the GeeDeeR. Hardly anyone among-ordinary-people knew about This Company, which, installed in-the-GeeDeeR in-close-collaboration with the-west, especially West-Germany, went about. . . . . its=work. Its activities took place !toodeep & !toofar away from anything the-people could imagine — anyone who whispered about it on either side of The Border was ridiculed as an ahistorical misstick and political muddlehead or: branded a re-actionary & a warmonger — which meant that this company could operate from both countries at almost no risk.

When this Bernhard Mandt had left my office, I looked at the pictures of the 4 murdered women from the crime scene for the umpteenth time. So far I'd noticed the peculiarity that the-perpetrator had washed the dead women carefully, especially the faces — now it occurred to me for the 1st time why he'd done that. But he hadn't been quite as thorough in his washing as we'd assumed : there was a trail of blood smeared with his hand across the dead, eyeless faces, as if the-perpetrator had crossed out the face with the women's blood —. And then he had to remove !this trace. But these clear traces were still visible in the enlarged photos. I'll get him, this man with-2-Ls=in-hisname. — The entry in my desk calendar for tomorrow, Tuesday 4 December, 8 am: *See the boss* 3 exclamation marks.

— *Deadlines are there to be observed. The same applies to agreements and contracts, whether written or unwritten!*

— *You're hardly in a position to make any demands. After all, I don't have to explain to you how one runs a business. You can leave the amateurism to your state lead* —

— *How dare you! I won't negotiate in that kind of tone.*

[*Tumult breaks out, muddle of voices, loud shouts of protest.*]

— *Gentlemen! Gentlemen!! Please: gen-tle-men!!! Let's be calm. Please.*

[*The tumult slowly winds down.*]

— *Let's not forget our good breeding. And above all the business interests of both our companies.*

— *So, gentlemen, let me summarize the situation at this
moment: you assured us production figures that you have not
met to this day. Although we understand your reasons, especially
the deadline pressure, we must insist on the fulfilment of the
agreed delivery contract. And this — allow me to recapitulate —
comprises ten products of Tariff Class One, five products of
Tariff Class Two and two products of the lowest tariff class,
Three. Everyone has the respective names. Instead, you have only
delivered two products of Tariff Class One, five products of Tariff
Class Two and two products of Tariff Class Three, and declared
the products in the latter two categories as being of a higher
grade than they are. So the delivery list is numerically correct, but
that's all. That, gentlemen, simply will not do! That was not the
agreement. But let's not say any more about evaluations of the
quality of your current selection — [speaker clears throat] —
that, as we saw earlier, will not get us anywhere.*

— *In addition, you had offered us products in categories two
and three that we can present on our market with a high accep-
tance level and to great effect in the media. None of this happened to a sufficient extent. So come up with something. Tighten
your conditions of production if you like, you've always achieved
excellent results like that. We don't care what you do, but if you
want our money, abide by our agreement!*

— *Because we don't document any of our conferences — and
I assume that you too, as men of honour, are keeping to this —
I promise you that none of what you will do to raise the produc-
tion figures will be made public. I give you my word of honour!*

— *The budget, just to remind you, is still 700,000 DM. Now
it's up to you!*

[*Extended silence interspersed with whispering — and finally tape noise*]

[*On the next tape*]

— *Comrades, I look with great concern at the attainment of the profit target. Von Ende is right: we have to come up with something. Our revamping trick didn't work. Now we're stuck with these shelf warmers. Our previous strategy doesn't work any more. We have to optimize our approach. Immediately! Otherwise the west won't play along any more and we'll lose our reputation. And what are we supposed to do with the excess goods we produced? I hardly need to tell you what that means for our foreign currency plan, comrades.*

— *Nikolai Gogol 'Dead Souls'!*

— *What's this? We're not here for a literature sem —*

— *Hangon! Justaminute!: the comrade's right. That's an absolutely excellent suggestion! Comrade Zeiger, now that's a corker of a job for your people in a big way!*

— *How so? I'm afraid I don't follow.*

— *So, comrades —* [*fat jovial laughter*] *— everyone has to read Gogol's 'Dead Soul' by the next report meeting in one week! It's literature by Big Brother, after all.* [*More fat laughter, several voices from the group chime in.*]

The scene back then, late in the day, in my office : dusk was gradually falling — followed quickly by the autumn evening with its shadows — the only bright island-in-the-room was the round spot of light from the desk lamp. Then all the sober, banal objects in that office were extinguished — desk, computer, rolling cabinet, chairs, clothes rack, the dishes in the sink still shimmering wanly with the rectangular mirror above — long ignored in their 20year ordinariness. Even the dust here&there was part of this decades=long unobtrusive presence. I listened to the recordings one more time —. And : !suddenly : a !light !biglight seemed to flare up — at=once all the evening's shadows were torn apart, all that was familiar about the furnishings that belonged to-the-routine of my service=years in that room : !gone —; and: desk, cupboards, chairs rose up in thisnewlight and suddenly detail-by-detail exposed other contours, dazzling and distorted but over-clear, painful to the eyes, the cruel reverse of all banalities. Their Other thereness was a malicious, sharp-hewn second life that had always been locked inside the-objects, but which I had never noticed.

I knew instinctively that there was ?Something fishy about these taped speeches, I sensed something in this language that I couldn't quite define, something like a 2nd layer of truth — ?What-the-hell was It : And now, in thisbigdazzlinglight, I experienced The Moment when I !suddenly, after listening to those tapes for the umpteenth time, recognized the !true content of all those terms once used at the ominous meetings between the functionaries of two states:

— Product (sometimes also called 'item' or 'accounting unit'): !people, !GeeDeeR citizens who were suitable to be ransomed by West Germany (the-FRGee);

— Product range : totality of people offered in the GeeDeeR's tariff lists & available for ransoming from the-prisons & work-houses by the-FRGee. — The tariff list covers the full social scale in the GeeDeeR: e.g. Tariff Class One would include an engineer or doctor, i.e. someone academically qualified, with a monetary value of 30 to 60K DM; by comparison, an unskilled worker — belonging to Tariff Class Three — would have a maximum value of 10K DM;

— Production figures : gathering GeeDeeR citizens to be sold:

— Conditions of production : creation of situations that would give the GeeDeeR's state security services possibilities for arrests, rapid sentencing with severepunishment & the later sale of these citizens-of-the-country to the-FRGee;

— Depletion : when GeeDeeR citizens, after already being classified as *products* & being put on the-product-lists (in cases already paid by the-FRGee), committed suicide for all sorts of reasons, sometimes out of panic.

And just as the ancient Egyptian hieroglyphs were deciphered after a handful of symbols enabled researchers to deduce the larger-remainder from those, this riddle was now solved:

— The market : the-FRGee as a potential buyer of GeeDeeR citizens:

— Excess goods : as soon as the-supply-quota for the-FRGee surpasses its purchasing power, consumer interest or the like, i.e. unsalable GeeDeeR citizens;

— Product reduction : targeted-killing of GeeDeeR citizens because of the high inflation rate (excess supply of people that resulted from the waves of arrests & therefore wouldn't disappear from the market in the foreseeable future). Because they'd already been put up for ransom, and thus necessarily knew about the-top=secret activities relating to the-ransoming, but weren't taken by the-FRGee, these citizens would have degenerated into human shelf warmers; they were entrusted to the-employees of COSUBO Ltd for *disposal*; that is, they usually died 'by-accident' or through 'suicide'.

— Delivery of goods : the completed departure of GeeDeeR citizens to the-FRGee after payment of the purchase sum agreed on by east and: west;

— Transaction, procedure : term for the successful sale of certain numbers of people, according to social classification;

As well as playing down & eliminating any feelings that may have interfered with the-transactions, such biznizspeak, like the language-of-bureaucracy, also served another purpose. That became clear to Möller & me from the-references to the 'Secret Operation "Dead Souls"' this undertaking, set in=motion purely by the GeeDeeR side of the negotiations, was the multiple listing & thus multiple sale either of GeeDeeR citizens already sold & then repeatedly sold as *new products*, or of citizens already falling under *depletion*, who underwent mercantile resurrection in the-product-lists. This method was so successful because it was agreed that there must be no record whatsoever of all=these *procedures & transactions* and !strict silence about everything. So there were no balances documenting such *actions*, either in-east or in-west, to=the-end. Only the secret tape recordings bear witness to *These Events.*

The greatworry about the-publication of these numbers & the currency subsequently transferred to the-GeeDeeR was also due to the-duty of the GeeDeeR & FRGee governments to-report to their respective occupying powers: the Soviet Union & the western Allies. That way such deals remained *!topsecret=procedures*, even within the respective state apparatuses. . . . .

But I was deeply mistaken about One thing & would later discover That : although we heard voices speaking from the-grave on the-tapes, the bodies & the deeds of these bodies were by no means dead and: buried: — — Right=Inthemud of this unpassed=past Today. No happy place where everyone has to keep Everything for all eternity. And never in=the-end — —

CHAPTER 4

The wanderer rests in a shelter.
He obtains his property and an axe.
My heart is not glad.

The date at the-registry-office had long been fixed, the-announce-ment made, friends relatives & acquaintances had been sent invi-tations for The Wedding Party. The-ceremony was to take place on Sunday in the first week of June 1992. Milan said he wanted to go and see his parents in Prague first, give them the-invitation in person, & anyway: see his parents again after-alongtime, before !such an event. He wanted to stay in Prague for 2 days, the weekend before their=wedding; he would return on Sunday evening. Milan left on Friday on the night train; Theresa, who stayed behind in Berlin, accompanied him to the station. When she tried to give Milan a parting embrace on the platform, he shrunk back with a movement of his whole body as if something had given him a shock, as if he had come from a differentworld. Then he leapt into the carriage with an exaggerated light-hearted-ness and coarse laughter, from-inside he waved cheerfully at Theresa through the window — his smile shaded by the dirty windowpane — then the train departed —. — Queasy cold crept through Theresa. !What had made this man ?recoil from her= touch : all those evenings in recent weeks — the started nights in which he didn't come-home; the meagre excuses about lotsof-work-at-the-institute; for-sometime the telephone calls, then his voice mechanically said *You've-got-the-wrong-number* (but he never hung up immediately) and afterwards the brittle sound of him clearing his throat — —. During these reflections, Theresa's chin crumpled into tiny folds as it always did when the-sobs were rising within her. She couldn't lift her arm to wave, just stood frozen like=stone on the platform. She stood like that for a long time —, and was still standing when the next train arrived. Only then did she leave, and went back to the empty & cold breath of the flat. — The following evening, Saturday, the telephone: Milan's parents called, asked after their son, he had wanted to visit them, ?could they ?speak to him — : — this attack of reality wouldn't even have been necessary. — Milan came back to Theresa's flat 1 day later than arranged, only on Monday evening; he-had-to-talk-to-her, he said while still at the door.

— You don't have to tell my Anything. — Theresa replied. — I know the score. — He acted stupid, asked in a wide-eyed voice: ?What's-the-matter —: men lie badly, and most-badly when trying to lie to women. — You should've stayed with *her* tonight, and every other night. I hope for your sake that you've known *her* long=enough that *she* will let you stay at *her*=flat. Because you don't have any business here at=mine any more. — Said Theresa & slammed the door in his face. The sharp gust of air struck his face, shattering his dim-witted stammering. She stood indoors, freezing shivering, leaning against the wall in the corridor, & listened to the man's steps down the staircase as they grew distant — and as the woman followed them with her ears, the echo of his quick footfalls inside her was not cowardly, not angry, not resentful, not remorseful or penitent, and not really stubborn or suggesting injured pride; the sound reminded her more of the early morning routine of a worker who had overslept & was now trying to make up for the delay by hurrying —: the most denigrating, callously stupid humiliation of the-woman. Finally the front door downstairs, open —; shut. Over. Those were the last sounds Theresa ever heard from Milan. When he came to pick up his=things from her flat days-later, Theresa made sure she wouldn't encounter him. Her father opened the door instead; handed him his=belongings, Milan's attempt to explain something to him was dismissed with a wave of the hand. Nowords were spoken between the two men. The date for the-registry-office was cancelled at short notice, the-announcement withdrawn, friends relatives & acquaintances received disinvitations, The Wedding Party never took place. Theresa was shrouded in silence. Cold bland silence, as if she were guilty of a moral offence.

That's how That must have been, that's how I imagine It. I'm just a copper=from-the-CID, but I've had my share of separations & cold farewells too. One as much as the other. Plus a case of Hans=Inluck or Riches to Rags. — Not much later her=professional-decline from-1-crappy-job-to-the-next began. First she lost her man, then her work & income; people hastily distanced themselves from this woman. A part of friendship is one friend's (secret) joy at the other friend's misery; her friends fell away like dust.

White covering all the shadows. The snow my wedding dress my skin, and: underneath themountains and canyons of my shame. The snow, my=beautiful white shield, has melted at the edges into a night the wedding dress burnt many nights before. My skin was pulled off my body — since then I've lain open, raw, like shame the naked red flesh the muscles sinews bones & in its ribcage the hopelessly bubbling heart. And anything that ever lived in a flesh in this great site of pleasure and mirth is dead today. Frozen. They look so peace=full. The-frozen. But 'The mountain is no longer happy'. THEY came here to bring me back. In white again : the narrow room with the high walls. The bedsheets, the walls, the light, trapped in a white glass ball floating above me, and the light the deathly pale discoloured light=Outside in front of the barred windows : white. *I shouldn't have.* Heads bend down over me, floating like moons with expert gazes. Mouths in the moons, each mouth holds judgement. Thefrost of my loneliness and my fading has not yet chewed up my whole mind, so I remember The Smile. — (Feel the tugging of the cold on the cracked skin of my lips, the needle-fine pain in the corners of my mouth — my face will be torn apart —) But this-smile doesn't belong to me. I took what was left of you. Milan. What was your=smile is now !mine, it was always just=for-me. I stole your smile. Milan. I cut your fantastic soft lips out of your face & attached them to my face. I didn't need any knife for that, any scalpel, neither needle nor thread nor scissors, the weapons-of-a-woman. ?What do I need a knife or a scalpel for when I have my=thoughts. !Keep your blood, I don't want it. You won't have noticed my=theft of your smile. And you'll keep smiling. But now they won't be your lips, twisting your face into the grimace of a goat. Now my smile is inextinguishable. Milan. Your mouth lives in=my=face, you'll never again be able to say to any woman *?Will you marry me* with this mouth. I'll be the last girl who heard those words from=you, I never forgot them. But you left me before you belonged to=me. You didn't give me any children that I could take from you now & give to-death. I've been spared the role of-Medea and the-unborn have been spared life. . . . . . *I shouldn't have.* Yet I took what was left of you for me, your=smile. Milan. And so I let your words flow through my new mouth and my new lips, words that you once spoke whispered wheezed with your panted breath as your semen shot into=me. — Wherever the search for work took

me after I was fired — the-stain of my=background was burnt
into me, what was left for=me was working at a call centre, as a
shop assistant in a shoe shop, a cleaner (but the-bosses-in-the-
administration whose rooms & hallways, and often=enough toilets, I cleansed of the arsedirt of businessmen, feared I might pore
over the-remnants of their=business in search of *secret knowledge*; so they dismissed me beforelong); then, consistently
enough, I was left with: toilet attendant at Alexanderplatz station, a top-job, other toilet attendants envied me for the-tips (but
there were barely any, more often the-customers took money
from the plate on their way out) & (probably, but the jealous
women didn't dare say it outloud) because of the male a-queynte-
ances —: that is the-path of a PhD historian, my=path : *inter
faeces at urinas*, the meat & potatoes of every history. — At each-
of-these-stations that the-sewerfloods of working-life flushed me
through, I was considered the-resident-whore. Prettysoon I didn't
care what They called me, as long as they left me in=peace. But
peace is a preciousthing. The-men told me I was *The-Best*, paid,
then these-Lohengrins all laughed the=samelaugh, the-laughter-
of-men, while they threw the condom into the toilet, pulled up
their trousers & swanned off. The-other-toilet-attendants hated
me, for that & for my=background, which stuck tome like
myshadow & thestench of disinfectant. And it was the-other-
women, the-colleagues, who reported me to the man-ager of the-
toilet-company, they said: She engages in *formal prostitution* at
the-urinals. They managed to say that, even though they could
hardly finish a sentence the rest of the time. !Formal prostitution
: THEY didn't mess around & kicked me out of that job too, my
last on the slide to happiness. . . . . *And now I've come here to
you, Father, at the end of my path: with Nothing in my hands
except my expectation of your love. But Father, I know I was The*

Best not only as a historian, but also as-a-professional-whore. I was The Best at the call centre, The Best sales assistant at the shoe shop, The Best of the-cleaners too. You, Father, taught me !how to do that, to be The Best. I took all my=thirstforhonour & all my=sympathies, of which you, Father, made me capable, & passed them on to your successors. So I always got rid of the stains on my white knee socks, the stains & the blemishes of everything past. And those who didn't understand me, I with-drew my sympathy from them & transferred it to the next. That, Father, gave me strength & hope, just as you taught me strength & hope in the years of my white socks. Even before I was made to know: you, Father, are not my real father and: were morefather to me than the real one, I'm waiting for here in thisnight. You !see what your daughter was capable of with her knowledge from those earlydays. But my white knee socks, they've got pretty damned !grubby from running rushing through the years & places of my humiliations — ?who will wash out the dirty shad-ows — to make the socks shine again like they used to: white for you, Father. White for you, Milan. And your words (which none-of-the-men I spoke whispered wheezed them to suspected were not my words, but yours, the words of a man, Milan, which I'd turned like the tables with the breath of a woman) : they worked on the strangeflesh like a sticky sweet attractant from the inside of salmon pink narcotically fragrant sepals — the strangers I took for=myself with your words. Milan. They sank into=me these strangers — dispersed themselves — & left me afterwards, thanks to !your words. ?Shall I tell you about the-men & the-times after you. Milan. ?Do you want to hear what allmen want to hear from the woman who had othermen after them. The knowledge of centimetres & geometry. Except I don't have thestrength to speak my words. They're lying in the cavity of my mouth like the semen of the-men I took with your words. Milan. They died there. The dead words of thedead. From my words new shadows. My long lie secure in these shadows. !Hold me=tight, shadows, I know you well. Whenever my=body was burning with cold and fear, you came to=me and enveloped me. Secure in shadows. For a while. I !could belong to=you= completely. The-other-people only see the past in you, it's always fullofscreaming, blood & revenge, crime & punishment. I screamed with them too, even wanted to be the-loudest & the-best — for suchalongtime. *I shouldn't have.* Thedays I spent among the-other-people, forced to break & be broken by humil-iations, they attacked me, ripped pieces of warm living flesh from my body, they burned too, like fire & fear thewounds gaped open to the night —; — the next morning they had healed, all visible wounds, the flesh grew back like the vulture-pecked liver of him who was chained to the rock. And the new skin stretched White over all wounds. So that I could get up from my couch of fire & fear, could return unharmed to the form of my painful ordinari-ness & and to be ripped anew by the-knives&teeth of-everyday-life. I broke a mirror into tiny splinters in the sink. 1 of them was oval, with a jagged edge. It looked like one of your eyes, Milan, when you said that One Thing to=me back then in the stiff wind Highup on the-skyscrapers in New York. Later I saw your gloomy eyes when you lied about a business trip and: you were really going to *her*, this otherwoman I don't want to know, for whom you left me and your smile. Since then I've cut your lying-eyes out of your face everynight, you gawked at me from stupidempty sockets. *?What's the matter with your eyes. Milan. I'd !never have thought your eyes could lose theirsight.* I'll have to smash many more mirrors before I find the 2nd oval fragment among the shards too. Then I'll place these two shards in your nightdark eye sockets and the shining light in your eyes will stay beyond allthelies beyond your death. Milan. Even your boneskull will eternally preserve your radiantly flashing pro-miss for you. Frozen in 2 mirror shards. For no one any more, my darling, except for the shadows & for time.

— I didn't know !That : ?Theresa — ?she's —!Here too in !thisclinic, in !intensive care. She's in ?verybadshape, you say = the-doctors say, might not pull ?through. She spent nights at the ?cemetery in the ice&snow, has severe frostbite. And that's why —. — The man was visibly shocked, tried to collect himself. Because of his bandaged eyes I couldn't observe what was going on inside=him. Sitting in the chair in the hospital room, he held his head up stiffly, his face turned towards an imaginary point on the wall opposite.

At first he spoke haltingly in a crusty voice. — I never saw Theresa again since-Backthen, since she threw me out of her flat and: our wedding didn't happen. And she'll never want to see me again. And I — (here a hiccup laugh) — — I'll never be able to see her again. — He pointed to his bandaged eyes. — I'm nearly-blind. I've had a few operations, but they didn't help. The-doctors may be quick-witted, but I think they're at their wits=end. No one knows ?why I lost my eyesight so suddenly — but things are going downhill fast. It started 3 months ago. First I had mosquitoes dancing before my eyes, whole swarms of black spots & streaks swirling around wildly. As if I were walking through cobwebs. Then my-vision started to blur, clouded over, dissolved —. First the left eye, soon after that the right. And noway to stop !that. — (A drop oozed out from under the right eye patch.) With great effort, the man regained his=composure. — — I won't be able to see Theresa again; she certainly won't want to see me. Impossible squared. — He made as if to cough. Then he said: —

I. — And immediately interrupted himself. Because the man evidently didn't want to carry on like !that. Nor did he know ?why a detective inspector was interested in him & his=story. (He seemed to have been=through a few-things in his time —.) And now he was searching for the words, once more a foreigner in this language.

Finally he began again. — In the years that I call My Life, I loved women. I was never Withoutawoman. And because all I wanted from them was their=love-for=me, not to possess them & pen them in with-children house-hold marriage=business, I got veryclose to women in their=love their=incredible patience & endurance and the cocoon of their=care. For a-certain-time. I learnt a lot about=myself that way during that=certain=time. But I never got any further, because I guess what I lacked for those women was what they call getting-serious-about-things, & everygame comes to an end, that's what they felt; the exact=thing that I wanted them and me to lack, and I never wanted it to end. The-game of man-and-woman. And what I learnt best about myself was my=cowardice, because I always ran off before thelove lost its spark. — He was silent for a moment, then continued.

— It was completely different with Theresa. Years-ago, I'd just got a job at the Historical Institute, I'd seen her often, but I suppose she'd never noticed me because she seemed to be busy with Other-Things, purely with her=career. That was no doubt her Biggest Pleasure Centre, ?what's a man by comparison. We hadn't spoken a word to=each-other either. She was a PhD historian & busy with A Study that people said was A-Hot-Potato. . . . . & whoever got !tooclose to Her would get burnt. I realized that the people talking like that didn't mean This ominous Study, but Theresa. So I took a closer look at this woman: outside of her=work, she struck me as a woman who'd been divorced for-sometime. Or her husband had died or otherwise disappeared. Anyway, when she thought no one was looking, she had this-typical a-peer-ance : pale, outwardly withdrawn, careful in her manner. The eyes in her narrow face sent out glances that spoke a palerestrained invitation, a late summer of her greatdesire, if you will. But how !wrong I was about every=thing. And one day at lunch in the canteen, she was sitting alone at a big table, in front of her plate, & was looking down at the plastic disc before here with that same late summer gaze. Thirst for honour makes a person lonely. She didn't touch her food, and although the canteen was overcrowded, no one joined=her at the big table. I must admit, those glances from women have an effect on=me; because I always sensed theheat of her desire and her longing, smouldering & glowing under the cold ashen layer of life's=deceptions. And !Thistime I glanced over-at=her until she !had to look up & meet my=gaze. Because she'd long noticed that I was watching her, of course — you can see that in woman by a slight twitch of the eyeballs, wherever they seem to be looking — as if there were little arrows striking their eyelids there —: so they look up. — Later we met for the first time: at the !toilets on the 2nd floor (?was it the 2nd), because she = who'd meanwhile been banished to-the-basement=to-the-archive, had to go there to relieve herself. Because in the basement it wasn't just her=career that was out of order, the loo was as well. Our=beginning was during the stage of her=end at the institute. —

Although the man couldn't see me through his thick eye patches, he certainly noticed my impatience, and especially my aversion to such long-winded foppishness. He twisted his mouth, as if he had bitten into the bitter core in the dough of his waffle.

— But with Theresa, — he said slowly, placing the words almost remorse=fully, — with Theresa there was my other,

165

quitedifferent cowardice too, the shabbiest form for a love=
her: fear. . . . .

— ?Fear. — I was genuinely amazed. — ?Why fear.

— Fear for my own skin. — The man said candidly. —
Political-fear. . . . . you'll hear more about It in a minute.

And because he couldn't dispel my amazement, he continued
as if speaking to cretins, where he'd always have to start-right-
from-the-beginning, always aware that the-whole-point-of-
the-story would slip through the crudely woven net of such a
dimwit's cognitive faculties. — ?Did it ever occur to you that this
ransoming of easterners from the-east = this-human-trafficking
to the tune of the who-money-tearian barrel organ, even the
dead-souls-scam was Nothing but a giant !smokescreen. — He
waited for new expressions of amazement from me, especially at
this unexpected twist.

— They say — he continued, — the blind see better, so I'm
curious !what I'll be laying eyes=on later on, once the last of my
light-bulbs have gone out. But that was what I could already see
Backthen with my healthy eyes, before Theresa had thrown herself into her=study, before she was thrown down for her=study,
& the Biggest Disgraces are always very simple in nature, because
they're essentially ancient, which means they're just right for historians. — He sat-up with a jolt, tightened his dressing gown; he
probably thought he was addressing an auditorium as he was
used to doing. He straightened himself out as if about to make
some great effort, as if not only his voice, but his entire body &
his arms had to reach out & dig deep down into thedust of ages.

A whore goes into thenight. One summer night manyyears
ago. Flowery scents a heavy, lush airdrink, within them the hot
city, the tram lines gleam like thin veins of liquid metal, soft

asphalt exuding tarsteam —, humid celestial paths spread out above themassofhouses; feet step through soft streets car tyres hiss bittergreasysmells of hot machines. — Father & I, we go deeper into the city. Blockhard strong steamheat between scarred house facades : stonewall beside stonewall, radiating glowing heat, like fires in furnaces burning behind thewalls. The vapour firm sugary hard, no draught moving it along, braced against people & vehicles, like awall of thick mud. Sweat coats the skin, a sticky film; sharp, biting in the airways the lungs & stomachs like smouldering plastic, toxifying the-senses burning like hooch with bad omens. Father's hand in mine, damp but not only from theheat; he seems nervous. — *Comeon.* He says in a thin voice. — *We !have to.* And guides me firmly with an iron arm from the evening-loud avenues into the sweet linden scent of silent side streets. Leafygrand green treetops tower high, overshadowing art nouveau villas in the Pankow street line. Father's steps hesitant now, I crumble along on his right in my new high-heeled red leather shoes; Father's hand reluctantly jolting pulling at my arm, telling me once again: — *We !have to.* (But I sense that this strictness is directed entirely at=himself.) When I look up at him, shock. Father (he's not really My=Father) now seems like a stranger on the outside: tall, gaunt, introverted with long dark hair, his face very pale, his expression broken up by concern and fear. I also hadn't noticed when we left home that he'd put on his oldest suit, a black one with an old-fashioned cut, & despite the heat had donned a long, likewise dark trench coat. So now there's a man walking next to me whom I don't recognize as My Father, holding my left arm he steers me through the streets of Pankow to the address of, as he remarks, a high-ranking-person who wishes. . . . . to see us & has therefore invited us to-dinner (and his voice, which I don't recognize as my father's voice,

becomes frail, shaky & splutters out syllables like a stammerer).
A life, slipped from his hands and his will, buried, struck by
everyday debris, now carried along, dragged away to his final
betrayal: of me. *But I know, Father*, I want to say, looking up at
his face, which is tired, but not from sleeplessness. *I know what
It's about with this High-Ranking-Person. We have to do what
THEY demand of you and: of me. I'm not angry at you for that,
you don't have to feel bad for me. !Come on, Father, let's walk
faster. Then It'll be over faster too.* — Now I want to pull !him
along by his arm, but he misunderstands, thinks I want to free
myself & run away from him; he yanks me hard back to his right
side, — feel wisps of my hair bouncing from the strong jolt, my
new short haircut; like a small-town girl before an opera gala or
a little=miss before the-youth-ceremony, I'D gone to the hair-
dresser especially for This-Dinner-Invitation=from-The-High-
Ranking-Person. I'd got myself a pageboy cut because Father told
me that the-High-Ranking-Person likes !that haircut in particular
on youngwomen. (That was all he needed to say.) / From the
wide road with the brightly shining granite cobblestones, an alley
turns abruptly to the right — the narrow street ends in a horse-
shoe bend. Grey-faced old bourgeois villas look down on us,
haughty and mute, on both sides of the path; at the middle of the
bend, a grand building reveals its entrance as a long-toothed maw
in the shape of a portico, — Father's arm steers me in there while
evening floods over us from the treetops, theshadows sink down
heavily like dark storm clouds. Theseshadows seem electrically
charged, I sense a quiet tingling running over the skin of my bare
arms, in my face too, then down my back. There also seems to
be something pulling us=in from theseshadows: apull that draws
us in — roaring in my head like the whirling of strong electric
currents — Father's legs running faster&faster, I follow him with

some effort — as if I weren't running myself any more, and the little cubes of granite were actually being pulled forward beneath our feet — closer and closer to the lordly old villa — through the wrought-iron gate (the white-gloved hands of a policeman standing guard outside the house open the side of the gate) — a few comfortable steps of grey stone lead up to the front door — then we, Father and I, find ourselves standing under the portico of the villa belonging to this High-Ranking-Person. The gateway is worked from heavy, dark-brown wood with fragile carvings, the two wings of the door have rectangular viewing windows with milky panes, engravings along the edges. I'm very excited & eager to enter There; Father is suddenly more hesitant, shifts awkwardly from 1 foot to the other like a supplicant; we wait under the portico. — *And you ?know !why you're Here.* Father's voice fearful & worried. — *Yes, Father.* I say. — — *And you won't tell !anyone about It. Won't ever breathe a !single word about It.*

— *No, Father.* I say. — *You don't need to tell me It'll go quickly. Father. I know the-score.* I add. (The famous 1st time : brief pain down=There, heavy body, twitching on top of mine, some wheezing against my neck. Sweat & saliva. Over.) My hand slips from Father's limp cold fingers, I approach 1 one of the rectangular frosted glass panes & because there's no doorbell or knocker, I bang my hand on the door.

Nothing happens. No one opens up.

Defiance wells up in me, outrage: I'm wearing my Best-Clothes, after all, even went to the-hairdresser; we've been invited, but !no one opens op for us.

Knocking on the door again. Nothing. Then, until they hurt, my fists drum on the wood. For that I move veryclose to 1 of the glass panes: ?maybe someone's watching us, and: I could watch the-watcher watching=us —. When my forehead touches the strangely hot glass, I have the impression of seeing 2 yellow eyes through the closed door. And again this force pouring out — — : theroaring=in-my-head returns — I feel thecentre of it in these two yellow eyes. I can't really see any eyes : but sense theforce of two gazes that slowly move across my face and my body, leaving a tingling vibrating a flowing humming warmth everywhere like a stream of hot breath — while a hard burnt smell rises, almost filling out the compact figure of a brawny man. I stagger 1 step backwards. But Nothing happens.

Father manages a sound, he wants to leave. He seems endlessly !relieved not to have been let in, as with some phone calls that one fears making, but then it rings umpteen times & Nobody answers, so one can hang up with a clear-conscience. But I'm angry & yell as loud as I can into thegreatsilence= aroundme & against the mute door: —!*Let !me !in*. I also bang my fist on the wood several times until the windows rattle. At the last bang I notice, in amazement, a change: the wood I was striking now looks shiny, as if freshly coated with blackish-red oil paint. After repeatedly banging my fist I hear Father's joyfully bright, grateful voice: — *There's Nobody here. Let's go.* — I find it —!outrageous to treat us this way: even if it were The-Emperor-of-China — one doesn't just invite people to=visit and: leave them standing outside the door. I defiantly leap down the steps of the portico, want to walk around the house — if He's in=the-house, he'll see me & let us in. Father, startled, rushes after me and tries to hold me back, looking fearfully in all directions like a thief —.

But I've already arrived at the back of the villa. Expansive lawns glide away from the villa into the depths of a park —. No doubt this park was once well tended and well planted; now the landscape is overgrown, fallen trees, thick moss and other growths, chaotically scattered among the highweeds with modern randomness, as if there'd been a battle between the trees with no winners. And the lawn soon turned into slush; stagnant water covered by duckweed, like green scabs, turned the soil into swamp. And as I turn around towards the villa, I see thick beads of black sludge around the windows on all floors, as if they'd been squeezed out through the window slits and dried in the sun. And hardened layers of mud have oozed upwards on all the windowpanes. Now I realise: Nobody's lived here in-ages. Or: Whoever lives here can't bear the light. / Iron darkness is always coming down from the brawny, big-headed wild wood. Father reaches for my hand again, and now I feel it: even he is burdened by thisdarkness as if by weights; first, fatigue forces us down on the lawn, then we lie down —. Lying stretched out beside-each-other, we just want to rest. But Something keeps us awake; we look up through the sparse foliage of thetrees into the violet sky of evening. — *Father: ?who is it that invited us.* My head is too heavy to turn towards Father, so I speak upwards into thedark in a quiet, tired voice. It takes a while before I can hear Father's voice. — *Possibly* —: and his voice stops, hesitates: — *Possibly — the devil.* It's strange, I'm not surprised in the-slightest to hear that. Even have to snigger. So !thedevil invited us to dinner; & Father wanted to bequeath me to the devil, for reasons known only=to-him: obedience or some advantage. Or: just to be allowed to stay-in-his=oldlife. !That's what I realize now. — *Father.* I say into=the-darkness, still smirking. — *You're like me.* It seems to startle him, a loud sound comes from where he's lying on the lawn. — *Yes.* I repeat. — *You're like me, don't you see: we're both lying on the ground. ?Can you ?imagine, Father, that you didn't lead me Here tonight, but actually followed !me.....*

171

Here. — And feel me and Father sinking slowly into the mud-soft lawn — —. My fingers, searching for something to hold= onto, grope around in the bed, stroke the sheets — find a long black hair, like a bristle of stubborn fur. I play with it for a while —, the hair leaps out of my fingers, springing into my face — on the bridge of my nose a sharp tiny prick, like from a needle or an insect sting. The next day in the mirror: the skin there is red, heavily swollen. He took my. I know My=Value. In my=dream of desire success & love. And the words fly out of my mouth as shadows. ?Are THEY still listening to me, the moonheads that were bending over me with expert knowsy eyes. Now I've already lost a few of my moons, there are 2 left, hovering above me insistently constantly in the chalkwhite of a hospital room. Moons pale as knowledge, owl ghosts from the antecages with explanations proofs sup-positions & theories. ?Can THEY hear me, these pale servants of the Why. ?Can THEY hear through the chalky walls of THEIR pre-judices THAT always purport to know Everything already. To avoid giving away Any of THEIR expert no-how, THEY wear white cloths over THEIR mouths. Masked breathing. ?Have THEY ever seen themselves=Inthedirt, lying mangled by harder kicks & fists than theirs, or ones that are more refined than THEIRS, but know !better how to kick to stamp with precision, Inthedirt like that : mashed to a greyish bloody flesh&bonepulp, and: no white cloth to hide THEIR shame THEIR cries THEIR crushed de-feet. If THEY have ears to hear, and whoever can hear shadows will understand me. *I shouldn't have lived.* And whoever can understand them will sometimes will occasionally hear these shadows say a name. A name, cleansed of all shadows. My name. Theresa.

— The thesis of her study — I still remember the subject: the-role-of-the-working-class-under-the-leadership-of-the-communist-party — (while speaking, he made a gesture with his right arm as if turning the handle of a barrel organ) — —: we heard that liturgical phrase ad=nauseam — (he said) — — and then: in historical class struggles in the 2nd half of the 20th century — : good lawd, !whata Cath Hedral of baroque buzzwords. But in every church, whether it's made of wood stone or slogans, there are spiders nestling & spreading their=webs; stupid flies get caught in them. ?What was I going to say. Ohyes: the thesis of her study was based on knowledge of documents from various secret negotiations between east & west (a !delicate-matter in=itself back then) : the-conflicts between the-socialist-camp — :!ha !camp — & the-capitalist-one got sharper during the period in question !not for objective reasons (as the state's representatives always claimed), but because the-means in thisdispute were sharpened on all sides. So the-battle didn't determine the-means, the-means determined the-battle. There are always parties everywhere who !don't want peace. — The speaker waited a moment for his statement to take effect on me, like the first gulp of alcohol, which hits the sober senses especially hard. — That was almost an academic approach. — The man continued. — Albeit academically=upside-down. But the aged state thinkers don't like standing on their heads : from overthrow to throwing-up. That was reason=enough for certain acadumbic blockheads to raise their malicious voices with self=righteously barbed tongues !against:her, Theresa. :But !that was just=!right for Theresa: it was the !verything that kept her going. In all that, we were already living together, she proved blinder than I am today. With all the material she'd collected, she felt politically energized, right=at=the=heart-of-power & in=the-right. Eve-&-

the-forbidden-fruit, you ?understand. At first she took the hostility at the institute as a confirmation of her=role, revelled in the certainty of her=resisdance to the corrupt party-bigwigs who nastysought to preserve The-Cause & themselves in-alcohol like a freak=of-nature. !The-Cause & !The-Idea. : !Those were Theresa's saints. She couldn't really help it, she'd grown up with That : !enlightenment, bringing !light-into-the-darkness (& darkness is always especially present where thelight glares too-brightly), True Socialism will !prevail & she, Theresa Herrmann aka Berger, is fighting on the !frontline with her files&ink for the 2nd revolution. That was how she felt & talked back then, — my silences became longer and morefrequent, because I knew her Serious Nature and: her unfathomable naivety. She wanted to be Top-of-the-Class again, trying to impress her father (who wasn't her father). — Incidentally, he was a lousy old rawmantic, if that's not a tautology, who hung on to The-Cause & almost hanged himself with it. To beg the-party-bigwigs for fairweather he'd even been willing to bring his adoptive daughter as an offering to one=ofthese Bigwig Scumbags who was into Young Girls. And the only reason it didn't happen was that just at-that-time, This Scumbag was getting some heat inside the party for his mmwell-inclinations, so he had to ease off a bit. Now !that's a nasty story. — The man interrupted himself & took a sip of water. — — But she, Theresa, was absolutely=convinced that Everything she elucidated with her=study would turn into gold, & that she only had to fill some sheets of paper with words that she took for !proof, & all=her=ideas would shine as an ever-lastinglight in the cathedral-of-communism. —:That was The Point where I gave up on her. The-party=machine launched itself !against:her, beat down on her with ironpower, I couldn't help her. No one could, and the-Majority didn't want to help anyway.

In the blink=of-an-eye, the Golden Gurl turned into Calamity Jane.

— And ?that's why you ?left her?

— Mm-yes — no —!No. — The man struggled inwardly, his face with the thick eye patches pointing straight-up as if invoking The Truth (which is always assumed to lie Above, funnily enough) with his nearlyblind eyes directed at the ceiling. — No. Not like that. Not because of that. That — was different and muchlater. — He swallowed. — You didn't know this woman beforehand. Sharp-witted, with a crafty sense of humour, aloof from all sentimentalities, she could sometimes be refreshingly irreverent, and I always saw the light hint of girlish laughter at the corners of her mouth & flashing in her bright eyes. She stood above everything as long as she remained the-victor. But when the-hostility at the institute began, this exterior hardened, it dug itself permanently into her face and the deep line above the bridge of her nose. She was the Golden Gurl, after all; when it came to defeat, she lacked practice & experience. And those who'd avoided her Before because of her=proximity-to-the-authorities avoided her Now, Inthestate-of-disgrace, for the same reason — just from the Other Side, you might say. So The-Annoyances built up=inside=her, she couldn't handle them, and then 1 lunchtime in the institute's canteen, when someone snatched away the last bit of stewed fruit from under her nose with a stupidgrin, that was !The-!last=straw. You know, Chief Inspector, the-human-being is a giant balloon filled with !bloody explosible gas, thegas of indignities, humiliations, defeats, losses & suppressed urges; — life squeezes All=That into=people. There's Thisgas under high pressure, more and more builds up; Thegas waits. Hold a little matchstick flame to it & !BANG : the wholegiganticboiler. . . . . !blows=up. And here the-matchstick was a stupid bowl of stewed fruit : she started sobbing and broke down. She didn't know what to do — was going crazy — felt surrounded by fire & poison —. !Blessed are those who can always !forget Everything that was done to them in-life. She couldn't; Theresa didn't know how to deal with defeat. . . . . Later she started dropping little notes with distressing cryptograms on them, I still remember 2 of them : *My life is ending. It is night inside me. I no longer see myself.* And: *When one steps on a beetle, no one hears it scream.* Underneath always her initial: T. :That looked like the-robber's-cross, and that was how she felt: nailed to=the-cross. How to ?help her, ?support her. I couldn't get through to her any more, was at a loss. And hurt. Because whatever I said to her, following old habits, she now=immediately twisted into an attack:against-her. — While the man spoke, all his helplessness from that time seemed to return: — So ?what is it that's making her scream & cry : her inability to deal with attacks and setbacks; her injured vanity because superiors doubt the gold of !her=study & want to turn it into scrap metal; that nobody wants to honour her any more, !her = the Eternal Number One —; instead attacks from-allsides, secret & open attacks. She used to dish it out with no hesitation, now she can't take Anything. And did she ask ?me even 1ce: ?how it was for !me, how ?I felt under the=attacks she subjected !me to as a substitute for her untouchable enemies.

Now the man composed himself and made a habitual wiping gesture across his face, shifting one of the eye patches. For a moment I glimpsed the festering jelly, the blood-clotted, sightlessly clouded eyeball like dirty glass, — then his hand hastily adjusted the dressing; he continued with some effort.

— To say nothing of The-Annoyances=at-the-institute that spilt over from her to me. Because what THEY keep purveying in pain-staking=detail is the-delusion of Original Sin, & the more secular things are, the more insistent the proponents-of-the-inquisition. : She didn't think !once to ask after !me, !never. !She was the-queen whose head everybody wanted now, I was just a prop, the straw mat under the career-carnage. I didn't understand her any more. Was at a loss. Didn't know ?how to ?help her. That was no longer the woman I knew; as if I had a completely different person before me now, a stranger to me in=everyway. ?What was I supposed to do. — He turned his face towards me as if to look at me. — The reason THEY didn't just get rid of her then, that was because of her background; her adoptive father was still Somebody. THEY didn't dare take as rigorous an approach with her as they did with others. — The man added. — And then the-GeeBeeR took place, the Great Bureaucratic Reshuffle. Now Everything went downhill onceand-for=all; now she saw onlyenemies=around=her, and I became her Worst Enemy, she made accusations and insinuations of infidelity that were still groundless back then. But sometimes accusations anticipate the deeds. — The man's speech halted as he searched for short words. — *She* was new at-the-institute, just out of uni, ten years younger than Theresa. I met *her* up=close for the 1st time in the paternoster after work. *She* spoke to me — and my spiritual lungs breathed freshair once more for the first time in-ages — the chest of my soul swelled without anxiety —: that was the beginning of what tore Theresa and: me apart for=ever.

Now I'd had enough of digging about in private laundry; and I knew the-rest. I wanted to talk about something Else. — Before, you mentioned thefear for your own skin, the political fear that drove you on & away from your fiancée. And then you spoke of a smokescreen regarding the-ransoming of GeeDeeR citizens by the-west. ?What was this smokescreen supposed to ?hide.

The man seemed very pleased by this change of subject; once again he sat up straight and started speaking in a comfortable, almost lecturing tone of voice. — There's a basic motif in the way all great rulers reveal their=nature at-alltimes. — He began. — Great rulers write new scripts for rulership, THEY reformulate POWER. For that, THEY must first destroy the places of the Old Powers & set up THEIR power centre in previously neutral places. That has been accompanied at-alltimes by massive urban construction. Akhenaten moved the capital of the Old Empire, Thebes, to the desert: the new capital was Akhetaton. Nero set fire to the Old Rome & after it burnt down He built His=capital with the *Golden House* among the ruins of the former sites. Russian tsars transferred Their residence from Kiev to Petersburg, then to Moscow & back to Petersburg. The Soviet tsars from Stalin onwards heaved themselves back to Moscow. And Hitler: his new capital, Germania, was supposed to rise from the demolition&war-ruins of the old Berlin on a grotesquely=gigantic scale. You ?see: the construction enterprises of ambitious new rulers, they bind the-forces in society & conceive, on=their-own-initiative & from ruins, the space of power over those who live There as the loyal & taxpaying citizen=masses.

— Although it's hard for me to follow you — I'm not a historian or a sociologist, after all, just a detective — I don't understand ?what !This has to do with that smokescreen of ransoming easterners. Let alone —

— Hang on, I'll get to that in a minute. But keep in mind the basic motto for the rewriting of power spaces : archi-tecture & war condition each other, the two are held together by the-need for an extremely high level of forced labour. Because where=ever such high-towering construction projects proliferate, incredibly !despotic powers will subsequently establish themselves —

slavery, whether physical or economic, for=alltime. That makes allrulers similar, & the !first ones to recognize that are always the-rulers, & they make THEIR theatre-scenarios about hostility towards other rulers in order to mobilize the-people for=themselves. And so in the 1970s, a new rulership script was opened in a —!seeming — rivalry between east & west, between the USA & the Soviet Union : the new joint residence=in-outerspace : the first space station. The unanimous aim: elimination or: rather abandonment of all troublesome=populations on earth in gigantic power conglomerates; instead, a formation of elites to carry-on=Inspace. And what we experienced at the end of the 1980s — the Great Bureaucratic Reshuffle : that wasn't an interruption in thisproject but its continuation by !superbly expand=able means.

The man, who couldn't see me but could hear me, could only guess !what I thought of his deliberations; he tried intensely to be understood. — Since-time-immemorial, dictatorships have sought populations that suited THEM. First the creation of new residences in empty earth-spaces, that reshuffles society — later THEY had to transfer populations —!ha !transfer —: now THEY !finally have the right techno-lodgies to create the ideal place-of-rule with the ideal rulers without a bothersome population : alone=with=themselves in the emptiness of outer space. !That's the !real goal: to sell of their own population, not to get rid of enemies, but to !finally be alone as rulers. Everything else is visual distraction, any con man knows that.

Now the man paused, and if he'd been able he would have pierced my eyes with his gaze. This way there were two eye patches staring at me like boiled eggs. But he hadn't finished his highly outlandish testimony yet. After a breather, with a sip of water from his bottle, he spoke again.

— What's interesting in this context, — he said, — is the forcible disparagement of this subject; conquering=space became an 'underclass' topic !exactly=at-the-time when the-logistics for the *New Ark Enterprise* were being worked out all the more purpose=fully & practically unobserved by the-project-leaders among the eastern & western chiefs-of-staff. ?Do you remember the whole arms-race-debates in the 1980s — all the-talk of the earth potentially being destroyed a dozen times over by arsenals overflowing with superweapons. So here's a question: ?what happened to all these arsenals, ?what happened to every 1 of those millions of killer weapons. I'll tell you: they didn't exist. 1 prototype of each at most, but even that's questionable. Theplans were there, but not the-weapons.

— And this woman, your fiancée, really found ?All=That out with ?her=research. — My jaw dropped.

— That & muchmore, but all by luck, like the proverbial dog having its day. Yes. — Replied the man & touched his eye patches. — Because !this is the weak spot with all the secret projects of rulers: because THEY !have to communicate about THEIR=plans, THEY have to !document them. Think of the !filth of documents in the-archives of past dictators. And documents can be !published. Literally Nothing is lost : that's The-Law-of the-Conservation-of-Infamous=Energy. . . . .

— But, — I objected, — ?where did ?themoney=allthat? money get to that — supposedly, as you say — had to be raised for the-armaments intentions in the east and: the west. — I looked at the man; he certainly noticed my gaze, said nothing, — then I concluded from his silence: — You ?think — — I don't think, I !know : Theresa had all=ofthat in black and white in her documents. Conspiracy-theory, !pà : conspiracy-practice, my dear man. By the time you grow-tired of something, It's long been full-grown & keeps growing further&further.

— So you're !claiming that in-reality, allthatmoney went towards !that !aforementioned space-project — ?what was it called. — — *New Ark Enterprise.* Yes: went towards=that so that the-elites=of-the-powerful could have their=second-lives=Inspace, while, for example, the-publics got tangled up in debates about armament & escapes-from-east-to-west like flies in=a-spiderweb. That's !exactly what I meant by smokescreens. For=the-people, the only !real things about the militarily fortified borders, the crazed flashes and fiery hisses of propaganda & persecution, are the despair & the dead. But all-thosepeople only see allthosedead allthatblood & thesmoke, and they get stuck in that. They miss the bigpicture. But anyone who listens long=enough & atten-tively to=thesedays will also hear thewhispers about the *New Ark*. And it's Here that you'll find the-!real-!criminals. . . . . Compared to them, the thieves conmen rapists murderers you presumably have deal with everyday, Chief Inspector, are, if you'll forgive me: less than a speck of dirt under a little fingernail. The-!real-!criminals: !THEY should be publicly skinned and impaled; but some of these=dirty pigs would probably enjoy being impaled, at least at the start.

I had long been sorry that Möller wasn't there; I would have loved to watch him making the greatest faces. But sometimes but sometimes ob-sessions and luna-see are precisely the ray of light that shines from thedepths of the future into thedarkness of the present —: it tells of realities that are not distant. —

But I !had to raise one point to the man after he had con-cluded his=power fantasies. — In all=these things you say you — found out there's Something missing. — — ?What. — He had probably expected some objections, but not !thisone: — The shame. — I said tersely. — People can feel shame, taking them off the rigidpath that would lead them deeper astray into shame.

At this, he turned his face towards me, not forcefully (as if looking through his thick eye patches in mocking surprise at an exo-tic animal & saying: *!What's this — a detective=inspector and: ?sucha !bighelping of morality-stew*). — — Theshame, — he slowly repeated. — Theshame doesn't save people. Theshame survives every nuclear strike better than rats & woodlice, and: it achieves Nothing. Nothingatall. — And his voice sounded indifferent, as if he'd already had to give this answer dozensoftimes, & now to a policeman as well. — Theshame is always precisely= the-stuff that helps to justify new mis-deeds. The capacity-for-shame must therefore be eliminated. — His upper body suddenly lost its-tautness, he collapsed in the chair, whether out of exhaustion or just because this subject had exhausted itself for=him. — —

(During the subsequent days, and into the many nights of porous sleep, these words reverberated within=me: space-elites — space station as a power centre — *New Ark Enterprise* — all rulers !finally !alone — theshame) — theshame will survive —

Your investigations into this ripper called Willfried — they resemble his dismemberments, you collect body parts that the killer left still warm with life, and use them to create a body that has to be the same as the murderer's. That's the !onlyway for you to recognize & catch him. Your investigations are perpetration — on the other side of-murder; what the murderer did, the dis-memberment, you will have to perform on him. I was examining the component parts of this body of bloody pasts, trying to remove them from their framework in order to understand how they had been able to combine and form this-killingmachine, with an effectiveness that outlasted the-former-taskmasters. For ?whom is this murderer killing !Today. *But what you're doing, it's much more than just gathering together the remnants of his killing, you're not a knacker; you add every piece of the murdered women's bodies to the body of the murderer, you equip his living flesh with the flesh of the dead, — so that the murder must finally emerge & stand there before:you as a real monster of dead and living flesh. This patchwork of his cursed acts, unfading, imperishable without atonement — and !that's what one calls the past: a wall, the Fleischbank of reasons, motives, irrefutable proofs. Even in-the-murderer's=deeds there is a logic.*

He was born in-prison, THEY tore his mother away from him; he had to believe from-Early=on that his=mother had left him. (But she was in prison.) *Women are beings that leave me.* He was forced to learn that. Hatred:for:women in=him, because women are always mothers too. He never knew his father. Father : it's an ideal. He also learnt that men, who can become fathers, love women. He couldn't love women, he couldn't love men who love women & become fathers; he could !admire men. He=Willfried is a man seeking admiration & awe for=himself. He can admire him=self, but he can't escape a guilty-conscience for rejecting all-women (already as a child, he translated this into his=love=of-animals: the guinea pig & his tantrum when it lay dead before him. And it was a woman, his attempted adoptive mother Hedwig Mandt, who presented the dead guinea pig to him). He tried to make up for his guilty-conscience, enriched by the love=of-animals, by, on the one hand, !crushing these feminine sensibilities inside=him and: on the other hand, by trying to protect his sister Theresa, who knows Nothing about his existence (from him=self and his=hatred=for-women, as if hatred were a 2nd person=inside=him, a shadow, his double, his incarnation=as-evil that his 1st person has to fight.) — — :I looked at this psycho-logical woodcut that I was awkwardly whittling with my conceptual woodcarving knife; the result didn't satisfy me.

Another attempt: — This boy had been through a number of children's homes, correctional institutions, youth detention centres; his attempted adoption — by Bernhard & Hedwig Mandt — had also failed; worse than that: they gave him back into custody likea broken toy being=returned to the-seller. And he was back Inthedirt. . . . . His=life-rage is a poisonous swamp from which the murderful gases arise, burn themselves into=his-senses, as the-violence that a body can command enters his= conscious-ness. Now he !can kill; now he !must kill: *because women are to=blame=for=Everything*. Then an authority in the state structure appears that requires his !exact skills : the firm for 'Commercial Subversion of the Opposition', COSUBO, a ltd company, — ½ western=business enterprise ½ state authority, with the maxim: power-to-the-murderers. . . . . For him, Willfried, all dams have broken — the lava torrents of his rage can pour forth unhindered — over all thresholds moral barriers & political restructurings. There only seems to be 1 thing still giving this free-roaming contract-killer-without-a-contract a purpose : his=quest for recognition & awe for his deeds; the-vanity of-the-murderer who wants to be taken=!seriously with his killing. He reduced his former quest for admiring awe to one for awe alone : he tried to push his=deeds-of-dismemberment to create=fear, an ever-greater fear of the-others towards HIM. He desired neither abso-lution nor remorse (let alone material wealth) on his increasingly narrow path ofviolence to=the-end of allhis escapes, but rather The Monument for veneration, the kind that people feel for space pilots who flew far=out=Intospace & never came back. They didn't give up ; he didn't give up. In the gleaming mirror of fire&blood — he could imagine himself like that, made-a-hero. *Sometimes the shortest path is the-longest —*

As I discovered this sentence, with a book lying next to my papers by chance, Möller entered, burst into my office, called out: — ?What offends a-fox the=most: when he hears the-hunter talking about him as if he were a squirrel. Then the-fox comes out of his den Fullofrage & runs in front of the-hunter's rifle. — Möller stood in front of me, a paper in his hand, & grinned at me joyfully.

— Until now you've always added your stupid — your jokes as a conclusion, now I suppose the-joke is the conclusion.

He didn't let this spoil his triumphant mood. —!Here, boss, I've got an !idea. —

— No !doubt. So then your=idea has taken over the role of your ?jokes.

He mutely handed me the paper; I read: *Manhunt! The criminal investigation department of Berlin, Mitte district, are asking for assistance from the population. The citizen Wilfred Berger is wanted on strong suspicion of 4 counts of murder* (followed by a description, age of 53, last suspected location & the phone number of our station). —:I was taken !aback: — ?*Wilfred* Berger — ?with 1 L and ?fred instead of !fried — : — And looked up at Möller; he was grinning like a Cheshire cat —.

— ? — ? —, !, !, !! : —!Cunning, Möller. Really: !very cunning. — I conceded without envy (especially as I'd been looking at the angle of vanity=among-murderers before, though I hadn't thought of !this conveniently=simple solution.)

— Wilfred — that's the name of some stupid=comedy-series on TV. — Added Möller, but I'd already understood. — Send out !this wording in !this=!exact form as an announcement & !right-away: to newspapers, television — regionally & nationally, to Interpol. But I don't think he's left Germany. — — Yes, sometimes it's not a bad thing in-the-city to be a country-boy. My father was a hunter, he often took me with him as-a-child. — said Möller, his voice still greased with pride. And as he left: — The-fox will come, boss. !Dead=certain.

Towards morning, in the faint twilight, a shadow appeared before my bed, a small wiry figure whose hair stood up wildly on one side. Not a sound from its unrecognizable face. The shadow gave me a few heavy blows to the shoulder with its right fist. I was shocked, wanted to get up, but was stuck, paralysed by sleep, stammering ?What is this ?What's going on I couldn't move. Then the shadow hit me hard on the left shoulder with its right fist. As if I'd been hit by a steel ball. Another. I realized: he'd keep on hitting me until I was dead. Full of horror and fear but unable to move, I gurgled in a voice husky from sleep: !HELP — : when I suddenly opened my eyes, the room lay empty in the faint twilight. Beside me my wife=asleep, lying peacefully still on her side —. Only the echo of my voice remained, like a rotten smell —

A policeman who whimpers for !help like a frail woman when a criminal grabs him. !Sad. !Pathetic. What !adisgrace. — All day long I kept my head down before my colleagues at-the-station, & whenever I had to leave my=office I looked carefully in all directions & avoided conversations so as to hide the trembling uncertainty in my voice. Because I firmlybelieved that everyone would notice the embarrassment of my weakness-from-last-night.

Yet nobody at-the-station would have found the time for such close observation that morning : noisescreamingtumult in=the-building, the rush of soles tapping along the high long corridors — & One thing kept on ringing out: *!He's !here*, they called out, *!He gave him=self !up*. — The wave of excitement broke & rolled up to the door of my office —; here thenoise suddenly ebbed away, everything went veryquiet for a moment —. — Someone knocked almost timidly and opened the door — : 5 policemen were holding a man=very=firmly who was showing no sign of resistance, but rather sank into the room like a wilted leaf; it seemed like he was dragging the 5 officers behind him — , the few-steps up to my desk. Here, in=the-grip of 5 men, the man we'd been seeking for-years now stood before me: Willfried Berger. — He was smaller than I'd assumed from the photo. Smaller and much less brawny. On the photo he was 19 — 53 now : a life had declined along that little dash. His appearance testified to resignation, to being worn down & generally to a waning of vitality. His haircut, short as stubble, was meant to convey military=firmness; the bald patches in the grey mirrored the ravages of misfortune. His face was a picture of exhausted rage; though before, I was told, he had been screaming around at-the-reception and frothing at the mouth, attacked the 1st officer he could find, yelled ?something about *My proper name* and about *the right to have my own name spelt properly* & such like in a foaming, cracking voice. That was why the 5 officers had to catch & hold him. Now hisrage had died down; in his face I saw the picture of someone who has long had only hollow spaces for hollow rage. But I could tell from his features that a new=real outburst could erupt from those dead hollows at any moment. So far the man was silent, so was I: ; :we stared at each:other. Time passed. Then I had him taken to the-interrogation-room; he had to wait in=there for a long time. I was happy to let Möller, who'd had the idea that led to this man's arrest, have the 1st interrogation. Then we'd alternate.

In the meantime, I gathered together all the material we had about=him — I was especially preoccupied by Theresa Berger's statements, admittedly somewhat muddled, about her unnoticed encounter with a man that night at the cemetery in Birkheim. For we'd been working on the assumptions that it was the murderer who had darted along the cemetery's avenue in the driving snow and that the imprint in the snow on the bench, next to Theresa, belonged to !him, Willfried. And for=us, Willfried meant: the murderer. I remembered Theresa's remark about the stranger on the platform in Stendal, that haggard man in a coat *the colour of coal dust* who didn't board the train Theresa took, but stayed on the platform & showed Theresa a razor-thin smile as she went past. This figure too, we had believed until now, must have been Willfried (Theresa didn't know anything to=that-day about a brother who was on her=trail, so she couldn't recognize him); her description fit him=perfectly. : Yet seeing his true appearance !confused me. I looked up the-train-timetable on the-Internet to check the connections from Stendal to Birkheim, & discovered that the train Theresa took was the only train to Birkheim in the daytime, there was 1 more that only went late in the evening, so in October it would already be dark as night by then. Other connections, such as the-bus, were either unavailable or so roundabout that it would be impossible for a traveller to get to Birkheim quickly. But the figure darting through the cemetery avenue was still recognizable in the shimmering twilight, so it would have been the afternoon. It was !impossible that this figure and: the-man-on-the-platform were 1=and=the-same person. And if the two weren't identical, but the imprint in the snow on the bench belonged to the darting figure, and that wasn't the murderer (because he hadn't hurt Theresa) but that same Willfried, then —

Möller dashed into my office with a confused, deeply pale face. —!Boss. — He called, breathing rapidly, beneath the overwhelming weight of heavy disappointment. —!Boss: it wasn't !him. We've got the !wrong one.

At a time when bureaucracies sprang up like tectonic plates, cracked apart, pushed together & piled up into new mountains of paragraphs laws regulations — then the supposedly constant& form measures for property & ownership were also overturned. That time was the year 1990, the time of the Great- Bureaucratic-Reshuffle. Whatever was writtenanew in printer's-ink-on-paper took effect with iron machines, burningsharp sunlamps, the clanging of work day&night, with coarse hands & screaming, to bring about the-New. The-oldbigwigs rushed off in armoured limousines, like cockroaches in squalid dives when thelights go on ; in armoured limousines, surrounded by police convoys, the New Bigwigs came along with lights flashing, black watchdogs of shining metal : 1 state goes ; a state comes. THIS ONE MAKES THE WORDS. And the hollow spaces between paragraphs were once filled with the blood & death of people, but Today blood&death have long since dried up in the New Books of Laws.

The only privilege Martha and Paul Herrmann were left with was the detached house in Berlin, Mahlsdorf South, a house they had once bought from a state because the previous owner had fled to-the-west shortly before the-wall was built in 1961. The property was transferred to the-Herrmanns after they had taken in and adopted the child Theresa. They moved from the cramped flat in the old building in Prenzlauer Berg to the spacious house on the outskirts, where towns already decline into-villages —.

Now, for 1st time in their lives, the two of them had enough room-to-live. They also took in Paul's parents, his father Max and his mother Franziska, to live with=them in the same house, because they didn't want the parents to. . . . . waste away in=a-nursing-home later on. *Getting old is !bad=enough*, they said, *then at least old-age shouldn't end=badly in humiliations and rough treatment from strangers. . . . .* — From that point on, three generations lived together under-1-roof as peacefully as they could. Until the year 1990.

One leek-coloured spring morning, the son of the previous owner appeared at the house in Mahlsdorf South. He didn't bother to ring the doorbell, he just went to the front door through the little garden gate & banged heavily on the wood, calling out !Herrmann. Max, Paul's father, was the only 1 at=home; perturbed, the 78yearold opened the door to the stranger — who, with atorrent of foul words, pushed the front door open, pushed his brawny body past the slender old man and stood in the hallway. He was railing away in a manner the old man couldn't understand; to him, the stranger might as well have been yelling in Chinese. What he was speaking was Notchinese, however, but a flood of legalese, talk of returning unlawfully con-fiscated property — he wants the-house-of-his-father = !this house !back, here&now=!immediately; he doesn't give a !shit where the old man & his=bunch would go, they're still settled here !unlawfully. He wants them !out, !away from here & right !now. The old man has to sign all the papers !onthespot: !Here = !there : !sign. The ballpoint pen floated eerily into his hand. — The stranger raised his fists menacingly; the old man managed to push the raging intruder out of the door & quickly turn the key-in-the-lock after him. When the stranger banged on the door again, the old-man=inside phoned his son Paul=for-help.

Paul, now 56 years old, feared for his job, which he still had; was scared to rush home & come to his father's aid during working-hours, so he advised him to call the-police. But the two old people didn't dare ask the-police, the-New-Police for protection; they suspected that THEY wouldn't want to protect them, people who used to have privileges. Now it was !their turn. Those were the gloating-whispers everywhere. ?Hadn't the-police refrained from coming just the other day, when someone broke into the neighbours' place, made excuses, hadn't wanted to help —

Days later, Max was at=home alone again, the noise of machines pushed up against the house in Mahlsdorf South : a bulldozer was moving towards the house, the son of the former owner in the driver's seat — flattened the little garden fence — then the narrow vegetable patch & flower beds, the little greenhouse shattered noisily under the coarse wheels. The bulldozer smashed the steps to the front door with its iron blade. The door flew open, Max stepped out, an axe in-his-hands, to confront the violent stranger. The son abandoned his attack, leapt off the vehicle & ran away. — In the meantime, Max, the old man, felt his strength fade, his heart failed and he collapsed in the doorway in front of the shattered steps. Neighbours who had watched Everything from=the-safety=of-their-walls, hidden by curtains, but hadn't dared to intervene, now followed the subsequent events : Franziska, Max's wife, clambered down the destroyed steps, rushed from the house to a phone booth (her own line had been cut by the bulldozer), in the 1st one she found, the phone was out of order: the cable hung loosely with no receiver on the end; Franziska=in-a-panic rang at the door of a house where she knew there was a phone. The door stayed shut, no one opened up for this woman who was screaming for=help (presumably they didn't want to be dragged into bigtrouble-among-strangers).

The old woman kept rushed on along the street —; — !finally: in this phone booth the phone was working. She called the-emergency-doctor, her son, the-police.

Theresa had kept her own flat in the city, so at=thattime she'd been living away from her adoptive parents for a long time. She heard Nothing of that defenceless day, learnt nothing of The Attack. . . . . on the home of Martha & Paul. Because the Two of them didn't want to drag Theresa Into-thisbusiness, they knew she had her=own-problems at-the-institute. And anyway, when-ever the two old people had to endure hardships, illness or other disturbances, they spared those around them all complaints & demands; as still as wounded forest-animals, they withdrew into=them=selves, back into=the-darkness, and if it were possible for them one day, they would even deny their=deaths. / Theresa was meanwhile fighting her=own=war at the Historical Institute, losing another piece of herself day-by-day. She felt as if her body were currently being broken up by tremendous paw swipes —, and exposed terrible wounds that Nobody and Nothing would ever be able to heal. And from ghastly=open wounds came the screams of voices, incessant choirs of rising yells & wailing, firing theirscreams against:&intooneanother, They weren't striving for peace and quiet; This cried out for JUDGEMENT & REVENGE, constantly, and: every word to the contrary was futile, the-verdict had long been reached the !very moment The Court convened. She was met with icy & shrill whistling from allsides, this woman became her own baddream. . . . . She felt as if trapped in quick-sand. Every movement she made in defence, in whatever direc-tion, only made her sink deeper and deeper. Sometimes the loamy sour taste of thesand already went into her open mouth — no air to breathe, damp rough sand pressed itself against her face, burning on cheeks in eyes and nose, and the gasped for air while wheezingchoking ; in vain ; she would suffocate in a moment. She knew that, in this dream that kept=returning, that didn't seem to end and was ultimately. . . . . notadream any more.

1 evening the phone in her flat rang. Martha. She didn't want to keep silent any longer, even though her husband had forbidden her to call. She, Martha, could no longer which her husband and his parents suffer because of thewar-over-the-house. Now Theresa learnt Everything that had been hidden from her until then. And now 1 more perplexed person; perplexed because she didn't know how to help Here either. She only knew one thing: now her support from home was gone too. Theresa's instinct scrabbled for a rescue, found something, & her=instinct said to her: !Keep !away from the war=athome. !Break away from the-others. !Fight !your=war. !Help your !self & !only yourself. — She longed for days=inthefog that would protect her, hold her, help her find innerpeace, fully=enclose her and make her untrace-able so that she could find herself within=her=self. But the days stood Inthelight; shrill, sharp & hot sunbeams cut through every shadow. The first heat of a premature summer suddenly erupted brutally into the city & over the people, then back to freezing cold with frosty blades in the evenings&nights. On allsides of Theresa, things were icy one minute and hot with poisonous fumes the next. . . . . The gold paint on her triumphs=ofpastyears, determined by other people, began to bubble and boil; beneath it was the naked flesh of a person forced to run up against theconcrete-of-everydaylife with her=will. Following every colli-sion the rock-hard tone: !YOU !MUST !NOTBE. No rest for her, no sleep. And so she kept away from the house in Mahlsdorf. — / — Meanwhile the former owner's son had returned several-times, made noise, shouted threats at the old couple, threw stones at the windows. (No doubt he realized that he barely had any

justifiable claims alongside the current owners.) One time he brought two pitbulls to the house on a tightshort leash — giant beasts of dogs, the coat of white short hair stretched like naked skin over powerful bodies & the tremendous muscles of those animals, enraged sharp-toothed barking with fullforce from snouts rough as fists, from their=primaldepths of hatred that they were only born as=dogs. As in a Grand Guignol horror performance, the raving stranger furnished every scene with brutish new touches — whoever wanted to could pour out their corrosive laughter with malicious=glee.

But now Paul & Martha plucked up the courage to rush home from work. The-policeman-on-duty who was supposed to process their=report didn't actually believe this woman, fear=fully railing crying in-her=distress; he refused to send a patrol to apprehend the stranger (:such an operation would probably get physical & perhaps the-policemen were worried about their crisply-ironed new uniforms). / Paul & Martha got to their=house almost simultaneously. There they found the desperate Franziska kneeling over her lifeless husband. When the emergency doctor finally arrived, all he could do was confirm Max's death. — *Acute heart failure. You should have called !sooner.* Issued the-death-certificate & vanished. 2 years after Max's death, his wife Franziska followed him. The house, which had been law=fully bought by Martha & Paul Herrmann — as proved by various documents — remained in=the-family, Paul & Martha Herrmann were able to keep the house; the disparate son of the previous owner faced a lawsuit for domestic disturbance coercion assault & criminal damage; — he ultimately abandoned his attempts to have the property reassigned to him. Now Martha and Paul lived in this house in Mahlsdorf South, just by them=selves, and avoided the-neighbours.

Theresa wanted to marry Milan. But Theresa's wedding to Milan did not take place.

After she had thrown Milan out of her=flat, Theresa became ill. All food induced nausea, often vomiting. She wanted to ignore her complaints, but what appeared occasionally at first became a constant malady; the illness grew worse, she could hardly keep any food down at all. She lost weight severely within a short time. The smooth skin on her cheeks was deepened by lines, which pulled the corners of her mouth downwards and gave her face a lasting air of bitterness and resentment. The-people around her eyed her mockingly, joked: *She's turned into a stomach.* And her condition deteriorated further; she had to stay home from work. In bed. She lay there for hours, in the daytime too, without moving without eating. Everything toxic in her=existence had to be !starved out. She stared at the ceiling with big fever eyes — figures with sharp outlines puffed themselves up in=white up-there, they wandered with Theresa's fever bouts, changing shape like summer clouds drifting bright across a bright sky. The scree field of dreams came hurtling down in Theresa's sleep, quarrel-some malevolent flickering barking voices from sneering faces, no difference between dream and waking life. . . . . The woman declined. The-hours full of dark shadows spread through the stuffy sick room. / Because they hadn't heard from or seen their adoptive daughter for a long time, Martha and Paul turned up at Theresa's flat 1 evening, they left their=war for 1 short moment to get into-the-war waged by their daughter — both=their environments were narrowed into poisoned cells in the every-day-prison. When Martha & Paul saw their daughter's state: — *A !doctor.* The Two of them immediately commanded. Theresa collapsed at the-touch of the doctor they had summoned, writhing in=pain. At-the-hospital, at the accident & emergency department, the examining doctor identified an *ulcus perforans*, a perforation of the stomach — operation !immediately. / dfgjlk-fjgdflkjgdfgklj ███████████████ / — Theresa, still drowsy from the-anaesthetic, was lying in-the-ward when the senior physician who had just operated on her entered the room & stopped in front of her bed. He recounted details of the-operation, gave advice for her further recovery, explanations that Theresa could barely follow in her sleepwalklike haze. She just-feltsick and she wanted to rest. — *You were !lucky.* She heard the senior physician say as he left. When she looked up at him she saw The Doctor's Smile. / The man often visited Theresa during her stay on his ward-at-the-hospital, asked after her in a caringly warm-quiet voice, gave her the-results of the-examinations, spoke of healing up well & fast. His visits to Theresa grew longer& longer. Then they talked about professional matters, and soon private ones too. Finally, seeing as Theresa was a historian, the man had a request: his 12yearold son, of whom he had received custody after the-divorce & who now lived with=him, was in urgent need of private history tuition for-school, because his-grades in that subject were very poor; ?would Theresa be willing to give the boy a few ?lessons, there'd be something in it for her too, the man added & smiled engagingly. Overjoyed that some-one else needed her again, Theresa agreed at once. / The 12yearold boy was an extremely fat child, good-natured, taciturn and intro-verted, he only had one pastime besides eating: he liked drawing, especially portraits of people; probably the only thing he was good at. A number of his drawings showed the same portrait of his disappeared mother. For a 12yearold, his drawings displayed remarkable art=istry, and he had acquired this skill without any-one's help. Theresa didn't ask why his parents had divorced. — The boy's mind was not slow, but he had no sense whatsoever of historical processes, no understanding of the logic-ofpower; to him, history was a confusing tangle of strange deeds with no recognizable sense, always=the-same without any sequence. He found it hard to retain historical facts — had to learn practically Everything by rote, like poems with peculiar rhymes, that he tried to remember with=the-aid of memory hooks. The boy went along with Theresa's tuition patiently & without complaints; but the memory hooks often failed to hold on to the facts. Then the boy sat obediently and quietly at the table & listened to Theresa as she tried hard to explain. A number of afternoons passed in this way. One time the session took longer than usual; the boy's father, the senior physician, returned from his duty at the hospital and met Theresa, who was still at his=flat. She had just finished the history-lesson; the boy, pleased, had immediately placed his drawings on the table in front of her with a new portrait on top: of Theresa. Upon entering the room, the senior physician noticed it at once. With harsh words to his son, he ordered him to put his drawings together & go to his room !immediately. The son obeyed silently, and the fat child waddled out of the room without complaining. Now the man turned to Theresa with a friendly smile. His anger over his son's drawing activities, the father explained, came from a fear that his son might end up being gay. . . . . / Theresa, she was sitting in an armchair, kept still as the man approached her and placed his hand on her shoulder. She kept still when his hand glided over his neck towards her breasts. She closed her eyes, feeling the tingling run down her inner body like a warm stream. His hands circled her breasts playfully, grasping them slowly and gently as if he wanted to mould them. Theresa surrendered to the flow of warmth running through her veins —. And turned towards=him when his hand reached between her thighs. — In the bedroom, as if she had

suddenly plunged into a different climate zone after the man
closed the door behind her : the man stood naked before her,
grabbed Theresa by her hips, overwhelmed her with theforce of
his body & threw her hard onto the bed. — Get your !arse up
you !bitch. — The man yelled & shoved her body into his=
preferred position. — You !pileofshit. !Don't you !dare move.
!Stay=like-that. Yes: !I'll show you. !Dirty pig. !Filthy beast. —
And the sweating man continued his raging & yelling & thrust
brutally into her arse. Then panting wheezegasping dripping
with saliva he continued to shower the naked female body with
his frenzied curses insults, & roaring with rough resounding
slaps of his flathard hands on the woman's trembling buttocks
he came in her anus. Then, still-inside-the-woman, he tipped over
sideways into the bunched-up bedsheets like a fallen sculpture of
sweat-soaked flesh. Panting hard against the back of Theresa's
neck, the man spoke: — Without a stamp — a file is worthless
— to the-German. Three matters taken care of — with 1 quick
— procedure. — The man wiped the spit from his mouth &
rolled on his side, trying to calm his breathing. Theresa turned
her gaze towards=him. Only=now, she noticed, with him lying
panting next to her helpless & sweating like a schoolboy thrown
down by someone stronger, was she able to look at this big,
athletically-built man, who still managed to appear youthful
despite his 50 years, in his=nakedness. And while he lay there,
his breathing now more regular, the woman was seized by a deep
compassion for this man, who seemed so utterly at the mercy of
his=brutality, a compassion she had only felt as a child towards
exposed or crippled animals. Clearly the man wanted to
take=revenge on the wife who had left him and his son shortly
before he had to enter his late years: when people are torn into
ever-smaller pieces by time, the arteries of life severed with ever-

cruder blades; and he was a coward, like all brutal people. She could barely hear what he was saying to her now, — but when he stopped & looked at her from the ruffled pillows and sheets, searching her face expectantly, it seemed to her also fearfully, waiting for her=answer, Theresa submitted to this man & agreed to do=anything he demanded of her. And It stayed like that between her and: the senior physician, his first name was Ullrich, who had saved her, always=thesame from the first time to the last : at the beginning the-lesson for his son, then the-smile of the doctor & the flesh — the-gentle-hands (the tingling in Theresa's inner body and the flow of warmth), at-the-end the-cursing, the-blows, the man's carnal rage & the bedroom poisoned to become a dreadroom. / The Great-Bureaucratic-Reshuffle in Central Europe in the early 1990s, paper-dry & vampiric, sucked fresh blood from the Southern European countries a few years later : the ethnobutchery in-the-Balkans, supervised by UN Blue Helmets, was already building up to a first bloody wave —:now Croatia's Adriatic coast was the ideal place for supercheap holidays: the-western-tourist=rabble stretched out in deckchairs on the-beaches, and 200 metres away from them, Croatian tanks=in-position. Ullrich and his son, accompanied by Theresa, went to the southernmost part of the Adriatic coast in Croatia. He had been coming here, said the man, for over 10years, they knew him in the village & he always got the same two-room cottage for a bargain price; this time, because there was war=allaround, the holiday was practically free. The smile of the-doctor. Theresa did-n't respond to any of his big talk. She now knew that he had spent the-holidays with the other woman & the boy in this-exact-place in the-years=of-his-marriage, slept with=her in the same bed, eaten off the same plates; the stranger's breath & her sounds were still stuck to the walls & ceilings of the rooms. Theresa felt

as uncomfortable here as if she were being forced to wear this
woman's old underwear. But !this-holiday=for-two-weeks was
one of the concessions the man had demanded from Theresa. —
Now she was here, and: if she thought the smaller room was for
the 12yearold boy and the bigger one for her and the man —
Theresa now found she was mistaken : the man firmly assigned
the small room to her and took the larger one together with his
son. Theresa took it for a joke; — it was only when the man
locked his door in-the-evening & thus denied her entry to his
room: — *You will not come in here !under !anycircumstances,*
Miss Herrmann (the man barked at Theresa; outside of the bedroom he always addressed her formally) — that Theresa understood —. — The man didn't touch the woman once; otherwise
he would have had to vent his=bedroomrage on Theresa within
earshot of his son, because he couldn't help himself. In-the-street
by day he always kept himself-&-his-son a few steps away from
Theresa; ?maybe he wanted to de-monstrate his man-hood to the
men in the Croatian village with this woman. Every morning
there was an envelope with banknotes on Theresa's bedside table,
with no explanation. The man barely spoke to her; but Theresa
had understood. 1 veryearly morning she packed her=things &
left, likewise with no explanation. After that she never saw the
man or his boy again. Theresa's compassion for this man was
burnt up; she didn't want to keep the ashes.

And when Martha, Theresa's adoptive mother, died in 2005
and Paul was left behind alone in the gloomy, lifeless chill of the
decrepit house in Mahlsdorf South, Theresa gave up her flat in
the city & moved back into that house to live with her adoptive
father.

Every time I want to tell myself this part of my story, after step-ping out of myself, with the words & eyes of a stranger, I'll arrive at !this point where I ask myself these questions: ?How often can you fall in the water, Theresa, without getting wet. ?Where do you draw The Line for what's bearable. And ?what happens at the moment when you have to ?cross This Line — with a step or with the unknown breadth of your remaining living time. Because everything=around-you dissolved into a quicksand-of-unlivability. But you, Theresa, kept going. One premature win-ter's day in October 2012 you left the house of your adoptive father, you know: for=ever. Went through the snow & ice into the nights at the cemetery in Birkheim, where you know the shad-ows of your real parents are. You wanted to cleanse yourself and your name of allshadows. But you couldn't know that another shadow had joined all=your old shadows in the meantime: the shadow of your adoptive father, who died at a police station at-the-feet of the inspector, who thinks you, Theresa, are dead, the 5th victim of a serial killer he is trying to catch, & for that he needs your=story, Theresa, & the stories of allthose who have followed you as your=shadows for your=wholelife. Now at the=end with alltheshadows you !can't fail any more. But for that you have to do !more than just meet your finalshadow, you have to travel through that finalshadow —

From the basalt block of thenight march the mummy-faces, their skin their hands & eyes bleached, with deeply carved grooves of metal-hard cruelty. THEY always have a lot to do in=heaven as on=earth. But when heaven, a white linen cloth, is grabbed by the hands of the mummies=on-duty & pulled up over me my body my face, then I've left the last ramp to visibility. Have become my=own=shadow, following you or rushing ahead & always=there, whatever light you might step into. And if you want to disappear, to abandon yourselves in=the-dark lose your-selves: shadows eliminate shadows, come inside. *I'm Here. I'm alive. But I won't say it any more. This=life-of-yours isn't worth living.* Because Nobody wants to speak to me before I leave, I'll sing the *Swansong for an Old Whore* to=myself.

Canto 1. ?!How can the once=present maintain their calm their equanimity their even balance when Damiens is about to be ¼ed and lets out soul-rending screams because four horses are pulling on his body in vain: he doesn't want to be torn apart, his=will is inside his muscles & sinews, they are toostrong even for four horses that are pulling, being whipped, flogged beaten for maximum performance their hooves striking sparks from the cobblestones, in vain — and this human screams !screams !!screams !!!screams against thepain against thefearofdeath & against thestrength of the four horses — hisdeath is long & longer than his body which thepowers of the horses stretch-a-part to grotesque proportions — and thescreams strike like chis-els shrill & sharp against the stone alleys of a city, it happens to be Paris, and I hear his screams because thesky left behind the frost on the threshold of an October night, and lets Everything trapped for-centuries in=clouds&ice rain down on a deaf mute earth that wanted to hide with all=its shadows beneath the white of a premature winter; an earth on which people-today waddle about, pushing shoving with the stupid=mocking quacking of their spirit-forsaken voices. ?!How, Father, can they live out their lives like that without feeling. !Faster than The-Light flies around the earth & deeper through alltimes than autumn soaks the veins of the leaves on the trees — pain rushes around the-world. I am ashamed for all those who carry thepain in=the-armour of their well-formedness further as indifferently as mules carry sacks-of-flour. !No end to the-hardship for them.

Canto II. Having hit the very bottom of my heaviest coldest guilt, I sense your approach, Father, as if reading word-for-word & line-by-line in an unknown book. But with each new-letter I can feel where they are leading, sense their=push in the faster flow of lines towards the One, the feared and: longed-for word. The word that I suspected would be written in this book. !Now It is there. This One Word, It's written here clearly before my eyes. I read It.

Canto III. Father. Now you're here. I recognize your form, which stepped away from the eyes of a 3yearold child and now reappears before the eyes of a woman in her mid-50s. But they're still my=eyes. I think, Father, when my eyes saw you for the last-time, your gaze was blurred by tears. I have no tears. The ones who have to conceal & hide themselves & theworld, it's always just the-living, who always want to understand and: always are understood. People-today, hostile in: the resi-stance of garrulous silence. . . . . Since being=Here I've been seeing clearly. But back then I was a child and: didn't know what to make of your=tears. ?Whom were they for. There was no one who could have explained it to me. Because I didn't know what explanations-for-tears might mean : wanting to endure & letting oneself be pushed deeper into defeat, into losing, slicing into one's own soul to reach the next slice ofdeath.

Canto IV. The white linen cloth over my body bulges up to the heat-white summer sky — a glass hemisphere over the sea — !O *white ocean* !O *wide sea* — your great hand, Father, a farmer's hand, lies in my childish hand. Our two shadows run entwined along the flat hard-flooded beach. Our feet only make weak imprints — the taut moist sand, in which I risked drowning in-my-lifetime, immediately and fastidiously erases the traces of our presence —. Beside us the silver-flashing flat ruffled surface of the sea lies spread out — the air tastes warm & salty, no wind — at the fine straight seam of the horizon, the sea enters thesky. I'm 5 years old, walking hand in hand with my true father : Everything turned out differently from what we know.

Canto V. Winter, snow swirling through the abandoned village street of Kaltenfeld one early morning in February 1959. Three black limousines, coming from the highway, turn into the village street —. The people in=the-house heard the engines of the three vehicles, 2 people sat there allnight in=fear&trembling, waiting for thedisaster to come : !Now It's here : those three limousines grimly threatening in=the-full-enjoyment of their= state power driving along from-house-to-house to find !that house number & !that name on their-writs-of-execution. With an eerily even movement traced slowly inexorably along the invisible band of-doom, with their toothy powerfully chrome-plated grilles they snort the snowdust out of their way — thus the three black limousines come gliding along. Fear is tugging at the two people's breathing, Irma and Alois Berger. (The 3yearold child Theresa is still lying safely=sleep.) The rope of greatfear tightens around their throats choking harder as the first of the three limousines arrives at their house, big rectangular shadow of shinyblack metallicdoom — but the three cars don't stop here, they go on, drifting past in gravelike silence & calm along the village street, slowly searching. — No storm in the sky, no lightning from the clouds. Only snow swirling over the earlymorning village street, now empty once more —

Canto VI. Indoors, at the Bergers' house, they can breathe more freely again, finally the noose offear is removed from the two people's necks. The woman tightens her dressing gown across her chest & hurries to her daughter's bedroom, as if she didn't trust the-calm; as if, while she had been sitting bound by her=dear, the-bailiffs had secretly taken away her child. — *She's asleep.* Breathing out deeply with relief, she whispers to her husband and to=her=self. — *Theresa's fast asleep.* And carefully closes the door so as not to wake the child. — *Fast asleep.* The man repeats, nodding gently. — *Then let's sleep too.* Both of them, the man the woman, go quietly to their bedroom. They didn't have to get up yet, it's still early this day. — I look up at this man by my side, Today and Here after somanyyears. — *And I'm still with you. Father. Your love —*

— *But One thing will !never happen.* Says the man and stops on the firm beach. — *What, Father: ? What will never happen.* — — *Wiping out the memory of this damned=life.* The man replies.

Then he grips his daughter's little hand even more firmly. — *Come.* He says. — *Let's go and find your brother and your mother. So that Nothing Bad happens to them.* And the two of them, father and daughter, walk silently on-their=way along the beach — further into the immensely high white heavens —. Their=way is still long. And the porcelain balls on the lampposts along the promenade are glowing. Little white suns — strung together on the invisible cord of the distance like immaculate pearls —. They glow steadily with their gentle lonely light that nobody needs, for it is day at-alltimes — —

CHAPTER 5

In the interrogation room I then heard the story of said Willfried Berger, who had come to the police station that morning of-his-own-accord or: rather : for reasons of deeply injured pride owing to Möller's idea for finding him, to rescue us from our=error that he was the wanted murderer of several women — & thus burdened us a-new with the duty to find the !true serial killer. Because what marks the end for the 1 will be the beginning for the Other.

But we didn't have to start right-from-scratch. In the man as he sat before:me in his life-armour, which had long since developed dangerous cracks, I still saw the glow of that mixture of anger & despair which had presumably driven him like a madman to the police station that morning — and only that enabled him to tell us what he presented as his=story and The Truth in his=story. But first he told us nothing new; the story of his childhood, those years that had been broken from=the-start, where any reasonable person would have said that to go on living could only be a-bad-thing, we'd already learnt that from Bernhard Mandt, who for 3 years had tried to be this institutionalized child's foster father and, together with his wife Hedwig, had been thwarted by the hardened stone block of hatred=in-this-child that had been carved early on. And what this man, who looked older than his years, now told us about Someone he had supposedly once been (at times he seemed taken aback at his own words, as if the events behind those words didn't belong to him, as if he were telling a totally=fictitious fabrication whose every sentence, like a tightly-stretched elastic sinew, stubbornly jolted this tale back to the bleak wasteland of so-called real events. . . . . Because nothing is harder than finding words for lies that are so beautiful that they can escape thepull of the truth for=ever; instead, everylie eventually plunges of its own accord into this maelstrom of sober act-uality —); I knew all=that already & it lined up fairly closely with the accounts of said Bernhard Mandt. And Everything returned, came to life a second time before my eyes & ears : the 1st pale images from the home for children made parentless by-the-state — gloomylightshimmers sparsely illuminated these memories, as if insufficiently strong light bulbs were glowing in chilly halls with nooks & niches sunk deep in the walls, inside a house boastfully rising like the misshapen decoy of a manor from the 19th century like a monolith in a flat landscape — and then especially !therage, the earlyrage, which blazed around the child's body unfettered always flaring up from mysterious ovens, as if his-inner-nature knew of the necessity to harden himself in the flames & to fashion anarmour for=alltime — then the real fires which the child started againandagain — (he only had a faint memory of the-night-with-the-knife, not because he was so ashamed of it that he had cast this event down into the deepest inner=dungeons, but presumably because, even then, Something had already shifted in him, something had emerged that still knew what right and: wrong meant, but the creature-controlling=him didn't give a !damn about that distinction, and over-the-years the memory had been worn away until the grown man no longer thought this event from his childhood was worth mentioning). — Finally the man, in his rather unimpressive voice (— as if a constant inexplicable rage was now also

207

pulling his vocal cords into thin-sharp overwrought heights &
stretching his lips to the point of reduced movability —) reached
the point in the story when his despairing foster parents Bernhard
& Hedwig Mandt gave him back Intocare & To-the-State. As the
boy grew up going from-institution-to-institution, considered
incorrigible, unreceptive to allefforts to form him into a social
creature, the time-of-punishments began: detention centre, forced
labour, beatings, solitary confinement & dark cells, boredom.
. . . . Growing insensitive even to the harshest punishments
(thanks to The-Innerarmour forged in thefire of his earlyyears)
— his abandoned training as a mechanic; without professional
skills he was only eligible for the most basic menial work at railway freight depots or slaughterhouses (years in the toughthick
cold bloodstench & liquorfumes) — military service in the-
people's-army; & at the end of that time the One Cut, the personal turning point in his life.

All I knew so far from !that=time was the photograph that
the young man had sent to his former foster parents like a trophy
: *The 19-year-old in a challenging pose: standing arrogantly with
his legs apart, arms on either side of his brawny body poised=to-
attack, his hands clenched into-fists. The features in the ascetic-
haggard face hardened, as if the taut pale skin had been
galvanized.* (This metallic hardness seemed to have moved out of
his body and into his voice over-the-years.) — And here&now I
learnt from the man that it was exactly=at-this-time, in his youth,
that he found out about his real parents. . . . . (!What had ?par-
ents been for him until then: something he'd never had and therefore didn't miss; everyone=around-him had no parents, so he
never learnt to *have-a-family*.) : The man paused at this point in
his account. Presumably he still had to battle the command=to-
keep=the-secret that was embedded firmly=within=him, even

Now&today. And from-then-on he glanced more often, more hastily around my office, growing ever-more uncertain, as if looking for secret=eavesdroppers & hidden bugs. In this respect he showed a trained eye : he stared at sockets, lampshades, the 1 vase on the filing cabinet, no doubt his fingers secretly felt under the table near him & under the chair he was sitting in. Quietly amused, I didn't stop him — (*!how could I have ?known then how !right he was* —) — and gave him time. Meanwhile, Möller brought coffee in paper cups, placed 1 in front of him too; he regarded the hot brown water with the same suspicion as the room, pushed the paper cup towards Möller & took his own, but still waited until we'd drunk some of the coffee. A shadow of yellowish pallor had been spreading across the man's face for some time, this colour drained from the-years of his pale life-sun, which made him look broken again, only a small step from falling apart. Perhaps he now sensed this danger himself & he held his right forearm tightly with his left hand (I saw the white of the knuckles against his tensed wrist) as if he'd arrested himself & was leading himself before an implacable tribunal, to force him to continue his story, neither defence nor prosecution, simply *his story.* . . . . But knowing that he could only expect One Thing from This Tribunal, the thing that awaited everyone without exception as soon as they appeared at The Gates of this Draco: the conviction.

— The turning point in my life: it was just before the end of my-army-time. — Slowly, only with great effort, this man now found his 1st words to continue the story, as if suddenly unsure whether it could actually be of interest to anyone Today, because the people in this Today feel so safe from everything they can euphorically call the past, and thus cut out of that same Today like the rotten bit in the otherwise perfect fruit of the present.

— Captain Frieder. — The hesitant voice continued. — That was how the man introduced himself: Captain Frieder. But he wasn't wearing a uniform. Was in civvies. A man who looked athletic. Tanned skin, casual light-coloured & crisply ironed shirt with short sleeves. I can see it as clearly now as if that stranger were sitting in your seat. He was sitting in the colonel's office, I'd been summoned there. Leaning back relaxed in the colonel's chair — gently turning the seat from sidetoside — grey, bright-grey eyes looked at me distantly. Neither hard nor sly. They just looked. Waited. A temple and an oval lens from a pair of mirrored sunglasses were sticking out of his breast pocket. Intheroom a heavy silence and the colonel's office smell: biting aftershave cigar & floor polish. With his casual manner, the stranger automatically made fun of this odour blanket, this stiff-musty working atmosphere in a crummy little army coop, which suddenly had an old boys' style to it, and it disappeared. And I felt like I was breathing air from a different atmosphere, one I'd never known before. — *(An atmosphere, I thought while this man spoke, that was so thoroughly synthetic, air produced especially for those=particular customers, which could only seem fresh & full of the world's air to someone who'd been forced to spend their=lifetime breathing the stuffy air of a country that turns to swamp like sludgethick watermush in a pond with no inflow or outflow. And anyone who thought the:collision between the two atmospheres would eliminate the sludgy, usedup=dead-pond atmosphere turned out to be wrong, because topping up that deadstuffiness with the synthetic could be taken further by enabling the-dead-part to simulate the-breath of the-reinvigorated through some synthetic airiness, in the same way that the famished desires of young men for everlasting glamour & wealth could be tricked with brand-name clothes & a few cartons of Camel.)*

— That was the 1st meeting with that man. — I heard Willfried Berger say now. — The colonel-himself wasn't in his office any more. He'd stormed out of the room after my usual show of obedience to a superior, it seemed to me with annoyed= angry glances at me & the stranger who'd made himself com- fortable in his office chair. Captain Frieder and I — we were alone in the room. At least, I didn't see anyone else. — The man's voice suddenly took on a rhythm like slaps to the face, with that even speed & force that aren't supposed to be painful so much as to guarantee submission to an all-encompassing power of con- trol&surveillance 1ce=and=forall.

With a casual gesture, the stranger who called himself Captain Frieder motions to the young man to stand at ease. Looks at him closely, saying nothing. And only starts speaking when the entire space of the colonel's office is so completely filled with silence — an atmosphere of seemingly civilian silence — that each of his words appears in it like a word written with a sharp quill. Now the man leans slightly forward in his chair to reach the file on the table. He takes it, leafs through it with appar- ent disinterest, skimming seemingly carelessly over the entries. He turns the pages with a regular motion; no sign in the man's face of any engagement with what he is reading.

— All right. — He remarks, closes the file & puts it back on the table. — I'll tell you plainly, Mr Berger — (:probably the 1st time the young man isn't being addressed as *prisoner* or *comrade*, but as *Mr*) : — You're well on your way to becoming a failure. With no professional qualification, but with avastnumber of bad conduct certificates, with a truly !exorbitant criminal record for your tenderage — (the man twists his lips strangely & nods his head, as if !such a rap sheet, like a list of sporting achievements, called for respect.) — And !that means you have !no possibility of a career in-the-ranks-of-the-People's-Army. After your basic military service it'll be !curfew=for-you in a few weeks. — (He gauges the effect of his words. Then continues:) — Soon you'll start smelling: of crime & jail. . . . . And !thatsmell sticks to=you, it stays like a skin, one you'll !never get out of. You won't get far like !that. Because with your history — (the man makes a disgusted gesture with his right hand, as if brushing dead insects off the file) — you've got *almost* no chance. — And watches with relish for the effect of his words in the other's face. The boy doesn't flinch. (But naturally that little word *almost* becomes a slim flickering flame inside him.) Skilfully, the man wants to kindle that flame. And then this man who calls himself Captain Frieder speaks to Willfried Berger with words he has !never heard before. He's expecting one of the usual=lectures, which always come either from surly, smelly, apopleptic, boozy functionaries in crumpled suits, soaked in decades-old sour officesweat, or from foul-mouthed=armymen firing their spittle along with repetitive accusations like *Unsocialistic Lifestyle, Antisocial Bee-haviour, Criminal Specimen* or *Hostile Negative Element*, each followed by coarse threats & mean=thuggish punytive rituals, the kind only ordered by authorities who believe with almost religious self=assurance that they are Intheright. : But instead he now hears Captain Frieder's words like sounds from a differentworld.

— YOU !WANT TO KILL.

The man tells him this in a decidedly factual voice. — Killing: that's been at=the-heart of all your aggressions from-an-earlyage, of all your roughness, of your boundless rage. Yes: you — want — to kill. Like otherpeople, you are neither good nor evil; I=personally don't think much of these theo-ries, don't think much of the talk of monsters; you are the way you and people=in-general are: lazy. Always looking for ways to improve their situation with as little effort as possible. Constantly trying to gain relief & advantages. Like Everyone. Even just before their execution : a man's standing up-against-the-wall, already blindfolded, the soldiers have their guns at-the-ready: but one of the condemned man's feet is standing on a sharp pebble that makes the sole hurt. Presently, in a few seconds, it'll be over for him — but he, this almostdead man, takes that tiny step to the side, off the pebble, to be more comfortable. —:That is how humans are.

(?*Why's this bloke talking to me about !firing-squads.....*) Willfried Berger knows that thesum of all his indiscipline, insubordinations and offences has to go beyond measure at some point —!end-of-the-road — and then he'll have to receive The Ultimate Punishment (so far without a real idea of what thatpunishment would be); & now&today, because of The Order to go to the colonel=in-person, thispunishment has to take place. (*But !yes: this country does have The Death Penalty : that 1 tallthin prison cell in Leipzig, bare, & the-shooter lurking behind the door : a shot in the neck.*) Willfried Berger readies himself; outwardly standing firm, inwardly shaking & flooded by waves of coldfear, he stands in the colonel's office. Before, on entering, he received his cold metallic-grey gaze, which went through him at close range, and could take it — and only lost his-composure when the colonel's brawny body stepped aside mutely heavily & with barely concealed anger to reveal a person lounging in the colonel's office chair: a civilian with a youthful athletic appearance & casual manner, the kind that's unknown here, especially in departments & offices. He knows every variety of sermon, reprimand and rant: from the kind=paternal homely tone to the scorn=driven screaming fit — but !this routine=today is completely !new for him. This=here !definitely isn't a sermon : !this must be the !sentencing. (*Wouldn't have thought The Death Sentence could be announced !so pleasantly.*) Now he tensely awaited The Verdict from this man.

— You want to kill. — But Captain Frieder resumed his speech.

— Without exactly knowing it, you might think that after killing people, snuffing them out with-your-own-hands, you'll feel better. And you're absolutely right. You !want to kill & you !should kill : people you have no connection to, except that they are people you can kill. People — that means neither honour nor awe towards them and their ex-istence; people, that's just a word with 6 letters, & you have the power & the permission to erase each & every 1 of them. By doing that — whether you like it or not — you are imitating nature. Murder is at the heart of all-nature. And no one can escape their=nature. I have no worries that your anger might fade, by the way : you=anger comes from the simple fact that you are forced to be a=live, & if you can be prevented from killing yourself then the flame of your=anger will keep burning as long as you live —. In=anger for life : that is your=nature. — The man makes a brief hand movement as if dismissing something long-known. — But just like nature in its raw state, you too, in your naturally=raw longing, must be !formed, you must learn a style & a direction for your will. That's the !only kind of human education that's worth !anything. And you, Mr — (suddenly the man seems to have forgotten the other's name; he looks at the file, emphasising his search:) — Will-fried-Ber-ger, will receive !this education if you make the !right decision. Already today you can begin the process that will turn your ex-istence into your=life.

Because Captain Frieder recognizes in the young man's eyes a muddle of confusion, incomprehension & also defensiveness

214

hardening into a *!What-is-all-this-crap*, he feels it would be appropriate to give him some concrete information. The captain quickly changes his voice from a more chatty tone to one of terse orders and protocol: — As soon as you complete your basic military service you will go to a facility where you will receive the necessary training for your further activities. And because you have nohome, no friends, no social life, this training facility will be !more than just a-home for you in all your needs. I can promise you nothing less than a !New Beginning.

— ?What sortof training. — The young man's voice still displays distrust and defensiveness. Captain Frieder knows this reaction, so he presents the hesitant youth with a few perspectives for his=further-life. For that his voice takes on a deeply serious, urging tone, as if wanting to convey that all of the following is something Very=Special & conceived !just for=!him: — I'm offering you membership in a newly founded organization, active both nationally and internationally, whose tasks in involve the neutralization of persons or groups of persons that — for whatever reasons — cannot be apprehended via-the-criminal-justice-system in the respective countries. Simply put: the persons in question are to be !liquidated by any available means. That is essentially what we do. We see ourselves as a political service provider and have an !international clientele. If you take my !meaning. We have no reservations about our clients. The employment that would be suitable for=you requires practical work directly=on-the-ground. You'll work in-a-pair and maintain contact with a superior. If you find yourself in-lifethreatening-danger, THEY will be able to get you out. You will be paid in equal parts with national & foreign currency. I can tell you that the payment is !considerable, and employees also receive special bonuses with the same terms after each successful assignment. Your training in theory & practice will last three years — your basic training in the-handling-of-weapons should be useful — followed by a 2-year graduate period, & once you have successfully completed that you will be a Full Member of our organization. Your promotion-prospects are considerable; more than a few of=us have risen to the highest circles of international government & business. To-the-outside-world you will live the life of a civil servant with your own apartment & all the conveniences that go with such=a job. Yees — (the man leans back in the office chair with satisfaction, as if after an extensive meal) — — We're simply Every=where. That's all the information I can give you for know. You will find out more as soon as you've signed your membership contract. Let me emphasize that Everything I've told you here&today is subject to the !strictest confidentiality. Maintain !absolute-silence, to your superiors=here as well. You are hereby !committed. ?Or do you want to become your own 1st case. — (The man's sardonic grin is meant to have an emphatically burlesque effect. But he immediately wipes that character from his expression.) And because he knows what conflict is flickering up&down in the youth in the face of !this decision, the reflexes of both flight and compliance that are driving him at=the-moment, the man temptingly spreads out the contract papers and returns to his original speaking tone.

— Consider that the ordinary path of a murderer, which is what you will be, is fullofdangers & full of oppressive fears, because the-ordinary-murderer is always=alone. . . . . He stumbles from one hazardous situation into the next; he is always=without-protection, more naked than naked; he is sent nightmares, set allsortsof traps & in the midst of treachery & traitors he becomes his own=worstenemy. Because someone who spreads so much death !doesn't want to die himself. Even thinks that with each of

216

his=corpses death moves 1 step further away from him. Nobody-in-the-world, not even God, is !so important that they have to be reachable around-the-clock, !except for the-murderer. The-murderer is always=Onduty, but also always=the-hunted. . . . . And so thefears grow and keep growing. He senses how themob of his pursuers is pushing along, getting closer, They chase him further and further, from one fear-scorched night to the next — he is hunted & he hunts himself, and deeper and everdeeper into thefear — to the point where he *wants* Them to catch him. Now the-murderer will do=Anything to make the endless=running & thefear !finally !stop. In a word: fear turns him into a nitwit. — !Do you want to become a ?nitwit, Mr Berger. — The man called Captain Frieder leans across the table, grinning, holds out his arm, a fountain pen in one hand and a paper in the other, shiningwhite like Temptation. The little box for Willfried Berger's signature is still empty : a pure empty space — an island of blamelessness — as tempting as the-promise of a New Life. —

— ?What's: the name of this — organization you want to recruit me for anyway. — Willfried's question sounds like a final, shyly grumbling objection, like the last threshold before A Decision that's essentially long been made.

— COSUBO Ltd — Captain Frieder answered tersely, without softening his challenging manner.

The young man, shaken tooheavily by the last halfhour, doesn't ask the meaning of the abbreviation in the company name. Nor does he ask for details of the contract once he is standing at attention again in front of the desk.

— By the way, after meeting you today, I'm determined to vouch for you personally; don't disappoint me. — (Captain Frieder speaks once again. The man's face now assumes what is meant to be a very familiar, amicable, almost affectionate smile.)

217

With that, he pushes the shiningwhite sheet of paper & the fountain pen close to the young man. As he leans forward, the man reveals a little more of the sunglasses in his breast pocket: an American brand name. Together with the invitingly extended arm and the fountain pen, that 1 temple seemed to Willfried virtually like the 1st instalment of a temptingly offered reward for his=future-activities, which he will henceforth be able to carry out with the rage that is his=own, but now within the big space of noholdsbarred with a pleasure that is equally his=own. And like someone drowning or falling from a greatheight — whose entire previous life races through the senses 1 last time in an avalanche of images — he feels individual scenes from his previous years crashing into his brain with full force — & he finds almost nothing in them except humiliations, indignities, constant lack, scarcity, exclusions, beatings; a murkyrancid smell of fat is already wafting from a few years of life, the furry mouldy feeling of rot all over his skin, already stuffed on disgust at 20. But Something Else rises up !againstthat in his mind: thedroning of an organ like a storm beginning to rage above him — and as violent as the storm rainfloods hail & thunder are, he is seized by an intuition. There could be !even=greaterthings in store for=him —.

Willfried Berger steps up to the table. He takes the fountain pen mutely & solemnly from the hand of the smiling man and —

— I signed. — The man sank back into the backrest of his chair.

— Didn't really twig any of what that golden boy was waffling on about back then. All I knew was: Ltd —:you !don't get that in=this-country, !that's ?something from-the-!west. ?What's that about, a western company here=in-the-east that's allowed

218

to employ people=from-the-!east. There was Somuch I didn't know back then. Believed in the-strictness of the border, the wall, the barbed wire, the firing=order & spring-guns. And the Big Opposition & essential=hostility between socialism and: capitalism — in other words, !that-bollocks THEY'd drummed into us from=an-early-age; still believed in what was said word-for-word. — He wiped his mouth with the back of his hand, as if to remove putrid saliva.

And while the man told us of the 1st days of his training=as-a-hitman in what they called a special camp, Somewhere among the boring pine forests of Brandenburg or in closed areas of the Thuringian forest & Erz Mountains or in Prora on the island of Rügen, I saw the image of that recruiter, the ominous Captain Frieder (:which was undoubtedly a fake name just like allthose aliases used by spies or prosecutors in political lawsuits with pseudonyms like *Lovejoy* or *Makepeace* or *Darling*). He fulfilled his task, namely, the-recruiting of so-called employees for COSUBO Ltd, with the-instincts of a scavenger, and was doubtless assigned exclusively to enlisting youths. !That was what THEY had equipped him for : speaking to the tattered emotions of the broken youth in this country; even then & already among the youth, for the unquenched longing for a life=of-mediocrity & embedded in that a well-being spiced up with glittering goods=from-the-west. And so THEY presented the still ½childish recruits they were targeting with this man called *Captain Frieder*, polished into an ever=youthful figure who could occasionally give the greedy goggle eyes of these youngmen a quick glimpse of accessories THEY equipped him with from the-stores, like the fittings from a playboy's wart-robe for light commie-dies: the mirrored sunglasses, the hand-sewn bespoke shoes, casually offering American cigarettes & chewing-gum; playing care=lessly with his smart clothes (whose material was so light & the cut so perfect that these suits shirts trousers adapted naturally to the shape of the body, giving the body inside them a relaxed posture=automatically, meaning that this character held the template-for-urbanity or: what people in the unworldly, closed-off valleys of the world, with their stiff uniforms and off-the-shelf-products might take for *urbanity*. And he was skilled at tapping into the youngmanly drives with his sparkling brew of ostentation & subtly emerging homo=erroticism) & therefore this=character could behave like whores of all professions who offered their buyable, heavily overpriced desires for men made stupid by a prematurely grey unsatisfied=life. Stupidity that comes from the personality, not the head. And so this=fellow moved about in the aura of messed-up youngmanliness, much as house-clearance specialists move about in the bits and pieces left behind by the dead, in this sphere of lost things, cooled-off things & death — in which they roam, plundering without consideration, like scavengers of all stranded life. . . . . . And who, as the years progressed towards the inevitable collapse after being sent *into-retirement*, met up in the squalid coves of their life's shore in grotty bars, holding on to the scuffed counters with frozen grins & with red-rimmed booze-eyes rattled out their=heroic-deeds-of-yesteryear, like old veteran legionaries, to some new arrival fascinated by this=milieu, shot through with over-loud laughter thrown coarsely across the tables & the counter — & when they poured enough hard lickor down their gullets for the-evening & the-night & got the-usual-brawl over with, crawled back alone to their holes with torn grimy clothes & bloody fists to have a kip in the TV chair & wait for death in=drunkenpeace. —

And he, this man in my office, was now playing the-film of his youth to me, the time of his training-as-a-hit=man somewhere

in one of the many Forbidden Zones in the forests of this country
— most likely all in facilities once set up by the-Nazis, & Today
these=facilities are used by people-today in=today's=way : we
don't have enemies any more, we're surrounded by enemies,
because with friends like !that, who needs enemies. In the training
camps THEY gave allthe young precarious types they'd recruited
the finishing touches that cut the grooves of carefreeness into
their hearts; they were meant to feel like an *elite squad*, modern-
day Spartans whose cohesion in this male=world was sealed by
sweat, effort, pain, blood, abstinence & absolute=obedience
towards The Superiors & The Clients for the operations
commanded.

— ?Women. — I threw him the question.

— ?!What.

— ?Did THEY allocate any !women to you. Even in-
Buchenwald there was a camp-brothel for the-best of the-
prisoners.

— Nah. Nowomen. Never. — The man's voice took on a
hard, proud tone.

— 1 proper kill, Inspector, & you'll know what a lousy substitute a fuck is. — The man had wanted to laugh, but changed
his mind with the last bit of his breath, so what came out was a
small wheezing cough. Only his face, for a moment, kept the
bright look of someone who's ready to laugh but has missed the
punchline. — Then his expression changed and he struck a different tone: — It was a world-without-women There. Inspector.
But the-queers got punished like deserters. During training there
was !nogoingout, !no contact-with-the-Outside, no visits from
relatives or friends either. Most-of-us didn't have the one or the
other anyway. And finally: a man's longing for a woman is never
greater than in the-absence of-a-woman. —

— We didn't live there, we were housed: we slept in metal beds, stacked I tightly I together in 3s, we ate and shat there in hangar-sized halls. Constant rumbling tumult under the huge arched ceiling, every noise blew up into a racket, every word into a yell — at 6 in the morning glaring floods of light came down on our sleeping=bodies from downlighters lined up on metal rails dozensofmetres above us and barred lamps, and at 10 in the evening the glaring light with went away with a hard bang of the master, the lamps faded with a red like twilight. Everyone had a metal locker and a mess kit. We received what was allocated to=each=individual, no one got more than that. Everyone knew everyone else's habits, Nothing was hidden from anyone; our existence followed the-ideal of transparency & publicity. We were constantly on=standby, biological machines waiting for The Command : then we leapt into=action. — That seems to ?disturb you, Chief Inspector. You think we ?lacked what people today call !freedom. But I'll tell you something: if you're living in=hard-ship on the outside, you have to go !verydeep inside=yourself to find your own space. What you find there will give you strength when you carry your=find to-the-Outside. That was the idea of this way-of-life. I think that what you miss isn't freedom, Inspector, it's permissiveness: an unpunished letting-yourself-go, laziness, weakness, indiscipline, a joy in being allowed to do-what-youlike — a pisswarm pensioner's ideal, that's what you call. . . . . freedom.

— Being constantly=inescapably close to the nextman was meant to foster trust, devotion, but also distrust & distance — this thin line was where we found community and: fires-of-anger & thedesire-to-kill held in=the-vice of the strictest conventions. That was our code of honour. We were expressly ordered to form friendships=with-our-closest-comrades; if Nofriend came along for someone, he was provided with His=Friend. None of the-trainees were allowed to stay Withoutafriend. THEY demanded unreserved trust from the-declared-friend; he was responsible for protection, help, support=in-every-respect — but any rebellious-ness let alone a wish to desert on the-friend's part were to be reported to The-Superior !immediately. Our language was made up of warlike terms, phrases about acts-of-violence & the-hunt. Those who turned out to be too weak or succumbed to homo-sexuality weren't removed from the-ranks-of-the-warriors, but could be made a *practice-enemies*: live demonstration-objects, ready for slaughter by their former comrades. . . . .

— The-training also extended to similar camps abroad — West Germany, the Middle East. Whoever wanted to go over=there to continue his training-as-a-specialist, which meant joining the Higher Ranks of the organization, needed all sorts of special permits, and those were based on outstanding deeds & flawless=conduct. To reinforce the enclosed character of those training camps even more, they used their own currencies as the only valid form of payment. Anyone who tried to circulate other currency, especially foreign ones, got the same severe=punishment as deserters or queers. It went without saying that deaths=within-thecamps were declared *accidents* or *heart-failure=in-the-course-of-duty* to any loved ones living on the outside; the-relatives always had to carry the funeral expenses, assuming any relatives could be found. (The bill was sent to them by the-People's-Army. But this authority knew nothing about the-facts of these deaths, because the name COSUBO Ltd. Wasn't mentioned !anywhere, not even within the-government & the-army : a phantom authority within a ghostly country.)

— In the-camp-world there was a strict, albeit flat hierarchy: the-trainees were at the bottom. Above them the-instructors, then their superiors, with a major at the top as camp commander. Administration, policing & legal matters were taken care of by the military leadership; the military court was the only = the final judicial awe-thority. — In parallel with that was the-business-hierarchy, because this company was a commercial entity & therefore organized like a western industrial-corporation with service tasks.

— We were sent out to complete the assignments we were given. We were elite-soldiers; we carried out every assignment, because we knew our=enemy better than ourselves. The-enemies could be any-where-in=the-world; and they weren't that different from-1-another. All you needed to understand them was the-ABC = of-human-nature : every cut of a throat, every deftly-placed poison injection, every handful of guts yanked out of the-enemy's body — as clear & simple as 2 + 2. That's why we carried out everyassignment with the desired result.

— ?What did you feel during your=work.

The man reflected for a few moments, as if listening for an inner=voice.: — At The-Moment I killed someone, my vision turned blue : a cold metallic blue. The feeling of ice crystals on my lips. I !love that blue, the taste of that ice. Inspector.

— And ?then. ?What happened after that.

— Then we returned, unrecognized without leaving anytraces, to-the-deadofnight in this or some=othercountry. We killed silently, our=victims died Withoutascream. That's the advantage of cutting=someone's-throat. The next dawn was our=triumph, the sun shone red & glaring like acry: !Our=Victory.

— Because nobody knew about Us, unless our=assignment required it. Our=signs & traces were the missing, the dead, either presented dramatically for=everyone's-eyes & their=horror or sunk deeper into the darkness than drowned bodies in the sea. Those bodies never surfaced. In boldness & strength=of-purpose We grew !far=beyond every normal lowly standard in the pussified world of clever-dick business types, dreamers, grovelling church mice & crybabies of both sexes —:but our=clients usually came from !exactly=!that mob : they wanted to do it but didn't want to do it themselves —!that's the longest-lasting joke of the last half-century. We still laugh about it today. — The man was audibly hitting his=stride while talking about The Deeds of his obscure outfit. — At 1st glance a very clear, uncompromising work: — but in-reality: far beyond complicated. As far as I could tell. — He added by way of qualification, perhaps to avoid certain questions in-advance. And immediately diverted the conversation towards the topic of camaraderie during his training; a subject that still provided him with pleasant reminiscences Today, and was the real reason for his appearance-in-my-office.

— He was almost the same age as me, had a completely different childhood from mine and came from Faraway. — The man began in a quiet voice, his head lowered.

— The childhood years=in-an-orphanage were the only thing we had in common. THEY assigned this man to me as *My-Friend*. That was a !rank that made us=all=equal. And like with anything in life, Inhere too *The Friend* had to prove himself to *The Friend*.

— ?What's the name of your friend. — I interrupted, but presumably the man didn't hear me, he had gone back too deep into-thattime (he was already saying *Inhere*, as if here were in That Camp right now). So I kept listening to him.

— One of the 1st tests was The-practical-training: THEY split us into two groups for the-exer-sighs: one group was the-attackers, the other the-defenders. The-attackers were given small-calibre weapons, the-defenders steel shields. Now within the group-of-defenders, one friend had to protect the other from the shots of the-attackers with !his shield; if the friend failed, the other was injured, and I saw some lying fatally wounded in the shooting area. —:That was considered 1 one of the early tests of friendship & demonstrated the usefulness or uselessness of a friend. It's only !Underfire that you see what kind of person is in=a-person. Other, much harder tests were to follow. But every time — every time the friend assigned to me proved his worth, & I showed him the same friendship. So we belonged together. — Suddenly he banged his fist on the desk. Möller was about to start towards him, but I held him back. The man, I saw, was no longer here, in this office; he had taken himself back to the time that he had felt driven to describe to us.

— And I — — I !betrayed — My Friend.

He spoke as if he were before The-tribunal of COSUBO Ltd, called to account for This Offence, in the knowledge that for traitors there could be neither extenuating-circumstances nor acquittal, only The One Verdict: death. So the man at least wanted to stand before His Judge with a clear conscience. I understood the situation & took on the function of the prosecutor in this play: — You !betrayed your friend. Describe !what you did. — Evidently I had captured the sharp, cold, shrill tone that was typical of former judges at the time, because the man continued speaking with his head lowered, eyes staring=wide into space & with an evenly guilt-ridden voice.

— As my first=real test I was given a !special assignment, still during my trainee period, that I naturally had to carry out. Assignments that were given had to be carried out no matter what they were, one !couldn't refuse. !Endofstory. THEY had given me the necessary documents for it. They contained the name, location and description of the target person, their habits & such details. I opened the file, read the names : they were the names of my real parents Irma & Alois Berger.

— But ?why were you supposed to kill your parents, your !real parents.

— No one who was given an assignment had the right to ask for the reason behind it. Assignments were to be !carriedout as well as we had learnt in our=training. I didn't tell My Friend about Everything that burdened me about !this assignment. We made our preparations for the chosen date and went to theplace where we were to perform our work.

The man was silent for a moment, as if he had to gather his thoughts. In the part of his face that was still lowered, I could see that he was reliving that hour at !thismoment.

— But I !had found out !why I was supposed to eliminate them, because I'd acquired some additional information about the two (secretly, without anyone finding out, even My Friend). And found out the last part of their story.

— After Alois and Irma Berger had been released from imprisonment in 1979, on different days, & were living together again, the first thing they tried to do was to find my sister Theresa & me. THEY had probably told them a few things about Theresa, but nothing about me, the jail-birth the prison-brat. Now they wanted to find us=both so we could !finally be afamily. During their-imprisonment THEY had offered to both of them, no doubt separately, to be ransomed=to-the-west. But these ransomees often knew nothing about the deal-with-the-west that had already been made; they only found out about It shortly before the handover date. But often THEY planted an informant in the cells of these already-ransomed prisoners a considerable-time before thatday. His job was to insinuate himself into the other's confidence — which wasn't hard considering the long solitary confinement; then anyone's happy to have someone else there speaking to=them outside of the-interrogations. . . . . And 1 of those infiltrators also informed my father that, if he was considered for-ransoming, first an official would come to ask him about his immediate goal after his-release. And if he then answered *To-the-west* — then !that would be thereason to re-arrest him right after release, practically at the prison-gate, because of intent-to-flee-the-republic. Instead, to avoid being arrested again (the informant revealed), he should reply to this trick=question *?Where do you intend to go after your release* by saying: *To-my=relatives-in-the-GeeDeeR*. I heard there was this disgusting prison poof, an arsecunt with a slimy mouth who sucked up to my father & pumped him for information. He had practice in-that-stuff & he didn't have to do much for my father to walk straight into the trap. And so That happened & so THEY released Alois and Irma Berger to the GeeDeeR. . . . . Even though they were supposed to have been ransomed by the west & taken Overthere. But far from it, THEY kept the two & sold 2 other people in their place. Who cares about names, as long as the-numbers add up.

— So after they had to report to the-authorities in Birkheim, their=search for us, Theresa & me, led them here to Berlin. They left Birkheim without the knowledge of the-authorities. They couldn't know that precisely this behaviour would ultimately be their=death-sentence : because for one thing, the-search for their=children underthesecircumstances amounted to *An unlawful act : child abduction*. . . . . And on top of that, they had left the area of residence assigned by the-authorities without permission. They were immediately arrested again in Berlin — originally probably with the-intention of flogging them off a 2nd time to the-west as part of the *Dead-Souls* enterprise & thus cashing in a 2nd time as well. Unfortunately —

The man's account came to an abrupt halt, he seemed to have suddenly awoken from one=of-those baddreams that bring images full of oldfaces, but where after waking up, None of them of disappeared, as if one were still trapped in those dream events & the eternal return of the-dreamt darkened both one's sleeping and waking time.

— Unfortunately — I repeated his last word to help him resume his story.

— Unfortunately my father, in the process of searching for me, had learnt of my membership in COSUBO. !Bad=luck for=him. Because the mere knowledge of! that organization's existence is mortally dangerous; all the more if there's any knowledge of individual persons, their duties & clients. That much knowledge is !toomuchknowledge. And now only one outsider has That: !you, Chief Inspector, & your colleague=here.

— I think we'll survive. But ?your assignment: ?where were you supposed to — ?strike that time?

— Maybe at first THEY had really intended to flog the two of them off to the-west again as *Dead-Souls*. They'd been informed of that. Too bad for them that there was a phase of product reduction due to a surplus of products for-the-western-market, you follow me Inspector; so the two weren't taken by the-west. Now they weren't just excess meat, they were knowing meat too. They were released from detention only a few weeks after their re-arrest, with strict orders to stay at their 'flat'. They were given — until their-departure=to-the-west, as THEY told them — a little hole in an old building in Lichtenberg: 2 stair-cases, 1 room w/kitchenette, toilet-in-the-basement, they had to share that with another tenant whose 'flat' occupied part of their shared hallway. Coal heating, leaky tiled stove, no double windows, one could stick one's hand right through to-the-outside under the window frames. The mortar was crumbling off the walls and there were straws sprouting through the ceiling. WE were supposed to nab them as soon as they were out of prison. THEY had given us, My Friend & I, the-assignment to fake the couple's double-suicide in this dive. Suicide-by-hanging. Both in the same night in 1979. ?Who do you think had seen to it that they got !out of jail again soquickly. That wasn't the-west with its=cash, it was !US. — The man remarked & looked at me provocatively.

— Nowonder: you couldn't just knock them off in-jail, that would've been too tricky even for people-from-your-outfit & most-importantly, too conspicuous. ?Right. — And now I stared him angrily in=the-face. We kept that up for a few moments.

Then I adopted the-voice=of-the-judge again: — And your ?betrayal. You !betrayed your friend. You said so yourself. ?How.

— Before we entered the house I left My Friend's side. I left My Friend in=the-lurch. I didn't go on. Just stopped. Waited. At some point thecity would come & get me. Thecity is as mute & deaf as stone.

— So your — ?friend ?did It ?alone.

— Yes, he had to carry out the-assignment !alone. he did It. And anyone searching for a reason for the couple's suicide would only have had to set foot in that. . . . . hole. But no one searched. Noteven for the two dead people. !Who was going to ?miss them anyway, they'd been vegetating alone among convicts & traitors for-severalyears. And so 2 shameful people died in 1 night in a shameful hovel : my mother my father : suicide-by-hanging, and:

I !wasn't there. That was All. Goes without=saying that I couldn't go back to COSUBO Afterwards. Since then I've had to stay hidden. Even Today: ?!what do you ?expect.

— ?Where were you ?hiding for allthattime.

— In the jungle ofthecity. With the-monkeyhordes in their caves. We got closer during collective grooming & other prayers. I'm a good monkey for the-monkeys. — The man replied full of bitterness. — — Because I'm !great at play-acting. But now that's !over. And the fact that I'm alive Today & was able to come here to you, that's definitely thanks to — My Friend. Who never betrayed me, even after my=betrayal. !That's real fellowship. And now&today I've betrayed him for the second time. That means I've condemned my=self. I'm already dead, I don't care about any other judgements.

— The !name of your friend. — My voice, without intending it, sharp & cold. The man-before:me gave a start. But in the reverberation of his shock, which broke open all the locks&bolts of his=fear (because now=at-!that-moment he would utter the name of his friend aloud, he would carry out with his voice the betrayal of this friend that he had already committed over fortyyears ago through his behaviour. !No turning back now.) He said very firmly: — If you want to find the murderer you're looking for: find the man with the name — (and he skewered the syllables like a knife) — —!Orfan !Batt.

—!What kindof funny name is that, ?eh. And we're supposed to ?believe !that. !Look here matey, if you're trying to take us for a !ride here, then —. — Möller stepped quickly & agitatedly up to Willfried Berger.

· He only looked up in tired defensiveness. — That's not his real name. He's actually called: Sunardi Orhan Battachrudin, born in 1960 in Java, Indonesia. He was the son of an Indonesian diplomat-in-the-GeeDeeR during the Sukarno government. The father was recalled to Indonesia shortly before the coup by Suharto in 1965 and, like manythousands of people, murdered by the-Pancasila-troops during the-upheavals. These death squads rampaged through the country wearing combat dress in the colours of burning petrol. Everywhere the bodies of those beaten or throttled to death, villages burnt down : the-right-to-kill had now changed hands. His mother managed to flee the country with the 5yearold boy, travelling by the route Malaysia — China — Soviet Union — East Berlin. But refugees will stay refugees, nobody wants them in their=country. And the GeeDeeR government had already expelled all Indonesian diplomats once the anti-communist Suharto had seized=power, that was a death sentence for most of them. — Willfried Berger took a deep breath. — The mother escaped expulsion, she died shortly after she & her son arrived in Moscow. The boy was immediately deported to East Berlin, there were supposedly relatives-of-his living there. But they had already upped&left by the time he got there. So THEY put him in a state orphanage for children of diplomats. Since then his altered name: from Sunardi Orhan Battachrudin to Orfan Batt. It was at that orphanage=for-privi-leged-children that he was later recruited for COSUBO. That was where we met. And since then he's been My-Friend: Orfan Batt. !He's the man you're looking for.

    — I know that — the man continued, — because I heard talk of His=Deeds in the bars where the-old-comrades hang out. You know: in seedy losers'-clubs where most=of-us sit around & now&again have to take on crappy little jobs so we don't go-to-the-dogs completely, usually debt-collecting & Suchlike — but everything !ab!so!lute!ly=!illegal, !ooh. — He threw his arms in

the air affectedly & whined like a moralizing TV-preacher. —
COSUBO folded long ago —!of course: the-GeeBeeR, the Great-
Bureaucratic-Reshuffle, wasn't without its successes. What
remained were small cells that operate like partisans for hire, or
sometimes like one-man-companies: Me Incorpsorated. That's
professional humour. Chief In-speck-tor. Killing just happens to
be a private enter-prize, that's why killing has become so mani-
fold & excessive. — Again there was a scraping sound from his
mouth that was meant to be laughter. But he resumed immediately. — But he, My Friend, has had !better luck. He's still doing
Good=Business nowadays, all over=Europe. So I heard.

— You still call this: Orfan Batt your ?friend :Today.

— Friend — that's once and for=Ever. You don't understand
!Anything = Anythingat!all, Cheef In-spectre & that's why it'll
be hard for=you to get to him. Because, as I said, since the
Ohsogreat Bureaucratic Reshuffle he's been doing !better business than ever before. And He'll go on as long as THEY need
him. You should hope that —. — But he didn't finish his sentence,
instead adding: — He is the man you are looking for. But you
won't find him, because His Disguise is !better than ever Today.
Arrest me instead, Chief Inspector : I accuse myself of murder in
so many cases that I've forgotten the number. Murders: for jus-
tasmany customers from east & west, I've forgotten that number
too. But the 4 women whose murderer you're looking for, I
!didn't kill them. From=now-on I'll say no more. — He held his
arms out to me for handcuffing. I motioned to a colleague, who
did so. And he did speak to me 1 more time, in that way I only
knew from Möller: — People who play with fire shouldn't throw
stones. — As the officers escorted him outside, the man turned
around and grinned at me.

When the man had been taken out of my office again by the same officers who had brought him in, some other part of him was left in the littlenarrow room along with the murky light of that December day, which seemed like an attribute of this man: something like a broken aura (emphasized by his grin, which stayed written in the stagnant office air like a visual echo), almost palpable. The man knew he'd been defeated long-ago, now he just had to fall. He soon would in=prison, because THEY'll get him there. . . . . His hunters were people for whom the statute of limitations is meaningless; traitors are to be dealt=with, & betrayal is !unforgivable. I'll try to do as he ask and arrange pre- ventive detention, for=his=own=protection (maybe the-principal- witness-regulation would be an option for=him); but he knew as well as I did that it was !impossible to guarantee such protection. But both of us wanted reassurance, & I wanted to give him that if peace was so easy to come by for-him. And both knew !what kind of peace. . . . . that would be, sooner-or-later. Hence his grin, I suppose which, in the face of an aging murderer, suddenly showed such a resigningly=understanding, almost sym-pathetic quality. The murderer's grin before his=murder. — This aura lay in the room like an electric field. I couldn't take being inthere any more, so I suggested to Möller that we got out & to a nearby bar.

— But ?don't you have an appointment now with the ?old — I mean: with the ?Boss=Upstairs. He'll be —

—!Come on, Möller. Let's beoffthen.

He looked at me in surprise for a moment — that was the 1st time in allthoseyears that I'd taken him to the pub — then hastily grabbed his jacket & coat and followed me — through the station building down the echoing staircases and out to Alexanderplatz.

The-Christmas-market was already there. Between colourful stands, sticky like gaseous syrup, the aroma of roasted almonds candyfloss & the foul smell of meat stewing in sizzling fat. This was jumbled together with wailing loudspeakers, muffled poprhythms, squeaking children's choirs joyshrieking Christmas carols — & people with bored faces, some twisted in inexplicable rage, covered by Santa caps, pushed their way sluggishly past all the junk of the-jolly-folks. Chunks of food disappeared into greedily opened mouths, mulled wine steamed from cups. I saw a man with bobbing plastic-moose-antlers on his cap bend down to a child & as if he wanted to puke, he yelled at the boy. Who started bawling. (:In 10 years, Pukedaddy, this boy will kick you in the arse.) Our festivities: yelling, tears & the stench of all things rotten. It began to drizzle from a dull sky —.

The bar Möller & I entered was the same one where I had first met Regina some 20 years earlier. But the place had changed its decorations & clientele in the meantime, & the wild ones from back then were now bank clerks, lawyers, estate agents. And because Regina couldn't be here=with-me-now, I suddenly longed for her=presence. The angular barroom was swimming in a murky-red light, and on the semicircular plastic-coated counter there were a few blobs of bright light in which full beer glasses with dew drops on the outside beckoned temptingly. Apart from us there were 2 figures sitting at a table in a distant corner (they didn't seem to be looking anywhere, weren't saying anything to each other, didn't move). No music —!whatarelief — I suppose there weren't enough guests for the barman; it was just after noon.

I downed the 1st beer quickly, as always. A few days earlier I'd learnt of the death of Lena, my first wife from my Hanover days. Murdered. The-investigation, they said, had been taken up.

Death —:*she's lying in the flat that's still familiar to me, that little cosy shelter with all its standing furniture (if the cupboard, armchair, couch, table and dresser had human faces they would already resemble our faces, the way old people resemble their old pets), and: in the room on the carpet a small bent figure, without breath, one cheek pressed firmly to the ground as if in desperate sleep. The hair messy, crumpled inwards like dull wilted hay. (:An icy pang-of-shock once when you abruptly fell to the ground in front of me on a busy pavement, as if struck by lightning, a form that suddenly looked bulky and misshapen in its helplessness. There she lies. Isn't moving any more. ?Blood. ?Was blood flowing from some ?wound. No. She was strangled. They say. She lies so still, so coolly in a rigid pose, in a state I never saw when she was still in=life. Disconcerting, eerie — so still and shocking — just as I was shocked as a child by the tears of adults.)* This woman, she had caused me muchgrief in the lastdays of our relationship, and I had done the same to her, otherwise she wouldn't have gone Sofar off the rails. The last I heard of her was that she had taken that black man into the flat, that stranger who had screamed out his=pain at the death of his friend in the street outside the house, and those screams, she told me, were the outer echo of her=own=pain. That was all. Her last words. That black man, who was living in her flat at the end, was quickly apprehended; he was !not the-perpetrator. There was no trace-of-the-real-perpetrator yet. *She was like a person standing at the edge of adesert who, for inexplicable reasons, doesn't choose the path to the life-saving oasis, but the other one: more than 5000 kilometres into. . . . . a sandy desert boiling by day frostridden at night. And she didn't go slowly along her=path=to-death, not with measured steps; she rushed, chased furiously like someone hunted, and when she fell, she slid through thesand on her stomach for some of the way, then picked herself up again & raced back into the infinity of sand —. As if she didn't want to waste a single minute until her=death. Her figure became smaller, ever smaller in the shining dazzlebright expanse, — a trembling, wobbly spot, then finally she vanished —. — All re-flection on death is really the idea of a life which was denied by death. Because there is One Thing humans cannot think: the sight of the world, without them.* — Tears set upon my eyes, I ducked down into the beer glass. *!Don't, !give, !up.* The blood pumped behind my temples. I drank. Waited once more for the gentlewarm ocean wave — rolling over the hard-lived beach of my emotions. (The effect of the beer already weaker now than with the 1st sip.) And I said the name of my second wife — Regina. Her name and her name — constantly, like an imbecile who's been left with nothing but this 1 series of sounds & has to repeat it incessantly. Because it belongs to the last person I loved. And although I knew that !this woman was there at=home (all I had to do was leave this murkyred hole & go back to my flat, then I'd be with=her —), I suddenly felt a stronger sense of loss when I remembered Regina than at the thought of the now-dead Lena. *Cold like fire on-a-theatre-stage.* Only the draught in my brain that accompanied the inner=utterance of her name filled this menacing emptiness inside me with her image. And this form, which ran through my brain in the draught of her name, now also gave me back the details of events that two=of=us had experienced together, along with the succession of thoughts and wishes, of emotion, of wistfulness, of jealousy & of anger — that whole excess of feelings from whose richness two lives re-form by the hour. But that — I now felt — because it seemed to have come from our own=inner-realities and entered=us in powerful, firmly developed forms, made me doubt Lena's death and also feel uncertain that I could reach Regina again. *!Don't, !let, !go.* Again the blood behind my temples. *Because fear and doubt came from the differences between the dimensions in which the-memory discloses its images. So a beetle, viewed up close, can crawl across a window-pane, cover up a distant mountain & make it invisible. I loved both women all the more now=at-that-moment precisely because Both, distant from me, were !there nonetheless; the one dead in the reality of my=memory and my=grief (which means the return of the feeling-of-love), the other in tangible reality, a presence I can envisage as easily as the returning presence of a dead person, even though she moved further away from me, but it was pre-cisely through their absences that my=love=for=them could be revived all the more strongly, such that the feeling-of-love towards the one intensified the feeling towards the other. For reality is what I can envisage. Because I, like manypeople, know my way around my landscape ofpain better than the pastures of joy, I sought my=solitude — it is the place where absence and anguish come together — which increased my suffering. And went back to Regina, who lives barely 2 kilometres from here and couldn't have any idea at that moment that I would return=to=her. (They say that the shrill tone in one's ear that one occasionally hears announces the presence of the very person one is thinking of, like the whistling feedback when a loudspeaker & a microphone get too close.)* And thelonging for this woman spread out-inside-me like a warm ocean wave rolling out — so great was this yearning for her, like in the earlydays. *She'd always been my favourite company, I could be=silent with her, didn't have to say-Anything about my job (which she hates, as I learnt on our firstevening. But she only hates the job, not me). So it's All=fine. Fine.* I said to myself. — *Peaceful emptiness now enclosed us as soon as we were alone together and time left us.*

Just= her just=me — on a slow imponderable peace of earth, green and light yellow at the heightofnoon — : — rare moments of time-free hours —. — And in this murky-red bar in an hour stolen from work, that feeling of happiness granted by unhappiness flowed into=me as if hearing the first distant sounds of violin music. — Moved and joyful, I raised my glass to Möller.

He was sitting on the bar stool next to me, frozen. He was probably very bored by now. I glanced over at him. (Had I ?spoken, the same way ?now with the returning memories as in=my-sleep). He gave a visible start at my toast. The sight of my unexpected cheerfulness must have seemed to him like the sight of a drowned body that had just been pulled out of the river, and whose face showed none of the agony of havingtodrown, just a constantly=peaceful smile. — The nearlyempty beer glass before him, with annoyance in his face, presumably because he had forgotten the-reputation I had among our-colleagues (:*the sophist-icated Chief Inspector who reads !novels* —: which to them was !worse than having a woman as their-superior). He'd stupidly followed my invitation & was now stuck=here, unable to escape. So he sat quietly next to me on the thin-legged bar stool, sipping his beer. For something unanswered formed the centre of the force field that had sent out its invisible rays in my office, & like the threads of a cobweb these rays clung to us & had followed us all the way here. And I realized that he was affected by something other than annoyance at my presence; Something was writhing about inside the man. — He took off. — Müller noted, as if that was the-conclusion from thiscase.

I knew it was that man, Willfried Berger, who had walked into the fool's trap Möller had set and had come to us at the station, given himself up & told us his=story, & That kept preying on his mind. Möller's mind was on the night when this man had to carry out the-assignment of knocking off 2 people who were said to be *his parents*. — ?Why did he take off. — Möller now insisted. — He didn't even know them, those two. He wouldn't have had any qualms about offing people in cold blood that he knew a thousand times better & were far closer to him than these two alleged parents. So ?why did he run away back then.

— He didn't run away. At least, it wasn't what one generally means by *running away*. — That was suddenly clear to:me.

— ?Didn't run away. But —

— And that's the !exact=reason why *His Friend*, whom he betrayed, hasn't eliminated him to=this-day. !That=reason is also the motive for the murders of those women. Once we know !that reason we'll be in the picture about the-true-murderer. We've got his name now, but we also have to understand his=actions. Because —

— Yes: ?because —

— Because the-killing=alone doesn't tell us anything. ?What did this killing achieve; ?what's behind it. !That's what we have to understand. Otherwise we've lost him. . . . . (And maybe in the process we'll find The-real-motive too, The-real-reason for the Great-Bureaucratic-Reshuffle. The words came to my mind. But I didn't say them.)

— All=That seems pretty — weird to me. — Müller continued haltingly.

— This-wholestory we've been served up about This killer-squad, these recruits & these contract killers on secret missions. And then that name: Orfan Batt :the whole thing's a pack of !lies. I mean: word would've got around about something like That over-the-years if people were disappearing from the neighbourhood or being carried off as corpses.

— ?Who's to say that word !didn't get around.

— But if something like That had got around, then the wholesecrecy & thefuss with this fucking firm called Cohsubbo would've been history. Then they would've done ?Something about it.

— And ?!what. ?Who would've done ?what about it. Wouldn't be the 1st time that neighbours have noticed their neighbours disappearing, getting PICKED UP, and: still done Nothing about it.

— And ?how do you explain !that.

— In any society at anytime, the-people only notice thehorror of events=around-them as long as that horror doesn't seem embedded in the ever-reassuring business-of-everyday-life. But once such events have become *normal*, they no longer get noticed, as if thosethings weren't actually happening. The more often such things happen, the sooner they become *normal* & the less the-people will be aware of them. And anyway, in thisworld Everything gets worn out, Everything perishes at some point, usually without leaving any traces; and there's Something that gets even more worn out, that perishes even more thoroughly & rapidly than everything else: the suffering of other-people.

— But this Willfried: he ran away —

And I realized that I didn't have to answer this question so much for my stubbornly insistent colleague, but above=all for myself. I'd long stopped just wanting to get-hold-of a murderer. One can understand a country and the-people=in-it from many angles, and I wanted to understand this country from the angle of its=criminals. But one can't understand anycountry with helicoptershocktroops-of-reason & by dropping a few murcenaries-of-justice in the hinterlands. One won't understand the country like that, nor will one win against it. !That was what the-Americans found out in Vietnam. So if I wanted to understand theseevents=inthiscountry, my only=option was to look closely, with as precise & cool a gaze as possible, the way a lab technician examines the bacterial cultures under the microscope (and no one would expect a lab technician to love those bacterial cultures or to have any personal investment in them). And whatever he makes out apart from the visible, those are the possibilities that lie within-the-visible.

    —!No. — I called out tooloudly (the two figures in the corner looked over) — — No. he !didn't run away. Not from his assignment and not from the fact that he had to kill the people who were supposed to be his=parents. That's !not true. It's All=!wrong. — (And tooloud again. I pulled=myself=together, leaned heavily on the bar and murmured to Möller:) — I see him before me on that distant night: he stops in front of that run-down dive, at his friend's side he suddenly doesn't go any further. Only this Other Man continues, he probably doesn't even turn around to look for him, goes straight into the house to carry out the assignment. He's been trained not to ask questions, so his friend doesn't ask him why he's hesitating, why he's stopped. But he couldn't stay there forever. So at some point he slips away while his friend takes care of. . . . . thejob in the house. But he doesn't creep away stooped & in secret; instead — & this is !crucial — he walks up=right with slow, large steps. And !that must have been The Moment when Something happened inside him. Probably the 1st sign was in his face. Everything would still have been in that youthful face, like before: the nondescript brutal hardness, therage with its almost metallic implacability, which, like a galvanic layer, made his features look empty and emotion-less —:All still there, All still ready, as it always=was, for !that

triggeringmoment = The-command=to-attack with taut muscles
—. But with 1 change, no: a darkening, as if the galvanic layer
for hardness & implacability had been corroded by an acid and
suddenly changed colour. And !That was The Moment.

?What moment. I mean, he still —

— Most of their 'jobs' would've been done at-night. In those
tar-coloured big city nights, theair congealed and thick. ?What
time of year was it when he set off with His Friend, as=ordered,
to kill his parents. ?Was it summer, ?winter — or one of those
indecisive times in between —. I forgot to ask him that. You
know, Möller : people kill in different ways during the different
seasons, assuming they have a-choice.

— I didn't know that. — He replied sullenly. No doubt he
thought I was trying to change the-subject.

— In the-summer the-knife, in the-winter the-bullet.
Everything=else in between. The fact is: he !didn't run off. He
stood still. Didn't know What to do at first. As if he's forgotten
?how to Gothere & ?what to do. Suddenly ?thehesitation that
made him ?getstuck in the tar-thick black=ofnight.

— That's it. That's what I've been saying the wholetime. And
that's why he ran —

— No. I still say: he didn't run away. And his=hesitation
didn't come from some advance sympathy, wasn't a delayed
remorse about all his=earlier-deeds. ?Maybe That was exactly
what he was afraid of: ?remorse, ?sympathy that could ?fly at
him & ?seize him at=the-moment when he was facing his parents,
his !true parents, for the 1st time, which would also be the last
time. Was he ?afraid that the human ?longing to be reformed, to
be cleansed of alltheawfulnesses & allthefilth that he = as a human
had received from other humans, with which he had soiled himself

when he cut short their lives so abruptly & threw them into= death's jaws like knacker's meat, was he ?afraid that this ?longing for reformation would now ?burst open in=him like an ulcer that was old, as old as humanity, & flood & poison him with the pus of ?sympathy for=alltime, which All=Inall would mean paying far more than he had ever owed. Yes: reformation & shame at his longing for reformation —:That was what he feared more than losing his life. He was even !more scared of That than of the sight of his parents, killed by his & his friend's hand, those two pathetic bodies that were condemned to perish miserably in their hole. But that !wasn't It. At least !not like that : reformation, shame, remorse. And more and more terrible tribulations came along, cutting his whole previous existence out of thedarkness of anonymous law=fullness in the most glaring light of hisguilt; an anonymity that offered its receptiveness as easily & carefreely as if he could effortlessly take off all the clothes burdening him, like in the cloakroom of a theatre or museum; for smallchange you can get rid of everything that's holding you back that- moment, and will only need once the-performance is over & you have to go back into the cold & the biting wind of the-outsider's- life. . . . .

— And !That's what this bloke was supposedly thinking. Do you ?really believe that, boss. Do you ?credit him with ?Thatmuch conscience, ?Thatmuch sensitivity. That'd be some- thing-new for these=types. . . . .

— I credit him with even more than that: ?maybe, in that blackglassy night, thickened to the point of stasis, he recognized something else that he had so far lacked (without ever seeing it as a lack or a flaw): ?where in all the infinity interwoven, matted & tangled threads in=, :I almost said: in=the-carpet of human existence, but it's really more like a mop, a giant flawcloth in human existence, and yet The Question: *?where in allthat immea-surable=infinity was ?my thread, ?my=!veryown trail that could have let me imprint something unmistakable on this inex-haustible lifemopmess.* So far he's given Nothing : had only ever taken; had eliminated & undone. But ?how to go on now. Was ?!That already=?Everything he'd ever manage to achieve: popu-lating the shadow world with more&more shadows, all of which had already started coming back to him with their iron weights of disgrace and shame. ?Was he about to ?feel That too. I don't know. But I think he was capable of all that, even if He didn't formulate it all in his thoughts, but only, as all=of-us usually do with the-crucial-things: *felt* it.

— But —

— Because there must have Something that made him give up on thatnight. Maybe in that tarblack darkness he'd perceived Something as clearly as if a light had suddenly been switched on in his narrow murder cell, and now Something in oversized letters moved before his eyes and he !had to see it —

— ?What's That supposed to have been, so powerful & so great that It could make this man's previous, well, life go off the rails.

— Maybe Something so universally understandable that someone who realized it for the firsttime could neither overlook it nor ever forget it. Because Yesterday isn't just over tomorrow. Yesterday will only fade when the-last-human has vanished from the-earth and from space. Killed, exterminated, died out like the-dinosaurs — whatever. When there's Nothing left of humans, less than a grain of dust in the memory —: only !then will allof-yesterday be over. Until then, Yesterday is just a different word for Today. And so he was suddenly forced to feel: *I'm not young any more — —*

— And you ?really believe, boss, that ?something could've bowled this guy over !sohard that he'd immediately —

— His whole measly life he'd always been very close todeath. And the words that can bowl a person over are always the simplest words; they look for the wounds in each individual person that won't heal, because allactivity reveals the futility of allactivity at some point. And already at 20 the realization *I'm-not-young-any more* —:that's thewound that can !never heal. !Those are the places that words attack. Like acid poured on raw flesh. *(And beyond the power=full-voices & all the bigmightywords, in your deepest darknesses allalone in your bones — you will now tremble before the next breath, before the slightest movement. With no courage for the next step, you are stricken with fever-cold rigidity. For the jaws of TIME are wide, with fearsome teeth. Slowly theteeth of our years chew up —)*

— So you think, boss, — Möller replied hesitantly — : — you think he became an ?adult that night.

— An ?adult. Yes. Exactly=that. And suddenly had to realize in the brightest light, in the midst of thedarkness, that all his & all the others' murderous deeds were & are !fartoosmall, completely !inept & even !laughably useless for him to stay there & carry on a minute longer. Yes: he resigned himself, that means: he became an adult from 1-minute-to-the-next. And as it goes with those erratic puberties: the heart only rarely follows thegiantleap properly; the heart can no longer supply the enormousspace that has suddenly opened up, which is suddenly too big for justdarkness justrage&anger, with sufficient blood. I don't mean the bodily heart, that vainly twitching muscle; I mean the-heart-of-the-soul, which strengthens the will & provides the imagination & all curiosity about life with the blood flow that only a few people even feel; blood that can't be tapped by any tube, and equally defies any scalpel cut through the artery from those who, at some place in life & at the point of highest saturation, say to=themselves: *I've had enough.*

Möller stared at me, sweat running down his face in broad streams. — I've been — been in your department for hic-years. — (He suppressed a burp.) — If I'd written down the stuff you said to me in alltheseyears, I could fill whole !bookshelves with it. — — But then you'd have to look after the-books too. — I replied in the same tone. — Because books are alive. And things that are alive want to — assert themselves. :?Don't you want to start writing down my words of wit&wisdom right now, ?hm. — And grinned at Möller. — For a writer, a bar likethis can be a real career launch. Or a good place to be really out-to-lunch. — — A ?good place. Then I'd rather not see a bad one. — Möller downed his glass in one —, set it down on the bar table, looked at me & grinned back.

I adjusted my position on the bar stool. Though Möller may have hoped I would drop the subject, I didn't. — But that's not Everything about this man at that moment of reflection. — I began, Möller actually slumped, turned his beer glass and stared at the foam oozing down the side of the glass (no escape). I continued resolutely: — Which means that he suddenly understood: *From now=on I won't be able to die. I can get rid of my body, but that won't let me stop living any more than I can stop dying.* : And this most !terrible of all terrible knowledge is always the !First thing that's drummed into the-adult; — most-people forget it later, the only trace is a scar at most, like from a fall on the pavement as a child, the scar that stays for a life=time, grows with the body, becomes fainter but never disappears. Skin & flesh have their=own-memory. Only sometimes, when life's weather changes, this scar begins to hurt — nonetheless: it remains there in=everyone, whether one knows That or not. After all, no one pays attention to the clip-clop of their heart or the-rushing of their blood, — & yet It happens: without interruption constantly. Until —. But then it doesn't matter any more. — (And sensed I had long=overspoken.) But now Möller interrupted me indignantly: —!Oh. ?Doesn't ?matter any more. — His big eyes suddenly stared at me from the side, and I sensed a hint of rough annoyance in his gaze, as if I'd tried to tell a joke but forgotten or messed up the-punchline. But I couldn't waste time on that; had to go on. — And that still isn't Everything. — I said boldly, as if I genuinely knew Something that compelled me with such urgency to talk about It now&here to my much younger, inwardly robust colleague. It was only this insistent, pressing feeling, which wanted to utter something that still had to be said, that kept me talking now.

— Consider this: thecity, where all those decrepit houses sucked up the-everydaylight & the-everydayair for the-everydaypeople like black monoliths and kept it scarce; & then thesepeople themselves, who didn't even ask themselves where That came from anymore, the thing that made them duck=down, that made their voices fall silent & their seeing eyes cloud over. Consider these !darkforces that are capable of Suchthings & come pouring out of the-pile-of-massed=people like gas; that mash people up into-allpeople like A monotonous mass that annuls every face — every TomDick&Harry in their preferred position: being-dirty & lying, with that eternal mindless rottentoothed !Naah in their mouths. But THEY needed them, these fartoomany, for all kinds of purposes in the political lacuna; not as individual beings, but in their=appropriate manifestation as MASSES; & so THEY drummed into them from-birth that they were value=able-people, God's image, each 1 of them a special little light, & because THEY wrote in the constitution that they had the right to develop their personalities freely, THEY !absolved each 1 of them from The Duty to account to themselves and their consciences for all their deeds & desires, & instead assured them of their entitlement to happiness, a bank account, a house, a car, a family, a career, a widescreen television & a flush toilet.

— And we=the-police have the job of making sure nobody barfs on their=happiness or their=carpet. And if someone does, we have to come along & mop up the puke. Because we, the-police, are truly !gifted mops, aren't we, & that's exactly how THEY treat us. — (I wouldn't have thought so much bitterness could already have accumulated in this still youngman.) I looked up & gazed directly=into-his-face for the first time that day. And I saw the anger already fading again, like when a strong light bulb is switched off but the filament still glows for a while —. And knew that this bitterness would never leave him; it got him at an early age. . . . . — And that's why THEY & they don't really !giveashit about right, wrong, justice. I continued along the path of my speech. — But ?who, I ask, actually ?gets anything out of right, wrong, justice. Because one of the simplest things in life is grasping one's situation: like the age-old song in-wartime and in-peacetime: the soldier at-war is supposed to kill & THEY honour him for that. From the 1st minute after-the-war, if he does something he'd done & been honoured for just minutes earlier — killing — he'll be punished. So THEY'll punish him too for the-murders he committed by=order of the government agencies that will now punish him — yes, THEY'll punish him !severely. But THEY'll only charge him for trifles, if they do at all, the way after the-GeeBeeR those responsible didn't stand trial later as state criminals but as tax-evaders, a joke or a big diversion. THEY can't charge him, the-murderer=in-THEIR-service, for those murders, otherwise THEY'd have to charge themselves overandover again as soon as they became THEY. THEY won't charge him, but THEY will punish him.

— But ?what'll THEY ?do to him.

— THEY'll — remove him. . . . . — I was silent for a moment, then: — And there's another reason why THEY'll punish him without mercy: because he's the living proof of the legacy of every=state: murder-by-order. But everything in the way of blood & corpses that comes from state crimes has lost currency Today; THEY show disgust & horror, officially at least, towards such relics from earliertimes, like bizarre instruments of torture in-feudal-museums. Today THEY kill differently: with computer programmes, databases & Babeltowers of bureaucracy. That conceals the-death the-blood the-bodies; executions have become hygienic. THEY don't want to see blood; THEY prefer a long process to the 1 shot, the 1 quick cut. Or rather: one no longer even needs bloodshed in these=parts in order to produce the necessary dead. Because everyperiod needs its=dead, so every-period has its=dead. But death-by-law&decree isjust more hygienic than bloodshed. And most of all, you don't get the-heroes & the-martears, the-icons for every up-rising, because those who are killed by-law, the-papercorpses in the longhall-ways of the-departments, there's nothing heroic about them. I often used to confuse the two terms: execution & executive.

— Aha. That's why, boss, you think Willfried Berger turned himself in Today. And !didn't run away back then, because —

— Because it would have been meaningless. Another very-simple thing : meaning less. People are capable of almost any-thing as long as they can give their=actions a meaning. Without meaning they'll croak like fish out of water. But the-catch is: they think that the meaning they 1ce gave themselves is always The-

Rightmeaning, for alltime. Thesepeople are convinced of that. That's why mostpeople, when they look back on the years of their life, can't admit that their life & the meaning they gave themselves for it were !wrong : they served the !wrong-master, yielded to the !wrong-yoke, thought the !wrong things & did the !wrong things; the-wholelife they lived was a !wrong life —: mostpeople find it !impossible to admit !That to themselves. Let alone to stand by their wronglife : I see that Everything was wrong, but !I lived that way. !Out of the question. The ones to blame are always the-others, the-time the-society the-circumstances. !Never them=selves. Their life drips from the sky as slurry; but their lies turn it into clear water. If this illusion goes to pieces, these-people collapse, they can't move a muscle. And so, in The Night of a greatdarkness, this man said to himself: *?Where am I supposed to run away and escape to. ?What for.* Anyway, he'd already reached his=goal : the monotony & unrecognizability of the MASSES. In THEIR noise-racked, stuffy, congested places full of sharp-edged lights. In the reverberation of THEIR din & the stench of machines & the flashing colours. In theconstriction of THEIR hunts, agitations, cowardice & shirking, THEIR lies & falsehoods & endless jabbering yammeriads whimpering : THAT gets squashed up into an impenetrable massmush like corned beef; whoever gets caught inside can't get out, but they can't be found out either. That's presumably how he survived. Until Today. — Well, — I conceded, — I think the old man, Theresa's adoptive father, knew where he was, maybe even found a place for him & supported him as far as he could. ?Do you remember the old man's last stammerings: *if someone gets hounded by the-mob — he has to at least have some1 who :protects him,* he probably meant to say. I expect he hid away in the-prefab-buildings =on-the-outskirts.

But Möller seemed unable to get over onething: — And you think, boss, THEY as the MASSES only needed to do what THEY do best: donothing, & that's why THEY did Nothing. ?Not even finding him & sending him to his doom —

— Being there, spreading out like a stagnant muddy pool with all dead things at the bottom, sitting around, staying & waiting. *Thou shalt wait* : that's the additional commandment to go with the dusty=age-old pap-pyrus, crumbling like it was from pharaonic times, *Thou shalt not kill* — that's not even funny any more. And Both of these — the commandment to wait & the ban on killing — were cunningly left without an object, so one can wait for Everything=for-ever, the same way one shouldn't actively destroy everything on-the-spot, but can let it perish slowly for-ever=amen. That way every virtue also has ITS=cheapjokes & ITS=trashy&dirtyliterature. So: !stand still & !Sit=tight. — I accidentally knocked over my beer glass with my arm —, — watched the puddle slowly spread over the bar —. Möller also stared at the spilt beer, mesmerised, the way one stares into flames —. Then the barkeeper hastily wiped the puddle away.

Now I had to finish It, to get to the-punchline, so that Möller wouldn't be disappointed. — And so it happened that thenight in which in which he had previously existed suddenly began to run — do you understand: it !wasn't !him who started running, because he said himself before: *I didn't go on. Just stopped. Waited.* : he didn't flee from thenight; it was thenight that ran away from !him, went out & took off — and gave him the 1st faint shimmer of life, which he'd have to live on from that point. To this day. Until he came to the station to my office and gave himself up.

— We have to start-a-manhunt for the bloke he called His Friend right=away. !Boss. — I heard my profession in Möller's

voice. I had hoped that by talking for long enough, I'd find out
!why he'd grinned at me in that strange way in-the-moment when
they took him out of my office in-handcuffs —. — But I didn't
find out, and it would have been pointless to ask Möller about
it, because at that-moment he had been standing with his back
to the prisoner. (— *and washed my hands downstairs in the crys-
tal-cold water jet to rinse thesmell from my skin that stuck to it
like the charred stench after a house fire —)*

— Er — ?What : yes. Start-a-man-hunt. I've already done
that. — As I automatically repeated those words my tongue
encountered a thin-sharp sensation, as if I'd just licked the elec-
trodes of a low-voltage battery. (— *the little curled-up letter of
her body on the ground, motionless, with strangulation marks
on her throat and her larynx broken. More than silence, deathly
silence, full of choked breath so dark. My hands trembled in the
ice-cold water jet. Couldn't get rid of thesmell, couldn't wash off
that —)* — — It won't take long now. — I said into the murky-
red bar light. Stood up from the thin-legged stool & put money
on the damp-wiped counter. Then we left, Möller & I, back out
into the grey shred of day full of Christmas stench, and back to
headquarters.

The staircases & the hallways in the massively-built complex
seemed unchanged. Floating light everywhere in the shade of
mild herbal tea in the evening in a hospital room. And when I
returned to my office, the small room was filled with people-in-
plainclothes, psyclopes wrapped in light-grey & brown; searched
their faces : recognized none of them : as if they had been poured
into the room, these figures filled it to the very last corner with
sluggish masses of flesh & faces eyes hands. Upon my entry,
thick-lipped mouths immediately let out sequences of words like
ancient formulas : against me. (I knew the-words, but none of

the speakers) : *Under arrest — strong suspicion — murder of your former wife —*, & because my name was spoken, there was no hope of a mistake. Rough hands reached for=me resolutely & with well-practised violence, bent my arms behind my back, forcing my upper body into a horizontal position withthisgrip. From my back the bright clicking of the handcuffs snapping shut. With the pain in my joints I felt nausea stab in=to=me, coming out of a fish-cold sensation. The forcibly-lowered head stared at the worn-out linoleum in my office, my eyes filled with tears from the effort : This is !not a dream. — Tried to call Möller, but nothing came out of my mouth except a croaking sound and a slim thread of saliva that dripped onto my feet.

Perhaps the oddly twisted saying & the strange grin of Willfried Berger earlier referred to these!exact circumstances, which he must have anticipated — as I said, an almost sym=pathetic grin. It seemed to me.

CHAPTER 6

Voices push against:me from pictureless dreams — they rise from
thedark of the expansive prison grounds : first like drops of liquid
metal, raining on the stone ground — 1, 2, then several, a shower
of hailstones with steely voices — freeze into balls — they roll
towards me from the massive cube of the building — down the
long hallways always the same path — from corners nooks cran-
nies like the rumble of approaching thunder —, clattering down
the iron steps as steel hailballs, throwing themselves along walk-
ways & corridors —, until they smash against this cell door as
rattling projectiles — : — VOICES. When they penetrate the tiny
rectangular hatch in the iron door, thevoices hurl themselves at
it unhindered against:me, tidal waves of noisy debris flood over
me, bury me, — and it feels like I'll suffocate break apart under
the tonnes of steel balls. Consistently highpressure from everything unfinished oflate. Oppressive duties, actions to perform,
outstanding forgotten tasks —:but even All=Those are not gras-
pable, have dissolved, They too are shapeless; — only thepressure
from Them has remains, and will remain and remain and grow
into a lump of clay that chokes all breath. —!*Air* cries Something
inside me *!!Air*, — *haa* —, *heeh* —, *khkh*, — *khh* — *h-hh*. Iron
shackles around my chest. Wildlythumping racing heart. Will
surely shatter burst. *Give me !!!air* —! . . . . . — —

These attacks have been recurring lately, since I've been locked
up Inhere. Dampclammy stench of hundreds of imprisoned men.
Sweat and limp tiredness later like after the hardest physical

labour. I'm not doing any work. Prisoners=in=detention-awaiting-trial don't work. Soon, once thevoices rise to shrill heights, they collapse again, stop abruptly, as if ?someone had choked them. And no trace of them afterwards. And Everything would start again; these charging voices solve Nothing, they change Nothing; repeat & repeat their clattering rolling wailing whooshing; all words with no rescue-in-the-One-clarifying-word, a Sisyphean= ordeal. And every time, at the exact=same point, the same fragments of words, the same-phrase: *Under arrest — strong suspicion — murder of your former wife* — \ :and here&now the collapse, the end. No more words — dark — no remembering. Therock slips from the bloody bruised hands of Sisyphus, — rolls back down the hill banging mockingly crashing, back to Square One, — & Sisyphus runs after it, down=the-path, staggering stumbling along furrows scratched carved deep into the soil, witnesses to affliction and all futile efforts, down the tormented path, the earth broken open brutally like a slain deer being ripped apart by hyenas, — and having arrived at the foot of the hill, Sisyphus takes his=rock once more and resumes the ancient path of his=work. There were times that saw *happiness*. . . . . in such work. But happiness without a society-of-the-happy is none; there wouldn't be enough stones for every happiness-seeker to have their !own=stone. End of the stone-age. Therock rough, the hands bloody. Voices speak — ruins hiss thevoices — —

I'm lying in the top bunk in my cell, staring up at the ceiling light with its chicken-wire bars, burdened=by thenightmare of a compulsion to remember something monstrous, formless with no shape to grasp — to touch It, to name it : *murder-of-my-former-wife*. This shadowyunresolved Thing, which weighs on me as oppressively as a 10-tonne rock. And so I wait for its next awakening, which will be like all the previous awakenings, and when in the morningdaytime&eveninghours I can no longer bear the glaring light from the one cell lamp on the ceiling, I shut my eyes tight & follow the electric sunball on=the-inside of them and the storm of colours with its flashing echoes-in-my-brain —. — And when these bursting balls grow weaker and weaker and finally dissolve and vanish like coloured mist in the wind, then other, real pictures enter the resulting void. Unfamiliar pictures. Disturbing sigh-ts. But even those are alwaysthesame, just as the hissing rattling words in the-phrases — *Under arrest* — *strong suspicion* — *murder of your former wife* — return unchangeably, as if out of allthewords left for me, those were the onlyones.

Unlike the black man she had taken into her home from outside out of com-passion for the pain he yelled unreservedly into the night, she had not screamed her own=grief at the pale tired street lamps in the nocturnal street; her=grief kept her Insilence, shut in and then died away between the narrow walls of a flat, in=the-dungeon of a curled dead body. No one had heard her=dying. Except for the murderer, who was supposedly me, no one had seen her in those lastminutes. Then the neighbours noticed the sicklysweet stench — a familiar one. That would mean !I saw her in her lastmoments. I, her murderer. (Once in a dream : *like a chick that had fallen out of its nest, then the little body lay still + dead. — My heart : but my heart is my dead wife. — My voice tripping up. The old man remained motionless, insistently held out his hand to me with the tiny dead body —*) And have been trying since then to imagine the face of this dead woman; its expression that was no longer changed by any inner flames, storms of tired pale suffering, only by putrefaction. And I was stared at constantly again&again unchanging by the same sigh-t : a resentment gone cold, something sullenly deeplyangry, a despair bleached in the rotten white of the eyeballs; and eternally staring disappointment, purged of allpain. And later only 2 slowly, blindly expiring gelatinous orbs —, and those too finally blurring together with the doughy mass of a corpse —. — As soon as my imagination (which selected its pictures from my years on the job & throws them together with her, my dead wife) presents me with this final picture too, Something always cries out inside=me, soloud sohard that It threatens to burst my skull, tears open my mouth the theforce of the pain charging at me —. But thepain doesn't come out, must be toobig for the mouth's little opening — I needed more farmore outbursts openings holes in my skull for thispain to escape —: and so I keep still, mouth torn open and panting, in=sleep in=waking in the longhours in the sweatfumes of despair. In mymuteness I reach across to her, to the dead woman (the dazzling flash of screams goingback& forth inside=me) — —

But I do not always remain mute. In the pictureless dreams in the suffocating dark of my nights lightningflashes of these-screams do occasionally reach the outside, they penetrate the prisoner vapours of unwashed skin and sweat-soaked uniforms, enter the sluggish-sour cellnight, — stab the other man out of his sleep in his bunk. But he never wasted a word on my nocturnal distresses; only the fists of the warden on duty sometimes bang on the cell door from-the-hallway-outside when, doing his rounds through the block shimmering in the faint night light, he passes this cell and hears my dark animal utterances. Cast back into wakefulness, I then lie Insweat in my bunk, and thisdark too remains without pictures. Musty odours from the-imprisoned stand like steel&concrete in the rage-smouldering thin sleep. I probe the eerie sensation that one can collapse even when lying down — a corporeal gradually fading sensation, like a cramp easing. And the same sight always appears, now too; becoming an endlessly-repeating sequence: the time our time=together, this garden landscape of interwoven commonalities, — then later, & starting with the-hour-of-my-departure from Hanover to Berlin, this joyful fabric, this once-flowering allotment=of-our=together-ness, seemed to burst apart, first slowly and almost imperceptibly in our earlydays; then unmistakably, with no laughter, none of our usual almost childish silly comments to gloos over it — : — the chasm between us became sinister, a blockhole with rockhard crusty walls of suspicion rumours presumptions & fears; what a bottomless chasm of the unspeakable, because every word in the other's ear had to be twisted into a lie immediately; a !never-before-imagined poison brew spills its corrosive wave crests at&against:us out of thisdark — — each moves further away from the other — withdraws into themselves; the poison waves are only absent Insilence, but thissilence is like a foul-smelling gas that suffocates us slowly carefully & mercilessly. That's the end. And now I have to retch again, as if thesepoisonfumes were entering my lungs now&here from the tightness of the cell to corrode my breath again&again. !No escape. Always=eternal return of !this 1 passage, like the stylus skipping on a damaged record, back to the same place time-after-time. But this broken record is inside my brain. . . . . And again and again the-ancient-phrases, the statement: *Under arrest — strong suspicion — murder of your former wife* —: only my=death would !finally offer release from this.

I'm not alone in this cell, in this room of maybe 12 m² : roughly 3 m wide & 4 m long; the walls, painted light grey, about 2.5 m. In the middle of the ceiling the barred light, & this electrically lifeless cell light galvanizes figures & objects equally; hands fingers skin, they shimmer like tin plate, the food seems metallic : the wrecktangular concrete sky with a sun, without stars. No orientation in all the grey colour-drained night journeys. Dreams and: waiting, notliving, just for a full stop. — while thewalls of this cell | all | around | me stand tight&firm, pushing pressing against:me, impenetrable; — the walls of my safety crumble, the fence posts point around my conscious-ness; everything well-founded from my years on the job sinks down, limp & rusty, rots disintegrates — finally It will break a part — —

When I was shown my cell weeks ago and stood in front of the open steel door, holding the laundry package in my hands, & the-order was given to go in, I entered the exhausted, breath-drained cell air & saw: left wall metal bunk bed ; right wall a table, 2 stools in front of it; a corridor between table and bed; to the left by the back wall with the high-positioned, iron#barred window a sideboard & a shelf, everything narrow & tiny, like for children or oldpeople tired of moving; directly to the left of the cell door a foulpissy small: the toilet, partitioned off by a screen, a wash basin next to it. / The bottom bunk was occupied by a lying form, an incredibly fat guy who didn't move when I came in, he just turned his face mudsluggishly in my direction, the narrow Asian eyes, 2 brown slits in a fadedbrown mask, sucked themselves onto=me, sparkling, appraising —. / This man, maybe early 50s, whose belly bulged out over the tightened elastic band of his tracksuit trousers like a flatspherical mountain of lard, seemed to me like a reptile that carries out all its movements extremely slowly. The heavy head with the greasygrey shimmering long hair, stuck to his skull as if wet, sat neckless on rounded shoulders, the bulging cheekbones seemed to squeeze his eyes into a permanent squint. A high forehead leads up his head from his fat-spongy, contourless face, its skin just as smooth, with no folds, but glistening like jelly. The cheeks podgy and loose; the chin broad and soft like a woman's; nose wide and flat; the lips, with a slight blue tinge, look as if they were painted with weak strokes on this skin, coloured like cocoa with dirty milk. Everything about this man seems sluggish, his skin seems permanently coated in a thin film of sweat, his body, heavy with fat, clumsy & the epitome of laziness — but that's a mistake : I saw him carry out the most vigorous actions unexpectedly, without any prior motion; powerfully & precisely. Because there was nothing calming about this sluggish stillness; it's more like the armoured lurking waiting of reptiles who, from their million-year-old capacity=to-exist-Onearth, have developed their=own cruelties=for-survival so that, unlike all later species, they can !suddenly leap up from their ancient stone&sludgequiet to carry out The-deadly-attack (his mouth with the thinblue lips is always open by a slit. Seems that, like all people who are tired of moving, he has infused laziness with economy. His dirt-brown face bore traces of the inscribed, immobilised pen-strokes of something brooding, once filled with an urgent will to explore everything impalpable unspeakable, but long since abandoned by all distress & now cooled off insubstantial full of unwelcoming indifference, like a moor in which even the largest boulders sink completely & are digested, and the muddy surface closes again over them to form an ever=lasting traceless uniformity ofmud. Just !those eyes : when they didn't seem almost closed, as they usually did, then something unexpectedly flashed in them like pieces of flint struck together, bright sparks. And when he keeps hisgaze fixed on an object or on people foralongtime, attentively examining, a fiery dark radiance appears behind his eyelids like ghost=lights glimmering from swamp gases. It's said that this man is here because of *Severe Tax Offences* & is awaiting his-trial. I didn't hear that from him (who hasn't spoken a word to me yet from the swamp of his half-wakefulness), but from 1 of the wardens, who evidently still saw me as a colleague. — But !don't ask, don't !ever ask him about *His Case*. Asking-things in general: for!getit inhere; !pull=yourself=together : you're not a-cop-any more. — His form and the bunk in which he lay almost motionless mostof-thetime, his left sausage-plump arm hanging over the edge, the right resting limply against the wall, chubby fingers spread out from his cushion-shaped hands like fins, already seemed to have merged inseparably in the few weeks he had been here.

?Why had I been ?put me in this cell — *partnered*, as they call it, with !this guy. ?Was someone trying to ?protect the ex-cop from violence from other prisoners through someone else's presence? Because an-imprisoned-cop is even more hated among=convicts than a pedo. . . . . !That information had got around before my arrival=Here, & the hooligans the vengeful-bastards were no doubt already massaging their fists or getting knives they had 'found by chance' out of their hiding-places to do me in, the dirtypig=Injail=on !their=terrortory, at the first opportunity. ?Maybe THEY'd just come into my cell Atnight & snuff me. ?Or did someone think I was ?suicidal. But ?how would anyone ?know; can't we even dream any more without ?eaves-dropping; ?where are our brains ?registered : even theconcrete has ears, thewalls are flesh, with mouths of stone THEY disclose what lives under the skullcap in=the-secrets-of-the-brain-fibres. Every word, every sound, every screaming raging yelling every fist blow, even the smallest breath is seized & entered in the-protocols — Outside, while we think we're living. . . . . I Inhere we're the skinless dogs we became Outside, now for the slaughter-house, open. . . . .

From the-1st-moment, That was the hardest thing for me to get=over : me = in a prison cell, & when the door closed behind me, I wasn't outside again in the city's gusting wind & flood of lights, didn't return to the office & home=to-Regina; but was stuck Inhere, locked up under a biting palelight in-enmity with thisbloke who says Nothing, this sluggish meatball with his cocoa-coloured, broad and fatslobby face and: narrow flashsparkling eyes, which were constantly inspecting me, even at night. *And I=the-newcomer can't ask him !anything. Say !anything. !Embarrassing.* As the-newcomer I had to wait until !he spoke to me. That's the law-Inprison.

Regina's first visit to the remand prison. (The authorization was obtained by the lawyer Regina hired for My Case. — Möller was denied permission, however, on the grounds that he wasn't a rel-ative. Shortly after my arrest, I found out, he had been transferred from the Berlin office to the-country. I never heard anything from him again.)

The visiting room at the remand prison : like a sports hall with grey-blue tiled walls, grey concrete floor, high Up below the ceiling a few wire-barred windows, 3 parallel rows of fluorescent lights above the 3 rows of tables for prisoners on 1 side, visitors on the other side, put an electrically cold block of light in the hall (some of the fluorescent lights humming like an innervatingly cir-cling insect). A large public clock placed above the entrance, like in the waiting hall of a train station. Normally the minute-hard progress of its black hand is inaudible in=here, it gets drowned out by the echoing voicestumult in the hall; today I'm alone Inhere, a warden motions towards a table and I sit down at it with him. Then he sits down at the narrow end of the plain piece of furniture. Thesilence, humming like a transformer station, the smell slightly oily. THEY had ensured that even at visiting times, none of the other prisoners could be in this room together with me, the ex-detective. The warden's features adopting the nothing-face of duty (quietly rattling his keys, it almost sounds like the music of the sfears), he stares straight ahead through the high-wide hall : *Now I'm truly on The Other Side : there's an immense emptiness coming from thiswidespace, grabbing, pushing, pressing down, I'm breathing against anightmare, fear, like before suffo-cating Underwater.*

I sit at the empty table like a schoolboy, arms shyly resting on the pale green Resopal top, palms sweat-moist, heart beating-wildly. The fingertips touch one another hesitantly, warily, as if meeting again after a longtime —. Waiting. Electricity humming quietly in the fluorescent lights high above me. The hands of the clock clicking goose steps. The right corner of my eye is occupied by the figure of the guard, a light spot like a disturbance in the retina. — At the back of the hall, opposite the entrance-for-prisoners, behind the steel door steps & clanging sounds, — the door opens, a guard walks in, and following closely behind him : !Regina : past the accompanying official she rushes across the hall to=me to the table. Under her light-grey unbuttoned winter coat, the duffle coat = her favourite coat she's wearing a plan dark dress. She wanted to rush towards me, to embrace me; but THEY must have instructed here : NO TOUCHING | She suddenly stopped as if before an invisible wall, frozen in front of the bare table in the tall empty visitors' hall (traces of acrid an cleaning agent puncture the stale air, only noticeable through the stirring effect of her steps). Now she doesn't dare sit down in the 1 empty, shabby chair opposite me at the table. She only sits down hesitantly after the warden urges her to do so. Her posture indicates — no doubt unintentionally — something like awe; but it may just be a fear of Everything=here, especially because she thinks that sitting amounts to a final acceptance of the whole situation; shuddering quietly, as if shrunken, she finally sinks down into the chair. — *Far far away from me* —. But she seems determined, even Here&now, to lose nothing of her vigorous, resolute manner. Suddenly her words, resoundingcheerfully, leap at the greyish-yellow tiled walls, cast themselves against the wire grilles in front of the windows, spring back boisterously as if from a trampoline and reverberate through the empty hall, bright colourful bags of words thrown across thefloor at thewalls theceiling, bursting into the pointillism of oversweetened gaiety. Her cheeks glowing red, the eyes big and glittering like candlelight in Christmas baubles (:ohyesright: it's Christmas-time now, Outside. That's probably why THEY gave her permission to visit.) Her loud-joyful voice bridges The Great Coldchasm. / Then, suddenly, as if she had reflected on the place & the circumstances, the bright cascades of her voice collapse; she pauses, sits very straight in the uncomfortable chair, looks at me with an open face, the skin above her chin crumpled into tiny wrinkles and tears trickle down her flushed cheeks. — I just want Everything to be the way it was Before. — That's all she manages to say, her voice chokes, she stays upright, rigid & straight (but seems to have crumpled inwardly).

Her sudden sadness hits me harder than insults or accusations. When I try to reach out to her across the table, the security guard intervenes. Without a word, with a greycaustic chalkface, he prevents our touch. / And once again I'm burnt by my inability to offer real comfort, hope and assurance like a caring hand over this woman who is despairing to her=core. That's never been one of my skills. So all I manage to say now is: — It'll soon come out that I didn't. — And couldn't continue; it was ridiculous. On top of that an idiotic — Butit'sallgoingtobe just=like-before — in an inane avuncular tone. Which isn't just a nonsensical statement, but also conveys an impression of complete indifference & insensitivity to hersuffering. — And that's exactly how Regina seems to read it; with a-woman's practical sense of emotional economy, she blows her nose into a tissue; oneortwo blows, then perfectly composed on the outside she doesn't waste another moment on her=sorrow (which she'll keep to=herself in future, as I've just proved unworthy of sharing; showing me further scenes of her=terrible-grief, exposing herself again before me and my inanity, would amount to pouring pearly tears into a cesspool) — but now speaks of everyday matters in a neutral voice: work, household, scraping together the-rent for the flat, paying the lawyer (who's being very accommodating about=it) —, lots of bloodless bustling, just about right for a lost man, for the husband being gradually disconnected from her=feelings (& if I were given a long prison sentence, I know as-of=Today&now that she'd get divorced. . . . . ; she's not so old that she'd have to fill the flat only with-her-own sounds & noises). — Soon she rises from the table, says a friendly goodbye, the way she'd say goodbye to a travelling stranger before getting off a train, having chatted with him non-committally for a few hours. And walks firmly across the hall, to the exit. (*?!Where is theflame, our=flame from Backthen, beneath these deadening ashes; ?what breath could make it catch !fire again* —). Then she's gone. And will even come back, but then she'll be a prisoner too (I'll never *see* her the way I did before), trapped=in-the-armour of misfortune and loneliness, her invisible walls in Theworld=Outside; palpable, understandable with simple words; but !never to be overcome.

Another visit from the lawyer. The man has the cell door unlocked, enters the narrow room with its stale air, a tall figure, almost a head taller than me. Must be around 40. (The smell of roast meat & the stench of powder seem to emanate from his heavy coat — Christmas, New Year's Eve and New Year's Day over, 2013 : a new year — and so I imagine that anyone who comes from-Outside must be smelling of festive food & gunpowder.) The presence of the other prisoner, sprawled on the bottom bunk as an immobile colossus of loamy fat, doesn't seem to bother the lawyer, evidently he doesn't pay him any attention. He quickly spreads out his documents on the narrow, wobbly table & starts speaking about my-case openly & without any preamble.

As he speaks the 1st words he casts off his heavy winter coat with a grand gesture —, as if peeling off a shell — and: his stateliness is gone. Now everything about this man seems small, tight, narrow & thin : shoulders, head on poppystalky neck (already stringy chicken skin under his chin), his greying hair combed with a crisp left parting & made into a wave, which, together with his strong vintage horn-rimmed glasses, gives him an off-putting air of a pampered snobbery that hasn't changed since youth. He often takes off his glasses, and then his dot-shaped dark eyes under severe brows are tooclose too each other; his little round mumblemouth with thin womanish-red lips, his nose skinny & sharply formed; his narrow chest seems sunken inside his overtight shirt, reminiscent of a soup chicken (like many puny men, he apparently wants to hide his scrawniness by wearing clothes that are too small, which always has the opposite result; *wouldn't surprise me if he had phimosis*). Occasionally a sharp sting of sweat comes from these clothes. Then his voice: always slightly rasping, with a high-handed dogmatic certainty. Amazingly small hands, he scatters further papers across the table with twitchy childlike fingers. In between the actions his hands & fingers remain restless, waving about in the air as if to chase away fruit flies. At the very 1st meeting, the first thing he said was that he would much rather be working on his books about the codes of civil & criminal procedure than acting as a defence lawyer. He made no bones about his disdain for all legal practice, much as some natural scientists in theoretical disciplines show contempt for applied work in their field: *If you haven't got a clue, applied science is the thing for you.* And left it to me to draw my own conclusions about his dedication in the matter of my=trial. — : — It was clear to me from the 1st word that this lawyer couldn't stand me, the way one animal despises another as soon as it catches sight of it & picks up its scent. Obviously he had only taken on my-case at Regina's err=gent pleading.

Indifference & reluctance strain his facial expression, as if he starts getting a migraine as soon as he faces:me. His quirk of abandoning sentences in which he sets out assertions & observations, then repeating parts of them like mnemonic phrases until they form a peremptory statement, now seems part of a secret agreement with the clanging cascades of noise from the prison building that enter in bursts, — a mechanical ran-dumb con-cert-with-1-voice.

For today's appointment, this man has evidently decided to give a keynote speech intended to end all his activities for-my-case. — In the past — you have — he begins, before repeating the opening immediately, — in the past you have described your version — your version of the-events in great detail. You have also — have also told me in great detail about your first encounter with the father of this missing woman — (his twitchy fingers dart across the paper) — this Theresa; then about this other family, the adoptive children as well as — as — this COSUBO Ltd —

andsoon andsoforth — we don't have to repeat Everything you
have told me now. And it's not necessary — not necessary to continue with that. — The childlike hands push various papers on
the desk together into a neat stack. — And there — there — and
there's no point in pretending, !all the-evidence is !against you.
— He pulls out one sheet, evidently the-prosecutor's investigation
report. He holds the paper in front of his eyes like a choir member holding his music, he reads out the words while his free hand
seems to conduct, emphasising every fact. — Your DeNA at the
scene of the crime: !fresh DeNA traces, please note, not ones from
the time when you were living at that flat in Hanover. Then: the
strangulation marks on the dead woman's neck match your
hands !exactly. Furthermore: neighbours saw you=at-the-scene
repeatedly, at different times of day&night. For the ascertained
time of the crime too, there are reliable statements from witnesses
who recognized you close to the scene of the crime. In short —
the man waves the report about, a sharp rustle & the lines he has
read out whirl about like swarms of flies. — In the light of allthis
evidence, there is !nohope for you. You have 1 last resort: plead
!guilty.

Now he's said It. Thestatement stands in the tight cell like a
red-hot metal block, a torrid burnt smell, theheat floods over me
like a roar from thelungs of a furnace: glowing sucking completely devoid of life; sharpdazzling sparks dance in my burning
brain.

Unmoved, the lawyer continues: — Plead guilty, then in-court
I can refer to your — can refer to your — to your special situation: the 4 unsolved murders of women, together with the great
strain of your professional & private life. But first — first it is
!essential that you confess. Only then can I — possibly I can then
— can then get some result for you. It'll be difficult.

— Is it ?impossible. — I interrupt him as a provocation.

— Nothing is ever impossible. — He replies with a detached reflex, twists his mumblemouth & shrugs his narrow shoulders indifferently. — But don't get your hopes up — a detective inspector who admits to murder, that's certainly a verygrave state of affairs. Though without your confession, your situation would be !disastrous. — He clears his throat, his face grows very red. — Even if plead guilty, I can't — I obviously can't — guarantee you that in-court — in-court you'll be given a more lenient sentence, agreements likethat don't exist, that's a myth. — Now he stops speaking, realising that he has stamped out any spark of hope in me; now he gathers up all the documents on the table. This Case already seems closed for him. I watch this man's actions, mute and defeated. He's probably inahurry to get back to his desk, to his manuscripts about theories of criminal & civil procedure codes. The-migraine lights up his face, twisted by eagerness. In this loreyer's childlike hands, the truth wouldn't even be turned on its head; it would simply rot. Truth, like a piece of raw meat left out toolong in the warm, stale air, would spoil, & I already sensed the glassy stench while having to listen to this man's disdainful words. All I have left is a peculiar sorrow; sorrow with the dross of anger at !somuch open indifference, as well as a profound pity for the truth, which is forced to spoil in such paws & the red-lipped mumblemouth like a carelessly-tormented creature, and: Nothing I can do about it. I once found these lines in a book: — *and trained animals are but of dust & damp swamp — an ember that burns in=us with unextinguished longing, the-dream of justice dies out, ever unattainable, and ash is all that remains.* — —

The rasp of the lawyer's voice interrupts; evidently he wants to follow his imperious address with a few words of reassurance, and remarks:

— You don't have to tell me this minute what you'll decide: guilty or notguilty. There's still time before the first day of trial. Nothing will be decided before then anyway. I'll visit you again soon. Or if you reach a decision earlier, let me know. — He is already back in the shell of his winter coat, catches the attention of the jailer-outside-the-door and leaves hastily & wordlessly. The cell door shuts noisily behind him, the key&bolt bang metal-lically: *!guil-ty —!guil-ty*.

— The lawyer's advice wasn't bad. — I suddenly hear a voice, whispering and delicate as if from a dream, and it seems to be speaking from inside=me. I turn around, see the fat man lying motionless in his bunk, his broad face on the shabby pillow like a bronze mask. The next words twist out of his unmoving mouth like spider's legs, whispering gently but forcefully nonetheless. — If someone needs proof, they will always find proof; THEY pre-pared the-crime-scene !well. No way out for you. And no cop can handle being=in-prison. — The whispering voice falls silent for a moment, theman takes a deep breath and his quiet gentle voice hisses in my direction again: — But it doesn't matter whether you plead guilty or not. You were condemned long-ago. You'll soon find that out. It-has-to-be. — Then the mask falls silent once again. This man accompanied his words with no movement whatsoever of his fat body or his glazed-looking facial features, making me uncertain whether it was really he who spoke to me. But now I pluck up the courage to ask him ?what he means by That, by my being-condemned, & ?who condemned me —. — But the man remains silent; and if that light I'd seen didn't occasionally flash between his narrow eyes, one could think he was asleep or dozing and completely absent. !But he spoke to me of his-own=accord —!who else could be speaking in=Here in this cell except him —, for the 1st time this mountain of flesh *directed* a few words at=me.

— Tell me your name. — I say to the mask. And am startled by my old professional voice: the-inspector interrogating the-arrestee; the-cop-voice with the monstrous echo chamber of the-state behind me, which gets a response of punches & kicks Inhere, sometimes a knife in the ribs. — But the man I'm addressing doesn't react atall; lies motionless in his bunk like a colossal idol.

— You know my name & have known it for a long time. — The gentlequiet voice finally reaches me.

— Tell me your name. — I insist, now feeling braver, with a strong smell of burning in the unclean cell air, suffocatinglysweet like boiling blood.

Without a trace of impatience or displeasure, the gentlequiet voice answers unchanged from the mask of flesh: — My name is Sunardi Orhan Battchrudin. For-manyyears I have been known as: Orfan Batt.

—!*Orfan Batt* —!*Orfan Batt* — *he's bigandfat* !*Orfan Batt* —

The mocking choir of shrill children's voices stabs the ears of the corpulent boy sitting alone in a corner of the dusty playground. A mere 6 years old, he was recently brought here = to the orphanage-for-diplomats'-children in the south of Berlin, GeeDeeR. He doesn't understand or speak German; for=him the children's shouting has the same shrill voice as thescreaming of the death squads in his native country when fire&slaughter ravaged his=home in Medan, the city in the north of Sumatra. First individual voices, — soon others joined in, taking up the rhythm of the-chants, and finally the-yelling-choir:

—!*Death-to-the-communists.* !*Strike them* !*down.* !*Strike them* !*dead.* —

Once again, the shrieks of individual voices emerge from the mass: — *The-communists want to ban all the-American-films & rock'n'roll.* — And again thechorus: —*!Strike them !down. !Wipe them !out. !Death-to-the-communists. !Death.* — Rushing along the street where he lives with burning torches & shouting. The-hordes in their battle gear with the colours of burning petrol, youngmen in plain clothes mingle with them, THEY cast screams & flames into every house, constantly yelling their litany-of-murder from frenzied firemouths:

—*!Death-to-the-communists. !Strike them !down. !Wipe them !out. !Death. !Death.*

By the hair & clothes, seized by fists, THEY drag pull kick men women out into the streets with their children wholefamilies, clingingto=eachother like creepers, beaten into heaps, throw them in thedirt — in the churning haze the swish of clubs & flames the shrill twittering of wire nooses around bared throats — screams pleading begging for !mercy, spitbubbly gurgling from tightened wire nooses — twitching feetscraping eyes bulging from sockets — then the bodies slump down, lie strewn wildly across the trampled streetdust like chopped-up blocks of wood, flies & dogs drawn to pools of blood & open skulls. The frenzied wave of pogroms by the-Pancasila-troops floods yelling raging throwing fire into more remote areas of the settlement; here the-fires comfortably continue to gobbleup the slowly collapsing, defenceless leftovers of houses — and a deathly calm descends on the places abandoned by the murderers, the dry squelching of flames & the wet squelching of dogs'-tongues-in-the-blood. —

His home was almost untouched, there was no fire nestled inside, the-flames from the torches couldn't do much, the house stands in the affluent-people's-quarter, is made of strong tiles and: not wooden boards & bast fibre like the huts of the farmers&

handymen in the poorer parts of the city. Only a phew window-panes and the front door were shattered by stones & boots, the thin stakes of the front garden fence broken like ribs. ?Where has the husband got to. The woman looks around hastily but can't see her husband anywhere. ?Did thesquads ?take him. Then things look bad for him. . . . .The delicate woman, a mother of three, grabs the little ones off the street where THEY had driven them from the house & kicked them into thedust. The mother's face is bleeding heavily; a broad flap of skin, the result of a knife cut, hangs from her cheek. This cut will disfigure her face forever. For now the woman pay no attention to it; they are all still !alive. Only her husband is missing. With arms outstretched, ignoring the stream of blood from her face, she woman drives her=children back into the house. — The father is there. : The woman screams, tries to cover her children's eyes, they mustn't see Anything, but 2 hands aren't enough for 3 pairs of eyes, the youngest has seen it: the father's head, placed in a fruit bowl in the hallway to form a still life, stares at his entering family with a shattered gaze and the sullenly irate features of the-beheaded. —The woman dashes out, the children follow her. The 5yearold Sunardi also tries to, but slips up in the pool of blood in front of the table-with-still-life, hitting the floor in the viscous blood goo from his father's torso. Everything !Red —:Red smeared on the little hands, the boy's body, his hair Red, sickly=sweet the cold stench of blood and the taste in the boy's mouth. Several times, trying to get up and run after his mother & siblings, he skids on the slippery floor —. He is anointed with his dead father's blood. — Then he is grabbed by hasty hands : his mother has returned & pulls her son from the mess. Outside, in the street in this turbulent darkness spilling over with yelling & screaming, while the woman fetched the boy from the house, she lost her other two children : military vehicles squashed the little bodies under their massive tyres (no doubt the soldiers in the vehicles didn't even notice, for such heavymachinery these two children's bodies=in-the-dirt were just 2 little fleas). She lost two children to save the one.

—!*Orfan Batt* —!*Orfan Batt* — *he's bigandfat* !*Orfan Batt* —

That same night, the woman runs through the streets & alleys of Medan, making her way mostly through side roads because, so she thinks, The-Mob isn't raging as terribly as in the avenues & squares. She wants to go to the Chinese embassy, her husband is —:*was* a diplomat, she wants to beg the ambassador for protection for=herself=&=her=child. — But the woman was wrong : in the alleys & side streets she runs into glaringlight. Like blocks of steel, sharp floodlights place metal-hard light against the night against wandering figures. There isn't just 1 woman fleeing but manydozens, fleeing into the narrowing streets, like a funnel, into thetrap : mouths wideopen, wanlight skins with bleeding cross-hatched wounds, flesh hewn out tattered, clubs sticks thrash beat slapping down on the falling fallen, heads faces burst open by clubs. The woman finds herself on the edge of a wide square. There used to be big rallies here on independence-day (until recently, banners with Nasakom slogans : *Unity of nationalism, religion and communism!* flapped in the trees & twisted in-the-wind as streamers —); now mass-executions : the-screams drowned out by shrieking military loudspeakers, commands & squeaking American rock'n'roll mewsick. The lined-up people collapse like rotten posts under-the-blows of cudgels axes machetes. Bulldozers then pile the naked the dead the mutilated the violated onto open trucks, which drive to the city's outskirts. Dump the bodies in big dug-out pits, earth maws — opened wide for lifeless flesh (theair thickening with the putridglazed stench

— heavy clouds hang over the-place): *were those ?!people,*
degraded once more sliding tumbling swinging into the nameless
end of a pit. The naked dead plunge down like streams of coins in
a great inflation — and swarms of insects. . . . . descending black-
furiously with shrill humming whirling from a glowinghumid
night sky (lightning flickering in the distance, a silent tropical
storm beyond the horizon) — pelting down like sudden showers
the chitin projectiles of gluttonous insects on the baked-up dough
of human flesh — dusted with tipped lime like ash from the-
netherworld. Done. — The-youthful-death-squads move on, the
sharp floodlights go out. And silence. Silence & darkness over
this place Afterwards, just isolated choking sounds from the
mouths of the not-yet-dead lying around, the odd arm stretched
upwards pokes through the limy haze, begging for-help. The
hectic mercurial stumblingrunningrushingonwards remained
silent beneath heavytropicalrain — —

The delicate woman, firmly reaching for the boy with an
iron=grip, drags him away with=her. Her touch holds a warmth
that flows through the little body —. She has taken flight with
her only remaining child, as if running into a black lightless
gaping maw.

But the woman is not afraid of thedangers-of-fleeing. The fat
stupid idol-of-flight, with his giant frog mouth & an insatiable
stomach into which his tentacles stuff the-defenceless, all those
he can catch — the omnivore of human compulsions. . . . .
:Whoever submits to him by allowing fear to well up inside=them
(the-idol recognises thisfear in the eyes of people who gaze dully
and dustpalely like the eyes of dying snakes) is lost from the-start.
But whoever resists fear resists their own extermination; they can
escape from the-idol. The woman's disfigured face seems to her
like a protective spell. She also feels surrounded by the dead : her

husband, two of her children — someone who deals with the-dead is in a state-of-death themselves, ?!what dangers should she ?fear !then. Being undead, all she wants is to keep her 5yearold son alive. Herflight from the country has begun.

The days are the first things to change. They have kept their corset of hours, they still cloak with darkness and illuminate the morning hours when they return — but !how these days !arm themselves; !how they have !lost their simplicity, their triviality and nonchalance : now the days are full of turbulence. They throw it at the fugitives like hailstones —!run !rush, ?what else. In the tightly-squeezes ironcages-of-hours they have to make sure they !get further, and don't get stuck clinging to the bars of time as it grows everscarcer like breathing air. *It has to be.* Says the mother to the boy, time after time, when she wants him to make particular haste. *!Come on. !Keep !moving. !It !has !to !be.* By that she presumably means wanting-to-stay-alive; lying or even sitting down at the wrong time would mean submitting to death. The days merge into a pulsating tube — like the peristalsis of a throat, the-refugee-masses retch their way through this tight, pumping intestine. They, as the woman probably suspects, are already in=the-belly of the gluttonous idol without realising. ?How could That ?happen: she took !suchgood care of her=boy & herself day&night —. ?Did she turn to the ?wrong person for=help once, bribe a ?traitor. The fat idol knows many helpers who supply him & are unconditionally willing to do him any-service. Yes, it happened, the idol-of-flight saw her=need and her fear, stretched out his tentacles & sucked her into his maw —. She can count herself lucky that the idol let her and her=boy live. (*!So manycorpses lying in the middle of streets & paths, bellies bloated & mouths gaping, flashing their greyish teeth, they lie there & stink, flies rats dogs are upon=them. We're still !alive. In*

277

our body we're in=the-greatbody of the idol.) Well, the fat stupid idol will digest them for a bit —, then he'll excrete or spit them out at some point, like thewhale did with Jonah in that oldstory. One knows about that. That sort of thing happens Every-where & allthetime. But until then, the fugitives are in the !greatestdanger inside the idol. . . . . Most-importantly, they must !not get themselves arrested. Then THEY would immediately throw them in one of the the-internment-camps, into the wretched-masses THEY keep=imprisoned behind-barbedwire until they die of thirst or hunger or fever or dysentery. And they mustn't get caught by marauding gangs either — THEY would strike them dead on the spot, as no one would pay a ransom for=them — or if they were human-trafficking gangs, THEY would take them to the-Malayan-slave-markets. . . . . And in=their=need the fugitives would also have to !unlearn their faith in other people, yet keep entrusting themselves to others : intheundergrowth by border rivers, on beaches, before straits or on mountain paths, in the slums of big cities & at harbours the cunning helpers flock to them like swarms of malaria mosquitoes, murmuring their promises to smuggle them through & hide them from-the-authorities with honeyed voices & grinding teeth into the ears of allthe-desperate, where they pop like soap bubbles : the inflation of those unfit-for-survival, withoutlustre withouthappiness: unsuspecting without cunning, low-spirited clumsy and in the way of life because they don't want to die, but stupidity makes them too soft on alltheothers and value themselves so little that they will always allow theothers=thestrongerones the 1 kick They need to keep on kicking, & haven't found anyone weaker to kick except themselves; freedom is as unaffordable for them as the delicacies in the lounges of posh hotels at benefit parties for the-persecuted-in-the-world —:those who live Every=where but are unfit for life, whom THEY always know how to lure & sew into-uniforms the way incenturiespast they were dressed in animal furs for the-arena: *!Into-the-sand !Into-battle* — : — pushed aside trampled, let them die they must die they will die. People die quickly in these parts of the world, where people sprout up again faster than mushrooms. In sweltering heat dulling suffocating, pressing on the lungs, in the yellow-moist sweat-fumes of fever and fear, the days weigh heavy on the fugitives, who drag themselves on, bent over —*!It !has !to !be* — in the twilight shimmer within the entrails of the terrible idol, who hasn't spit them out yet, who doesn't yet want to forgo these two fine specimens of the epitome-of-flight: a worn-down mother with the only one of her children that's still alive. !How moved the idol is by this story. So he's happy to watch a little longer.

The woman has a goal. She remembers former colleagues of her husband, the diplomat, in various Asian cities where European & North American representatives-of-state-interests reside. That is where the woman wants to go with her child, she wants to break out of thestream-of-the-lost, she seeks a foothold & support from the political caste to which she feels she belongs. (After all, she went to numerous diplomatic receptions at the embassies & consulates in-her-husband's-company Backthen.) !What a boring story this is going to be, thinks the idol-of-flight, !what a predictable result. To spice it up a little, he adds an infection to the wound in the woman's face, now a fever is already entering her delicate body; without medical attention, she is at risk of septicaemia & a slow, agonizing death. !So. There we are. And now let's see how these former colleagues of her murdered husband, these fine diplo-matic gentlemen in their nice air-conditioned residences, !react to this injured woman with a 5yearold brat-on-her-arm, helpless run-down sick homeless, washed up at their doorstep from the immeasurable flood of roving wretched unfortunates. The gloating idol is already looking forward to this, even though he has long known the-outcome of this episode. Too often has he the idol-of-flight seen heard this peeved dismissal, people being told that the-gentlemen are notathome, these stupid lies & behind politically-infused set phrases (*At this junkture our-country !cannot afford any conflict with the new rulers of Indonesia. The-situation is much too !serious for us to — Our government has already sent a note-of-pro-test, with e!specially !clear wording, I can assure you, to the new rulers in Jakarta so that our politickal misson —*), the pathetically-concealed excuses in their uni-form steely=bureaucratic coolness during the last thousandyears, as long as there have been refugees, for him to set the dull straw of his emotions on fire with a single spark of interest. — But thefever this woman has; thefever drives her into thejaws of the other, the bigger, more power-full idol: death. *!That !must !not !happen.* The woman kindles these words, each one a !torch, in her=brain as an opposing fire to fight the flames of the fever spreading inside=her. . . . . Her face has grown even narrower, tapering down to a pointed chin, but is not gaunt or haggard. The skin of her cheek next to thewound is smooth, it appears in a tiredyellow shade. But her eyes, though the fever gleams through them, have life in them. She gazes at her son with strange eyes. Watches him. The child, the little 5yearold bloated with parasites now sitting asleep at her feet, remains so oddly calm, submissive, during allthistime-of-deprivation, of being-hunted, of hardships; immersed=in=himself, he has long since run out of tears. He barely steps outside. He is haunted by A Dream Image, even when not sleeping (the burrowing hunger robs him of allpeace anyway) : his father's severed head, placed in the fruit bowl, appears to him again&again, the eyes, wideopen but blinded by death stare directly=at=him. ?Why didn't anyone

!close his eyes. ?Must Father now stare=at=him for ?alleternity.
. . . . This preoccupies the boy, more than Everythingelse=around-
him. What he'd like-most would be to turn back immediately, to
run to the house in Medan, to that hallways & do what the-
killers neglected to do with his father's head. But the boy also
knows that his father's head would no longer be in the fruit bowl
in the hallway & staring into=nothingness with his wide-open
blind eyes —:probably the new residents have already thrown it
to the-rats to=eat along with the rest of his body. So he, the boy,
would be !toolate. This Toolate, this ultimate missed opportunity,
leaves the boy nopeace. And so he resolves: When I'm Grown-
up & can kill people myself, I'll close every dead body's eyes
& all the holes in their heads !tight. so the-dead don't have to
see Anything, hear Anything or say Anything, & most-of-all: so
they can't stare at !him anymore. When I'm Grown-up there'll
be. . . . . peace, with thetaste of his father's blood indelibly in his
mouth. (The boy utters a quiet sound.) And The Impatience also
rises inside=him: he can hardly wait to !finally be a Grown-up.
— The quiet noise, like the squeaking of a mouse, makes his
mother take notice. And because she feels unobserved, her gaze
rests on the child at her feet. This gaze (not intended for anyone
except the child) : not feigned, not put on, not rehearsed, but
genuine, a look of deep pity, as if nature were gazing with these
eyes (but pity for ?what: for the-life that might be ?awaiting
this child), a dark concern and a great bewilderment, as if looking
at this child for the 1st and last time. But in the darkness of her
gaze there is also a quiet caring for this child — her=caring for
this boy will extend so far in time, far beyond her=death. The
woman, she has forgotten herself entirely, one looks inside=her
as one looks through a door coincidentally left open to see the
interior of an unknown house. —

With gradual but inexorable determination, thefever burns up the mother — herface swollen, fattened, the wound festering and oozing from scabby openings, a ghastly sight ill-suited to moving anyone she might beg for=help. *The-leper* (many who see the woman think she has the-plague or leprosy) *had better !disappear=!rightnow. !Away from our door, !Away from our house. !Away & !out of town. Now, if she were an !appetizing refugee woman with a !cute little child, like on the posters-asking-for-contributions by the-refugee-charity — but not a hag like that with a cut-up mouth & carrying an ugly fat kid like a sack on her back —!No thankyouverymuch. Hey: !police.* Now the woman-with-the-child is an-outcast for good. Even the gluttonous idol-of-flight doesn't want to keep her any longer, he spits her out, spits her far away. And here, at this point, Everything would be over, it would be the-end of Everything that counts. But It still goes on. *It has to be.* The woman only dies in Moscow. That's how !far the idol-of-flight spat her & her=boy — over menacingly-towering jungles with prickly vines & poisonous creatures — over thewatermasses of the sea, the shiny backs of the waves rising to the far-flung firmament, torrents of rain lash down on the fugitives in their tiny boat from clouds puffedup like timpani — they plunged through Allthis on the trajectory spat by the idol-of-flight, whirling floundering through the rapids of these times, often going under, then seized from the-furnaces of thefever by the paws-of-chance with the upward force of *!It !has !to !be*, then flung away out of disgust at the dying woman & onto dry, stony land. Monsters floods hot dry storms like never-fading screams over steppes & tundra, sharp-toothed mountain edges tear shreds out of smooth celestial heights, & storms again, sharp scorching, dust clouds drift over burnt-out rocks like saw blades, cutting the horizons to pieces —. But here there are railway tracks, roads — where there are rails, there are trains, roads know the anonymous dashing of car metal — the two fugitives are picked up. Then there are localities, smaller towns with stations, and finally the looming capitals of countries with their old names Yerevan — Tiflis — Grozny — Kerch — Taganrog — Rostov. Finally the Trans-Siberian Railway brings the woman to Moscow to die. Before her life fades out, the woman (who strikes the-representative-officials as mysterious, hence suspicious; they surround the-deathbed day&night, her imminent death is the only thing preventing the-representatives-of-the-state-authorities from dragging her out of hospital & throwing her directly in=jail) provides 1 last address: relatives of her dead husband in Berlin, GeeDeeR; they've lived there since her husband became ambassador-of-Indonesia. They should send the boy there, to this address. The woman dies shortly afterwards, thinking that her=child will be in-good=hands with their relatives. And because it was her last belief, this woman will keep it For=ever. — But when the boy arrives in Berlin, GeeDeeR on one of the flights for Soviet-embassy employees, these relatives are no longer to be found. They were recalled to Jakarta under-strict-secrecy (It is said) a few days ago. And for the lonely boy, theworld morphs into a monstrous empty cave. . . . . Cold winds whistle as they sweep over his face. ?Where is this meanwhile 6yearold child from Indonesia to go now. There is a place for children=like-him.

    —!*Orfan Batt* —!*Orfan Batt* — *he's bigandfat* !*Orfan Batt* —

For the boy, this recurring and incomprehensible refrain shouted by his age-mates at=the-orphanage just south of Berlin, GeeDeeR is a long steel needle. (All he understands is the-rhythm of malice & mockery in this shouting) — a thorn that pierces his skull — going in deeper and deeper with each repetition —;

besieged by pain, the boy presses his little fists against his ears.
Now he has to listen to the shrill calls as a dull blubbering. He
can't get rid of THEM. Red waves of anger froth up in the boy,
spilling sorely against the brain pan inside his head. The round
little childish body, carried by two short fat legs, is already filled
with rage & resentment after his experiences of murder death
humiliations & thedangers on his almost year-long flight cling-
ing-to-the-hand-of=his-mother, before finally having to come here
to this unfamiliar, strange country with restrained vegetation &
baffling people who mock him with incomprehensible sounds.
The death of his mother before-the-end-of-their-flight instilled
glowing red-hot streams of lasting despair in the boy, because
even a child can already learn that no one has a chance against
death. So the plump little body has already been filled up with
such a brew of pain fear & disparagement; it won't take many
more such humiliations that he doesn't want to hear, but has to
hear nonetheless; so it will soon erupt, hisanger. . . . .

   —!*Orfan Batt* —!*Orfan Batt* — *he's bigandfat* !*Orfan Batt* —

?!Which of the 6yearold inmates of that institution would
have known !what 'orphan' means in order to twist the name
Orhan into !this ?word. :It was the-minders & the-teachers who
mangled the boy's real name. So !they had given him up to the
other children's appetite-for-mockery, the-minders & the-teachers,
by giving the stranger, the other this mangled name as taunting
material : divide & rule, the !bestway to discipline an institution.
Because humans are moronic from=an-early-age: in their=wishes,
in their=drives & actions, in every ordeal they inflict on others :
dogged=in-their-insistence, with no care for the suffering they
cause. Fullofrelish they prod & prod again, they harass, torment;
repeat their=I-deas-for-torture until they turn ash-grey —. Once
they find someone for their=will to humiliate, the-whipping-boy

on whom to take out their anger&insolence, then they stick=to=him like leeches, even when this results in harm to them or the threat of destruction. Even while=dying they carry on with their=acts, like the sheep at the-slaughterhouse that collapses in a fit of twitching after being shot by a bolt gun, yet carries on to its Last Breath doing what it spent its=life doing: chewing. From=an-early-age, humans are not fundamentally evil, devious, malicious or back=stabbing; above=all, as already stated, they are stupid. Trapped in a compulsive repetition of whatever allowed them to gain pleasure 1ce. Because the-will=of-humans= to-pleasure is A Greatpower.

The 6yearold, holding the heavy hammer with bloody clumps of skin&hair stuck to it, stood motionless over the boy sprawled out on the smoothcold tiles of the showers. Waves of twitching still went through his body, bloody threads of saliva ran from the trembling mouth. A few moments later, the boy lay still. When the-staff, fetched by screaming children, appeared in the showers, the 6yearold was in the process of calmly sewing up the dead boy's eyes with a steady hand. The-minders stood speechless, frozen, before this scene. Then, after a longtime, one-of-them dared to extend his hand to the 6yearold, who had almost finished his sewing work — (another was meanwhile dragging the hammer carefully out of the child's reach with his shoe) —; in a slow, calm (but inwardly trembling) voice, he called the 6yearold by his proper full name: *Sunardi Orhan Battachrudin.* The boy's reaction was friendly. Perhaps !that was !all he had wanted to bring about: to be called by his proper name Here=at-the-orphanage too. — *It has to be.* He said in a quiet & clear voice, as if someone had asked him the-reason for his bloody-deed. But presumably the-minders who had rushed to the scene were !tooappalled to ask a stupid question like *?Why did you do* *that.* The 6yearold let the-minder lead him out without any resistance. And later, several years later, this orphanage too in the south of Berlin, GeeDeeR, was visited by certain men with aliases like Makepeace, Darling, Lovejoy, emissaries of the-state, — they showed greatinterest in such murderously=talented-children. — And was, as he told me himself while he was My-Friend, with COSUBO = during the bestyears of my life.

— That was what I wanted to tell you as *Willfried Berger,* Chief Inspector, that day in your office. ?Can you still ?hear me.
— —

— —!A call : my name — and open my eyes. Blue light in the cell night, with no visible source, like paint on the compact air block. And !again : my name. A few figures entered while I was asleep; they emerge from theblock of the cell night. Fill the tightness like stakes. Heads seem to be mounted on these stakes, like skulls of the decapitated, planted there for the triumph of the overpowerers & the terror of the lowly people. And the faces in these skulls gape like masks at a carnival of the worst convict-faces — they wobble & push their way through the shimmering blue sweat-fumes of this cell, over to me, lying tied up on my bunk. Close to my head, the face of a man. A !tube stuck in the crook of my left arm — ?!What's going on Here. ?!What's going to happen to=me. — With great effort I turn my head slightly — : in front of the cell wall, I see thefleshmass of Orfan Batt flowing from a stool.

He sits there, the back of his head with the grey smooth greasehair leaned against the wall, his inert doughy face seems to have been observing me for a long time; now too, the narrow eyes, sparkling between rolls of fat in the colour of hardened molten metal, prove his constant vigilance in the conviction of his own invincibility. The skin stretched over thisface with its flat nose, in the bluish shimmer of indifference like a mask made from a strange, unknown metal, an ore-of-the-future that will one day be extracted from mines on the moon or Mars, a metal already fashioned Today into a mask whose form must come from times & epochs mucholder than the-formulas for black-smithing as we know it; and the metal for this mask contains unspeakable forces & testifies, through its bluish shadowy radi-ance, yet-unknown possibilities of cruelty horror & death; only a few sounds, spoken whispered murmured through the mouth slit in this moon-hard expression of cosmos-filling indifference towards any inferno, just 4 words are enough to unleash devas-tation: — It has to be. — No more than that from this mouth slit in themask. Calm, careful & quiet, an exhalation of metal. Sharp-burning cold casts itself over me, a wash of mortal fear.

Now a further figure among the men who entered steps up to my bunk. It seems he has already been talking at me for quite-sometime, the way a bored judge reels off the endless list of the-delinquent's charges & offences or a priest mumbles the-lines of his prayer for one-condemned-to-death; I see the lips moving, but can't hear what he is saying. The sight of his face also distracts me : constant storms flicker through his face, as if a film projector were casting every conceivable facial expression of which humans are capable onto this=1 face in rapid succession. — I was meant to stop here. I won't stop, I'll continue, overrun my=time. — Behind this one, other faces now move forward : a broad fleshy face full of dark-red fire scars with a rugged copper nose; then a little yellowy rat-face, the eyes nose mouth look as if they've been drawn together with a strong thread, as if the little beastly mouth were meant to cover up a far-bigger hole in this skull. — The one who's clearly the eldest in this group slowly building up in front of my bunk is also the smallest, barely 5 feet tall. Above his sunken slim ribcage I see the wrinkled, undeveloped face of a sick child; flat drained face. Leftover twines of hair on an oversized head, his skin looks like mouldy fruit in the blueshimmerlight. The sight is reminiscent of creatures veget-hating in lightless clammy backyards in the-slums of big cities, the palepoisonous progeny of sprawling lumpenproletarian families, humanoids cast incesstuously into the world, gathered around the fleshmass of a so-called father; early-too-early manybeatings bits of firewood broken shards scolding bawlinginfants snot screams & tears, the-police-radio-patrol constantly returning. The Graves-diseased eyes wide apart in a fish-bright gape, the near-toothless little mouth twisted into a devious grin, have made all that is profoundly evil in children come to the fore in this character over-the-years, cunning out of early hardship. — These faces are what was carved out of justice & leftover Today as its inhairitance, the-grim-asses. Age=long scratching burrowing scraping away at humanness, like bulldozers digging up waste from the soil to bring to=light a daily lie-f of revenge & retaliation, has deformed humans; like tools of extermination, both of others and themselves; constant, cold, poisonous, with murder on their tongues. Manifestations-of-constancy emerged from all the changes, bureaucratic reshuffles & modifications enacted in=this-country during the mostrecent periods; inseparably visible truths that attach themselves neither to Yesterday nor Today nor Tomorrow, but are&remain=the-same . . . . . as they=always were. Which means that The-Human-World is shaped not by figures-of-high-rank&importance, but by the ability of The-Human-World to absorb practically allthefigures that were ever active in it, to assimilate them, & thus to help them gain dominance &

importance, even though those same ones were meaningless creatures before. The-void=in-them produces thepower to carry on under allcircumstances. — A chill not felt inhere for a longtime, blue-faced & sharp, creeps inside=me. Makes me freeze 1ce again. Now no more resistance to The-Injustice being inflicted on me — *It will soon come that I didn't* —:the thin voice of a child shouting at thestorm. It was awall=sostrong that a child could lean against it for a while. But suddenly thestorm stopped, the child had to fall, unheard. And that's why those-creatures are in the right: the-manipulated-right . . . . . It-has-to-be. So be It. —

The elder's clawpawy monkeyhands now pass a small case to the man with the twitchy face, who opens it carefully and takes out a further syringe. Undoubtedly !this one is meant for=me as well. And now I can make out his words, can hear what he's saying to me in an unexpectedly calm, almost soothing voice while fierce storms constant erupt on his face. And see the-colossus Orfan Batt rise slowly from the stool against the wall as if rising from his throne, themask with the heavy, tragic expression, cast in bronze flesh, now likewise steps up to my bunk & with reptilian serenity, he too seems to listen to his comrade's words & follow the progress of the execution. The One. He will outlive His=Time.

It goes without saying that this cell is bugged too; the usual cameras & microphones leave no corner of this deathspace unseen. (Everything WE can know, WE !want to know. . . . . : he always wipes his backside with his right hand, in the morning he has an erection, but ignores it. Many of his nights are full of screaming —.) After he was taken here as=planned, following the-tampering with the crime scene = the flat of his ex-wife in Hanover, I was given the task of observing this prisoner, the former Chief Inspector. After giving=myself up to this inspector under the name *Willfried Berger* — the real Willfried Berger was eliminated long ago. . . . . — I had already adopted his name and his=history, I put myself in his skin, as Many others will after me. And thus became an heir to what is associated with that name, just as the-crimes of states are passed on to their successors. Every name is just an empty shell, and whoever fills it out with their flesh must do whatever needs to be done in=that-name. His=knowledge is now mine; the-domestic-intelligence-service is particularly inter-ested in the years at COSUBO. As for who I am, I had to forget that for professional reasons — and after receiving a 'visit' from some gentlemen-in-uniform at the-remand-prison, THEY gave me the-choice: a longprisonsentence or collaboration. What's most-important is to accept situations that one can't change and see the Better Possibility. THEY pitted my knowledge against the knowledge of this inspector. Whatever I can report, I will report — whether it's arse-wiping, erections or his moans & screams at night, I operate on the same side of coldness & precision as the-bugging-devices : my=service to ourtime. The man who previously pursued Willfried Berger with his oldmethods — each of his suc-cesses brought him closer to=his-doom — now I'm pursuing him with allthenewmethods, a question of routine, to his final breath. It sounds different for each person. Now I'll listen for !his.

Now they're standing in a semicircle close:to his bunk in the diffuse blue light of this cell night. One-of-them starts speaking. — Calm down. No more cause for excitement. You managed It, you remembered well. Did what you could & what We expected of you. Did more than a police inspector is capable of. So there's no need to be ashamed. To be afraid. It won't take long now. — You want to ?say ?something. Go ahead.

— ?What was it=all for : the roundabout route, the long-pursuit thewaiting and hesitating. ?Why didn't you just knock me off muchsooner. Allthistime such an !effort. ?Why. And won't someone ?investigate. Afterall: a cop dying in jail.

He turns his head effortfully towards the previous speaker, his straggly greyhair flat against his skull. In his eyes, in his whole posture, I recognise thefear that he is trying to suppress with moreandmore questions, to draw out his=time. The-dawdling of the-condemned before execution.

— Whether mouse or elephant : the-hunt is better than the-catch. And no-hunt can match thehunt for a human. — Answers the man with the injection. — Your death: 1 of many drugdeaths= Injail. A former policeman who couldn't take it any more Injail. Just the-usual. But just lie calmly. Relax. It is time. Your work ends=here. You'll never have to work again. For mostpeople that would be the !best possible news. And you'll already leave this prison today.

I see that he is genuinely surrendering. He stretches out obe-diently in his bunk & even holds his bared arm out to the man with the syringe for him to tie the tourniquet. And looks tensely at the crook of his arm with the vein. The needle enters — a fine jet of blood immediately shoots into the tube. Then the plunger is pressed, the deadly serum flows into his body —.

A few minutes pass. He still wants to say something, but his voice is heavily weakened; he whispers haltingly: — ?Why ?me — the smallest — — player —

The man who gave the injection looks around from his flick-ering crazed-hasty features, doesn't seem to know this simplest of answers.

The fireface steps close=to him & speaks directly in his ear: — Whether small or Big : whoever gets close to Us has got too close to Us. Like those 4 women: whores who learnt too much about Us from their=customers & wanted to make=money with it. They wanted to blackmail Us. So simple and: you spent such a longtime looking for reasons. Always money&moremoney — life amonghumans is so boring & dreary that one would rather die now than later. You should be grateful to Us for re-leaving you of theburden of life's tedium. You'll have It over with in a moment. And truly being=human only occurs in=death. In short, those 4 women had to go. The-customers too. And that was all.

—!Enough now. It-has-to-be. — Orfan Batt suddenly intervenes; thewholething is taking too long for Him, too much chitchat.

But he doesn't stop. He'll keep asking questions for as long as his=strength allows. — But — he stammers quietly, — those — mutilations — those gruesome —. — His voice is only a breath now, the voice of a dying man.

And once again the man with the fiery face answers him. Hastily this time, otherwise he'll be speaking to a corpse: — That was simply for pleasure. Every profession has its own art. Sometimes just the arse of art. Questions & more questions, to the last gasp, Chief Inspector: the Art of Askery. If you try to find a reason for everything, you'll lose yours. — He looks at Orfan Batt & adds, presumably in the hope of still reaching the dying man: —!Nip it in the-bud. !Stamp out the embers. — And pulls the tube out of his arm.

Then Orfan Batt spits in the face of a dead man.

The-murderers get the Last Word. One day in the unexpectedly hot April of 2020, the-prison-gates open for Orfan Batt —: that's what one used to say. Today it's the prison door that discharged prisoners have to pass, like the shop-bought door to a block of flats; His fleshmass is almost toomighty. He skweezes laboriously through the narrow doorway. — Outside, The Day thawing in bright light — above, the sparkling, dazzling sun-embers and the still spring-cool air stand swaying in blue masses, reaching up to the sky like a morning sea —. — The fat old man stops below, on the dawn street, breathing heavily, & slurps=up this trickling air in deep draughts, like a drink. The drink from an otherworld.

Outside of the-prison He seems awkward, out of place, Out=Here the bronze quiet of his mask almost seems like fear. He ventures his next steps tentatively, carries his incredible bodily mass further, cautiously probing and withdrawn, not looking around him. And so He doesn't notice me, His-Friend, who betrayed him on 2 occasions manyyears ago & will do so a 3rd time before this days is over. He drags his immensebody along the street, indifferently passing house fronts carbide-grey like badly-brushed teeth —, the jailcase in His hand seems woman-ishly=small like a handbag. ?Where will He go. ?Will He seek out the-place where The Boss ?expects him to go : where WE will expect Him.

A few street lamps are still glowing in the last bits of night-gloomy dawning avenues. His=shadow is agile, it follows Him with ease, leaps about in front of Him, dodges aside, rushes ahead — the way shadows are, lighter than the spring air. But no power in the world can move shadows if they aren't moving by themselves. I, in the name-shell of Willfried Berger, am one of His shadows that He drags withhim into the earlycold morning hour of a city that has grown foreign to Him during the-years=of-his-imprisonment. He'd been inside for a longtime, moneybag= states punish tax evasion more severely than murder, because for such=a-state there are always fartoomany people, but never enough taxes. The sun hasn't yet driven out the nightly chill from the deep cuts in the roads&avenues, the V-shaped valleys of the housing blocks lying-in-wait, nor bitten completely through the fog above them; and so thecity shines above the-streets & rooftops in a veil of glistening solar haze, with the rows of awakening windows squinting. Different tools for different crimes are required Here, ones He can't know about. His heavy, waddling steps become slower, He's unused to walking so long and often has to stop and rest. But I keep following him, sticking secretly to His heels; pause when He pauses & walk when He walks. I, His=shadow, don't want to catch Him up, He isn't meant to notice me; but I want to see if He will reach His final destination. (Thestone of betrayal weighs heavy from a previous life, all my transgressions still glowing & theguilt gnawing inside=me like a vulture's beak. Want to see Him sink into the deepchasms of this-time — into=!nothingness, into=!oblivion with Him. Only then will I be quiet.) Meanwhile thecity pounces on Him in too-mult from the slowly-warming morning hour —

Mild earlylight smoothes edges, rounds off the spiky brittle edges&corners of the houses. There are still delicate clouds of steam rising from the night-cold asphalt in little spirally mists, — then the delicate veils are shredded by the flaring wheels of car bodies, the grinding din. Small shops & big department stores businesses & factories tower high from the-hours of quiet, push down the 5-storey houses in their sandstone colours, steps whirl rushing from doors into other doors, push along-pavements, up down subway entrances, into buses for the morning bodystream of thebigcitycrowd. Petrol-yellow taste on their tongues while the sun's arcs above sandstone & glass facades slide down & are crushed by hissing tyres into spraying bow waves of light dust. *A roller coaster of emotions!* Bouncing along the viaducts the metallic canon of commuter trains, longdistance&freighttrains, light that slipped away from the morning stroboscopes through the carriage windows, the card-punchers for the early shift, delayed rabbits dash into-the-vegetated-depths of parks, dogs hastily paw their way along the flagstones from corner-to-corner (time&again lifting a hind paw —:!how can they piss thatoften), children jerked away by mothers fathers, bawling flailing displeasure & stubbornness into the earlyhour, the viaducts drone with the tiled bass of old clinker bricks, a spill of soapfoamy rinselight from a shop door —, leaves a darkwet tongue on the granite flagstones. *Tell us yourself, Consumer Berger: is that still fast food?* — Every advertising poster people pass addresses thosepeople=purrsonally, by name & sometimes in a flattering, sometimes in a boisterous voice; me as well & everyone else, except Him. No one knows Him or His name Here, He has no customer profile; He was locked away in=nothingness toolong for theadvertising-industry to target Him. So He drags himself along, unmolested & anonymous, although a few passers-by have already noticed that the machines didn't address Him; He doesn't pay attention or: He doesn't even know that !such a circumstance is suspicious Nowadays (: 1=ofthese ?anti-consumers); I follow Him, the grotesquely waddling wobbling body-bubble — as He stops open-mouthed & gasps for air. The shabby clothes, Hisbodilymass seemingly poured into them, are reminiscent of jail. Panting sweating He continues his path along wide avenues, beneath towering church steeples that suddenly smash their sonic shards out of the hourblock from 2000year=depths & clash them down on the heads of the passers-by with an iron racket — ***Pure entertainment and nothing but the best! Especially for you, Consumer Berger*** — the flood of city tides washes thecrowds from the residential areas to the hot springs of busyness in offices shops factories — the hoarsely rustling wingbeats of printed adverts&newspapers chased with sighing gusts of wind across pavements & gutters **SALE EVERYTHING MUST GO CONSUMER BERGER!** — *Clearance sale! Up to 85% off! Consumer Berger, pay us a visit! We'll be expecting you with great offers, just for you!* — the letters numbers pictures with colourful paper feathers whirl in the suction-of-the-drains lurking for eager wills to rekindle an ever-new glow in the rapidly-fading eyes — CONSUMER BERGER: COME TO US AND FIND THE LOAN OF YOUR LIFE — while in quasi-suburban residential areas, the low noise-tide spreads as if at the bottom of a tide-worn sea of pensioneresque daily quiet — every bigcity is first-of-all a small town; inside every city-dweller there's a villager. Then it finally rises: theday. — Rushing feet, hot & still business-sore from yesterday, humming brains, thegazes duty-strict, pro-fessionally-flashed red-bordered smile-teeth like the chrome radiator grille on fancy cars — *You too can have new teeth, Consumer Berger, at a great price!* — call out make noise ascend in communicating vessels frothing fill the busily-churned air. And spring swims in this air, the gonads skulk in=the-service-of-the-drives, induce risky man-oeuvres, women girls offer more of their winter-pale skin than usual to the-prying-eyes — *Love in full swing! The worldwide theatre hit has now come to our city too. Let us entice you, Consumer Berger, your happiness is dear to us!* — gin-light umbels in fresh green shadowed branches of whisky-yellow pollen poured out over stone streets & asphalt emitting their spicy aroma-floods into the smelt-out nostrils in glassy eyes, tongues roll re-tasting glandular moistness, eyes flail along hips-thighs-necks, swirling limbs, stuttering world pollu-tions *Beautiful breasts affordable for every woman!* (:That's how far things have come, now they leave out the personal address)

— between the slickly boastful letters-of-advertising-slogans from the chemical scent-buds of sickly-sweet perfumed spring *LA VIE EST BELLE* the high city birds' voices in a constant twittering of young=girlishly rhythmic pop music as trembling swirling sequin-glitzy layers of haze infiltrating even the subway tunnels of all unconsciousnesses, hurled up in rows & columns of doctored account balances to strict irrefutably convincing stock market prices, above the streets the gilt-edged cloud-banks & hard-nosed effete creatures with energetically clean-shaven jaws, their necks tie-dily=constricted, larynxes pumping intensely (!always keep the top button !done up) poured out over the-places like a rain of meteorites as snappy slogans in the voices of heavenly heralds, people only have to open their mouths to-slurp this celestial nectar & the-happiness from the-heaven=ofmoney-&-speculation enters them via payment in extra-cheap instalments & lines of credit. The warm glistening tingling happiness of all belongers, who be=long as long as they can pay; & pay & pay & — JUVENILE™ *A little younger every day Consumer Berger. Now mature men too can preserve their youthfulness so easily* the over-affectionately=stroking industrial female voice informs me as I pass —; the smart shopping bags from the luxury boutiques swing along the-avenues, moving widely & energetically, alongside perfectly-formed women's legs stockinged with a hint of nylon —: this is where all the tentacles begin that quickly or slowly, almost imperceptibly, wrap themselves around the-happy-ones to be devoured by The Great Gullet of New Crimes & New Slavery. Manycorpses of happiness, thousands of hecatombs, but absolutely without bloodshed or any reek of putre-faction, justquiet nicesmells & noscreaming, all deaths invisible, transformed into electronic signals, pulsing withoutinterruption through thick bundles of fibre optic arteries in the bignetwork of permanent hygienic world peace. . . . . *The Golden Curtain this year for* | Orfan Batt : the bronze age of your=crimes is !over. Here&today your mask is powerless. !What is your ?mask next to a !matricks. Your corpses from formertimes are of no interest whatsoever to the cabaret, to comedy, to a tribunal & even to the-memorials for remembering the-crimes-of-humanism. You, trapped in this absurd bodily mass, drag the-bankruptcy of allflesh a few metres further through This Other World where you no longer belong. Only your path still ploughs through thestreamsofpeople, as a ship ploughs its soon-vanished trail into a large body of water. As if you, with your roving mass, wanted to curse thecity & the people in it one lasttime by your presence. Because cursing is so easy and has long stopped have any effect; yet you still seem to believe in thisforce. You : the immoderate fatso, dinosaur from the-Jurassic of crimes. . . . . — You often have to stop & catch your breath in the middle-of-the-street —; then people avoid you, because they don't want to collide with you & run into yourflabbymass : then for a moment the hard-closed faces burst open, some of their eyes poisoned by illnesses and imminent death, & the people walk-around-you, therock= inthebodystream of this city, annoyed shocked amused indifferent to thisobstacletoo —, & have already forgotten you a moment later in the flash of other short-lived desires & effemeral sensa-tions —; — and soon the surging crowdstream closes once more over your trail to form an undulating swirling com-packedness, erasing the last memory of your presence. — Now I know where you're going, I can tell where your ridiculous waddling steps are taking you, interrupted by heart palpitations sweating attacks breathlessness. You want to visit the-old-haunts of the-COSUBO= alumni, the scabby bars with the cobwebbed stories in frozen grins. But those bars are long gone Today, the doors have been crossed out with nailed boards, pasted over with hip posters for cinemas&popmusic; the 1 place became a daycare centre — from a murder club to a mothers' club : a sign of thetimes. And so you stand facing:it : your=past & all the futilities of your=life. *!Me-old-terror*, the way one says *!Me-old-mucker*. In the hard high light of noon, cut deep & sharply into the city by blades, every shadow-circle has a zero radius — now it's time: I reach for the mobile phone; I call the taxi, as ordered by the boss in a disgusted voice. Time for=you to stop.

Soon the large pale-yellow taxi with dark-tinted windows pulls up next to him at the roadside. He stops in bewilderment. The driver gets out, stands in front of theman and addresses him by throwing his head back. His mouth agape, theman stares at the taxi driver, this tiny little man. ?Does he suspect danger. . . . . ?Might this=dwarf be a ?danger to !him. he doesn't move, his bulky body doesn't budge an inch. The taxi driver, an aging man with an unshaven birdface, leaps to the side of his car chattering affably & opens the sliding door to the box-like interior. The door — the floodgate to falling darkness. Nolight from inside, a big black space. Theman hesitates. The taxi driver stands next to the open door like a guard, waiting patiently & quietly. Now he seems to understand; he looks around quickly, but can't find any-thing suspicious (I = hisshadow, invisible in the other shadow, stay in a gateway). Now thebody moves, the great hollow-mouthed opening looms towards him, he steps slowly & heavily into thedarkness as if stepping through the entrance of a wide, fathomless cave, one of the deepchasms in=the-rock-oftime with the meat grinder for Everything that must go. The car's suspen-sion sags as theman enters the car & takes a seat inside. His face turns towards the light=Outside 1 last time for a moment: the bronze features seem dull & faded, the thin lips move incessantly as if whispering longformulas. Finally I think I hear his last words. Because he has already said them sooften, he will speak them now too: *It-has-to-be.* — Then he disappears in darkness; the taxi driver shuts the sliding door hard. And the spacious vehicle with the dark windows & the-silver-star on the front, almost like the-symbol for eternallife, drives away quickly — it will drive veryfar out of town.

As far as the outskirts. . . . . Where a constant draught sweeps over barren soil & asphalt — dust flying about in the wind tunnels between old dilapidated 10storeyblocks from prefab days. They stand in the landscape like giant abandoned bunkers from some war-or-peace, sometimes these buildings just collapse & crush the last in-habitants, the outcasts, the impoverished & neglected, the illegal immigrants — no one to miss or mourn them, not even their own people. Brutalized ex-sistence burns as if from oil puddles behind dirty windowpanes. It used to be that people only dumped unwanted pets Out=here, Today it's also children that were born but not meant to be. Surplus life. Many of the abandoned pets survive & go wild, form packs & roam the cities looking for prey; the abandoned humans don't survive. A knacker's yard of tiny dead bodies, the stench of cold rotten flesh, all breath suffocated. Mutated & crippled scavengerbirds drift about this terrain in desolate flocks beneath the rough slapping of their dirtymoist wings, feral dogs stray about, tearing at skin&sinews, hurriedly dismember and rip apart the corpses, antssnailsworms take care of the rest — and soon only stripped little bones remain, scattered like lost Mikado sticks; scavengerbirds dogs insects always do a greatjob. Bulldozers a little later, they clear away the debris & piles of bones, their shovels churning up the corpsesoil. Then caterpillar tracks smooth out the surface & soon afterwards new housing blocks appear on this wasteground, 10 storeys high. Andsoforth. Speculators' property. Rarely any people on the windswept streets; only towards evening, then figures ooze out of smashed doors : marauding child gangs & crazies, rapists, blood=lustful psychojunkies — they flood along in droves between the housing blocks to flock together for their looting&murder rampages through the inner city, through the-evening through the-night; any stranger still walking the streets won't live long. The gangs surround the stranger in tighter&tighter circles, trapping him on-all-sides, silent withoutasound & with the relentlessness of machines in=action THEY throw him to the ground. THEY are pleased by the massivebody served up to them by-taxi; that way the fun will last longer. . . . . THEY will pounce on him &, as if THEY were the scavengerbirds dogs insection, THEY will shred him —. That man Out=There. . . . . who was encircled & killed in the cold cursed places of murderous hordes & lunatics, in=my-dreams that always used to be me. !Now&today it's !your turn : Orfan Batt, My-Friend; your remains for the-vermin. I'll be rid of you for=ever.

And the abyss and the emptiness are tempting with the magnetic breath of thesilence, which opens wide before my senses while faroff=inspace satellites-in-geostationary-orbits register these events too in their databases, converted into a few columns of 1s and: 0s. Invisible cloudpillars of the two digits rise noiselessly & constantly from allplaces allpeople & thicken into electronic clouds, the old misdeeds & never-punished crimes evaporate. The fangs of past curses become the seed for the soil of the light, unblemished fields : databases for the-modern-Boeotians. As boundless in their force as if theforce=of-the-thoughts=themselves could burn up all the dross, the whole remainder of crusted f-acts & old lies, scatter them to papery greasy ashes, already

disappearing with the next gust of wind or ordered deletion —.
New weapons new murderers. And lets the-dragonsteeth germi-
nate in the silicon-smooth guilt-freed ground of all displays for
the pay-triarchs of a New Thebes. Columns of 1s and: 0s : 2
scrawny digits create terror for this time. Everything else just dust
and shadows for Electronic=Eternity. . . . . It is done. *Perseverance
brings good fortune to the wanderer.*

Now I can be quiet.

Some of the descriptions and references in this novel to the events in Indonesia during the 1960s are based on Joshua Oppenheimer's documentary *The Act of Killing* (2011).

MAIN CHARACTERS

Irma Berger (née Mandt)
* 1936 in Kaltenfeld
† 1979 in Berlin, buried
  in Birkheim

Alois Berger
* 1930 in Kaltenfeld
† 1979 in Berlin, buried
  in Birkheimin

CHILDREN

1. Theresa
* 15 April 1956 in Kaltenfeld
† 2012 in Berlin

2. Willfried
* 13 September 1959 (during Irma's imprisonment)
† ?

Hilde
* 1912 in Aue
† 1989 in Aue

Gustav
* 1910 in Aue
† 1988 in Aue

Franziska
* 1915 in Berlin
† 1992 in Berlin

Max Herrmann
*1912 in Berlin
† 1990 in Berlin

CHILD: **Martha**
* 1935 in Aue
† 2005 in Berlin

CHILD: **Paul**
* 1934 in Berlin
† 2012

The Chief Inspector
* 1953 in Hanover
† 2013 in remand in Berlin

Sunardi Orhan Battachrudin alias **Orfan Batt**
* 1960 in Medan (Sumatra, Indonesia)
† 2020 in Berlin

Page 19, Mittelstrasse: 'Middle Street'. Mittel also has the meaning of 'means', either in the material or the methodological sense.

Page 50, *'The wanderer comes to an inn . . .'*: *The I Ching or Book of Changes* (Richard Wilhelm and Cary F. Baynes trans.) (London: Penguin, 2003), p. 218.

Page 156, *'The wanderer rests in a shelter . . .'*: *The I Ching or Book of Changes*, p. 218.